NEW YORK TIMES BESTSELLING AUTHOR

LINDSAY McKENNA

OUT RIDER

"Fast-paced romantic suspense that renders a beautiful
love story, start to finish… McKenna's writing is flawless,
and her story line fully absorbing. More, please."
—*Library Journal* on *Taking Fire*

New York Times bestselling author

LINDSAY McKENNA

takes you to Jackson Hole, Wyoming, where love always finds a way out of the darkness...

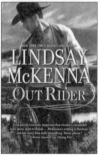

Pick up your copies today!

ISBN-13: 978-0-373-78861-3

HQN™

www.HQNBooks.com

PHLM0516IFC

LINDSAY McKENNA

OUT RIDER

HQN™

ISBN-13: 978-0-373-78861-3

Recycling programs for this prcduct may not exist in your area.

Out Rider

Copyright © 2016 by Nauman Living Trust

This is a work of fiction. Names, characters, places and incidents are either the product of the author's imagination or are used fictitiously, and any resemblance to actual persons, living or dead, business establishments, events or locales is entirely coincidental.

This edition published by arrangement with Harlequin Books S.A.

For questions and comments about the quality of this book, please contact us at CustomerService@Harlequin.com.

www.HQNBooks.com

Printed in U.S.A.

Dear Reader,

This is a bittersweet note to all of you. *Out Rider* is the final book of the Wyoming series. Like you, I've grown to love Iris Mason of the Elk Horn Ranch and feisty Gus Hunter of the Bar H, the other matriarch of ranching families in Jackson Hole, Wyoming.

In this book, I've tried to tie up a bunch of loose ends so that my loyal readers know "what happened next" to some of the other characters. I had a lot of fun doing it and I hope it brings out a few chuckles and smiles from you.

The entire series is being put into Audio.com for those who love to listen instead of read. Just type in any of the titles and they'll be there for your listening enjoyment. I want to thank senior executive editor Tara Gavin for shepherding these last two books of mine (*Night Hawk* and *Out Rider*), because it was pure joy working with her in our creative synastry.

I wanted to write Sloan Rankin's story for a long time. Most people don't know that the US Forest Service has rangers who are farriers. They go around trimming and shoeing the mules and horses utilized by the Park Service. And I wanted to highlight their service because it's an important one.

Sloan was a great character to play opposite Devorah McGuire, a US Forest Service ranger. Dev's story happens more than one would think. She was in the military, a combat dog handler who hunted for IEDs in Afghanistan. Getting a job as a ranger and tracker is a dream come true for Dev. With her trusty female yellow Labrador, Bella, she's running away from a dangerous situation, turning a page and hoping for a new start out in the Tetons. Only Dev didn't expect to meet a man and his dog in a highly unusual way. But you'll have to read the book to find out what happens next! Happy reading!

And thank you for taking this journey with me to Jackson Hole, Wyoming. It's a place I visit every other year with great joy. And I hope I've transferred some of the beauty of this magnificent area onto each of you.

Subscribe to my newsletter that is chock-full of exclusives, a giveaway and so much more at lindsaymckenna.com.

Lindsay McKenna

To Tara Gavin, senior executive editor, who has shadowed my 36-year career with her magic. What a team we were in the past (1980s–1999) and then now (2013–present). It's a pleasure sharing this ongoing journey with you.

CHAPTER ONE

OH, HELL! Devorah McGuire gripped the steering wheel of her truck, knuckles whitening as she felt the unexpected sway of her horse trailer behind her. Automatically, she tensed, taking her foot off the gas pedal and signaling to move onto the berm on the four-lane highway leading into Jackson Hole, Wyoming. The traffic at 9:00 a.m. on a Tuesday going into the popular tourist destination was fairly heavy. Everyone was heading into work, she supposed. Her buckskin mare, Goldy, was in the back of a two-horse trailer. She hadn't heard one of the four tires blow out, but she'd sure felt it. Her trailer had two tires on each side to carry a horse's weight.

Slowing, Dev eased the truck off onto the shoulder. It was wide enough to be able to pull the trailer safely out of traffic, and would allow her to walk around and inspect the trailer to see which tire had blown. She was worried what Goldy, her ten-year-old trail mare, thought about the sudden blowout, but Dev didn't sense the horse was agitated. If a horse was stressed, it shifted nervously around in the trailer and it could be felt by the driver. The May Wyoming sky was threatening rain and she hoped to reach the Grand Teton National Park, about twenty miles north of Jackson Hole, before the cranky weather arrived.

Climbing out of the truck, dressed in Levi's, a red

flannel shirt and work boots, she pulled on her heavy winter coat because it was near freezing.

"Hey, girl," Dev called to her mare as she walked to the blue-and-white trailer. "You okay?"

Goldy whickered, turning her head toward her.

Dev saw the blown tire right away. The trailer had a double axle to bear the weight of two one-thousand-pound animals. The front tire on the driver's side was shredded. More concerned about her mare, Dev went to the other side, opened the side door that led into a small compartment where she could check on her horse and stow hay and other items. Dev smiled at Goldy. "Hey, girl, how you doing?"

Goldy whickered again, sticking her black nose forward toward Dev's extended fingers. The mare had on a bright red nylon halter and the chain beneath it was fitted to a solid iron loop so she was not loose in the narrow stall.

"Did that scare you to death?" Dev asked her, gently rubbing the mare's white blaze that divided the front of her dainty face. Goldy's large brown eyes looked a little more unsettled than normal and Dev couldn't blame her. Petting her and leaning forward, extending her hand across the mare's thick winter-haired neck, she moved her long black mane aside. That touch would quickly settle her friend down, and so would her soothing, husky voice. The mare's ears flicked back and forth and she began to relax once more beneath Dev's long stroking motions across her neck.

"Heck of a welcome to our new digs, isn't it, girl?" Dev asked, smiling at Goldy. The mare snorted and tossed her head.

Dev grinned and looked up, seeing a dark blue Ford

pickup truck with a cab on the back of it pull up behind her. "We got company, big girl." She gave Goldy one last pat and exited the compartment, shutting the door.

She noticed a tall man wearing a beat-up tan Stetson in the driver's seat. On the side of his truck she saw the sign: Sloan Rankin, Farrier. He was a blacksmith. Rubbing her hands down the sides of her jeans in the cold wind, Dev watched him climb out of his truck. There was a big dog on the passenger side, looking somewhat like a German shepherd, ears pricked, watching intently through the windshield, fully focused on her.

The man was in his late twenties or maybe his early thirties, the Stetson he wore sweat stained around the crown and shaped so that the brim was set low over his pale blue eyes. He wore a green canvas barn coat, jeans and beat-up cowboy boots that were scuffed and well aged. Most of all, Dev liked the kindness she saw in his square weathered face. He wasn't handsome but rugged looking, his eyes wide spaced, large and intelligent. His dark brown hair was cut short, brows straight across his eyes. She relaxed because she saw a faint smile tug at the corners of his well-shaped mouth as he approached her.

"Howdy, ma'am," he said, touching the brim of his Stetson. "I saw you blow a tire back there," he continued, gesturing behind him. "You all right? Your horse okay?" And he halted about six feet from her, lifting his chin, sizing up the horse in the trailer.

"Yes, I'm fine and so is my mare, thanks. You must have good eyes to have seen it happen that far back." She gazed up at him. The look in his blue eyes reminded her of a soft midday summer sky, and it warmed Dev for no obvious reason.

He shrugged. "My ma and pa always said I was part eagle." He held out his hand. "I'm Sloan Rankin."

Taking his gloved hand, she said, "Dev McGuire. Thanks for stopping."

"Let me help you change that tire?" he said, releasing her hand. Looking toward the gunmetal-gray sky, he added, "Going to rain or snow shortly. Where do you keep your jack? In the forward compartment of your horse trailer?"

Dev nodded. Her heart wouldn't settle down. The man had a soft drawl, not quite full Southern, but he was definitely not a northerner by the inflection in his deep, unhurried tone. "Yes, forward compartment. I can help you. I'm really used to doing this on my own." She flashed him a slight smile of thanks as they walked toward the trailer.

"Well," Sloan drawled, slowing his lanky pace for her benefit, "a woman shouldn't have to change tires if she doesn't have to."

Dev pushed some of her shoulder-length black hair away from her face, the wind carrying it around her. "I appreciate the help, believe me."

"Where you comin' from?" he asked, halting and opening the door. He pointed at the license plate on the rear of the trailer.

Dev leaned down, drawing out the tools to fix the tire. "From the Great Smoky Mountains National Park. I've just been transferred from there to out here, to the Teton National Park."

Picking up the tools, Sloan's brows moved up in surprise. "You a forest ranger?"

"I am indeed."

He shut the door. "Well, this is your lucky day, Miss

McGuire. I just happen to be a ranger at Teton Park." He gave her a grin as he walked around the trailer.

"Seriously? You are?" Dev leaned down and picked up rocks the size of cantaloupes and placed them behind and in front of the four tires. It would stop the trailer from rocking back and forth as he worked. Or if Goldy shifted. It was a safety measure.

Sloan gently patted the gold rump of her horse as he walked by her. "I'm dead serious," he told her.

"But," Dev said, frowning, "it says 'farrier' on your truck door."

"Oh, that." Sloan crouched down on the dry, gravelly soil, using his glove to make the area clean of small rocks that might bite into his knees. "I'm officially a US forest ranger and I'm in charge of shoeing all the mules and horses for Grand Teton Park and Yellowstone Park. On my days off, I pick up some money on the side by shoeing at the local ranches around the valley."

Dev quickly found more rocks. She placed them around the tire next to the blown one. It was critical when changing a horse trailer tire that it be stable. "Wow, what luck this is, then." She smiled as he knelt down and slid the jack beneath the frame of the trailer. If Goldy had been on the side that had blown the tire, Dev would have had to unload the mare. As it was, she was on the other side, taking most of the weight off the left side where Sloan would be working. The wind was icy and Dev slid her hands beneath her armpits, wishing she'd put on her gloves.

"Quite a change," Sloan told her, quickly putting the trailer up high enough on the left side to raise the blown tire off the soil, "from the Smoky Mountains to the Tetons. You probably know we get eight months of

winter out here." He moved his gloved hands with knowing ease, quickly removing the lug nuts and pulling the
tire off the axle and setting it aside.

"I was warned," Dev said. "I've got the spare. Hold
on, I'll get it for you."

She hurried around and found it in the front compartment, lugging it around with both hands in front
of her. Sloan met her, easily taking it out of her grasp.
"Thanks," she said.

"No problem." He settled the tire on the axle, pulled
off his gloves and put on the lug nuts to hold it in place.

Dev watched him work with speed and efficiency.
Sloan had long, almost graceful-looking hands, but
they were the hands of a farrier, for sure. She saw the
thick calluses across his palms and on his fingers where
he held his tools to fire and shape iron horseshoes. He
wasn't heavily muscled. Most farriers she'd met were
short and on the thin side. Sloan was tall and lean. For
whatever ridiculous reason, Dev wondered if he was
married. Most likely. And from his easygoing nature
and genteel drawl, he probably had a bunch of kids, too.
He seemed like a fatherly type: calm, quiet and patient.

This man was a far cry from her stalker, Bart Gordon, another forest ranger at the park she'd just left. She
couldn't help but be deluged by memories, especially out
alone like this. He too was tall, with dark brown, alert-
looking eyes. But his face resembled a mean horse's face:
eyes set closely together, small and malicious looking.
As Dev stood nearby, watching Sloan quickly tighten up
the lug nuts, she automatically placed her fingers against
her exposed throat, her skin cold to her touch. Gordon
had stalked her for a year, always trying to corner her,
touch her, ask for a kiss, which she'd refused to give him.

Don't go there. But her heart automatically began to pound as Dev starkly recalled the evening at the ranger headquarters when she had been alone, getting ready to close up the visitor's center. Gordon had waited, hidden, when she went into the back room to put the money in the safe. He'd jumped her, then knocked her down and started tearing at her shirt, popping the buttons off. Dev closed her eyes, willing away that terrifying experience, the fear skittering through her like a knife blade sliding through her tightening gut.

"You all right, Miss McGuire?"

Sloan's low voice was near and it startled her. Ever since Gordon had jumped her, she'd been filled with anxiety, afraid of her own shadow. With a gasp, Dev's eyes flew open and she leaped back. Staring up at him, she saw confusion and then regret come to Sloan's expression.

"Sorry," he said. "I startled you." He turned and pointed toward the trailer. "Tire's fixed and you're ready to go."

Gulping, Dev whispered, "I—I'm sorry. I didn't mean… I…" She gave him an apologetic look. "I'm just jumpy."

Nodding, Sloan said, "Understandable. You're in a new state, new area with a new job. That's enough to make a polecat wanna leap around."

He pushed the brim of his hat up a little, studying her. Dev McGuire had gone pale on him except for two red spots on her cheeks from the near-freezing temperature. His low, soothing words seemed to calm her and her eyes no longer reflected menace. There was nothing threatening around him that he could discern, so Sloan wrote it off as that blown tire. It would spook anyone when

they were carrying a beloved animal in a trailer. It took
a damn good driver to safely bring a horse in a trailer
to a standstill after a tire had blown. She had the skills.

"C-could you tell me how to get to Teton Park, Mr.
Rankin?" Dev said, trying to collect her strewn thoughts.
Every time she had a flashback on Gordon jumping her,
she was shaking for the next few hours. She could feel
her stomach curling and tightening, her breath a little
ragged and shallow. "I need to put my mare, Goldy, in
the barn area."

"Call me Sloan. I'll do you one better than that," he
reassured her. "Follow me. I'll take you right to the barn.
That way, you won't get lost. Sound good to you?"

Did it ever! Dev gave him a grateful look. "Wonderful. Are you sure I'm not taking you out of your way?"

"Naw," Sloan replied, pulling out a cell phone from
his worn back pocket. "I was going to shoe Triple H
Ranch horses today, but I'll call 'em and let 'em know
I'll be a tad late. They won't mind."

Tension bled out of Dev and her stomach unknotted.
It usually took hours for her to relax. Did it have to do
with Sloan? He didn't seem like someone who got rattled about anything. But then, her knowledge of horses
and blacksmiths told her that the men and women who
entered that trade were all like him: calm, quiet and pos-
sessing a low voice that just naturally put tense horses
and mules at ease. Hell, he'd put her at ease! Smiling to
herself, she said, "Great. Thanks. I'll just follow you,
then." She walked quickly around the trailer and climbed
into her truck.

SLOAN WAS MET by a whine from Mouse, his brindle-
colored Belgian Malinois dog on his front seat. The dog's

cinnamon eyes danced with excitement, his pink tongue lolling out the side of his long, black muzzle. After patting Mouse, his dog moved over to the other side to allow Sloan into the cab. He was excitedly thumping his lean tail.

"She's kinda pretty, isn't she?" Sloan asked his companion.

Mouse whined, thumping his tail even harder and faster.

"You probably think I'm talking about that good-looking yellow Lab she owns hanging her head out her truck window. Don't you?" Sloan grinned, roughing up his male dog's dark brown fur. "Two nice-looking females," he agreed as the dog sat obediently as he closed the door.

Sloan pulled his truck around Dev's and signaled, easing into the nearest lane. Right now, there was no traffic coming their way. He watched through his side mirror and saw Dev McGuire was right behind him, but keeping a safe distance between the two vehicles. Smiling a little, Sloan rubbed his recently shaven jaw, thinking that she was one fine-looking filly of a woman. He liked her raven-black hair that shone with blue highlights even beneath a gray rainy sky. Her oval face had a strong chin and he could sense stubborn resolve in her after the tire had blown. Knowing she'd have successfully handled the changing of a tire, Sloan liked that Dev had allowed him to step in and aid her. She might be stubborn, but judging from the look in those deep forest green eyes of hers, she was intelligent and had the good common sense to accept help from others.

Dev was built slender, reminding him more of a willow, although he couldn't tell much beneath that navy goose-down winter coat she wore. The woman definitely had a fine pair of long, long legs on her and that heightened Sloan's interest in her. He'd always liked tall, willowy-looking women. But he darkly reminded himself that more than likely, she had a man in her life, even though she wore no wedding ring on her left hand. Most of the female rangers at the Teton station were either going with someone or married. Him and about ten other younger rangers were single. They were all looking for the right woman. He was not. His ex-wife, Cary Davis, had cured him of ever wanting marriage again.

As Sloan drove at a reasonable speed, he noted again that Dev was easily keeping up with him. Once they entered Jackson Hole, the four-lane highway bustling with locals and tourists, Sloan remained in the slower right-hand lane for Dev's sake. Trailering a horse required 100 percent of the driver's attention. Plus, they never drove near anyone else's bumper because they had a lot of weight and a thousand-pound horse pushing them forward even after brakes were applied. Trucks and trailers didn't stop that fast as a result.

Sloan kept trying to ignore the fact he caught the fragrance of her hair or skin, a subtle jasmine scent. It made him inhale deeply, as if he were inhaling a woman's scent for the first time. Well, that was partly true. After divorcing Cary at twenty-seven, it had taken Sloan nearly three years to recover from the damage it had done to him. And just recently, he was beginning to feel the ache of wanting a partner, or at least a woman to be in a serious relationship with, in his life once again. But no marriage. Just a relationship. Sloan wasn't the kind of man to have one-night stands. He never had been that type, and wasn't about to start now. He'd always had long-term relationships and never went into them with the thought that they were going to be shallow or time limited.

There was a haunting softness to Dev McGuire that called powerfully to him. Maybe an innocence to her? She looked college aged, but Sloan was sure she was probably in her late twenties even though she didn't look it. The maturity she had told him she was older. She wasn't some giggly young twentysomething. No, Dev had dealt with him in an adult way, although Sloan swore he had seen her interest in him as a man. Maybe that was his imagination? Sloan knew he was no pretty boy or magazine cover model. He was country born, backwoods raised on Black Mountain, and lowlanders referred to his kind as hillbillies. There was pride in being raised in West Virginia, in the Allegheny Mountains among the Hill people whose blood ran through his veins. Black Mountain was a harbor for his kind. These were good people who lived off the land, worked hard, took care of themselves as well as their neighbors. And despite the stereotype where outsiders thought Hill people were dumb and illiterate, nothing could be further from the truth. Minds were changed, however, one person at a time.

So why the sense of innocence around Dev? Sloan pondered that question as he drove slowly through the town. Maybe she got married early, in her late teens. Again, he assumed she was in a relationship. Damn, she was pretty. He liked her beautifully shaped lips, their natural fullness. Her wing-shaped black brows emphasized those glorious, large green eyes of hers. They were alive with life, dancing and fully engaged with him when they spoke to one another. Sloan had tried to ignore as best

he could the heat that had streaked straight down to his
lower body when Dev had smiled at him.

Sloan thought back to his growing-up years in an
old log cabin that sat on top of a tree-clad hill deep in
the woods of Black Mountain. They had electricity and
every night his mother, Wilma, would read to him as a
young child. She loved myths and in particular he remembered Helen of Troy and how beautiful she was.
Sloan thought that Dev could be a black-haired version
of her. What bothered him, however, was her reaction
when he accidentally scared the bejesus out of her. She'd
reacted violently when he'd approached her. Looking
back on it, he did walk quietly and Dev hadn't heard him
coming her way. Sloan felt bad about jolting her. The
woman was under enough stress hauling a horse halfway
across the United States, then having a flat tire, which
could all have contributed to her reaction.

It was the look in her green eyes that had struck him
deeply, the raw terror he'd seen in them. Her face had
gone completely white except for her red cheeks caused
by the cold weather and wind. He'd seen that look in Afghan villagers' eyes too often, particularly the women
and children who had been terrorized by Taliban who'd
come through killing and torturing fathers and husbands.
And raping the women. It was a look he'd never forget
from his deployments. And it was reflected in Dev's
eyes. Why? Shaking his head, Sloan couldn't put it together. At least, not yet. And probably never.

As they reached the outskirts of the town, there was
a long, long hill they had to climb. On his right was the
ten-foot-high elk fence. Below it was the valley where
thousands of deer and elk were fed all winter long so they
wouldn't die of starvation. On his left rose a thousand-

foot hill, rocks craggy and gleaming with wetness from small springs that wound unseen and then oozed out of the fissures and cracks on the surface.

Sloan could always tell a lot about a person by the animals they kept. That buckskin mare of hers wasn't jumpy, nervous or tense. She was real relaxed in that trailer, alert but not jerking and jumping around like some horses did. That was a reflection of Dev's real nature, for sure. Animals always mirrored their owners, plain and simple. So his initial sense of the woman was that she was grounded, quiet and mature. Just like her horse. That was a good combination in Sloan's book. Giggly, flighty, nervous women made him tense. But then, Cary had been like that, hadn't she? But that was because she'd been high on drugs and he hadn't realized it until much too late.

Sloan had only caught a glimpse of the yellow Labrador in the front of Dev's truck. By the fineness of the dog's large, broad head, she looked to be a female. He'd find out soon enough, he though, and then he grinned over at Mouse, who was decidedly an alpha male. "I think you already know that good-lookin' yellow Lab is a female."

Mouse cocked his black head, his large, intelligent eyes dancing with excitement. He whined. His tail kept thumping against the seat.

Reaching out, Sloan petted his combat-assault dog that had, for two years, helped save his ass over in Afghanistan. When he got out of the Army, he was able to bring Mouse with him because the dog had developed stress from too many IEDs and explosions. He'd been a brave dog, often going after fleeing enemies in nights so dark Sloan couldn't see his hand in front of his face.

Mouse would nail them, take them down and grip a leg with his teeth until the Army soldiers could arrive to take the screaming enemy prisoner.

Now his brindle dog was eight years old, well past his prime, but he was in better shape than 90 percent of the dogs in the United States. And Mouse had slowly, over time, let go of his combat-dog training as Sloan gently but firmly got his best four-legged friend to adjust to civilian life instead. As he moved his long fingers through the dog's short, thick fur, Sloan smiled a little.

"Hey, this may be your lucky day, fella. That woman has a yellow Lab and who knows? You might get to befriend that dog of hers." He chuckled. "And I might be able to befriend her owner."

Mouse thumped his tail mightily, ears up, eyes on the back window where Dev's truck and trailer were visible. He gave a long, excited whine.

Sloan knew Mouse could see the other dog through the windows, no question. The Belgian Malinois was one of the most intelligent dog breeds on the planet and nothing, but nothing, escaped Mouse's attention.

It made Sloan grin. Giving Mouse a last pat, Sloan wrapped his hand around the steering wheel, urging the truck up the long, easy slope of the hill. As they crested it, the mighty Tetons sat on his left. They were clothed in deep white snow with blue granite flanks and skirts of evergreens around their bases. May was still a winter month up here, but Sloan knew come June 1, the tourists would descend like a plague of locusts on this park and Yellowstone, which sat fifty miles north of them.

Mouse whined. His thin, long tail was whipping against Sloan's thigh.

"Patience, pardner," he drawled to his dog. "We're almost there. As soon as we can get this gal and her horse over to the barn, I might let you out and we'll introduce you to her dog. But no promises. Okay? Gotta see what the lady wants to do with her horse first."

The dog's tail hit Sloan with great regularity across his hard thigh. They were bruising hits.

"Calm down," he told Mouse. "Easy." And Sloan slowly stroked the dog's long, powerful back. He felt the dog's muscles relax beneath his stroking fingers. Mouse stopped whining. If Mouse thought he could crash through that rear-window glass, run across the bed of his truck and leap up onto the hood of Dev's truck, he'd do it. Such was his dog's type-A nature. Belgian Malinois were basically sheep-herding dogs in Europe. And their nature was to bring everyone together in a nice, tight, safe group, with the dog prowling around the edges, watching for bears, wolves or apex predators from the sky.

Sloan couldn't lie to himself. He was mirroring his dog. Only Mouse was a helluva lot more obvious about it than he was. No question, Dev turned him on. Caution told him not to put much stock in first impressions. He'd fallen so hard and fast for Cary, married her three months after meeting her in a bar, and look what had happened. Sloan frowned; he knew the price. And it was far too much for him to ever pay again.

CHAPTER TWO

DEV FELT NOTHING but gratefulness for Sloan as he pulled into the large gravel circle in front of a dark green three-story barn. She'd seen the headquarters building, a two-story yellow-brick affair on the right, after they'd passed through the area that allowed visitors into the park. Her heart picked up in tempo and she felt anticipation and relief while she parked the truck and trailer in front of the open barn doors.

Bella, her yellow Lab, whined, her head stuck out the window, her long, slender yellow tail beating happily against the seat.

Patting her rump, Dev said, "Stay here, girl. First things first. We have to get Goldy out of that trailer and into an assigned box stall in that barn."

As she opened the door to climb out, she watched Sloan ease his tall frame out of the truck in front of her. There was a casualness about him, as if he hadn't a care in the world, but Dev saw something else. He seemed to look around, not in an easygoing manner, but in a way that suggested he was thoroughly checking out the territory around him. Further, her own senses told her this man wasn't who or what he seemed to be. That was unsettling to her because Bart Gordon hadn't been, either. He was a stalker, a sexual predator beneath those good looks of his. Only she'd found out too late.

Dev compressed her lips and shut the truck door. She waited for Sloan to walk up to where she stood. A rocky hiking and horse trail existed beyond the barn area. The Douglas firs stood tall and straight everywhere she looked on that side of the path. Inhaling deeply, she drew the scent of pine into her lungs. The air was cold, the breeze brisk and there were patches of white snow everywhere, telling her spring had yet to make an entrance into this area of Wyoming.

"Welcome home," Sloan said, gesturing to the barn. "Let me connect with Charlotte Hastings. She's our supervisor. Chances are her assistant, Linda Chambers, will know which box stall has been reserved for your mare." He pulled the cell phone out of his pocket.

Nodding, Dev looked around as he made the call for her. She could feel Sloan's quiet power radiating around him. Bella had poked her head out the driver's-side window, panting and watching Sloan. He seemed to draw women like bees found flowers. Somewhat skittish, Dev walked away from Sloan, wanting to get out of that warm, sunlit aura that surrounded him. It was too tempting and she was too raw from Gordon's attack on her. There was no way she could afford to trust this ranger, even if he seemed helpful. He might have ulterior motives toward her, too.

Dev hated that she thought that way since Gordon's attack. Now she was looking at every man who approached her as a potential predator. Dev knew not every man was out to get her like Gordon did, but she couldn't stop the emotional internal reactions that automatically popped up whenever she was around a strange unknown male. And worse, the rangers she worked with at the other park, she began to question and distrust them, as well.

Rubbing her furrowed brow, she walked around the back of the trailer.

Goldy nickered.

"Hey, big girl, we're going to get you into your new home in just a bit," she promised, patting her mare gently on her big golden rump. Dev liked the black dorsal stripe that ran from the mare's withers, or shoulders, all the way across her back and connected with her long black tail. Buckskins, depending upon their genetic history, often had the dorsal stripe. Goldy also had the black horizontal bars across her upper legs, another indicator of mustang genes far back in her family tree. She was a true mustang buckskin in color and personality.

"Hey, we've got you a box stall," Sloan called, coming around the corner, tucking his cell into his back pocket. "Stall number five." He gestured toward the opened barn doors. "It's down at the other end of the aisle on the right. Do you need any help unloading your mare?"

"No, I'm fine. She's an easy hauler," Dev said.

"Okay, let me get down there and I'll slide the door open to that stall and make sure she's got water. Want her to have a bit of alfalfa or some timothy grass hay?"

"I've got some grass hay up in the compartment," she said, waving in that general direction. "With the stress of trailering, I only want Goldy on regular grass hay for now." She saw the pleased look come to Sloan's weathered face.

"You know your horses," he praised, turning and walking up the slight gravel slope to the barn.

Dev tried not to feel good about the compliment in Sloan's blue eyes and low voice. She felt that sense of warmth surround her like a wonderful, protective blanket. It startled her and she tried to figure out what was going on between them. After she opened the latches, the door to Goldy's side of the trailer swung wide. Going to the front compartment, Dev quickly snapped a nylon lead on her halter and freed her from the trailer tie. She patted her mare, who was more than ready to get out of the trailer.

Dev hurried to the rear and removed the rubber hose and chain safeguard that kept the horse from backing out of the trailer too soon. Patting Goldy's rear, she moved quickly up to the compartment. She squeezed in beside her mare, clucked her tongue and said, "Back."

Horses didn't understand English per se, Dev knew, but they associated sounds with a particular command and knew what was being asked of them. Goldy daintily backed out and Dev followed with the nylon lead in her hand. Once the mare was out of the trailer, Goldy perked up, lifting her chiseled head, eagerly looking around, her nostrils flared to pick up all the new scents.

As Dev walked to her side, smoothing out her long ruffled black mane, Sloan reappeared at the entrance to the barn. "Is it ready?" she called.

"Sure is. Come on in."

Smiling a little, Dev led her mare toward the barn. Already, she could hear the welcoming nickers of other horses who heard the buckskin coming their way. Horses were social animals and always preferred being in a herd. Dev was sure that Goldy would make some good friends soon.

"She's a nice-looking animal," Sloan said, walking with her down the clean, swept concrete aisle between the ten box stalls. "Mustang?"

"Part," Dev said, watching Goldy as she swung her

head one way or another as she clip-clopped down the aisle way. "Part mustang and part Arabian."

"Nice combo," Sloan said. "You're slender and delicate, and so is she. A good match."

Dev wasn't sure she was small at five feet seven inches tall, but she supposed in comparison to Sloan, she was. "I wanted a trail horse that had her instincts," she explained.

"That's wise," Sloan agreed. He stepped out of the way because she was going to have to swing Goldy wide to step into her awaiting oak box stall.

The whinnies of the other animals grew in volume, a pleasant horse chorus welcoming Goldy to her new home. Her mare whickered back in a friendly fashion, as if thanking them for their welcome. All the curious horses had their faces pressed against the wide iron bars across the upper half of each of the stall gates, watching their progress. The sweet smell of alfalfa and timothy hay made Dev inhale deeply. It was like perfume to her. She spotted the open door at the end, on the right stall. The other enclosures were all filled, probably with either USFS-owned horses or horses privately owned by some of the rangers.

It was warmer in the barn due to the body heat of the ten animals. The breeze was cold, flowing in and out of the barn. Dev was pleased to see thick cedar shavings in Goldy's new stall. To her left was a steel watering bowl that had a heater in it to keep the water from icing up when below freezing. Hanging in a net in the corner near the bars at the front was a flake of timothy hay. Goldy eagerly stepped up into the roomy stall, plunging her nose into the large watering bowl.

Looking around, Dev wanted to see if there were any

nails or other items that could accidentally injure her mare. The stall was bright, large and airy with a second window opposite the sliding door. Horses hated being in dark stalls. They got depressed just like a human without adequate light. Slipping the snap off Goldy's halter, she pulled the door halfway shut and slowly examined every oak panel in the stall. She could feel Sloan's silent interest, her back prickling lightly where his gaze rested upon her. Before Gordon's attack, Dev wouldn't have reacted to any male interest with anxiety, but now, she did. Moving her hand along the wall, fingertips skimming the sanded, honey-colored hardwood, Dev told herself that Sloan was not Gordon. Or was he? Looks were so damned deceiving. Feeling guilty because Sloan did not deserve this kind of paranoid reaction from her, Dev turned and walked to the other side of her mare, who was lifting her muzzle from the bowl, water dripping from it.

"This is nice," Dev said, pointing to the water dish. "Not only self-filling, but with the temperature gauge in there, it will keep ice from forming over the top of it."

Sloan leaned against the stall and nodded. "I think you'll find everything in the stall in shipshape. Charlotte is a nice lady, but she's strict about keeping the animals clean and safe, too. She's a good supervisor and I think you'll like meeting her."

Pushing her hair away from her face, Dev patted Goldy on her broad wither one more time and then slid the door open and stepped out. The horse next to her, a big gray gelding with a black mane and tail, had his nose pressed between the iron bars, wanting to say hello to Goldy. But Goldy was more interested in that clean-smelling timothy hay in the hanging net after sating her thirst.

"I have an appointment to officially meet her tomorrow morning at 10:00 a.m.," Dev said. Glancing at her watch, she said, "Next order of business is to find my new apartment. I leased it over the phone after going on the internet and looking at what was available in this area."

Sloan took the heavy oak door and slid it closed, and then latched it so the mare couldn't possibly get out. "I'll bet you had sticker shock on the prices of an apartment and condo here in Jackson Hole."

Groaning, Dev said, "Yes. Even worse, I have a dog and most places don't allow you to have a pet, so it got pretty worrisome." She rubbed her hands down the thighs of her Levi's and hung Goldy's red nylon lead on a horseshoe that was attached to the door.

"There are two places that allow pets," Sloan said. "The Pines, where I live, and a condo group known as Winterhaven. Which did you rent at?"

Dev walked slowly down the aisle toward her truck at the other end. "I took a two-bedroom apartment at The Pines. It was a lot cheaper. I mean, it wasn't really cheap at all, just less than Winterhaven."

"That's a good choice. It's a nice place. I live there with my dog, Mouse."

She smiled a little, feeling a sense of protection coming from Sloan as he walked at her shoulder. He'd pulled his gloves off and stuffed them in his back pocket. The male grace of the man told her he was in top shape, although pretty much hidden from the waist up with his utilitarian Carhartt heavy canvas jacket. She could always tell a real rancher or farmer from the wannabes. That particular line of clothing was built tough for hard-working men and women. Instead of buttons, they were fastened with rivets. Dev had a dark brown Carhartt jacket packed away in her suitcase and would always be wearing it anytime she was working in the barn or around Goldy when it was cold. "What were the chances we'd meet each other on that highway? And that you'd be a ranger like myself? And then we end up living at the same apartment complex?"

Sloan shrugged and slanted her an amused look. "Dharma? Or Karma, depending upon how you take it all in."

"Kismet," Dev said. His low, husky teasing flowed through her and touched her heart. She chided herself inwardly for thinking Sloan was a wolf in sheep's clothing just like Gordon. The warmth dancing in Sloan's blue eyes made her feel safe. And since the assault, Dev had not felt safe at all. Anywhere. With any man. Except Sloan. Frowning a little, she tucked her feelings away, concentrating on leaving the barn. Above, some sunlight managed to peek through the gray fluffy clouds gathering with what looked like rain or snow.

Sloan lifted his Stetson, ran his fingers through his short hair and settled it on his head. "I'm going that way. Got to get out to the Triple H to shoe some of their horses. Want to follow me?"

"Yes, you're really being a guardian angel for me, Sloan."

"Okay, but first, back your trailer over there." He pointed to five other trailers that sat in a neat row east of the barn.

Dev was used to hauling and backing up her horse trailer. It wasn't hard to do, but one had to know how to turn the wheels on the truck to back the trailer straight and next to the red-and-white one at the end. "Got it."

"I'll help you."

"I appreciate it," she murmured, climbing into the cab of her truck. Horsemen usually helped one another and Sloan wasn't disappointing her at all. She turned on the truck's engine and then drove around the circle, jockeying her truck and trailer. Within minutes, thanks to Sloan's hand signals, she had her trailer parked. By the time she got out of the truck, he had lifted the trailer hitch off the truck and had it standing and ready for the next time she would want to hook it up.

"You're going to spoil me," Dev said, smiling up at him. "Thanks." She saw that gleam come to his eyes again, and she swore she could feel his care and protection once more.

"Horse people always help one another," Sloan said, shrugging a bit. "What building and apartment are you in, do you know? There are three units to The Pines."

Frowning, Dev pulled out a note from her jacket pocket and opened it up. "It says 'unit two, apartment 224.'" She saw his brows rise, and a surprised look come to his face. "Why? Is this not a good apartment?"

A grin edged Sloan's mouth. "You aren't going to believe this, but I'm in the same unit and my apartment is directly across from yours, 225."

Her lips parted and Dev wasn't sure she felt good or bad about that news. "Well...uh...this is really something, isn't it?"

"I guess so," Sloan said, shaking his head with amusement. "Look at it this way. If you need to borrow a cup of sugar, I more than likely will have it on hand. It'll save you a trip to the grocery store."

"At least I'll know one person in Jackson Hole," Dev said, stunned by the development. When Sloan smiled that slow, lazy smile of his, heat flooded her lower body. The reaction surprised the hell out of her. The man was not flirting with her. He was simply being a gentleman, trying to help her out, her heart told her. He was a ranger, and so was she. Sloan was just doing his duty was all. But the heat in his gaze for a split second unnerved her Dev wasn't even sure she'd seen it. Maybe she wished she had? God, she didn't know—her emotions were still a tangled mess within her since Gordon's attack.

"Come on," Sloan urged. "I'll get you over to the manager's office at The Pines and then I'm going to ske-daddle down the road to go shoe those Triple H horses."

Without thinking, Dev reached out and briefly touched the sleeve of his jacket. "Thanks...really. I truly appreciate the time and care you're giving us, Sloan." Her fingertips tingled slightly and she saw his expression darken for just a moment, as if he hadn't been expecting her to reach out and make physical contact with him. Maybe she had overstepped her bounds with him? "I'm sure your wife can also loan me anything I need," she added.

Sloan said, "Not married. I'm divorced. Me and Mouse are the only ones in that apartment and I don't think my dog, as smart as he is, is up to pouring you a cup of sugar." He cracked a grin.

"Point taken." She saw Mouse with his head hanging out the passenger window of Sloan's truck. "Pretty dog. What breed is he?"

"Belgian Malinois," Sloan said, slowing his pace for her sake. "He used to be my combat-assault dog when I was in the Army." Hitching his shoulder, he added, "But that's another story for another day. We got places to go and people to see right now."

The first raindrops plopped around Dev. She glanced up, seeing the clouds had lowered and become dark and threatening. "Good timing. Looks like it's going to pour any minute."

"Oh, it'll turn to snow up here real quick." Sloan gestured south as he opened the door to her truck for her. "Jackson Hole will more than likely get rain because it's a thousand feet lower in elevation than where we are here. Follow me?"

Dev climbed in. Bella whined and tried reaching across her to smell Sloan, but he left too quickly for her to get a friendly and curious sniff. As she petted Bella, the yellow Lab placed herself on the passenger side, her brown eyes alight with excitement. "Soon, we will have a new home," Dev promised her dog.

Bella thumped her tail, watching Sloan climb into his truck. Her eyes, though, were on Mouse, who was craning his neck out the partially opened passenger-side window, staring intently at her.

"You already have an admirer," Dev teased Bella, putting her truck in gear and slowly following Sloan out of the barnyard. And she almost added that *she* had an admirer in the form and shape of hunky Sloan Rankin. Did she really want that kind of attention? No. Not right now. Dev was still sorting out the assault, trying not to take every male she saw as a potential attacker. It was a terrible thing for Dev to see her once overly trusting self shattered and destroyed by one man. Gordon had changed her life in those moments. Forever.

SLOAN TOLD HIMSELF to slow down with Dev. What the hell were the chances they'd meet on a highway and then find out their other connections with one another?

It was almost scary. Certainly surprising. As he drove through Jackson Hole at a crawl, tourists everywhere, he told his body to settle down. There was nothing to dislike about Dev. His mind churned over things she'd said. Damned if she hadn't looked relieved when he told her he was divorced. Why? Was he misreading that look? Was Dev personally interested in him, man to woman? Or was it wishful thinking on his part, because he was lonely and craving a serious, healthy relationship with a woman once again?

Mouse sat on the seat, his nose stuck out the open window, sucking up all the scents he could find. Sometimes, Sloan wished life was dog simple. They ate, slept, exercised and slept some more. Human lives weren't so straightforward. Because he'd worked with his dog for two years in Afghanistan, Sloan had developed a powerful intuition. He could sense people even if their faces were completely unreadable. Sometimes, he could feel Dev wanting to warm up to him. And then, she'd retreat for some unknown reason. He'd sensed her wariness about him, too. Not that he'd given her *any* reason to distrust him.

Something was going on and damned if he could figure it out. *Yet.* And because he was drawn to her, rightly or wrongly, Sloan wanted to know why Dev's reactions and signals toward him were mixed and confusing. He'd already figured out she was either single, divorced or widowed because the apartment was for her and Bella, her dog. There was no man with her. Sloan knew he shouldn't be happy about that realization, but he was.

Mouth thinning, he took a left turn and drove down a street that would lead them out of Jackson Hole. It would be a mile down the road and another left to where the

newer condos and apartment buildings were located. The
rain was splattering more heavily now and the gray pall
hung over the hills clothed in evergreens in the distance.
The beauty of the area always lulled him and made him
feel relaxed. He drove by a huge power pole on his right.
Up on top of it was a huge osprey hawk nest and there
were two adults in it. Soon, they would have eggs to sit
on, and would raise another generation of fishing hawks
that would ply the nearby Snake River for food.

His body was heating up and Sloan groaned inwardly.
Dev was pretty, no question. He was eager to see her
without that big down-filled coat, see her hips and her
upper body hidden beneath it. He was such a fool. Suddenly, his body, which had been pretty much dormant
since the divorce, was coming back online with a vengeance. All he had to do was look at Dev's soft mouth,
that winsome smile that had tugged at the corners, and
a sheet of burning heat flowed powerfully through him.
She wore no makeup. Her black hair was straight with
slightly curled blue-black tips. He liked her oval face,
those high cheekbones giving her large eyes a slightly
exotic look. Sloan had a lot of questions for Dev and
found himself starving to sit down over coffee and ask
her them. But that would be rude. His parents had taught
him better than that. He needed to give her space to acclimate to a new apartment, new area and new job first.

Glancing to the left, Sloan saw Mouse sniffing up the
rainy air, his sleek muzzle now shiny and wet. Maybe the
best way to get to know Dev was slowly, to try to figure
her out a step at a time. With that unexplained wariness
of hers in place like a shield between them, Sloan knew
patience was going to get him what he wanted. If she
wanted anything to do with him, that is…

That was the great unknown.

Hell, did he really want to get involved with a woman? Again? Sloan's brows lowered as he turned and headed down Moose Lake Road, condos sprouting up as tall towers on his left and a blocky three-story apartment building coming up on the right. The rain was worsening. No surprise there. It was going to be an all-day rain, too. It would turn yellowed meadows into lush green grass for the wild animals. All of them looked close to skeletons, their thick winter coats peeling off them now. The animals were looking forward to that nutritious grass peeking above the snow.

Sloan never lied to himself anymore. He'd lied to himself once, when married to Cary. He pretended her quixotic moods that always kept him off balance were just a natural part of her effervescent personality. Going home to her at night was like entering an emotional battlefield that never ceased. Sloan yearned for a woman like Dev to come into his life: someone who was thoughtful, stable, had a good sense of humor and shared some of what he loved, such as trail riding, having a dog at his side and enjoying the healing silence of nature.

Dev fit the bill so far. Did she have a significant other that she'd left behind? Maybe a long-distance relationship still between them? Maybe the guy was trying to get a transfer out here to be with her? Sloan's head filled with all kinds of scenarios that would stop him in his tracks from getting to know Dev better. Rubbing his jaw, he slowed his truck as the turn came up for the unit-two apartment building in the crescent-shaped complex. Sloan didn't feel any guilt about hoping Dev was completely free of any relationship obligations. But one look into her face and Sloan was sure that wasn't going to be the case. She was young, pretty, fresh and confident. Any man worth his salt would be attracted to her.

Slowing, he pulled his truck next to an open parking spot so Dev could turn in beside him. The rain was constant now, the day turning a depressing gray. Depressing for some, but not him. Easing out, he kept Mouse in the cab and shut the door. He walked around her truck and opened the door for Dev. He then pulled up the dark brown corduroy collar on his coat to stop the rain from running down his neck. She had already pulled up her collar, grabbed her leather purse and pulled the strap over her shoulder. She told Bella to stay and the dog promptly sat down on the seat.

"This way," Sloan urged, pointing her toward double glass doors to the left of them.

Dev nodded, slid out and hurried to get under the eave of the cedar shake roof. Waiting, she watched Sloan shut the door and trot in beneath the eave, as well. He moved around her and walked to the glass doors, opening one of them for her. She slipped in, thanked him and wiped her boots on a coarse mat before walking into an office where a woman sat behind a desk. She had red hair, with green eyes and a welcoming smile, and looked to be in her midforties.

"Hey, Sloan," she called, grinning. "Wet enough out there for you?"

Sloan returned the grin, took off his Stetson and cupped Dev's elbow, guiding her up to the desk. "Sure is, Carol. Hey, this is a new tenant, Dev McGuire."

"Oh, yes," Carol said, shaking Dev's hand, "we've been expecting you, Miss McGuire. Welcome."

Dev smiled. "Thanks. And call me Dev. If it weren't

for Sloan here, I'd probably have had trouble finding you folks."

Settling his hat on his head, Sloan looked at the women. Pinkness had flooded Dev's cheeks after he'd cupped her elbow. Why had he done it? Out of a desire to touch her? His body was growing tight against his zipper. *Damn.* "Gotta go, ladies. You're in good hands with Carol," he told Dev.

"Great...thanks, Sloan..."

"I'll drop by tonight after I get home to see if you need anything." Again, there was that wariness in her eyes. She tucked her lower lip between her teeth for just a moment. "Well," he said, giving her a warm smile, "let's do it the other way around. You know I'm across the hall from you. Just knock if you need anything." Instantly, Sloan saw her worry disappear. He filed that reaction away and would chew on it later.

"That would be fine," Dev murmured. "Have a good afternoon."

Sloan headed for the door. "Hey, I'll be inside a dry barn doing my shoeing. I'm a happy camper. See you two later," he said, and he waved goodbye and slipped outside.

CHAPTER THREE

BART GORDON SAT at one end of the U-shaped counter in Mo's Ice Cream Parlor in the main square of Jackson Hole. He was nursing his cup of coffee and noticed how the place was bustling with customers. At 9:00 a.m., tourists were filtering in for breakfast. He'd already eaten his eggs, bacon and hash browns, and was now content to watch the flow of traffic. One corner of his mouth ticked upward. Wouldn't it be hilarious if Dev McGuire waltzed into this place? He wouldn't want to be seen by her because it was far too early for that. Still, he relished the thought, his mind taking flight, imagining the shocked look on her face when she spotted him. A sense of satisfaction raced through him. All he had to do was see her face in his mind or say her name, and his body ignited with desire for her.

He was angry at her for getting him fired from his forest ranger job. Claiming assault with the attempt to rape her. *The bitch.* So he had been a little rough with her. The women he knew liked it that way. It made him feel manly. In charge. A woman should always be controlled, and he enjoyed it. Moving the cream-colored ceramic mug between his large hands, he tasted rage over her reaction to his wanting her. He'd been a forest ranger for seven years after coming out of the Army transportation command. At thirty, he was hanging his hat on doing his twenty years with the USFS and collecting a nice pension that would be the bedrock for his old age. But Dev had destroyed all his plans. Utterly. Revenge warred with desire for the woman.

Dev wasn't just any woman. He liked black-haired women who had spirit and were confident. And he liked his women to be fighters, giving as good as they got. That turned Bart on. His mouth quirked and he scowled. How the hell could he have known Dev was going to take his advances like that? Every other woman *wanted* his strength, his mastery, and wanted to be tamed by him. They liked being subjugated. And they all liked rough sex. So did he.

This morning, he had an interview with Blake Rivas, owner of Ace Trucking. In the military, he'd been in transportation and had driven the big trucks. A semi truck was no different. He could call upon those four years' worth of skills and convince Rivas that he would be a damn good driver for his huge company. Bart was desperate to get a job. He'd purposely come to this town because Dev was here. A hard anger congealed in his gut. He was going to make her pay for what she'd done to him. Only this time, she wasn't going to live to go to the police and hang his ass a second time around.

Sipping his coffee, watching the sunlight dance through the large picture windows that showed the busy square, he smiled to himself. First, he'd get a job. Then he'd rent an apartment. Lastly, but most important, he'd begin to shadow Dev and watch in order to learn her habits. Then he could plan to kidnap her. It would take time, but he was patient. Above all, Bart didn't want to be connected to her murder when someone discovered Dev's naked body tossed into the woods. In fact, he was planning on learning the grizzly territory around here, planning on letting one of them use her dead body as food. His smile widened as he thought about how his revenge would be set in motion and getting even with Dev. He could hardly wait to see the look in her eyes when he caught her, took her somewhere private, had his way with her, kept her chained up so she couldn't escape. He would degrade her. Then, and only then, when he tired of her, would he get rid of her once and for all.

DEV TOOK A deep breath and rose from the seat in the outer office of the USFS superintendent's office. The assistant smiled and gestured for her to go through the closed door for her first interview with Charlotte Hastings, her new boss. At her side was Bella, in her work uniform and harness as a working dog. She wore a lightweight nylon jacket that said Tracking Dog on it. Dev had placed the black nylon martingale harness across Bella's broad chest and over her shoulders. Not liking a chain collar around her dog's neck, Dev used a leather one that hung comfortably around Bella instead. She gripped the nylon leash and nodded her thanks to the assistant. Bella walked calmly at her side, alert.

She got her first look at her new boss. The fifty-year-old blond-haired woman in her Forest Service uniform sat at her large maple desk. The office was located on the second floor of the building, in a corner where large windows allowed in a lot of light. It was a beautiful place for an office, Dev thought as she closed the door and turned around to greet Charlotte.

"Come on in," the woman called, smiling and standing. She moved from behind her desk and shook hands with Dev. "I'm Charlotte," she said. "And this must be your tracking dog, Bella?" She reached down and patted the dog's head.

"Yes, ma'am, it is," Dev said.

Charlotte straightened and gestured to a chair at one corner of her desk. "Have a seat, Ranger McGuire."

Dev took her seat and Bella sat down next to her. The HQ was parallel to the main highway that led into the park. A lot of cars moved slowly past the building because they'd just come out of paying the fee to enter the park. Across the way, Dev could see the newly built three-story visitor's center opposite of the HQ. She pushed her left palm down her green trousers, getting rid of the dampness. Hastings sat down at her leather chair. Supervisors, she'd found over the years, came in many different stripes. It was rare that a woman was at the top post at a park. She didn't know what the woman's agenda would be, but she'd find out shortly. Her supervisor seemed efficient because there were a number of stacks of files on her desk. They weren't messy, but rather organized.

"Ranger McGuire," she said, folding her hands over Dev's opened file, "you come to us highly recommended. We've been needing a tracker and tracking dog here for this park for some time now, so I'm personally glad to see you here."

Dev felt some relief. At least she wasn't going to get stuck in some office, away from the outdoors. Which could have happened. "Yes, ma'am," she said, "I'm happy to be here, too."

"Every year between May and October, we get at least fifty calls for lost children, elders or adults here in the Tetons." Charlotte scowled. "And it takes a lot of my personnel halting their jobs to go off looking for these individuals." Looking at Dev's file, she said, "You and

Bella have an excellent record of finding lost souls in
the Smoky Mountains region. I see no reason why you
won't do as well here."

"I anticipate we'll be able to do the same here," Dev
said.

"Well," Charlotte said, raising her head, "we have
grizzly bears out here and the Smoky Mountains only
have small black bears. There's a huge difference between them. A dog barking at a black bear will send it
running away." She pointed at Bella. "If she barks here,
the grizzly will take it as a challenge and go after your
dog."

It was a grim warning. "Bella doesn't bark."

"Not even when faced with an elk? A deer? Or a black
bear?"

"No, ma'am." Dev saw some relief in the superintendent's blue eyes.

"Well," she muttered, "I hope that's true because grizzly bears *hate* dogs. They see them as a certified threat.
That means if one sees you and the dog, they could stalk
you or just outright charge you, Ranger McGuire."

"I need to get up on grizzly behavior before I go out
to track," Dev agreed.

"You will carry the following on you whenever you're
tracking, Ranger. A rifle, a pistol, a quart of bear spray
and a radio. We keep constant monitoring of the bears in
this park for good reason. But there's always new ones
wandering into the area we don't know about. On a given
search for a lost person, you're going to work closely
with our bear-tracking unit. That way, you're on top of
where the bruins might be located. But on any given
day, a grizzly can travel twenty miles to find food." She
wrote down a name on a piece of paper and pushed it

across the desk to Dev. "This is the ranger you want to talk to about grizzly behavior. I'd suggest the next time he's on watch, you introduce yourself to him if you can?"

Dev picked up the paper. The name scrawled across it was Sloan Rankin. Her heart pounded, underscoring her feminine reaction to him. "I'll make a point of finding his schedule and talking to him, ma'am."

"Good. Because it could save you and your dog's lives. We ban dogs from this park for the very reason that the grizzly hate 'em. They interpret a dog as a wolf. And wolves are their natural enemy."

"Got it," Dev said, tucking the paper into the breast pocket of her long-sleeved uniform shirt.

"For the next two weeks, I'm putting you over at our newly built visitor's center. You need to get acquainted with the tourists. We get them from around the world. Most are completely ignorant of the grizzly bears that populate the Tetons."

Dev's heart sank. She hated office duty. But Hastings was right: she had to see the type of people coming to the park, get to know them and understand the general lay of the land.

"Ranger Rankin is our farrier. He's also been here for two years and knows every trail in the Tetons. I'm going to keep you on an abbreviated schedule at the visitor's center. You'll spend four hours over there on your shift, the other four hours working with Ranger Rankin. I'm paralleling his schedule with yours so that the other four hours you two can ride the trails. You need to get acquainted with them as soon as possible. I've already talked to him about being your mentor and helping you, earlier today. Before you were assigned here, he always headed up any searches via horseback, to look for lost tourists. Now I want him shadowing you on *every* tracking assignment for the next few months."

Dev frowned. "Is this because of the grizzly threat?"

"Precisely. You will go nowhere without a partner on any of these assignments. Ranger Rankin will be carrying weapons also. He will be your guard should you encounter a grizzly. He's your chief defense because I want you tracking and paying attention to your dog. You'll be distracted if you have to divide your awareness between watching for a grizzly and trying to track a lost tourist."

"That sounds like good common sense," Dev agreed. She was glad it was Sloan. She liked him more than she should. He was someone who was calm and didn't appear easily shaken up in a dangerous situation. Even though she wondered how Sloan had taken this assignment, Dev was sure she'd find out sooner or later. Did he feel like a glorified babysitter for her? *Probably.*

Charlotte pushed a paper toward Dev that had her next two weeks of shifts on it. "Now, since Ranger Rankin is our shoer, he's usually pretty busy. We've gone over a trail planning session already and he knows where he has to take you. There are some areas where we have lost more tourists than others. So, he'll be with you in those primary locations first. His office, if you can call it that, is over at the main barn. You might try to catch him there now, and make introductions."

"Yes, ma'am."

"Questions?"

Dev knew better than to overstay her visit to the boss's office. "No, ma'am."

Charlotte nodded, closing the file. "Welcome to the Tetons, Ranger McGuire. Stay safe out there."

Rising, Dev saw Bella stand at her side. "Thank you, ma'am. I intend to do just that."

Leaving the office, Dev felt better. The tension in her shoulders had bled off and even Bella looked a little more relaxed. Her dog instantly knew when she was upset. Stopping at another office on the first floor, Dev got a USFS truck assigned to her. It would be her wheels around the park from now on. Plus, it had a ball hitch on it so she could trailer her horse to where people went missing in the park.

After finding the truck parked outside the motor pool's area of HQ, Dev signed off on it and put Bella on the passenger-side seat. As she climbed in, Dev noticed how the morning was warming up. She took off her dark brown nylon jacket and placed it between her and Bella. The sky was clear and it was looking like a nice day after last night's rain. The air smelled intensely of pine and Dev smiled as she pulled the door shut. She rolled down the window because she wanted that cool, fresh air to circulate that heavenly fragrance within the cab of the truck. Even Bella was appreciatively sniffing the air.

She pulled out into traffic between tourists' cars. The barn and corral area wasn't far and Dev wondered if Sloan was around or not. She probably should have called his office but took a risk. Even if he wasn't there, she wanted to check on Goldy and see if her mare was happy with her new digs. Pulling into the parking area in front of the green barn, Dev saw the doors were open at both ends to allow air to circulate through the barn. No one was around. Where was Sloan's office? Probably inside. She got Bella out on her leash and they walked into the barn.

There was a door open halfway down on the left. Dev

peeked in and saw Sloan sitting at a beat-up desk, busy doing paperwork. He looked up.

"Hey, good morning," Sloan said, standing.

Dev was touched by his courtly manners. In some ways, Sloan reminded her of a knight from a bygone era. "How do you get away with not wearing a ranger's uniform," she teased, meeting his smile. Instantly, her heart beat a little harder and she felt heat flowing down through her, wrapping around in her chest.

"Lucky, I guess," Sloan murmured, looking down at his Levi's and his blue chambray work shirt. He had the long sleeves rolled up to just below his elbows. "I assume you saw Charlotte?"

"Yes. She told me to look you up."

He gestured to the chipped and old-looking aluminum chair off to one side. "Have a seat."

Bella came in, wagging her tail, nosing around the desk to lick Sloan's proffered hand. He petted the dog with genuine warmth.

Dev sat down, noticing how much Bella liked him. She was a friendly dog by nature, but she had favorite people, too. Obviously, Sloan was on her short list. She tried not to stare at him, but the sleeves of his shirt were rolled up, showing off his lower arms. Rankin was nothing but pure muscle, but that wasn't surprising given his job as a farrier. Hefting around a heavy hammer, dealing with metal, shaping it with his large hands and inherent strength, this all showed in the lean, ropy muscles that moved beneath the sprinkle of dark hair across his skin. The Levi's fit him well and she saw he wore the same scarred old pair of boots as when she'd met him yesterday. There was a green USFS baseball cap hung up on a nail behind him. She saw the holster and pistol that rangers were to wear hung on another nail.

"Your office is hardly larger than a telephone booth," she said, looking around. A naked lightbulb hung above the desk, the only light to the place.

Sitting down, Sloan said, "I'm not in here any more than I have to be." He gestured to the papers in front of him. "I don't like office work, either, but today's the day to handle it."

"You'd rather be outdoors."

He grinned. "No secret there."

Dev pulled out the shift schedule and pushed it across the desk to him. "Charlotte wants me to shadow you or vice versa for the next two weeks."

Picking it up, he looked at it. "Yes. She nabbed me earlier this morning here in the barn, telling me what she wanted done to acclimate you and Bella."

"Do you want to play babysitter?" Dev wondered aloud, crossing her legs and leaning back on the chair. There was a glitter in his blue eyes, most likely amusement. His mouth twitched as he looked up to regard her.

"Now, don't go down that path, Dev. Charlotte's worried that because you've never been assigned to grizzly country before, that you need a little watching and training is all. Besides, we can't lose our tracker and her dog to a bear, can we? We just got you." He chuckled. "Charlotte's been beating her drum for someone like you for the past two years I've been here. She's over the moon you've arrived."

Bella laid her head in Dev's lap and she petted her dog. "And how are you with having to teach me the ropes?"

"Hey," Sloan joked, gesturing around his tiny office,

"it's better than being stuck in here in my telephone booth, don't you think?"

Dev saw the laughter in his eyes, the wry curve of his mouth that made her go hot with longing. The man's mouth was to die for. And she wondered what it would be like to kiss Sloan. His face was deeply tanned, with fine, feathered lines at the corners of his eyes, all proof of how much time he spent outdoors. Again, she felt that invisible sense of protection surround her. Bella felt it, too. The dog lifted her head, looking over at Sloan, who was putting all his papers into a drawer. So, Dev wasn't imagining it. Yes, she felt safe in Sloan's company. Maybe more than she should? Her heart liked being around this lanky farrier whose hands mesmerized her. Dev was sure if she told Sloan he had the most beautiful hands she'd ever seen it wouldn't go over too well with him. Men didn't consider themselves beautiful. She kept the remark to herself.

"How's Goldy?" she asked.

"I got here at 6:00 a.m. and checked in on her," Sloan said. "She was fine. I'm the one that feeds the horses stabled here. Goldy had finished her flake of timothy from yesterday and was more than ready for another one this morning. Why don't you go on down and visit her while I finish up duties here? It'll take me about ten more minutes. Then we'll hitch up a trailer and load Rocky and Goldy, and then trailer them up to the first area where we get a lot of lost tourists."

"Sounds good," she said, rising. Bella was out the door first, as if knowing Dev was going to see Goldy. The dog tugged at her leash. Smiling, Dev knew her mare and Bella were the best of friends. She wondered where Mouse was at. Did Sloan leave him back at his apartment for the day?

Goldy had her nose pressed between the iron bars and nickered softly as Dev approached. Bella whined and leaped up on her rear legs, paws on the front of the sliding door to the stall, happily licking at Goldy's velvety black nose. Dev positioned Bella at one side of the stall and like the good girl she was, she sat down. Bella knew when Dev gave a certain hand signal it meant stay and sit. Now, Dev could bring Goldy out and put her in the crossties to give her a brushing, clean her hooves, and the dog wouldn't move from where she'd placed her.

Her heart lifted with silent joy as she led her buckskin mare to the crossties and hooked the panic snaps on either side of her red nylon halter. Goldy's black mane had bits of cedar shavings in it, indicating she had lain down and rested at some point during the night. That was good, because two days of riding in a trailer was tiring for any horse. Grabbing her grooming kit from the tack room, Dev met Sloan on the way out.

"While you're cleaning up Goldy," he said, "I'm going to get the trailer hitched up."

"Sounds good. Do we saddle them before putting them in the trailer?"

"Yes. But we'll put the bridles on them once we arrive at the trailhead."

Her heart wouldn't settle down because Sloan had just given her an intent look. The sensation she'd felt was as if he was mentally photographing her. It wasn't uncomfortable, but rather made her feel desired. And darned if her body wasn't taking off and reacting favorably to that heated look. When he settled the Stetson on his head, it made him look like a cowhand, not a ranger. Trying to ignore her body and silly heart, she quickly cleaned up Goldy, who enjoyed all the attention.

They worked like a well-oiled team, which surprised Dev. She quickly saddled her mare and led her out of the barn, the bridle in her other hand. Rocky, the big gray gelding with the black mane and tail, was Sloan's horse. He was a rangy horse like his owner, probably part Thoroughbred because he was a good sixteen hands high. Of course, Sloan was a tall man and needed a bigger horse than she did for her size. Rocky was just as placid as his master. Dev waited outside the barn, allowing Goldy to nibble at the grass poking up here and there. She liked to watch Sloan move. He was graceful in a masculine sort of way.

"How old is Rocky?" she called down the aisle.

"He's ten," Sloan replied, running a comb and unsnarling Rocky's long, thick mane.

"Is he a USFS horse?"

Shaking his head, Sloan said, "No, he's mine."

"He's a nice-looking animal."

Grinning as he patted his horse's long, slender neck, he said, "I'd like to think so. Can't be a farrier and not be paying attention to the all-important conformation of a horse's legs. He's got near-perfect legs, but so does your mare." He glanced in her direction. "Says something about your horse knowledge, Dev."

Heat fled up Dev's neck and into her face. She was blushing from his praise and the warm looks he gave her. Sloan finished grooming Rocky and unsnapped the gelding from the crossties. All the man had to do was lower that voice of his and Dev felt like he'd reached out and stroked her with one of those beautiful male hands. To say she was befuddled didn't even begin to describe her body's reactions to being around Sloan Rankin. He was amiable, genial even, but not being a flirt or trying to let her know that he liked her.

Dev was positive Sloan liked her. With a groan, she took Goldy to the trailer. Both doors were open and she led Goldy into her narrow stall and snapped her halter to the chain in front. Moving up to the compartment, she watched Sloan throw the halter lead across Rocky's withers and cluck to him. The horse moved into the stall without hesitation and then stood quietly until Sloan got around to his side compartment to snap the lead to the trailer.

"That horse is used to hauling," Dev said, impressed. Not many horses would just hop into a trailer without being led in by a person.

"Rocky doesn't get upset about much," Sloan assured her. "Kinda like me…" He stepped out and shut the door. Dev followed. She went to the rear and watched Sloan close and lock the rear barn doors.

"Ready?" he asked, meeting her gaze.

"Very. I'm excited to get out into these mountains." Dev smiled a little, looking up at the massive peaks that were lined up in a row, north to south. "This is such a gorgeous place to work."

"Sure is," Sloan agreed, meeting her smile. "We're going up to the Moose Lake area. Lots of tourists get up in that area and get lost. I have no idea why, but it's a hot spot for us."

Snorting to herself as she climbed in the cab of his truck, Dev thought Sloan was a hot spot for her!

As they drove northward on the main two-lane highway through the park, Dev couldn't stop her curiosity about Sloan. She asked, "You have a sort of Southern drawl. Where were you born?" She saw him slant a glance in her direction and then return his attention to driving.

"I was born in the Allegheny Mountains of West Virginia," he told her. "Place no one's heard of, Black Mountain." Opening his fingers on the wheel for a moment, he added, "Most people, when I tell them that, think I'm a hillbilly."

Dev caught the amusement in the inflection of his voice. "Nothing wrong with that."

He raised a brow. "No?"

"No. Why would you ask?" Dev felt him teasing her and she enjoyed watching the corner of his mouth curve upward a little.

"Curious as to how you would respond to the label."

"Do most people catalog you because of it?" she asked. When he glanced at her, she saw thoughtfulness in his gaze. The man was easy to read. Unlike Bart Gordon, who always smiled, who always showered her with compliments, telling her how beautiful her hair was or how pretty her eyes were. It got so she hated to be in the same building with him.

"What does the word *hillbilly* bring up for you?" Sloan asked.

Shrugging, Dev petted Bella, who sat on the floor between her legs. "Actually, lucky, because they were born in rural parts of America. In more natural surroundings, rather than the big city or suburban areas."

"And you weren't born in nature?"

She grinned. "Technically, I was born in the suburbs of Casper, Wyoming, but out in back of our house there was nothing but fields that went on forever. I felt like I lived in nature."

"So you're a tough Wyoming-bred woman?"

The way his voice caressed her, Dev had to shake herself out of the sensation of warmth surrounding her. It was as if Sloan had invisibly embraced her. But he hadn't. "I don't know about tough," she said, "but yes, I'm used to long winters."

That brought a smile to his mouth. "Yes, you would be. Where I come from we have about three months, but then it starts warming up."

"Did you learn your farrier trade from your father?"

"Yes, I did. You're pretty astute."

"I find in some families that skill is passed down."

"So," he mused aloud, giving her a quick look, "you're a pretty observant woman. How did you get that way?"

"People interest me," Dev admitted, hungry for this kind of intimate conversation to better explore Sloan. She didn't look too closely at why.

"You're an extrovert?"

"Mostly, although—" Dev looked out the window at the passing grassy meadows and the evergreens skirting around them "—I consider myself half and half. My mother is an introvert. My father is an extrovert. I think I got a little from both of them. What about you?"

"My pa and ma are both introverts, so I got a double dose of it."

She smiled softly, absorbing his clean, rugged profile. There was nothing weak about Sloan Rankin. He was, in her book, a man's man. "You like quiet, no crowds and not getting peopled to death daily. How on earth did you get into the Forest Service, then? Most of our duties, with a few exceptions, involve interfacing with the public on a daily basis."

"They hired me for a couple of reasons. I don't think

it crossed their minds that I was a total introvert. I came
out of the Army and was a combat assault–dog handler.
Plus, my pa taught me to be a blacksmith, and they were
looking for someone good with animals and who had
farrier skills." He smiled a little, slanting a look toward
Dev. "Most of the time, I'm with animals, not humans.
They never stress me. But put me on the visitor's desk?
Then I'm tensed up tighter than a riled copperhead."

She chuckled. "So you were in the military?"

"I was. I guess I fit the profile of a dog handler at the
testing phase and got shuttled out of basic and into dog
training. Ended up with a few two-year-long deployments to Afghanistan with my boy Mouse."

"Those had to be intense deployments," Dev muttered, frowning. "Dangerous work every day."

"It was. I wanted out of the Army after my four-year
enlistment was up. My dog had a nervous breakdown of
sorts. We got attacked on a hill with RPGs being thrown
at us from three directions. My dog couldn't handle it."
And then his mouth thinned. "None of us could, so the
dog's anxiety was merely a reflection of all of ours. He
just showed it outwardly. The rest of us stuffed it deep
down inside of us instead. Animals are more honest than
most humans, I've found."

Dev felt tension and grief surround Sloan for a moment, and then the sensation dissolved. It surprised her
he would allow his feelings to show and wondered why.
Did he trust her? Or was he that way with everyone? "I
was in the Marine Corps for four years," she admitted
quietly. "I was a dog handler, too. Only I was out on deployments with bomb-sniffing dogs, not like what you
did. Your kind of work was far more dangerous than
mine."

"So, you were in the Corps?"

"Now, you aren't going to throw labels on me, are you, Sloan?" she teased a little, watching his shoulders come down to their normal position. Just talking about those dangerous deployments had tensed him up. Dev understood fully.

"Me? Nah. I believe in letting a person show me who they are through their actions, not their words. Still, I find it interesting we were both in the military and both dog handlers, although in different capacities."

Moving her fingers across Bella's sleek, golden head, Dev smiled softly. "I loved my work, but the heat was brutal. Bella here is my second dog. She got injured in a bomb blast and I got to take her with me after I got out."

He scowled. "Were you injured, too?"

"Just shrapnel. Bella's the one who took the real injury." Dev held up her right arm. "The doctor picked out a bunch of shrapnel from my lower arm and shoulder. I'm good as new now. Bella took a big piece in her left shoulder. She develops a bit of a limp if we're out tracking more than six hours. Other than that, she's in no pain and is great at what she does."

Sloan's brows drew downward, his mouth flexing, as if unhappy. A powerful sense of protection washed over Dev and this time she knew it was from Sloan, how he was feeling toward her. Never had she felt this kind of a reaction from a man. She wondered if he was aware of it. Glancing at his profile, he seemed intent on driving. Oh, how humans hid things from one another. With an internal shake of her head, Dev knew full well she had been hiding her real feelings and reactions from the day that IED had gone off, sending her and Bella into the air, blown ten feet backward from the blast wave. Even now, her hearing wasn't back to normal.

It had ruptured both her eardrums. And even Bella's hearing wasn't perfect, which was why the Marine Corps had released her.

"Well," Sloan drawled, "I'm fairly sure you're glossing over your time in the military. On any given night, I can have a nightmare and recall every last detail whether I want to or not."

CHAPTER FOUR

THE GRAVEL PARKING lot near Moose Lake was huge. There were steep trails that led to a waterfall halfway up the flank of one of the jagged, snow-dusted Tetons. The sun was warm on Dev's back. Both horses were frisky and eagerly trotted toward the narrow, rocky trail that disappeared quickly in the fir trees. Bella happily trotted behind Goldy, keeping pace with them. Dev had a leash but didn't use it in such tight quarters. Besides, her dog was voice trained and Bella would obey her without hesitation. The air was pungent with the scent of the evergreens, and Dev thought it was one of her most favorite fragrances as she followed Rocky and Sloan up a steep switchback. They disappeared around the corner for a moment. Dev noted there was spring runoff snow from further above. The soil was slippery. On top of that, rocks appeared out of the mud and crisscrosses of roots snaked horizontally across the trail.

As they moved more deeply into the woods, always staying on switchbacks and climbing ever higher, Dev absorbed the muted silence of the forest surrounding them. She heard a blue jay calling in the distance. In front of Rocky, who had settled down to a plodding walk because of the nature of the challenging trail, she saw a robin on the path, pulling a worm out of the ground.

Dev tried not to appreciate Sloan's broad shoulders,

which were pulled back with natural pride. But now she realized it was a military posture, too. The fact that he had been an Army combat-dog handler made her feel good. Why, she wasn't quite sure, but because of her own experience it served to tell Dev that Sloan was a patient, kind person. A dog handler had to be sensitive, fully aware not only of themselves or their surroundings, but of the dog who was working and keeping the rest of the soldiers safe from hidden IEDs planted by the local Taliban.

Just the swaying movement of Goldy between her legs lulled her into a relaxation, more like a meditation, that Dev loved. The morning was perfect in every way. And the man in front of her tugged at her dormant heart. For months, Dev had been wrapped in anxiety, nightmares and sleeplessness after Gordon's attack on her. Her male supervisor had wanted her to go get therapy, but Dev had refused. Her mother, an airline pilot, was a very strong, confident woman. Dev had never seen her buckle under any loads she carried, and she wasn't about to buckle under hers, either. She'd just had to gut her way through it.

About a mile into the trail, it widened and Dev noticed that two trails to the east and west branched off from the one they were on. Sloan halted his horse and turned around at the juncture.

"Nice riding, isn't it?" he asked her, watching as Bella came and sat down nearby, panting and looking happy to be out in the woods with them. Big dogs needed big exercise to stay happy.

Dev wore her dark green USFS baseball cap. "Yes, gorgeous. It's so peaceful here." She smiled fondly, looking around, absorbing all the smells and sounds around them.

Pushing his Stetson up on his brow Sloan said, "This east trail goes to the waterfall about half a mile above us." He gestured toward the upward slope. "The other trail goes down into Lupine Meadow. It's a very large meadow about a quarter of a mile from the waterfall." He pointed to the signs. "You can see they're well marked. What happens is that parents with small children who go to the Lupine Meadow trail are pretty bushed by the time they arrive at the spot. Once they get into the meadow, which is very large and wide, they let the children run around. Nothing wrong with that, but if you got more than one child to look after, distraction occurs and the parents tend to lose one of 'em."

Nodding, Dev lifted her leg and curved it around the saddle horn to ease the stress on it. She hadn't ridden in about two weeks, so her legs needed to get their muscles back. "Are we going to the meadow?"

"Yes. First, I'll take you to the waterfall area and then there's a small, unmarked trail that goes directly to Lupine. Most tourists don't find it because it's pretty well hidden. Plus, there's a grizzly whose territory is around there and she has two one-year-old cubs with her. We don't mark that trail nor do we want tourists on it. The construction teams use it, though, when we pack in equipment on the mules to repair trails or other areas that need fixing after the hard winters we get around here."

Taking off her cap, Dev pushed her fingers through her loose hair. She saw something in Sloan's eyes but couldn't translate it. Her body, however, did respond to that millisecond look as she slid her fingers through her hair. "Okay, I'd like to see that trail, too. Has anyone ever gotten lost on it?"

Sloan shook his head. "No, thank God. Because the

mother grizzly has a den up about one-tenth of a mile off it and the Forest Service doesn't want anyone up there. Right now, we've got grizzly warning signs around the waterfall area where she comes to get water. If she's spotted too often by incoming hikers, we'll shut the whole area down until midsummer when she's not so hungry as to be looking at tourists as a food source." Sloan grinned a little.

"Do grizzlies really want to eat a human being?"

"Not really. But if the human gets in their territory, then the bear perceives them as a threat and will attack. You ever seen a grizzly?"

"No. From the sounds of it, I don't want to, either."

"Oh," Sloan murmured, "you'll meet them soon enough." He glanced over at Bella. "And what's worse, you have a dog in tow. Bears really get agitated when seeing a dog and that's why they aren't allowed in either the Tetons or Yellowstone Park. Grizzlies, I think, see them as wolves. They aren't, but bear perception is such that they are seen as a definite threat." He touched the quart of bear spray hanging off his left hip. "This is why whenever you take Bella with you, you have bear spray as a deterrent. And you have to make sure she won't go bark or charge the bear, either, because that will only worsen the situation."

"Do they like to eat horses?" Dev asked, running her fingers gently through Goldy's black mane.

"The scent will attract them," Sloan said. "Usually, we get bear and horse attacks on riders who are staying and camping overnight in certain areas of the Tetons. Grizzlies are starving to death when they come out of hibernation, which is right now, and they will eat anything they see. Horses look like big elk to them and elk are their favorite meat source on the hoof."

Mouth tightening, Dev looked down at the leather sheath beneath her left leg. There was a .30-06 rifle in it, loaded, with the safety on. It was a bear rifle and would stop one, if necessary. Not that she wanted to kill one of those magnificent bears, but Sloan had said they could range between six hundred to a thousand pounds. And that was a threat to Dev, pure and simple. Her horse weighed a thousand pounds. She couldn't imagine a brute of a grizzly weighing that much, but Sloan assured her they were around, and plentiful among the females of the population.

"I just don't want to run into one," Dev muttered, frowning.

"You will. Guaranteed. And if you're tracking to find a tourist, it's what you do with Bella that counts the most." Sloan regarded the yellow Lab, who had lain down in the muddy trail to cool off. They had ridden for half an hour, a constant climb. Right now, they were at seven thousand feet. The horses were breathing heavier, too, so it was a good time to allow them a rest. "Has Bella had confrontations with black bears where you were assigned before?"

"Yes, quite a few times. The trails in the Smoky Mountains aren't like these." She gestured around them. "They're wide, clean paths in comparison to this stuff." Dev wrinkled her nose. "When tracking, I always had Bella on a long lead from my horse I rode. But here, it's impossible to do that."

"It's rough country," Sloan agreed, placing his hand on Rocky's rump and stretching a little. "As long as Bella is a hundred percent controllable by voice commands, you'll be okay. And she doesn't bark, so that's in her favor. Bears get riled and agitated in a hurry when a dog is barking at them."

"Probably reminds them of wolves calling back and forth to one another?" Dev suggested.

"Yep. That's it in a nutshell. Well? Ready to move on?" Sloan smiled.

Heat skittered down through her lower body, his smile warming her, the corners of his eyes crinkling. There was a sultry, inviting sensation enveloping Dev right now and it felt like a big fuzzy blanket embracing her. When she knew Sloan better, she'd talk to him about this feeling that came around her at times when she was with him. Maybe he could explain it, because she sure couldn't! The fact that she willingly absorbed the sensation confused her, as well. "Yep," Dev said, uncurling her leg from around the horn of her saddle and slipping the tip of her boot into the stirrup, "I'm ready."

SLOAN COULDN'T KEEP his gaze off Dev as they sat near the roaring waterfall that fell over a hundred feet into a pool. They sat on the grass and ate their midmorning snack. The horses were both trained to ground tie and knew they had to stand where they were placed. Bella had eagerly lapped up the water and now sat next to Dev, who was on a bank, her long legs hanging over it. She had taken off her baseball cap, and her black hair was shining like a raven's wing beneath the sunlight. It was cold at nine thousand feet where the waterfall sat but they were bundled in their brown down-and-nylon jackets.

Sloan sat about four feet above Dev on the slope of the rocky cliff. Below them, the dark green pool of water was in constant motion from the falls. Sometimes, when the breeze changed, some of the mist would come their way, but it didn't soak them. The sunlight was bright and blinding. Sloan absorbed the heat, liking it against the chill of the morning temperature. In May, he knew too well that even if one moment there could be sun, the mountains made their own weather. Clouds could swiftly gather, dark and heavy with snow and rain, and dump on the eastern slope.

Dev was nibbling on a protein bar and had her canteen open near her right hand. He covertly watched some of the black strands of her hair lift and play in the breeze. Her hands were long and artistic looking. Sloan wanted to ask Dev if she was an artist, too. He wondered about her time in the military, about getting wounded by the IED. From his own experience, those events branded a person forever. He wondered how jumpy she really was because it hadn't shown up—yet. Though remembering that split-second terror in her eyes a day ago, Sloan wondered if it was connected to the PTSD from the blast. Right now Dev didn't appear anxious. But then, he thought as he looked around in appreciation of the area, the Tetons usually encouraged a person to let down their guard and relax. Nature had that effect on tense, overstressed human beings, he'd observed.

"Tell me more about your parents," Sloan urged her, figuring it was a safe enough topic. He saw Dev give Bella the last of her protein bar and rest her hand on her dog's back. Clearly, she loved her Lab. Sloan found himself wondering what it would be like to feel Dev's hand stroking him like it was stroking Bella. Whatever sizzled and popped between him and Dev was not only alive but more intense every time he found himself around her. And Sloan had never felt this kind of connection with a woman before. It reminded him of a pot on a stove, getting ready to boil at any given moment. Something was bubbling between them.

Dev turned. "It's a story light and dark," she said with a shrug. "My parents met in the Air Force. My mom was a captain and a pilot of C-130 transports. My father was a captain in the maintenance section on those types of aircraft. They fell in love and stayed in the military for seven years. When my mom, Lily, got pregnant with me, she got out. She was thirty when she had me." Dev smiled fondly. Then, her brows drew down a little and her voice lowered. "My father, Pete, had a problem with alcohol. While he was in the military, it was a hidden secret from my mom. She was always flying and not at home that much." She plucked a couple strands of grass, moving them between her fingers as she spoke. "My mother was more than ready to get out of the military. Once she had me, she was hired by a regional airline and she flies with them to this day. My father, however, didn't adjust well to civilian life."

"What happened?" Sloan asked.

"Well, as a kid growing up, I didn't understand he was an alcoholic. My mother didn't get it until I was a year old. She found him hiding whiskey bottles all over their house, stashing them away. I think, looking back on it, my father needed the rigidity and boundaries that the military naturally provided in order to keep his drinking halfway under control, and to still be able to fully do the work he did."

"Did your father come from parents who were alcoholics?" Sloan wondered.

"Yes. But my mother didn't find out until she discovered his secret. I remember growing up with them yelling and screaming at one another. My father refused to stop drinking. My mother, because of her airline shifts, wasn't at home to raise me. I had a lot of babysitters and maybe that was a good thing." Dev allowed the torn, twisted strands of grass to drop from her fingers and fall to the nearby rocks.

"Why do you say that?"

"My father resented me being in their lives." She gave Sloan a sad smile. "I didn't know why my father didn't like me…or love me… I just felt as a child he didn't want me underfoot or around. He had a job with a metal manufacturer in Casper and had shift work. When he had a night shift, he had to babysit me during the day and he really hated that."

Sloan frowned. "How do you know that?"

Dev picked more strands of grass because it soothed her. She twisted the long lengths between her fingers, staring down at them because she didn't have the courage to see the look that was probably in Sloan's eyes. Why was she telling him this? She'd never told anyone about it before. No one knew. Why him? Compressing her lips, Dev said, "I remember him telling me to stay in my room, not to dare going outside. At that time, I was seven years old, and I loved being outdoors. I used to sneak out through my bedroom window and run in the fields while he was drinking. When he drank, he'd fall sleep on the couch, and that's when I'd get out of the house and escape outdoors."

"You were seven?"

Dev heard the growl in Sloan's voice and looked over at him. His eyes were banked with censure and anger. She knew it wasn't aimed at her but at her irresponsible father. "Yes." Hitching one shoulder upward she said,

"Don't worry, I grew up fast. My mother would be gone
three or four days at a time, depending upon where she
was flying. My father would sleep six or eight hours
when drunk. We had a dog, Ghost, and I'd go out with
her. She was a white husky with blue eyes. She was so
beautiful. She was like my teddy bear growing up, and
always protective and caring of me. We'd go out into
the meadow and just go explore for hours. When I got
hungry, I'd walk home and go to the kitchen and make
myself a sandwich."

"Did your father know you did this?" Sloan tried to
remove the anger from his voice.

"No. I never told him. I had his drunk schedule down
pat and knew when I could do it and get away with it. I
never told my mother, either, because if I did, they'd start
screaming and yelling at one another. I couldn't stand
their anger. Whenever they'd fight, I'd run to my room
and Ghost would come and lie on my bed with me and
give me a doggy hug."

Shaking his head, Sloan said, "I'm really sorry you
had to live through that. Did your father ever hurt your
mother or you?"

Dev felt a powerful sense of protection wash over her
and understood now that it was coming from him. Maybe
she could equate it to the doggy hugs that Ghost always
gave her when she was feeling isolated and alone. "He
never laid a hand on me or Mom, thank God. When I
was old enough to realize he was an alcoholic, I ruthlessly researched the disease and what it meant. I wanted
to understand why he was the way he was. Why—" and
Dev choked up a little, avoiding Sloan's intense stare
"—he couldn't love me. He never hugged me or kissed
me or told me he loved me. He just didn't have it in him.

Frankly, after I grew up and matured a little, I saw why he couldn't. My father couldn't even love himself. So how could he reach out to love me?"

"But your parents are still together?"

"Yeah. Figure it out. I can't. I don't know why my mom never left my father."

"Do you go home at all?" Sloan asked.

"No. I talk to my mom on Skype and we send emails back and forth, but I won't go home. I know my father doesn't like me around. And I don't want to be around someone like that." Dev gave him a wry look. "Life's hard enough without going out and walking into the lion's den to get bitten again."

Shaking his head, Sloan said quietly, "I'm sorry, Dev. You deserve a helluva lot better than that."

"I don't know many people who have completely happy families, Sloan. Mine is completely dysfunctional. But so are a lot of other families. There are no happy endings from what I can see, for most people. We're all wounded. It's just a question of whether the wounds run our lives or not." She dropped the shredded grass by her side, pushing her hands down her Levi's. "I refuse to let the wounds my parents gave me run my life. I'm working through them, one at a time. I'm slowly winning my freedom…"

Sloan stretched out on the grass, an elbow propping him up as he studied her. "I'm pretty lucky," he told her. "My parents gave me a happy childhood in comparison to yours. I was an only child, by the way."

"Tell me about it?" Because Dev found herself starved to know more about Sloan, how he had become the man he was today. She saw amusement linger in his blue eyes as he pondered her question. "I could use some *good* news," she added with a slight grin.

"We didn't have much money," he told her. "My pa, Custus, is a farrier, plus a leather, saddle and harness maker. Between these skills, he had a nice business and was able to support our family. My ma, Wilma, stayed at home, gardened, canned, cooked and kept us in clean clothes and a clean house. She loves cooking, baking especially. She was also a seamstress, and often other Hill people would come to her to make special clothing, like a wedding dress for a daughter that was getting married, things like that. She also makes school-age clothes for the Hill children whose mothers didn't have the talent my ma has."

"I love to sew, too," Dev said wistfully. "Your mother sounds like she's incredibly skilled at it. I don't know anyone else who could make a wedding dress." She saw Sloan's dark features begin to relax as he shared the story of his parents. She was glad that someone had parents who loved them. She was beginning to understand why he was so calm and at ease and confident with himself.

"She also does tatting, crocheting, knitting and needlework," he offered. "There're some beautiful doilies made by my grandmother that my mother uses to this day."

"Those things should be cherished forever and handed down from one generation to another," Dev agreed. "She sounds wonderful."

"She is," he said with a slight smile. "Now, she has her bad days, and I grew up hearing my parents argue, but they discussed things. They didn't get angry and yell at one another. And I think that makes a huge difference for a child."

She raised her brows. "Oh, I think it does. I grew up thinking everyone, when they got angry, screamed and yelled at one another. It was only when I'd do sleepovers with my friends at their houses that I realized my parents were not the norm."

"My pa is a pretty stubborn man," Sloan said, amusement in his tone. "My ma calls him mule headed upon occasion. She said I take after him."

Dev grinned. "So far, I haven't seen you be mule headed."

"I like to think I learned from my pa's stubbornness at times, and modified it a bit."

"Where did you get your calmness, Sloan? From your mother or father?" Dev wanted to delve deeply into this man who made her feel incredibly at ease in his presence.

"From both of them. My ma never gets rattled and neither does my pa. I guess I have a family calmness gene?" He laughed a little.

Dev chuckled. "Well, whether you know it or not, when you're around me, I always feel that deep sense of calm around you." More shyly, she added, "And it helps me ramp down, take a deep breath and just be."

"You seem mighty calm from the outside," Sloan noted, searching her eyes.

"It's a game face," Dev admitted. Opening her hands, she said, "I can't remember a time when I didn't feel anxious."

"Well," he drawled, "you grew up in a household where there were threats and you were in survival mode. It would make any innocent and vulnerable child feel unsafe, don't you think?"

"I guess I never quantified my childhood like that," Dev admitted.

"Do most people make you feel edgy?" he asked.

"Yes, if I'm truthful." Dev sighed and gave him a confused look. "But with you, Sloan, I let my guard down. I relax. I don't feel anxiety when I'm around you. It's really odd. That's never happened to me before." She saw him give her an assessing look, a momentary burning expression in his eyes that quickly disappeared and was replaced with a hint of kindness.

"That's a nice compliment. You know, farriers are good at soothing a fractious horse or mule they have to shoe. They generally work real quiet and slow around an animal to get it to relax and get it to trust them."

Dev straightened, his words filling her heart with a new realization. *Trust.* That was it! For whatever inexplicable reason, Dev trusted Sloan. And on the heels of that, she suddenly realized for the first time that she had never trusted her father, and that had directly led to her always feeling anxious around him growing up. Even now, when she thought of him her anxiety would amp up. And just as quickly, when she was around Sloan her anxiety dissolved. Instantly. Always. It was *trust.* Moistening her lips, she said softly, "You're right. Farriers can calm the most scared horse or mule." And he could calm not only her general anxiety, but mysteriously dissolve the fear of men she'd developed since Gordon's attack.

Sloan slowly sat up. He gazed up at the waterfall, appreciation in his expression. "I could stay here all day," he confided to her. "There's just something about running water, the sound of it, that fills my thirsty soul and sates it." He slanted a glance in Dev's direction. "What about you? Does water have that kind of effect on you?"

"Oh, yes. I remember as a kid we had a creek that ran through that large meadow out behind our home. When I was feeling really upset, me and Ghost would go to the creek. There's a part of it where there's a little two-foot waterfall and I always used to sit down there. I'd cry, get out whatever I was feeling, and then let the water heal me. I always felt better being around water, Sloan." And she almost blurted, *You're like water to me. Healing. Wonderful. Soothing my soul.* But she didn't.

"I wish I'd known you growing up," Sloan said, rising and brushing off his lower legs. "I'd have let you cry on my shoulder and just held you."

His piercing gaze cut straight through to her opening heart and Dev felt Sloan's protectiveness and something else that she couldn't define. It made her go all warm and fuzzy inside. When he offered her his hand, she slipped her fingers into his. She felt the thick calluses on his fingers and palm, the strength that he called on as he pulled her to her feet. There was a storminess in his eyes and she sensed he was upset for her about her childhood. Sloan didn't try to mask how he felt and that was refreshing to Dev. Reluctantly, she pulled her fingers from his large worn hand. Her heart wanted her to move closer to him, slide her arms around his neck and broad shoulders. The ache within her lower body caught her by surprise. He was so tall, so solid and reassuring to her emotionally that Dev found herself falling into his blue gaze, reading that he wanted to kiss her.

That snapped Dev out of her reverie. A kiss?

They barely knew one another, her head warned her. Dev took a step back, suddenly unsure of herself, not of

Sloan. She had no idea what was taking place between them because no man had ever affected her as deeply and wonderfully as Sloan did. And yet, Dev knew he wasn't stalking her. He was casual. Not chasing her. This cowboy was the opposite of Gordon. Night-and-day difference.

CHAPTER FIVE

Bart smiled a little. He had the weekend off as a truck driver for Ace. He'd been working for two weeks, showing his boss he had the right stuff. Rivas, the owner, seemed happy with him, and that was all that counted. Even better, Rivas had given him a cot in a back room near the repair bay, a place to stay, until he could find somewhere to live. There was more to it than that, of course, Bart thought as he drove in his silver Dodge Ram. The day was sunny even though the sun was sinking in the West across the Tetons. The mid-June weather had been welcoming and warming. No more snow flurries, thank God.

He was driving down Moose Road toward a set of condo buildings on the left. On the right were apartment complexes sticking out on the flat land. So far, he'd found out that Dev Blake was at the Teton Park HQ. They wouldn't give out her phone number or address and so he'd hung up on the person answering the phone. He had learned that, yes, Dev was working at the visitor's center.

Today, he was going to check out the condos and the apartment complexes. The only way to find out where she was living was to go into the condo office and ask for her. So far, he'd turned up nothing. His mind roved over other possibilities, such as Dev living with another woman ranger and splitting the rent somewhere in town.

If it was a house, she was going to be harder to trace. Bart was hoping she had opted for one of these places on Moose Road because he'd exhausted all other rental properties, working from southern to northern Jackson Hole. He'd gone east and now he was finishing up by going west. The bitch had to be living somewhere.

And finding out she was working at the visitor's center was a piece of good luck. If nothing else, on his day off, he could hang out in the large parking lot and observe. Bart knew Dev McGuire owned a blue-and-white Ford pickup truck. It was another piece of vital info he needed in order to find out where she was living. Making a right turn, he decided to go into the apartment complex and parked near the office. Bart climbed out of the cab. He had made sure he looked like a tourist in a red polo shirt, a fisherman's hat and ivory chinos.

"Hey," he called, coming in the door and smiling at the young blond-haired woman behind the desk, "how are you?"

"I'm fine," she said. "May I help you?"

Folding his hands on the pine counter Bart said, "I'm looking for a friend of mine. Dev McGuire. By any chance is she living here? I'd like to connect with her." Bart saw the girl's young face redden a little as she put the name into the computer behind the counter. Bart knew she would not give Dev's apartment number or phone number. That was just the way it was.

"Why…yes, she moved in here two weeks ago."

"Great," he murmured, rewarding her with a flirty look. "I'll get in touch with her, then. Thanks. Have a good day."

Once in his pickup, Bart grinned and decided to drive around the three major parking lots to the three apartment towers. He tapped the wheel with his index finger, feeling a surge of triumph. The bitch thought she was done with him? He chuckled, feeling a sense of overwhelming victory.

There was no blue-and-white Ford pickup parked in any of the lots. He glanced at his watch. It was 5:30 p.m. He wasn't sure what shift Dev had. And those shifts changed every three months, anyway. As he got out, his gut told him to park at the first tower. At his back was the second tower and parking lot. Seeing a number of people coming home for the evening, he figured the mailboxes just inside the door would have names on them—possibly. That wasn't always the case, but he'd find out.

He went up to the main entry door but found it locked. An older woman in her fifties approached. He pretended to be looking in his pockets as she drew abreast of him.

"You know what?" he said, smiling at her. "I can't find my card. By any chance, can you let me in? I just moved in three days ago." Bart knew his megawatt smile always affected women. That was how he lured them in. The woman flushed and nodded.

"Oh, moving is so rough. Of course I can." She went forward and slid her card into the slot. The door clicked.

Bart moved toward it, opened it and gestured grandly for her to go in ahead of him.

"Thank you," she said. There was a bank of elevators to the left and she headed toward them.

Spotting the row of aluminum mailboxes, Bart quickly peeled off to the right, eyes narrowed, hoping to find Dev's name. Each one had a number. Some had names on them, too. Others did not. About half were just numbers. He was frustrated. If Dev was in this tower, she had a number only. *Damn. So close...*

SLOAN PARKED AT the complex and got Mouse out of the cab of his truck and onto a leash. He immediately noticed a tall red-haired man leaving Tower One, hands in his pockets. The stranger gazed around, as if trying to find someone. Sloan closed the door and stood, watching him. Mouse suddenly became alert. His dog was basically psychic, moving into that state of superawareness. Sloan knew most of the residents. He'd lived here two years and he made it his business to know faces and cars. The man briefly glanced in his direction and then swiftly looked away when he realized Sloan was studying him.

Something didn't feel right about this fellow. Sloan watched the man walk to a big silver Dodge Ram, climb in and then leave, heading south on Moose Road, toward town. Rubbing the back of his neck, he saw Mouse watching him, too. The dog was getting a hit, just like he had. And that was why Mouse was so good at what he did. The leather leash was wrapped around Sloan's hand. "Come on, let's go in, Mouse."

The dog wagged his tail, following him.

Sloan's mind drifted to Dev. Since that trail ride two weeks ago, it seemed that life was doing everything it could to keep them apart. He rarely saw her, except when she came into the barn to take Goldy for a ride on one of the nearby trails. He was always either leaving or coming back from shoeing assignments for the Forest Service. No one had any idea how many mules and horses the USFS had in this area. The rangers always rode horses and the mules did the heavy lifting. The mules carried shovels, pickaxes, quick-drying cement, and loads of posts and nails where needed.

Sloan wanted to see Dev. Where was she? He knew she was still on the day shift. Maybe she'd gone into town to do some grocery shopping? Dammit, he missed her. Missed hearing her husky voice, seeing the sparkle of gold in her dark green eyes, the way she tilted her head, the way her sleek black hair curled across her shoulders, emphasizing the natural beauty of her face. Those lips of hers teased his senses.

With a groan, Sloan took the stairs to the second floor, Mouse at his side. Maybe he should leave a note on her door? Invite her over for a glass of wine after dinner? He preferred beer, but Sloan had found out in their conversations she was a white-wine lover. And last week he'd bought a bottle that she liked and stored it in his fridge...just in case.

Opening his door, Sloan pushed it wide and took a look around. Old habits died hard in him. He'd breached a lot of doors of Taliban homes in Afghanistan. He could feel Mouse tensing, as if ready to be sent in to find and attack the enemy. Patting his dog's head, he unsnapped the leash and Mouse bounded inside, heading for the kitchen where there was a big bowl of water. By the time Sloan got in, locked the door, and found a pad and pen, Mouse was noisily lapping up water. Sloan smiled to himself and wondered how single people managed without a dog or cat to lighten their lives, make things better. He'd been raised around farm animals, dogs and cats all his life. Sloan would be lonely without an animal to keep him company.

He scribbled the note, found a piece of tape and

opened his door to walk across the hall to stick it on Dev's.

"Hey," Dev called, waving to him as she walked down the hall. Bella, at her side on a leash, wagged her tail upon seeing Sloan.

Halting, Sloan grinned. She was in her ranger uniform and looked a little tired. "Hey, yourself." He lifted the paper. "I haven't seen you hardly at all in the past two weeks so I was going to put this on your door and invite you over for some white wine, if you wanted." He liked the smile coming to Dev's face as her cheeks flushed. Her hair was in disarray and it looked like she'd been outdoors.

Dev held out her hand. "I'll take that invite. I *need* it tonight." She opened the door and said, "Let me change. You pour the wine and I'll be over in two heartbeats."

Nodding, Sloan felt his heart expand. "You got it."

"Is it okay if I bring Bella over?"

Mouse always enjoyed Bella's company. Why not? "Sure." Dev's green eyes lit up and Sloan's lower body instantly tightened. Her smile always made his heart beat a little faster, his yearning increase.

Entering his apartment, Sloan felt lighter. The injured part of him fought with the delicious, dizzying happiness that tunneled through him. He put all his bad experiences aside. Dev interested him and he craved her company. Looking at Mouse, who was wagging his tail as if reading his mind, Sloan chuckled and walked to the kitchen to get the wine and pour her a glass. "You're going to get some company, too, partner."

Mouse whined, his dark brown eyes shining with anticipation.

That was about the way Sloan felt as he poured the

wine and then got himself a cold beer out of his fridge. He decided Dev might be hungry, so he sliced up some Gouda cheese on a plate and added some crackers to it. Might as well go all the way. As he placed the plate on the kitchen table, there was a light knock at his door. Sloan tried to ignore his heart bouncing in reaction.

Opening the door, he saw Dev had changed into a pair of baggy gray workout pants and she wore a loose pale green tee. Bella was at her side on a leash, wagging her tail and panting, her eyes sparkling, too.

"Come on in," he invited, standing aside. This was only the second time Dev had been in his apartment. As she walked by, Sloan automatically inhaled her scent, evergreen combined with her own sweet fragrance that made him groan internally. Good thing he was wearing Levi's, but that didn't make the ache of his erection feel any better as it pressed against the zipper, encountering fabric resistance.

Bella remained at Dev's side until she unsnapped the leash and gave the Lab a hand signal to go join Mouse, who was ever the gentleman, sitting near his big doggy bed in the corner of the large living room. They sniffed and smelled one another in greeting, tails moving excitedly back and forth.

Sloan gestured to the kitchen table. "I don't imagine you've had dinner yet?"

Wrinkling her nose, Dev took the chair he pulled out for her. "No…and honestly? I don't feel up to a full meal just yet. The cheese and crackers look good, though." She glanced up, smiling at him.

Sloan saw that Bella was lying down near Mouse, both of them panting and gazing adoringly at one another. Mouse was better behaved than Sloan was feeling right now. Dev's dark hair was smoothed and brushed. Her cheeks were flushed and as always, his gaze dropped to her mouth for a split second. Sloan sat down at her elbow, sliding the cold beaded glass of white wine toward her. "What happened? You looked a little stressed earlier."

She nibbled on the cheese and then took a sip of the wine. "Right before 5:00 p.m., an older lady fainted at our desk. Out of the blue. Scared the hell out of me."

"What was wrong with her?"

"I think a stroke, but I'm not sure. I ran around the counter after she collapsed and with the help of Becky, who was also working a shift, we got her lying down with her head tipped back so she could breathe."

"I'll bet the other visitors were upset," Sloan guessed, taking a drink of beer, the bubbles feeling good in his mouth.

Dev rolled her eyes. "That was the worst part. The woman's daughter went ballistic. She was shrieking and screaming, completely losing it."

"People never know what they'll do until they're faced with a crisis," Sloan mused. "Could you talk the daughter down?"

"No," Dev said, blowing out a big sigh. "I told Becky to deal with her while I stayed with the unconscious woman until the ambulance arrived. A third ranger, Randy, quietly moved all the tourists out of the center and stood guard at the door, giving us some privacy and space."

"Sounds like you handled it the best you could."

"Yes, but it really shook me up," Dev admitted, picking up a cracker.

"It would anyone," Sloan told her gently. "Don't be

hard on yourself, Dev." There was something in her eyes, deep in the recesses of them, that Sloan couldn't define. That same terror he'd seen weeks ago was lurking in their depths. Dev's brow creased as she frowned and she took a deep drink of the wine. He could see a slight tremble in her fingers around the glass stem as she set it down.

"Well," Dev muttered, giving him a worried look, "there's more to this, but you probably realize that."

Sloan sat back, stretching out his long legs beneath the table. "I can see you're upset, Dev. What did this event trigger for you?" He might as well try to get her to talk about it. Even though they hadn't had a lot of time together, it was obvious he and Dev shared something good between them. Would she trust him and let her guard down with him? Sloan didn't know. He could see her struggle with his question. She pushed her fingers through her hair and he was beginning to understand that with Dev, it was a gesture of nervousness, of not being sure about something.

So, he waited. Sloan had learned a long time ago when dealing with fractious horses that hated being shod, that just standing quietly and patiently, letting the animal get it out of their system, was the best course of action. And he thought Dev needed that same kind of response from him if she was going to share whatever it was that had triggered the terror in her eyes again.

"Well," she mumbled, wrapping both hands around the wet stem of the wineglass, "you're right. It hit me a lot harder than I expected…the noise…the screams… the ambulance…"

Sloan met and held her eyes, seeing the trepidation in them. Dev compressed her lips. "You were in the Marine Corps," he offered quietly. "And from what you've told me, with that IED going off close to you and Bella, plus getting wounded, you probably have a little PTSD from the event. It would be expected, Dev."

Her mouth thinned further, one corner pulling inward as she gave him a swift look and then returned her gaze to the wineglass in front of her. "I do have PTSD. It wasn't half as bad as it is now, though…"

Frowning, Sloan remained relaxed, although his instincts told him that Dev needed to be held. Her fingers opened and closed constantly around the stem of the wineglass. He could feel the tension in her because his sixth sense was finely honed from years working in Afghanistan, where every minute he and Mouse could have died if they weren't careful. His hyperawareness wasn't something Sloan wanted many people to know about because it usually made them uncomfortable in his midst. Some accused him of having X-ray vision. Or being a mind reader. But it was neither. He just had very well honed instincts at an animal level he'd used to sense out situations that might have been lethal to him and Mouse. Even after leaving the Army, that skill remained online to this day.

The feelings he sensed around Dev were devastating to Sloan. Strong emotions, intense and shattering. What the hell had happened to her? He keyed in on her statement that her PTSD was worse now than before. What did that mean? Had there been another incident in the Marine Corps that had deepened it? Made it worse? He knew there were so many dark emotions that came with their military work in an enemy-rich environment.

Sloan had to stop himself from reaching out and enclosing his hand around Dev's nervous fingers, now wet from the beads of moisture sliding downward off the wineglass. Even more telling was that Bella had come over and sat down, feeling Dev's stress. Dogs picked up in a heartbeat on how their human handlers were feeling. Even the Lab looked worried as she studied her mistress.

Dev reached over, giving Bella a pat on the head.

Sloan watched Dev gird herself, straightening her spine, and then she gave him an apologetic glance.

"I guess this incident triggered something that happened to me six months ago."

Sloan nodded, saying nothing, not wanting to stop her from speaking.

"I was…well… There was this red-haired ranger named Bart Gordon at the HQ where I worked out of in Smoky Mountains National Park." Dev lowered her voice. "He was always smiling at everyone. He worked with me at the visitor's center sometimes. It was the only place I ever saw him. Bart had a way with women. If a little girl was crying, he'd come around the counter, crouch down and speak to her and she'd stop crying. He had a kind of magic with women, no matter what their age."

The terror rushed forward in Dev's eyes as she spoke, her voice as strained as her expression. Bella moved closer to Dev, placing her head in her lap. Dev automatically stroked her worried dog.

"I was usually out doing tracking with Bella, but I'd heard from my boss that Bart was really a great PR person for the Forest Service because he had a way with words and people."

Dev gulped and swallowed, her eyes trained on the glass. Something had happened and Sloan's mind instantly leaped to a place he was reluctant to explore. "What happened between you?"

Dev snapped her head in his direction, her eyes widening. "Am I that obvious?"

Sloan gave her a warm look meant to ratchet down her tension. Instantly, her shoulders dropped. "No. Just my farrier sensing," he drawled. Dev nodded, tearing her gaze from his.

"I keep forgetting that. I know farriers have almost a telepathic link to the animals they're working with."

"Yeah," he said, a slight hitch in one corner of his mouth, "it's all about safety."

"You're right. It always is." Dev gave Sloan a searching look and admitted, "Gordon started stalking me. I had only stood duty at the visitor's center with him a couple of times, but he became fixated on me."

"Did you want his attention?"

"God, no... Even Bella didn't like him. And she likes everyone," Dev said, giving her Lab a loving look, nervously stroking her head and neck. "I tried to stay away from him as much as I could, Sloan. But damn, it was like *he* was psychic. Bart could pick up on when I was going to be coming back to HQ. He'd always be around at those times and it started triggering my PTSD because he felt like an enemy stalking me. Wanting something from me..."

"Did you inform your supervisor?" Sloan asked. He saw her give a jerky nod.

"I went to him and he laughed it all off. Told me it was my imagination." Dev glared at the wall in front of her for a moment, seemingly wrestling with escaping emotions. "I filled out a report on it, anyway. He deepsixed it. After three months of no action, and Gordon following me around like a lost puppy, I put in for a lateral move to come out here."

"Men protecting men?" Sloan wondered, watching her expression carefully because he could feel how upset Dev really was. Just talking about it was making her edgy and tense. How badly he wanted to get up, move around to her chair, pull it out and draw Dev into his arms. But that wouldn't be wise because now he knew another man had done something bad to her. And for him to try to hold her could backfire. Dev might see him as a would-be stalker, too.

She grimaced and took a jerky sip of wine, wrestling with barely held rage. "Always," she gritted out. "I did *nothing* wrong. I'm not a flirt. I wasn't in a relationship. But that doesn't mean I'm out trying to get a man, either."

"Did your supervisor have a friendship with Gordon?"

"Oh, yeah," Dev whispered, shaking her head. "One thing you learn real fast about Bart is that he knows how to lure you and then hook you with his smile. With the way he maneuvers you. God, he gets inside your head." She touched her brow, her voice incredulous. Turning, she met Sloan's hooded stare. "When I was in Afghanistan, I met plenty of CIA operatives. One thing I found out in a hurry was the way they ingratiate themselves with you in order to gain your trust. Get inside your head."

Raising his brows, Sloan nodded. "It's a basic CIA tactic to gain someone's trust. Find out what they like, what interests them, and then they adopt the same likes and dislikes you have, so you'll trust them. After all—" and his mouth hooked upward a bit "—it's a human frailty to fall in with someone who is like-minded. Right?"

Dev saw the gleam of understanding in Sloan's thoughtful stare. "Yes. That's exactly what they did. I hated it. I saw it and I'd call them on it. And then—" she rolled her eyes "—I meet Gordon and he was exactly like that. He asks you a bunch of questions, feeling you out, and then he suddenly feels the same way you do on everything."

"Was he possibly a CIA agent?" Sloan asked.

"I don't know," Dev uttered wearily. She sipped her wine. "All I know is that he ingratiated himself with anyone that he thought had power. I watched him do it. I recognized what he was doing."

"But he was stalking you?"

"Yes… God, I hated it. I knew he had our supervisor in his back pocket. I knew if I went to my boss, he'd bury my protest and not protect me."

Sloan slowly unwound from the chair, walked to the fridge and pulled out the bottle of wine. Coming back, he refilled her glass. "Come on, you need to eat something," he urged her, catching her glum, dark-looking eyes. He wanted to do a helluva lot more than pour Dev some wine. She gave him a grateful look and sipped it. Then she picked up a piece of cheese with a small cracker, beginning to nibble disinterestedly on it.

Sloan felt good about the fact that he could affect Dev positively. But his mind spun with so many questions. Was she this trusting with everyone? Was that why Gordon had stalked her? Because she was gullible? As Sloan walked to his chair and sat down, he felt terror and sadness surrounding Dev. She had gone pale as she'd confided in him. There was a lot more to this, he realized. Dev was fragile. Despite her outward appearance of confidence, Sloan felt the wound she'd received, and it had done major damage to her as a person. Perhaps as a woman? He really didn't want to think Gordon had raped her. Just the thought turned his stomach and tightened it into a painful knot. His fist flexed and Sloan forced himself to remain relaxed. After all, Dev was a dog handler, which spoke about her sensitivity, her all-terrain awareness. She wouldn't have survived those deployments if she didn't have that outer awareness every soldier, every dog handler, developed.

"I'm sorry that happened to you, Dev. You didn't deserve that kind of treatment."

When she turned, her green eyes had a sheen of tears in them. It tore at his heart. Sloan could feel a huge storm of emotions bubbling barely beneath her control. Her lower lip trembled.

CHAPTER SIX

WHY DID SHE suddenly want to burst into tears? Dev blinked a couple of times, forcing back her reaction. Was it the compassionate expression on Sloan's rugged face? The burning look of care in his narrowed blue eyes? The sensation of Sloan invisibly wrapping her within his strong, safe arms even though he was sitting several feet away from her, sprawled out, relaxed, but focused on her? The sensation was so real Dev closed her eyes for a moment, her fingers tightening around the slender stem of the wineglass. She hadn't had *that* much to drink. But maybe her stomach was empty, so she was more susceptible to alcohol.

But the real truth, whether Dev wanted to admit it or not, was that she thoroughly enjoyed Sloan's easygoing, comfortable company. He was the direct opposite of Bart Gordon, who reminded her of a wild animal on the prowl, hunting for his mate, willing to do anything to make her his. Her gut clenched and she kept her eyes closed, trying to will away the terror that never seemed to leave her. It would steal upon her at odd times. Unexpected ones. Like right now. She should be happy to be with Sloan because he always lifted her spirits. He was kind. Unselfish. Interested in her, but allowing her, from what she could sense, to pace whatever it was between them. He didn't push her like Gordon had. He didn't close in on her, making her feel claustrophobic, which she was. Maybe it was because on bad days when her father wanted to drink heavily, he'd push her into the clothes closet in her bedroom and lock the door.

To sit in that darkness…the dankness…the lack of fresh air. Dev lost count of how many times she'd cried softly so she wouldn't be heard. Because if her father did hear her, he'd come and rip the door open, bellowing down at her, telling her to stop crying. Big girls didn't cry, he'd scream at her. *Suck it up. Wipe those tears away.* And he promised to come back in a little while—which was hours later—and let her out.

Dev felt herself begin to unravel, lose control, and she couldn't do that. Sloan really didn't know that much about her. And he'd probably lose respect for her. In the Marine Corps, Dev had tried so hard to keep it together. But her commanding officer was an alcoholic, too, and it was as if she'd stepped back into being a seven-year-old shoved into a small, dark, smelly closet. The only light leaking in was beneath the door and she'd stare at that light, willing herself to watch it, because it meant hope. Hope that her drunk father would eventually come and let her out of the closet. And God help her if she peed her pants because she couldn't hold it any longer. Or if she got so thirsty she couldn't cry any more tears. Those years were horrifying for Dev, and being in the military, she'd sought freedom from them.

Only she'd traded them for an alcoholic CO, Major Terrence Paddington, who had scared the hell out of her. He didn't like or trust the women in his company. He didn't care she was a highly trained dog handler who was good at what she did. He didn't like women in combat, pure and simple. And he tried to keep her safe so that his blemished record wouldn't look worse than it already did. No one wanted a woman to die in combat. That was a huge no-no. A black mark on her CO's personnel jacket. And Dev had felt like she had been in that terrifying closet once again: trapped. Only with Major Paddington, he wanted to keep her imprisoned in that invisible closet for her entire deployment.

Dev began to see an overall pattern in her life: one of being crammed and hidden away by men. By the time Gordon had come along, she'd simply wanted to be out in nature, enjoying fresh air, the sun on her face, and doing her job tracking. But Gordon… Oh no, she could *not* cry! Dev's fingers curved inward into her palm as she sat there, head tilted forward, her mouth compressed to stop the memories.

The memories came, anyway. But she could feel that invisible blanket sliding across her shoulder, warming her, protecting her, and she knew it came from Sloan. He sat there quietly and she felt no urgency to speak. Her throat tightened. A desperation surged through her like a clenched fist ramming up from her wildly beating heart, into her throat, past the forming lump, and leaping into her mouth. And then…

"I hated Gordon always watching me," she began in a desperate tone. Dev kept her eyes shut, not wanting to see what lay in Sloan's eyes. Just the sensation of that immaterial embrace of his, that sense of utter safety surrounding her, allowed the words to tear out of her, never heard by another human being until now. "I could… I felt…his eyes… His eyes were always on me. I swear to God, I could feel this hot, burning sensation on my back when he came in and found me. I felt his eyes following me and the feeling that came with it…" Dev shuddered, the words jamming up in her aching throat.

"I—I could feel him wanting me. It was dirty. It was…awful. It was sexual, and he scared me. I tried to deal with it. I told myself it was in my head, that I was imagining things, that is was me, not him. I tried to convince myself that it was me." Her voice broke.

Dev felt the beaded coolness of the condensation on the outside of the wineglass beneath her fingertips. She focused on it because the emotions writhing within her threatened to overwhelm the dissolving control she had over them. "But it wasn't me," she said. She hung her head, chin against her chest, fingers tightening around the stem. "Three months went by and he would quietly come into a room where I was and come up behind me… God," Dev whispered unsteadily, wiping her eyes and opening them, staring sightlessly and straight ahead. "He never announced himself. He would always find me when I was alone, in a back room, when no other people were around. He was stalking me. Waiting. I didn't know why, except I felt so damned scared my brain would freeze."

Dev forced herself to lift her head and looked up at Sloan. The urge to get up and run into his arms nearly overwhelmed her. Somehow, Dev knew Sloan would open them, haul her into his embrace and hold her tight. Hold her safe. It suddenly dawned upon her that since Gordon's attack, she had felt like raw meat with no way to shield her natural vulnerability from anyone. He'd stripped her. Humiliated her. Overwhelmed her with his brute physical strength.

Dev drowned in Sloan's stormy blue eyes, helpless to tear her gaze away from his. It was almost a hypnotic look, one pulling her in, pulling her closer, but she felt no terror. Just...safety. And it allowed her to give voice to something she'd never told anyone.

"Gordon kept after me for six months," Dev continued in a low tone. "I had tried to get my supervisor to stop him at three months. And I knew in my gut that Gordon was aware I'd written up a report on him. That I had accused him of sexual harassment, inappropriate touching..." Dev swallowed hard, looking away, because she couldn't handle the sympathy burning in Sloan's eyes. She said in a hoarse voice, "He...found me... I was out in the barn, up in the hay mow on the third story one evening. I was running late. I'd needed a bale of timothy hay for Goldy. We'd just gotten off a successful mission to find a lost twelve-year-old boy. Bella had found him. It was almost dark. I had Bella in the truck. I'd cleaned up Goldy and put her in her stall. And when I realized there was no hay down on the first floor, I hurried up the ladder to get a bale from the third floor."

She pushed the wineglass away, clenching her hands. "I didn't hear Gordon coming..."

Everything came roaring back to Dev and suddenly she was in a flashback, no longer there with Sloan, but back on that shadowy third floor of the barn. She had been hefting a hundred-pound bale of hay and had dropped it in the mow. She remembered the sweet fragrance of the alfalfa hay encircling her nostrils like a perfume, wishing she could just collapse into that mattress-like dried hay and go to sleep. She had been tired. So tired. It had taken nearly twelve hours to track and find the lost, frightened young boy. Dev had been physically exhausted, emotionally stressed and mentally whipped.

Not allowing Bella to go into the barn with her had

been a mistake. She'd dropped the bale next to that huge amount of loose hay, removed the two huge iron hooks from it and pulled her Buck knife from the leather scabbard on her belt. Leaning down, Dev had swiftly cut the three taut strings of twine that held the bale together. It had sprung open. She'd slid the Buck knife into the sheath, snapped it shut and leaned down to pick up a flake for Goldy.

A man's hand had snaked from behind her, his long, powerful fingers gripping her nape and then twisting her to one side, shoving her backward, off balance and into the mow. Dev had gasped, her arms flying upward, shocked by the assault. She hadn't known who it was until she'd landed on her back, the air knocked out of her.

Gordon's eyes were slits as he approached her. He had a grisly, triumphant smile on his full mouth as he jerked open the leather belt around his jeans, yanking at the snap and unzipping his trousers as he halted and lorded over her. Dev couldn't move. She lay helplessly, gasping like a fish out of water, terrified by the crazed look in Gordon's eyes. She saw him jerk down his jeans, the thick erection pressing against his blue boxer shorts. He pushed his Levi's below his knees. And then grabbed her by a shoulder to keep her pinned. He jerked at the snap on the waistband of her Levi's. He yanked them downward, grabbing for her panties, ripping them off her. Dev cried out, adrenaline suddenly firing through her like an explosion.

Gordon cursed at her, calling her a bitch, his fingers digging painfully into her shoulder to keep her trapped. Dev lifted her legs, fighting back. She arced her left hand upward, her fist slamming into his prominent nose. Instantly, pain shot up into her hand and her wrist.

Gordon winced and shouted out a curse, surprise flaring in his eyes. He reared back, his nose bleeding, the blood running swiftly across his lips and down his chin.

It was the break she needed! Dev wrenched her shoulder away from his grip. He released her and she swiftly rolled away from Gordon. His other hand was below the waist of her jeans, grasping at her crotch. Screaming in terror, Dev kicked out, throwing him to the floor as her boots connected with his chest. She shoved to her feet. Disoriented, in shock, she hesitated a split second, pulling up her Levi's, trying to find a way to escape him.

Gordon snarled and grabbed at her arm. He jerked Dev down into the mow once more. She shouted for help.

Her head slammed into the soft mow, Gordon's weight coming down on top of her. She kept screaming, desperate for someone to hear her. Her elbow felt immediate pain as she connected with one of the hay bale hooks lying nearby as he shoved her deep into the mow, fingers digging into her thighs, forcing them open. She saw the rage in Gordon's slitted eyes as his hand wrapped around her throat, holding her as he positioned one knee between her legs.

Bucking, kicking, Dev refused to give up. Panic seized her as he ripped her shirt open, exposing her white bra, then her breasts.

No!

Dev shrieked, her fumbling fingers locating the wooden handle of one of the huge iron bale hooks. His hand pinched and squeezed her breast, a victorious smile on his face. Everything began to turn gray around her as he deliberately shut off her breathing.

Desperate, Dev knew she was losing consciousness. With all her might, she jerked her hand upward, arcing it into his back. The hook point sunk deep into his upper back near his right shoulder blade.

Howling in pain, Gordon lunged upright, his left hand clawing wildly at the hook embedded deep into his flesh.

Dev scrambled away as he tilted to the left, losing his grip on her. Panting, scrambling to get to her hands and knees, she spotted the ladder, lunged for it. Her shirt was torn open, bra exposed. Her Levi's were sliding down toward her knees. Grabbing them, she yanked them upward and surged toward the opening.

Shaking so much Dev thought she'd fall off the ladder, her knees nearly buckled beneath her. She heard Gordon's curses. Heard him struggling to his feet.

The next thing she knew, he'd thrown the huge bale hook at her. It glanced off the silvery wooden wall of the barn, barely missed her head and went sailing silently down past her then clanged loudly against the wooden floor far below Dev.

Hurry! Hurry!

Gasping for breath, Dev didn't dare look up. Her feet slipped several times on the ladder, her hands gripping the sides. Splinters jammed into both her palms, but she felt no pain.

The moment her feet hit the second floor, she sprinted for the next ladder which would take her to the main floor of the barn. And escape! The thunking of Gordon's boots were heavy on the ladder above her.

Oh, God! No! Small cries tore out of Dev as she raced toward the last ladder. She wasn't sure her weakening knees would hold her up. Dev hit that ladder at a run, leaping down into the large square opening. She didn't care if she hurt herself at this point or not. It was better than getting raped!

Her boots skidded and slipped on the worn wood and she fell the last three feet to the first floor, pain arching up her right hip. Hearing the heavy thunk of boots on the second floor above her, Dev scrambled to her feet. Outside was her truck. Weaving, arm flailing to keep her from falling, holding up her Levi's with her other hand, she raced down the wooden ramp to the slope where the truck was parked. Everything was shadowy and dark, and her heart was pounding so hard in her ears that she couldn't hear anything. Though she jerked a look over her shoulder as she stumbled down the slope, terrified Gordon was right behind her, Dev didn't see him.

Yanking open the door to her truck, she hopped in, grabbing for the keys she'd left on the dash. She slammed the locks shut.

Bella whined. Then her eyes were riveted on the barn, hackles up on her neck and back, growling menacingly.

Dev got the truck started with a badly shaking hand. She jammed her foot down on the accelerator, the truck roaring and leaping forward, skidding, a plume of dust rising in its wake. Wrestling with the truck, Dev glimpsed a shadowy figure racing out of the barn toward her. It was Gordon! Teeth clenched, her eyes on the highway ahead, she knew she had to escape! Her breasts ached. They felt bruised. She could still feel his kneading, hurting hand around them. Oh, God…

IT TOOK EVERYTHING Sloan had to sit still after Dev told him what had happened to her. He watched her struggling not to cry. He realized she could very well misinterpret his wanting to help her in a moment of need. She gave him a quick look, swiped at her eyes and sniffed.

"Did you go to the police?" he asked hoarsely.

"Yes, but it was a lost cause. The sergeant at the desk looked at me and asked if Gordon had raped me. I told him he'd tried. And then he said if he had raped me, then I needed to get to the hospital and get a rape kit done." Dev shook her head. "He didn't believe me. I showed him my hands. I had so many splinters in them. Funny, I couldn't feel any pain in them at that point…"

"It's shock and adrenaline," Sloan explained, his voice low and taut.

"I couldn't go to the hospital because I hadn't officially been raped. Nothing would show up on the rape kit. I told the sergeant I wanted to press assault charges against Gordon." Miserably, Dev whispered, "My shirt was torn open and I was holding it closed with one hand. The sergeant said he didn't see any assault on me except that I had splinters in my hand from sliding down that last ladder. He told me it would end up being a he-said-she-said court case. That there were no witnesses. Gordon's word against mine. It was useless for me to fill out a report."

The look of defeat and devastation in Dev's eyes tore at Sloan. It would do no good to get angry. She might take his reaction the wrong way and she was the victim still suffering from the experience. "And that's when you went to your Forest Service supervisor?"

"Right," Dev whispered. "And he didn't believe me at all."

"Did you ever file a report against Gordon?"

Dev gave him a rueful look. "You have to remember, there are men who are backward as hell about women. The sergeant argued with me that I could have gotten splinters in my hand from anywhere, for a lot of different reasons. There were no witnesses." She touched her neck. "I told him he was choking me, trying to make me unconscious so he could rape me, but at the time I went to the police station, my neck looked fine. It was hours afterward that the bruises where his fingers had been started to show up."

Sloan clamped his lips shut. Dev had been railroaded. A bunch of men had stuck together to make her look like she was setting up an innocent man to get him in trouble. "I'm sorry," he said, knowing how lame it sounded. The terror in her eyes was still there. It was torture to sit there, not move, not get up and walk over to Dev. She needed to be held. Needed to feel safe.

"I—I went back to the police department," she growled stubbornly, her fingers on her neck. "I was angry and I wasn't going to let this go. The same sergeant was at the desk and I showed him the bright red and purple bruises around my neck. I'd taken a picture with my cell phone so it was part of the proof that Gordon had jumped me. At that point, he got a woman police officer and I went into a back room where I showed her the bruises on my abdomen, the bruises showing up between my thighs where he'd groped me. She took pictures." Her voice lowered. "It was humiliating. I—I've never been treated like I was a liar. Never been attacked like that, Sloan."

"I wish you'd had a friend who could have been there to support you."

"So do I. But my best friend, Tanya, was on vacation at the time."

"What did the police do then?"

"They took my complete statement. Then, they went and got Gordon at his home and interviewed him. He denied being there, but he didn't have an alibi to prove he wasn't at the barn. He had gone to a local doc-in-the-box to get the puncture wound near his right shoulder blade looked at. When the police asked him about it, he lied and denied it. They didn't have a warrant to force him to show them his back wound, so they had to leave. The woman police officer went out to the barn the next day, though. Up in a mow, there's always a lot of dust."

Sloan nodded, feeling pride for Dev's grit in her attempt to get Gordon. Tension ran through him and he had to force himself to relax. Dev needed a friend, someone she could talk to, to get this out before it ate her up alive. And Sloan knew something like this would do just that if she didn't talk it out. "Did she find his footprints?"

"Yes, she had a forensics team with her, and it clearly showed boot tracks from my boots and Gordon's boots, that there was a fight." Some satisfaction rang in her voice. "And then the same woman officer called around to the area's medical facilities and she found Gordon's name on an entry form. She got a search warrant, went to his house and he was forced to show the wound I'd given him with the baling hook. It was the proof I needed to charge him with assault." Flexing her hand, forcing herself to relax, she uttered, "It was enough. I got him convicted on assault, not rape. I couldn't prove he was stalking me, so that charge was thrown out of court. The judge gave him a thirty-day sentence," she said, disbelief in her voice. "And he was forced to have a parole officer, to check in with him weekly for the next three years. Plus he had to wear an ankle bracelet for the next year."

Sloan felt the anger around Dev. "He should have gotten a lot more prison time than thirty lousy days."

"Well," she said wearily, "Gordon's supervisor, who

was protecting him, was forced to fire him because a ranger can't have a felony assault on his record." Her mouth twitched. "Before he left, Gordon told me out of earshot of anyone else that he'd get even with me. That it was *my* fault he'd been fired."

"The guy is mentally unstable," Sloan growled. He saw relief in Dev's eyes as he sided with her. "And because of that incident and Gordon's threat, you demanded a change of assignment?"

"Better believe it. I didn't trust Gordon. He'd stalked me before, and I knew he'd try to get even with me. God, every day my stomach was tied in knots and I was afraid I'd meet him at the grocery store, at my apartment... I felt like if he could, he'd get me alone and kill me. It was that palpable. I got a restraining order against him, but I know they don't work worth a damn."

"And where is he now?" Sloan couldn't help the bitterness in his voice as he watched the helplessness in Dev's eyes. Her hands were trembling and she could barely sit still in the chair. She was beyond agitated. And he couldn't blame her.

"I don't know. I didn't want to keep tabs on him, Sloan. I just want as far away from him as I can get." Shivering, Dev wrapped her arms around herself. "I never want to see that bastard again."

"How can I help you?"

The look on her face told Sloan so damned much that it sent a blade of pain down through him. Her father was an alcoholic. Her mother had a demanding career and basically Dev had been abandoned by her early on in her life. The stark look of being abandoned was clearly etched in her eyes. She was feeling alone. Again. Only this time, she probably felt as if no one at all was there to have her back. Protect her. He damn well would.

"You're doing it now," Dev said, blowing out a breath of air. "Thanks for listening, Sloan. I—I've never told anyone about this, until just now." She gave him an apologetic look. "I don't know why, but you're easy to be around and I feel like you really listen to a person. I guess I needed to get this off my chest."

"My ma always said I had a broad shoulder to cry on." Sloan eyed her tenderly, feeling his heart turn. The devastation and the need in Dev's eyes nearly unstrung his strong sense of control. She didn't have any friends out here, Sloan realized. Everyone was back East now.

"Well, that's certainly true. But I think it's your farrier nature showing itself. Your ability to observe, listen and feel out an animal or—" she shrugged "—in my case, just listening to me, one human being to another."

"Anytime," Sloan said, holding his anger in check. "Listen, we've got tomorrow off. I was heading out to the Elk Horn Ranch to do some shoeing. Would you like to come along? Iris Mason is the owner of the ranch, and she's a good person. She's like a grandmother to everyone she meets. I think you could use some new, loving family around you. Iris is a very kind, astute person. Sees through people and knows how to support them in positive ways. Would you like to meet her? She's got a granddaughter, Kamaria Trayhern-Sheridan, who lives on the property with her husband, Wes, and their son, Joseph. They're a big family and Iris just kinda takes strays like myself in, and automatically assimilates us into her family."

"She sounds really nice," Dev murmured, rubbing her

arms as if she felt chilled. "And I do need to start making some friends."

"Yeah, it's lonely being alone," Sloan said, grinning a little, watching her cheeks grow pink, getting some color back in them. He could see the depth of stress that Gordon's attack had caused Dev. There was more to this issue, and he'd known it. She had been in combat and gotten PTSD like just about everyone else thrown into war. Getting wounded put a person in a different frame of mind and Sloan understood that better than most.

"Since the attack," Dev said hollowly, "I've been paranoid about men. It's silly because not all men are like Gordon, but my mind… God, my mind, Sloan…" Her voice trailed off in frustration.

"Listen, there's a real nice woman by the name of Sky McCoy who also lives out at the Elk Horn Ranch. She was an RN in the Navy and worked at Bagram Hospital over a number of deployments. Sky is married and works with her husband, Grayson. He's a former Navy SEAL and is responsible for the wildlife center on the ranch. They have a young daughter, Emma, who is six months old. Sky is easy to talk to, Dev. And she had a lot of rough experiences on her last deployment, too. I'll introduce her to you. While I shoe over in their main barn, you two might chat a little." She needed a woman friend in whom she could confide. He got how it was difficult for Dev to reveal everything to him at this point. He was a man and not to be trusted fully. At least not yet. Their trust was tenuous and slowly being woven together.

"I'd like that." Dev gave him a sad look. "I find that civilians don't understand us military people at all. We have experiences they could never fathom, much less understand. It's not their fault. It's just the way it is."

"I know. And it's important right now that you be around other vets. We do support one another, Dev."

"There weren't many at my other assignment among the rangers," she admitted.

"Well," Sloan said, forcing himself to remain relaxed, "Iris makes a point of hiring men and women coming out of the military as ranch employees. And so does Talon Holt, who's a former SEAL himself, over at the Triple H Ranch. And Griff and Val McPherson at the Bar H. Maybe some other time when I go back over there to shoe their horses, and if you have the day off, you can ride over with me. Meet Cat, Talon's wife. She wasn't in the military, but she was a firefighter paramedic for the Jackson Hole Fire Department for seven years. She knows combat of a different sort, but we consider her one of us."

Smiling a little, Dev said, "I should hang around with you. It sounds like you know just about everyone around here."

"Being a farrier does that," Sloan said, seeing a little hope leak into her darkened green eyes. He could easily understand how alone Dev felt right now. He didn't blame her under the circumstances. It was good that she had Bella, who was probably a lifesaver for her in an emotional sense. Dogs always knew when their owners were depressed or stressed-out. "Want to go?" He tried not to show how badly he wanted Dev to accompany him. It would help her. He watched Dev as she considered his request.

"Do you think I could bring Bella along?"

"Sure. Iris loves animals. Just keep her on a leash and that should be good enough."

"Right," Dev agreed. She gazed at Bella and softly stroked her head.

Bella thumped her tail.

"I'd better go," Dev murmured. "I've got a lot to do tonight. What time do I meet you tomorrow morning?"

Sloan stood up. "8:00 a.m. okay?" He walked over and pulled the chair away from the table so that she could stand. How badly he wanted to place a hand on her shoulder, gently turn Dev around and gather her into his arms. Sloan knew that's what she needed. But to try it now would frighten her away and break the thin threads of trust that lay between them. More than anything, Sloan wanted Dev to continue to come to him. As he walked her and Bella to the door, he wondered if he was any different from Gordon. Sloan wanted Dev, too.

"Fine. See you then," Dev said, opening the door. She hesitated, giving him a look of gratitude. "Thanks for everything, Sloan. I'm glad you were there…" She swallowed.

Just seeing the sheen of tears suddenly come to Dev's green eyes made him want to embrace her. Kiss her senseless. Take her to his bed and love her until she forgot everything except the pleasure Sloan knew he could give her. "I'll always try to be there for you, Dev." And Sloan would. She just didn't realize the depth of his commitment to her was all. Given the circumstances, patience was going to be the key to her. There was no way she was going to fall into his arms, even though Sloan knew Dev was as drawn to him as he was to her. Too much stood in the way right now.

Worse, his mind angled toward the question of where

Bart Gordon was today. Was he still back East? Or a worst-case scenario he didn't even want to contemplate: Gordon coming out here to even the score with Dev.

CHAPTER SEVEN

NEAR NOON THE next day, Sloan was halfway through the horses waiting to be shoed. He wiped his sweaty brow with the back of his arm as he walked down the aisle of the barn, looking out over the busy Elk Horn Ranch. It was Saturday and the six dude ranch families who were visiting headed to the wrangler's dining room for lunch. Tomorrow, that group would leave in the morning and Iris and her family would welcome six more families to stay a week for the ranch experience. He smiled a little, spotting Dev sitting with Sky McCoy, her daughter, Emma, on her lap, at one of the benches along the small medical facility near the main office. The moment he'd introduced the two women, they'd gravitated to one another like opposite ends of a magnet.

It sent warmth through him as he removed his leather apron and folded it over a bale of hay sitting in front of an empty box stall. Dev needed some women friends. The two sat on the same bench, watching people walking by. Emma, at six months old, was crawling between their laps, both women's hands protective as the baby wobbled back and forth between them. Sky had married Grayson McCoy three months earlier. They made their home here on the ranch, with their daughter the center of their attention. Iris, who was more than generous with her employees, gave each one a five-acre parcel where they could build their own house. Sloan often came out here and helped Gray pound nails and put up walls on their new home. Wes Sheridan, who was ranch foreman and husband to Kamaria Trayhern-Sheridan, brought out a couple of wranglers to help, as well. Kam then brought her three-year-old son, Joseph, along to feed the hardworking men. The house was now enclosed and next week everyone was meeting to put the steeply angled tin roof on the large two-story ranch home. Then, Sky, Gray and Emma could move into it.

Taking off his battered Stetson, Sloan wiped his brow once more and settled it back on his head. As he walked down the slope, he saw a lot of trail horses being unsaddled in the large sandy arena in front of him. The families had just come in from a midmorning trail ride. His gut grumbled. He was starving after working on the horses all morning. As he moved to the sidewalk, he saw Dev lift her head and pin him with her gaze. Sloan saw happiness in her eyes, a soft smile coming to her lips. He felt good about getting her together with Sky.

"Hey, you two," he called out. "About time for lunch. You gals hungry?"

Sky smiled up at him. Her hair was in two long, ginger-colored braids over her pale blue tee. "How'd you guess, Sloan?" She gathered squirming Emma up into her arms and stood, gesturing toward the main ranch house. "Iris wanted you and Dev to join us for lunch at their home."

Raising his brows, Sloan said, "That's an invite I'm not going to refuse." He looked at Dev. "You game?"

Grinning, Dev stood up and said, "Sure am."

Sky patted her daughter's diaper. "I'm going to change her first and then Gray and I will join you. Tell Iris we'll be there shortly?"

"Sure," Dev said.

Sloan led the way and fell into step beside Dev, leading her toward the large one-story cedar-log ranch house. "Well? You two have a nice chat while I was shoeing?"

"Yes. Emma's adorable. I just love babies." Dev met his gaze. "And you were right. Sky and I immediately took to one another. I really like her."

"Good. Did Iris drop by and introduce herself to you?"

"Oh, yes. She's such a dear person. She is like the fabled grandmother you always wished for, but never got."

Nodding, Sloan understood the weight of her admittance. He knew Dev didn't want to say much more with Sky within earshot and he was content to follow her into the large, roomy mud porch at the main entrance to the Mason home. As they cleaned off their boots and entered the main house through the huge living room, Sloan could smell what he thought was beef stew and baking corn bread in the air. He hoped he was right. He ushered them into the dining room, his stomach growling like a starved wolf.

Iris was seated beside her husband, Timothy, along with her son, Rudd. Sloan raised a hand in greeting and took off his hat, hanging it on a nearby wooden peg.

"Sloan? You and Dev sit next to where Gray and Sky sit." Iris gestured farther down the long oak trestle table covered with plates, flatware and glasses filled with water.

"Yes, ma'am," he murmured, pulling a chair out for Dev. She would sit next to Sky and Gray. There was a baby chair positioned between the two adult chairs, waiting for Emma. Sloan knew that would make Dev feel more relaxed since she didn't know anyone else at the table. Wes nodded hello to them from where he sat next to his wife, Kam. Joseph was in a toddler chair between them. It was a buoyant family atmosphere and Sloan always enjoyed eating with the extended Mason family.

Gray and Sky arrived with Emma, telling everyone hello and apologizing for being a bit late. Gray took his daughter and placed her in the chair between them. Sky smiled, said hello to Dev and sat down next to her. There were already thoughtfully placed warm jars of homemade baby food sitting in front of Sky's plate so she could feed Emma. Iris was picky and wanted only organic, homegrown food on her table. She was especially vigilant with the young ones in her expanding family, often preparing their food herself in the kitchen.

A young woman, Jenny, who worked as a sous-chef in the kitchen, brought out steaming bowls of beef-vegetable stew to each of them. The chef, Millie, a woman in her midforties, placed a huge sheet of steaming hot corn bread in the center of the table so everyone could reach for the recently cut squares slathered with butter. He waited like everyone else because Iris always gave a short prayer of thanks for the food. A bowl of fresh salad was the last thing to come to the table. Iris thanked the women. She then asked everyone to hold hands. Sloan felt greedy and maybe a touch guilty about holding Dev's hand. He really ought to be focused on Iris's short, heartfelt prayer. Dev's skin was soft and Sloan hungrily absorbed the brief contact with her through his fingers.

After the prayer, everyone dug into the steaming platters of food. Pretty soon, the talk died down as they hungrily ate the hearty beef stew with the fragrant, buttery corn bread. Occasionally, Sloan would slant a glance in

Dev's direction. She was eating well. And he could see there was no tension in her face any longer. The family surrounding was helping her. Coming from a dysfunctional family like hers, this had to be a very special meal for Dev. There was laughter, joking and gentle teasing going on at the table. Joseph was hungry, stuffing a piece of warm corn bread with butter into his mouth. It brought nice memories of his own family gathering for a meal in their log cabin, in the Allegheny Mountains of West Virginia. That same family warmth, that love that took many forms in his own parents' home, was here, as well.

Sloan watched Dev's face soften as she watched Wes and Kam's son eat, his face powdered with crumbs of cornmeal. It made her smile. And then she devoted her attention to Emma. She was a delicate child, pretty and lively. Dev would make a good mother someday, Sloan realized. There was a lot of sensitivity in her, as well as deep compassion. And secretly? Sloan wanted Dev for himself. He didn't try to resist daydreaming of them being married and having children just like Emma and Joseph. But that was all it was, Sloan sternly told himself, a dream. Just a dream.

DEV SAT WITH Bella between her legs. Mouse sat up on the truck seat between herself and Sloan as he drove them home. It was nearly dark and the cab smelled of sweat and horse, neither of which were offensive to her, but a wonderful perfume to her nose.

"Well?" Sloan drawled. "Did you enjoy your day out at the Elk Horn Ranch?"

Dev smiled. "Very much. Thanks for bringing me along." She stroked Bella's head. "It was fun going for an early-afternoon ride with Kam and Sky. Bella loved it, too. She got to stretch her legs."

"You need times like this," Sloan murmured. "It will help you relax."

"You're right," Dev admitted, looking out the window, the gray outline around the sharp pointed peaks of the Tetons in the distance. "I guess I didn't realize how tense I always am until today."

"What do you mean?"

"I've been feeling anxious since Gordon attacked me," Dev said, frowning. "I don't sleep well at night. And if I feel claustrophobic or shut in, I get panicked. Today, at the lunch table with Iris and her family, I felt really happy. At peace. Even now, I feel calm inside. My anxiety is gone."

"That's good. What do you think helped you the most today?"

She smiled a little, placing a kiss on Bella's head. "Just being around family again… I mean…a real family. A family that honestly loves one another and is glad to be in one another's company. Their two children were so precious…"

"Unlike your own family?"

Dev felt sadness move through her heart. "Yes, unlike my own. I guess I've always pined for a real family. A happy one. And at the Mason ranch, I felt like I was a part of it. They made you feel welcome, as if you were important and counted among them. And they wanted to hear what you had to say. What you thought."

"A healthy family usually does all those things."

Dev glanced at his rugged profile as he drove down the hill toward Jackson Hole. "Is your family like that?"

"Very much so," he murmured.

Frowning Dev mumbled, "Sometimes I think I got dropped off at the wrong address."

"What do you mean?"

"That the stork dropped me off at the wrong house number," Dev murmured, with a little embarrassed laugh to go with it.

"I wish I could take you home with me. My ma and pa would dote on you. They always wanted a daughter, but they got me instead."

Heat moved through her lower body at the gritty response from Sloan. Dev yearned for his touch. When he held her fingers during the brief prayer Iris Mason gave, she'd felt like a starving emotional glutton absorbing the feel of Sloan's roughened hand. "You turned out well." The idea of going home to meet his parents fed her heart and Dev couldn't understand why. Sloan never crowded her. Nor did he look at her like she was sex on two legs, as Gordon always had. She still, to this moment, felt invisibly enveloped in that sense of safety that he gave her. One day, Dev wanted to tell him about it, discuss it, because she'd never felt anything like that before. She was grateful to have Sloan in her life.

Sloan's mouth hitched upward as he slowed the truck, driving into town. All the bright lights of the many restaurants, the main plaza lit up with hundreds of tourists crowding the area, seemed to make him more alert than usual. "I was a handful, though." He chuckled. "But they loved me, anyway, and eventually I straightened out. My pa started taking me with him to teach me farrier skills when I turned nine years old. He decided learning to deal with horses was a big adventure and he was right. I'm always fascinated by horses, how they think, what they see and how they're processing it all."

"That's why you understand human nature so well." At least, Sloan understood her. Last night when she had divulged Gordon's attack on her, Dev had so badly wanted to crawl into Sloan's arms. She saw it in his eyes to do just that. Her throat tightened. Sloan had so far proven he was reliable and steady. Not once had he made her feel terrified. Just the opposite. Her lower body clenched and she recognized that familiar feeling. Somehow, Dev sensed Sloan would be a caring lover. Her fiancé from so many years ago, Bill Savona, had been like that with her. Heart aching, Dev realized she'd never found a man like Bill. He'd been killed by an IED in Afghanistan, two weeks short of leaving and returning to the States to marry her.

"I think some people have deeper insight than others, don't you?" Sloan asked, guiding the truck to the south side of Jackson Hole.

Dev gently put her memories of Bill away. She'd been twenty years old and had fallen helplessly in love with the Marine K-9 handler. It had been instant attraction, just as it was with Sloan. Was this something similar? Or was it because she was so lonely? Or that she wanted to be loved once more, and to love someone in return? Or a mix of both? Rousing herself, Dev said, "I do. I think anyone who works around animals like we do has an extra smidgen."

"Animals bring out a human's sensitivity," Sloan agreed. The traffic lightened as he drove them out of the town, heading west toward the shadowed Tetons in front of them. He slanted her a glance. "You're a very sensitive person. How did you manage in that family situation you were caught up in?"

"I don't know," Dev offered quietly, remembering

those times. "I know I always felt stressed-out anytime my parents argued with one another. Which was often. I wish I'd had a shield or something to protect me from feeling all the things I felt. I could feel their rage, their frustration…"

Giving her a quick glance, Sloan asked, "Maybe you're an empath."

"What's that?"

"My ma has the Sight. Among the Hill people, she's known as a seer. She helps people all the time because she can see the aura and colors around a person. And people often come to her when they're sick. She lays hands on them and they always feel better afterward. She works a lot with our Hill doctor, Poppy Thorn. She lives on Black Mountain."

"Is your mom an empath?" Dev wondered, unfamiliar with the word.

"No," Sloan said. "She doesn't take on or absorb other people's energy. She knows how to protect herself from it."

"Is that what I do?"

"Sounds like it. Do you know if either of your parents are psychic?"

"No, not that I know of. Is being an empath bad, Sloan?"

He gave her an apologetic look. "Sorry, didn't mean to upset you with that observation. Empaths are just supersensitive individuals, and usually they tend to be female. They are sort of like a sponge and they absorb other people's feelings whether they want to or not."

"Well, that part is true about me," Dev admitted unhappily. "I hated when my parents fought with one another. I always had an upset stomach. I felt like I was being bombarded with bullets."

"Right," Sloan agreed. "And you took it all in and you couldn't help it."

Dev frowned, mulling over Sloan's explanation. Was she absorbing *his* energy? Feeling his sense of protection, his calmness enfolding her, helping her anxiety melt away and dissolve? Dev needed to know. He braked and turned right into the apartment complex. It was dark and she could see the stars that always looked so close at this altitude. "Sloan? Ever since I met you, I've felt like… this…invisible embrace, like arms folding around me, when you've been close to me." Dev opened her hands as he glanced at her. "It wasn't bad. It's always been a wonderful feeling. As if… As if you were tucking me into this warm cocoon and it makes me feel protected." Her mouth quirked. "Am I imagining it? Or is it really happening, Sloan?"

He parked and turned off the truck. The sulfur lamps invaded the truck and he saw the confusion in her face. "Empaths can pick up on good energy around people, too," he said. "It's not always about picking up bad vibes or negative human feelings around someone."

She licked her lower lip, holding his gaze. Right now…Dev could feel a powerful wave of energy swirling around her, so calming and yet, incredibly melting and loving. That feeling startled her because she knew what love felt like from falling in love with Bill, and it had been a lot like this. Sloan's narrowed eyes were focused and intent upon her. Yet Dev did not feel threatened. If anything, the incredible warmth was making her feel insulated from the world and shielded. The feeling was like drinking water when she was dying of thirst.

The sensations were life fortifying to her. Never had Dev felt what she was feeling right now. It was so alive, so good and so healing. Her hands tightened momentarily around Bella's collar. Dev was afraid to ask, but knew she had to. "Are you—are you doing this on purpose? I mean, do you visualize this energy and *send* it around me?"

Leaning back, his arm going across the top of the seat, Sloan smiled a little. "No, you're just picking up on my feelings is all, Dev. Nothing more."

"It's a wonderful feeling," she whispered, suddenly shy in his presence.

"Better than the other type, right?" Sloan teased gently.

Just the way he looked, the soft amusement reflected in the depths of his eyes... Dev nodded, her throat going dry. "If I'm an empath, how do I protect myself from picking up bad feelings people have around them?"

Sighing, Sloan confided, "I don't know. My ma said these folks were special, that they were born with that supersensitivity. She did say that they should try to always have calm and quiet surroundings because they couldn't handle a lot of strife and stress."

"Great," Dev mumbled, shaking her head. "So I'm a walking sponge that absorbs everyone's feelings."

"But I'll bet because you have that sensitivity, Dev, you and Bella were great at what you did in Afghanistan. You saved a lot of lives in the process. You do realize that, don't you?"

She studied Sloan's serious expression, his low voice riffling through her like a lover's caress. "That's true. Bella and I would pick up on the same threat at the same time. No one else around us did, but I did. I guess it's not all bad." She rubbed the back of her neck. "Like at lunch today? I just loved feeling the people around the table. Everyone was so happy. I felt lifted. High, maybe."

"See?" Sloan said. "Being empathic has its positive points, too."

Dev frowned, moving her fingers nervously across Bella's shoulders. "The feelings I feel from you, Sloan?"

"Yes?"

Her heart beat a little harder because Dev was unsure of herself. "Are the feelings I'm picking up from you how you're feeling?" She tilted her head, searching his eyes. There was a dark, liquid look in them and it made her lower body yearn for Sloan. His physical touch must be as wonderful as the feelings she felt around him right now.

"My ma said empaths can sense emotions around another person."

Dev didn't have the guts to ask a follow-up question. She still carried a raw, open wound from Gordon's assault. And while she trusted Sloan more than any other man since that attack, she was too scared of her own inability to trust what she read in people. Instead, she asked, "Is that why I was always so upset and stressed with Gordon around? I was picking up on his intentions toward me?"

"Could have been," Sloan admitted. "But people like him are wolves in sheep's clothing and they tend to send out mixed signals to people. They don't want anyone knowing who they really are or what they really want. They hide."

"Well," Dev admitted, "I was confused by him at first. I could feel him hiding something from me. He always had this big award-winning smile and I fell for it. But then, when I had to spend some time around him, I felt like this oozing sleaze was pouring over me. It was the worst feeling, Sloan. I used to shiver, a cold feeling sliding down my spine when it would happen. I would try to get away from him, get into another room, another building, to escape it."

"You were more than likely picking up on his intentions toward you, but also who he really was beneath that mask he wore."

Rubbing her face, Dev muttered, "God, it was *horrible*, Sloan. Sometimes, when I was in Afghanistan, going through a village, I could pick up easily on men who hated Americans. I felt them. It was so visceral."

"Right, you would." Sloan gave her a gentle look. "This is something that's a part of you, Dev. You can't help it and you can't turn it off or on. It's automatic, like breathing."

She wrinkled her nose. "I wish I didn't have it."

"Maybe you'd feel differently if you hadn't had such a rough childhood. My ma knows an empath, Poppy Thorn, our Hill doctor. She lives happily with her two daughters plus a son-in-law, Gabe Griffin, on the other side of Black Mountain. They love one another, so that's the difference between what you grew up with, your parents not getting along. Poppy's family situation is the opposite of what you experienced, so she's not stressed-out like you were."

"Does Poppy ever get exhausted by being around people all day long?"

"Ma told me once that Poppy sees people only a few times a week. Gabe drives down to Dunmore to pick up groceries and run errands for her. She doesn't like doing it because it wipes her out for days afterward, due to all the human contact. And we're talking about physical energy. It just leaches it from Poppy when she's around crowds of people for too long a time."

"Ugh, that's me." Dev rolled her eyes. "I'm always glad when my time is up at the visitor's center. I left every day feeling wiped out. I'd much rather be riding on a trail or tracking a lost person than be behind that counter. Nature doesn't wipe me out. Crowds do."

"Well, maybe you found out something new about yourself today that you didn't know before?"

"Yes." Dev gave him a warm look. "Thank you. I just didn't ever know what was going on within me, or why."

"Well, I think this is enough for tonight. Let's get inside."

Dev opened the door and put Bella on a leash. She gave the yellow Lab a signal and she gracefully leaped out from between her legs, cleared the truck and landed on the pavement. Sliding out of the cab, Dev heard Sloan order Mouse to come. The Belgian Malinois was on a leash, too. As she shut the door, feeling the cool wind, Dev looked up to admire the twinkling stars embedded in the black velvet night sky above them. She felt Sloan approaching before she saw him. Maybe being an empath wasn't always a bad thing. Sloan felt safe. The man turned her on and made her body ache with need. He was a strong, silent person whose internal gentleness beckoned to her so powerfully she almost couldn't stop herself from wanting to touch him…kiss him.

They walked through the main entrance of the second apartment tower. And Dev, like Sloan, chose to take the stairs, not the elevator. Both dogs eagerly bounded up the wooden stairs. Dev could smell different things cooking as they walked quietly down the carpeted hall past other apartments. She halted at her door, bringing out the key from her pocket.

"Are you doing anything tomorrow?" Sloan wondered as he opened his apartment door.

"No," Dev said, turning. She saw a glint in Sloan's eyes, a half smile lurking at the corners of his kissable mouth. "Why?"

"Feel up to a fortifying trail ride? We could start out about nine, but first, I'd take you to my favorite breakfast restaurant on the edge of town, and buy you the best sourdough pancakes in the world. Are you game?"

Her heart leaped. Game? Dev wanted to throw her arms around Sloan's broad shoulders and hug him. Resisting, she said, "We can bring the dogs?"

"Of course. Well?"

"I find being in nature is the most healing thing to me." *Except*, Dev silently amended, *being with you*. She felt helpless to stop her heart from liking Sloan so much. Now that she understood the ugly, toxic feelings around Gordon, Sloan's energy felt like clean, healing sunlight in comparison. Dev wanted to be around him because Sloan fed her strength and calm. She watched his lips curve.

"Okay, gal, you got it. I'll come knocking at your door at 8:00 a.m. tomorrow morning. Good night…"

She watched Sloan turn away and almost reached out to grip his upper arm and stop him. Dev wanted to thank him for all he'd done for her today. In her heart, she knew it was because Sloan was trying to help her up and over the experience she'd shared with him last night. Sloan would never admit to that, but it didn't matter because Dev *knew*. Just having him tell her that she was an empathic person, a human sponge of sorts, had suddenly enlightened her as few other things ever had.

Dev followed Bella into the apartment. Closing the door, she turned, and Bella was sitting, patiently waiting for her to unsnap the leash from her collar.

"Is that why you like being around Sloan, Bella? Because you're picking up on his incredibly healing energy?"

Bella panted and thumped her tail, her eyes shining.

"So? Are all dogs empathic, I wonder? That will be a good question to ask Sloan at breakfast tomorrow." Laughing softly, Dev hung the leash on a wooden peg on the wall.

CHAPTER EIGHT

SLOAN COULDN'T GET to sleep. He lay naked in his bed, hands behind his head. Tiny slivers of moonlight peeked in around the drawn blinds and heavy dark green curtains. The clock ticked away on a mahogany dresser opposite his king-size bed. His heart centered on Dev. Damn, she was excruciatingly innocent in a world that ate empaths up and spit them out for breakfast. No one had ever realized her high sensitivity to other people's emotions. Dev felt like she was a human being without skin to protect her. Sloan was glad he'd grown up with Poppy Thorn as their Hill doctor. Poppy had also been his mother's best friend. He'd seen similar reactions in Dev, and that was what brought him to the realization that she was truly unique among most human beings.

Sloan couldn't shut off his mind as he wondered how in the hell Dev had managed two deployments to Afghanistan in the thick of combat situations, looking for IEDs that could kill her or her squad, with that kind of wide-open sensitivity. That was probably one of the reasons the Marine Corps had placed her as a K-9 handler. Dev's sensitivity had shown up on the battery of tests that they performed on every recruit. Maybe living through that hellish family dynamic of hers had grafted a kind of skin that somewhat protected her during her combat deployments?

Closing his eyes, he thought about the threat of Bart Gordon in her life. Sloan wasn't an empath, but he had his Ma's intuition that warned him that Bart Gordon was someone who would seek revenge. And Gordon would seek it from Dev, no question. Sloan wasn't sure how much he should emphasize this possibility to her. She was already stressed-out enough, still recovering from the assault and the police department of good ole boys who hadn't taken her claim seriously. He wished he'd been there at Dev's side to see her through that demeaning and intimidating process. Yet Dev was showing him that deep down she was tough and could gut it out when necessary. Although now, Sloan was sure he was seeing the fallout from extruding such strength from within herself. Dev was tired and he could see it, from the smudges beneath her rich green eyes to the way she easily tired by the end of a day.

Dev was good at putting on a game face, Sloan realized. But around him, she was letting it down, being more herself, maybe trusting him a little. His palm fell across his fast-beating heart as he thought about her in sexual terms. Yes, he wanted her. In every possible way. He wanted to feel how soft and lush her mouth blossoming beneath his would feel. To hear the softened sounds catching in her slender throat as he pleasured her. Something told him Dev was a woman who enjoyed and luxuriated in her sensuality. She would be hot, assertive and enjoy sex just as much as he did. Sloan would bet his life on it.

A bit of guilt ate at him because although he was sexually drawn to Dev, he also appreciated her on so many other equally important levels. Sloan liked the way she saw the world. Liked her innate gentleness and that soft, husky voice of hers. He could see her confidence clearly, but with him, she allowed him to see a little of who she was beneath it and that thrilled him as little else had in a long, long time. He wondered about her life. Had she ever been married? Divorced? God, he had a hundred questions for her and didn't have an answer for any of them. Maybe tomorrow, if it felt right, and she was relaxed, he'd ask. More important, now that Sloan realized the pressures on Dev, he was going to make damn sure he didn't trod like a bull on a rampage into her life. Pacing and timing with her was everything…

DEV GASPED WITH delight as their narrow, twisting riding trail opened up into an oval meadow with a small lake in the center. A cottontail rabbit startled near the only tree, an old oak, and it took off for the evergreen forest not far away. Both dogs' ears pricked up, but they remained with their riders. Mouse whined.

"I think he thinks it's a ball to chase," Sloan confided, grinning over at Dev. She wore her USFS dark green baseball cap, but everything else was civilian, from her jeans to the long-sleeved pink blouse. The sun showed it was near noon, and it glinted down upon the loose black hair that framed her face. He tried not to drown in the happiness he saw reflected in the green depths of her eyes. And as his gaze fell to her lips, his entire lower body reacted. Too many nights lying awake, imagining kissing her, dammit. He dismounted. "Come on. Would you like to have that picnic under that old oak tree out there?"

"Looks perfect." Dev sighed, dismounting. "Is it okay to give Bella the signal to go snoop around? Or do you think there are other rabbits around?"

Sloan's eyes narrowed as he absorbed the tree line, looking for anything that appeared out of place. He glanced over at her as she came and stood at his side, the reins in one hand. "Tell me what you feel. You're an empath. Do you feel anything threatening around here?"

She quirked her mouth. "Oh, I don't think I have that kind of skill, Sloan. If I did, I sure as heck would have felt Gordon sneaking up on me." His grin grew.

"Well, you might have a point." Sloan lifted his hand, gesturing around the meadow. "A little lesson here, because you're still learning about this area. The first thing you want to be aware of is the willow stands. Moose feed on willows. But elk, and especially elk mothers with their newborn babies, will hide in them. So will a mama moose, with her babies, too. Either way, if you see willows, there's *always* a chance that there's a grizzly hunting them nearby. You'll never hear the bear coming. They might sometimes weigh close to a thousand pounds, but you will not hear them until it's too late. Even elk and moose, if they're distracted, won't hear them approach, which is how they lose their offspring. Or their own lives."

"That's awful," Dev murmured, frowning. "I don't see any willows around here."

"Right. One of the reasons I wanted to ride up here today. Grizzlies naturally gravitate to the willow stands because that's where their meat source is at. Here, you have a wide-open meadow, with no place to hide. There's one tree, which isn't enough cover for elk or moose. And the pond is small and ringed with reeds."

"So? It's safe?"

"Yep." And then he chuckled. "Unless, of course, you

actually see a grizzly walking through the meadow. Then we would leave immediately."

"I don't see any."

"But the possibility of them being around is very real," Sloan cautioned, clucking to his horse. "Let's get to the tree and check out the whole meadow before we decide whether or not to let the dogs snoop around. We don't want a grizzly around, unseen. If he sees a dog, there's going to be a fight, and a bear weighs more than we do."

"We never had this kind of issue in Smoky Mountains Park," Dev said, falling into step with him, glad that Sloan was with her. The dark blue surface of the pond was dappled with sunlight, like jewels leaping and sparkling along the surface. There was a mallard duck couple at one end, opposite the oak tree. The grass across the oval meadow was lush and plentiful, barely ankle high because they were at eight thousand feet. Spring came slowly at higher altitudes, she knew.

"Black bears are easy to deal with in comparison to our grizzlies," Sloan said. He halted at one end of the pond, observing the other half of the meadow. Both dogs sat, panting. He gestured to the other line of evergreens. "Hear that blue jay in the distance in that direction?"

"Yes."

"Jays start screaming when they see a threat. Now, it could be a cougar, a bobcat, but it could be a grizzly, too."

"So keep the dogs on a leash?"

"Right. Jays often will fly over the threat and keep calling to warn the surrounding area. And if he continues to call and he's coming closer to us, then—" Sloan turned, placing his gloved hand over the butt of the .30-06 rifle in a leather sheath beneath his stirrup "—we might have to use this."

"But…" Dev stumbled, searching his tense face. "You wouldn't kill a grizzly, would you?"

"Not unless I have to. Often, if a grizzly hears humans, it'll turn away and head in the opposite direction." He pointed to Mouse and Bella. "But if the bear picks up on either of their scents, and if it feels threatened, it will charge the dogs, trying to kill them."

She patted the quart of bear spray on her hip. "You said this will deter them."

"I've seen it used on a charging grizzly," Sloan said, gesturing for her to follow him. "It works. But dogs often provoke a bear with barking and that's when the bear turns ugly. He'll go out of his way to kill a barking dog, bear spray or not. It reminds the bear too much of a wolf pack, and they're natural enemies to one another."

Dev leaned over, petting Bella's back. Her yellow Lab wanted to go run, smell and explore, but under the circumstances, it might not be a good idea. She followed Sloan to the tree, to the shade from the gnarled, ancient branches that had probably seen over a hundred years of harsh winters. To her they looked like arthritic arms and hands.

Sloan led his horse, Rocky, to the bank of the lake. Dev followed. Both horses thirstily drank their fill, their muzzles dripping with water as they smacked their lips afterward. Walking them beneath the oak tree, Sloan dropped the reins to his horse. Rocky was ground-tied trained and wouldn't move. Sloan kept his hearing keyed to the blue jay, and the sound seemed to be lessening, as if the bird were moving away from their area. That was a good thing. He wanted a nice, peaceful lunch, without having to deal with a pissed-off grizzly. The dogs lay down side by side after drinking their fill of cold, clear water. They looked beautiful together, Mouse's black-and-caramel-brindled coat next to Bella's golden short-haired coat. Sloan pulled out a plastic case that held their lunch, handing it to Dev.

"What did you make us?" she asked, standing back as he spread a small red wool blanket on the ground beneath the shade of the tree.

"Nothing fancy. Tuna fish." Kneeling down, Sloan smoothed out the blanket and looked up. "You okay with that?"

"Sure am," Dev said, handing him the container. Going to her saddlebags, she reached into one of them and pulled out a large plastic container and carried it back to where he sat cross-legged. Sitting opposite him, she said, "Chocolate pudding for dessert?" She held it up toward him.

"Great. You'll find I'm a human garbage can," he reassured her, opening the container and handing her a carefully wrapped sandwich. "I'll eat anything as long as it doesn't move." And his mouth twisted. "Well, I should amend that. There were times Mouse and I were up on ten-thousand-foot ridges in the Hindu Kush, having gone through all our food, and I'd send him out to hunt. He always brought back something." He opened his sandwich, taking a bite. "No fire, either."

Wrinkling her nose, Dev said, "Ugh. Let's talk about something else."

Sloan gave her an apologetic look. "Sorry. What would you like to talk about?"

"You."

Swallowing his surprise, Sloan saw the dark green of

her eyes and she reminded him of a dog on a hunt. And he was her target. He shrugged. "Told you about my family. What else is there?" He kept his voice light and teasing because today he did not want to stress Dev. Sloan wanted her to enjoy the day without any pressure. A light danced in her eyes and he had no idea what it meant.

"Well," Dev hedged, wiping the corner of her mouth where a bit of mayonnaise was stuck, "I have a question for you, but maybe it's too personal? And you don't have to answer it if it is," she added hastily.

"Okay," Sloan said. His instincts told him this was far more serious than what he had in mind. Clearly, it was important to Dev, so he gave her an easy smile and said, "Fire away." He saw her cheeks turn a deeper pink. She was blushing. Why?

"You're too nice of a man to not be married. I guess I was wondering if you ever were?"

Sloan kept his face carefully arranged, mulling over her question. He hadn't prepared for it because he hadn't known whether she was curious about this facet of him. And why was she? Because she might be thinking of some kind of a relationship with him? He didn't know. Sloan always thought he knew women and knew their minds, but his ex-wife, Cary, sure as hell had destroyed all his confidence in that department. "Yes, I was married once." He gave her a wry look. "My ma counseled me to marry when I was older, rather than when I was young. She told me I really didn't have the maturity or experience to tell a good partner from a bad one when I was in my early twenties."

Sloan lay down on the blanket, propping himself up on one elbow across from her. "I'd just gotten out of the Army at twenty-two and I was messed up with PTSD.

And maybe—" he hitched his one shoulder "—I was needing to feel alive again. I met Cary just after I got a job with the US Forest Service. My first assignment was the Grand Canyon in Arizona and she was a waitress just outside the gates of the park where I used to get breakfast every morning, before I went on duty."

Sloan saw the seriousness in Dev's eyes. Her legs were crossed, her elbows resting on her knees.

"I was pretty dead inside from those deployments over to Afghanistan. I wanted to feel something…anything." He lifted his chin, looking across the quiet, beautiful meadow for a moment. "Cary was a live wire. Always smiling. Always up. Always on. Unlike me. I felt like I was a robot, numb, not alive at all." He heaved a sigh and studied Dev. "It was the PTSD symptoms. I'd seen too much in combat, gone through too much, and my emotions were numbed out. Much later, after I got treatment for my anxiety with Dr. Jordana McPherson, who is a physician and head of ER at the local hospital, I began to realize what had happened. My cortisol was far above normal. It works in concert with adrenaline and shoots into our bloodstream when we're under threat or think we're going to die."

Dev groaned. "I should get tested, too."

Nodding, Sloan said, "More than likely a test would confirm the same thing in you. Your job in Afghanistan was never safe, either. You pulled two tours. That's enough to make anyone's cortisol shoot through the roof."

"Once I settle in with my new job, I will get tested. So," Dev said, grappling with his story, "you were drawn to Cary because you felt numb inside? And she made you feel things again?"

"Something like that," Sloan grudgingly admitted. "I just wanted to be around normal people again, I guess. I wanted to try to be like them. But I had a hole in my body as big as a crater and I couldn't feel anything. Even Cary couldn't do it for me. My ma was right: I was young and stupid. I thought being around Cary more would make me feel things again. I just wanted to feel normal. And I put all my chips on her, and married her." Sloan saw her flinch. "Yeah, bad choice for the wrong reasons," he added wryly.

"Twenty-two is young," Dev agreed softly. "You did the best you could at the time."

Grimacing, Sloan smoothed out the wrinkles in the blanket before him with his long fingers. "I was still learning how to read people, and I sure didn't read Cary right." Pain drifted through his heart. And sadness. "It took me three years to realize she had a cocaine habit. She'd been addicted to drugs since she was thirteen, but I didn't know anything about it until much later." *Years later.* Years of nothing but pain for him. He forced himself to look up at Dev. He saw anguish in her eyes.

"That's awful…"

Tell me about it. But Sloan didn't say those bitter words. "When I took Cary home to my parents, my ma pulled me aside and said there was something wrong with her. She couldn't put her finger on it. I laughed it off and married her, anyway. It was a pretty bad decision on my part for a lot of wrong reasons."

"Had you ever dealt with someone who was addicted before?" Dev wondered quietly, searching his saddened expression.

"No. Way beyond my personal life experiences." His mouth slashed into a grimace. "But I sure as hell learned about drug addiction. When I caught her using unexpectedly one morning, all hell broke loose. She turned angry, blaming me, saying it was my fault for the way she was. That she couldn't help herself. She needed her cocaine."

"That's the drug speaking," Dev said gently. "My father would blame my mother for his drinking problem, too. Same old story."

"I took it personally. I had no idea how to deal with an addicted person."

"They'll lie to you with a straight face," Dev muttered.

"Cary lied to me all the time," Sloan admitted. "But I never knew it. I tried to get her to rehab, to help her, but she didn't want to go. She said she was fine, that she was happy with the way she was."

"When they don't want to fix themselves," Dev said, "that's the stance they take. If you have a drug or alcohol addiction, you gotta wanna."

"What do you mean?"

"You gotta wanna quit," Dev said with a slight one-cornered smile, opening her hands. "And most addicted people don't want to quit. It doesn't matter if they spend a lot of money buying the drugs, or what it does to their loved ones or their children. They really don't care about anyone except themselves. It's an awful situation."

"Yeah," Sloan rasped, "it sure as hell was. After two more years, I divorced her because Cary used me as her whipping post, blaming me for everything, the way she was, said that I was making her unhappy…"

"Because you were trying to get her well, and she didn't want to go there. So, she used her anger to push you away from her, Sloan. I saw that happen between my mother and father. But my mother never divorced him, and I don't understand why to this day. I watched her disconnect emotionally from him. Now, they're like two strangers living in the same house. There's nothing that I can see between them anymore."

Shaking his head, Sloan looked up at her. "I had five years of hell. I can't even begin to imagine eighteen years of living in that kind of toxic environment." Dev might appear innocent and vulnerable, but Sloan knew from his own experience with Cary that she had to have some serious underlying strength. Otherwise, she would not be as resilient, would not have a healthy way of living as she did today. "Being empathic, you had to absorb all their tension."

Dev snorted and looked up at the puffy clouds drifting overhead. "It left me exhausted every night. I tended to hide in my bedroom to stay away from them. There was so much unspoken rage between my parents," Dev said, "you could cut the air with a knife. If my mother wasn't screaming at my father, or he was angry and shouting back at her, that toxic silence filled the house instead. There was always ugly energy between them."

"You had a continual war going on in your house," Sloan muttered darkly. Pain came to Dev's green eyes.

"Yes, and I went from an eighteen-year war inside my home, then stepped into the Marine Corps and went directly into another kind of war in Afghanistan. I made some bad decisions, too. Go figure…"

"It's all you knew," Sloan said gently, seeing the anguish in her expression, the way her lips compressed for a moment.

"But you came out of a good family, Sloan. And you didn't know Cary was a druggie. I've discovered that, coming out of an alcoholic's household, I can spot an addicted person a mile away."

"At least you haven't married one like I have. I had no experience at all with people like that. I do now and I agree with you. I can spot an addicted person real easy nowadays. Helluva lesson."

"I'm sorry you had to go through it," Dev told him, meaning it. "It's a special emotional hell. I would never wish it on anyone. All an addicted person does is tear up their own life and the lives of their loved ones." Her mouth curved downward. "The loved ones, the children, if there are any, all come in second place to them getting their drugs. It's a terrible situation..."

"It is," Sloan agreed thickly.

"You divorced Cary when you were twenty-seven, then?"

"Yes. I couldn't get her to change. The more I tried, the angrier and more accusing she became."

"You hung in there a long time," Dev said quietly. "If I hadn't been a kid, I would have walked out of my home situation long before age eighteen." She laughed bitterly. "In fact, I was always running away. I didn't realize why. I felt trapped and suffocated in that house. I felt like I was slowly dying. Starting at ten years old, I drove my father nuts. I'd pack my knapsack full of clothes and food, slip out my bedroom window and head on down the highway. I didn't know where I was going, but I just knew if I didn't run away, I was lost to myself."

Sloan studied her, the silence hanging between them. "Your spirit was dying." He saw her tilt her head, giving him an understanding look.

"Yes, but as a little kid, you don't realize that. All I realized was if I didn't try to run away, to leave my father far behind me, I'd feel like I was going to die. It was a terrible feeling to have, Sloan. I loved my mother, but she was gone three to four days at a time because of her flight demands. I was alone with him and he didn't try to hide his drinking from me. He'd get so drunk, he'd pass out on the couch or bed after a while. I was relieved when he did. Those were the only times he left me alone."

"What do you mean?" Sloan asked.

"He'd scream and yell at me. Tell me I was underfoot. That he wished I hadn't been born. That I was a pain in the ass he had to always take care of."

"Damn," Sloan growled, feeling anger flow through him.

"My mom wasn't around to protect me," Dev said simply, smoothing the blanket out in front of her knees. "And when I tried to tell her what happened when she got home, she didn't want to hear it. I think the long hours, the flying and knowing she was coming home to a drunk husband was just too much for her. I was the straw that broke the camel's back. I was just one load too many for her to carry."

"I'm sorry," he said. "You were caught in a trap that wasn't of your making." And then Sloan grimaced. "Unlike me, who walked into it with his eyes open, as an adult."

"Don't be so hard on yourself, Sloan. You had *no* experience with a drug-addicted personality. They're chameleons. They become what you need them to be when you're around them. When you're gone, they revert back to who they really are. It usually takes people years to figure out what's going on because they're so good at manipulating other people's minds and emotions."

Sloan gave her an admiring look. "What impresses me the most about you, Dev, is that you not only survived that family hell, but look at you now. You're making a good life for yourself. You learned a helluva lot of lessons growing up in that snake pit. And you do good things for people." He gestured to Bella, who sat near her. "You save people's lives. That's a pretty strong statement about who you are. You care. You're connected with others. You serve in a positive way within society."

"I didn't want to be like my father," Dev said sadly. "To this day, I'm angry at him for what he did to me, to my mother. I just can't understand why they're still together."

Sloan raised his brows and ventured, "Is she an enabler? That's what I learned when I went to a drug counselor to start understanding Cary and myself. I learned I was enabling her." Shaking his head, Sloan muttered, "Those counseling sessions showed me how I was contributing and feeding into her behavior."

"Yes, but Cary knew exactly what she was doing to you, Sloan. If she really loved you, she wouldn't have done that to you. Druggies see their entire life through a drug filter. They don't really see you. Not ever." Her voice grew hoarse. "My father never saw me. Nor did he see my mother. Not to this day..."

Feeling her anguish, Sloan rasped, "I can't imagine the pain it causes you, Dev. I really can't, because I had a good family who loves me. I went back home after divorcing Cary to try to get my head screwed on straight. My parents had seen her behavior, but they hadn't ever seen a drug personality around and couldn't identify Cary's issues any more than I could. But we sure all learned from it." He picked up a dry piece of a pine twig and snapped it in two between his fingers. It was symbolic of his broken marriage. Of the bad choice he'd made. "And," he said, "I was fighting PTSD. I didn't un-derstand what it was doing to me except that I felt numb."

"And where are you today with that numbness?"

"I'm feeling again," Sloan promised, seeing hope spring to life in her eyes. "Dr. McPherson has helped a lot."

"So you can feel anger? Happiness? Everything in between?"

"Yes, the whole gamut." Sloan sighed, relief in his tone. "I never thought I'd feel as grateful as I did when I felt my emotions starting to come back online as the cortisol reduced back to normal levels within me. I wel-come them all back. I'd rather feel them, even the nega-tive ones, than feel dead inside."

Dev nodded, frowning. "Maybe I should go talk to her soon, then. I have my feelings. I never lost them. But I hate this constant state of high anxiety I wrestle with when I'm awake. I have trouble sleeping, too." She pointed to the darkness beneath her eyes.

"Ask her to help you get your cortisol down to nor-mal," Sloan advised her, "and you will sleep like a baby at night. It also made most of my weekly nightmares go away, for good, too."

Dev pulled out her cell phone and clicked on her ad-dress book. "I'm sick to death of feeling like this. I'd like to have a normal life again." She wrote the note to her-self to call Jordana tomorrow. Dev managed a choked laugh. "Not that I've ever led a normal life…"

CHAPTER NINE

DEV KNEW SHE wasn't a normal person, at least inwardly. Just seeing the understanding come to Sloan's eyes at her last statement made her heart flutter. "I feel like I've done nothing but make one huge mistake after another," she admitted. "I see now that the war in my family made going into the Marine Corps, and then deploying to a combat zone was more of the same pattern being played out." She opened her hands. "When I got that, I left the military. I'd taken on a physical wound to mirror the emotional wounds I received from my family."

"Those wounds are never easy to see," Sloan agreed.

"Right." Dev lifted her head and held his sympathetic gaze. Sloan made it so easy to talk to him. There was never judgment on his part. He simply listened. "The one good thing that happened in my life was meeting Sergeant Bill Savona. He was a Marine K-9 guy who helped me get my feet under me on my first deployment over in Afghanistan. At that time, I had a different bomb-sniffing dog. His name was King and he was a beautiful black Labrador. Bill showed me the ropes and would go out on patrol with me." Her voice fell and Dev felt old pain move into her heart. "He was a good person, Sloan. I eventually fell in love with him."

"Well, if he was in the K-9 corps," Sloan said, "there had to be a lot of good things about him going on.

Animals like those who are highly sensitive and they wouldn't tolerate what I'd call a flawed human being."

She smiled a little, her gaze moving to the mirrorlike pond. "You're right. I had nine months working with Bill and we just sort of fell in love with one another over time. Not that we meant to or anything, because personal relationships aren't encouraged by the military, as you know. It just happened."

"What kind of man was he?"

The corners of her mouth softened. "The best. He was the one and only healthy guy I'd ever met. He came out of an Italian family in New York City, was street-smart, and that's what he taught me out there while we were looking for bombs buried in the dirt. Bill could read the villagers and he showed me that how a person walked, their facial expressions, their body language, was making a statement we could understand. Many times, Bill would talk to a villager and he'd come away with so much good intel. The Marine company we were in always relied on his insights. He was phenomenal in that way."

"He also saw you."

Her heart fell. "Yes, and to this day, I don't know how. All I do know is I was in love for the first time in my life. Bill made me laugh. He was such a joker. And he didn't play mean jokes on people, either. He had this ability to pull a smile or laugh out of everyone. He really lifted me. Made me feel good about myself, who I was."

"Did he know about your family life?"

She grinned wryly. "Bill was like his dog, forever snooping around and testing the air. Yes, that's how we met after I got assigned to his company. I guess I was looking sad or something and he came over, pulled me aside for a walk and asked me why. I'd just seen my mother at an airport she was flying into before I left on a military C-5 for overseas. I'd finally got up the courage to ask her why she wouldn't leave my father." Rubbing her brow, she glanced at Sloan, whose expression was concerned. "She said my father was like a sick animal, and she could never leave a sick animal because he needed help."

"That's enabling."

"Yep, sure was. By that time, I'd gotten some counseling myself and understood what enabling was. I think I cried half the way to Afghanistan over her answer. She was just as trapped as he is. Still is…"

"But Bill pulled you out of it?"

Nodding, Dev said, "He had a way of getting to the heart of the issue. And he was a good listener like you are, Sloan. Bill never judged me. He just listened and didn't say anything until I was done talking." She reached over as Bella crawled onto the blanket and placed her head on her thigh, her brown gaze reflecting concern. Dev knew Bella was picking up on her emotions, none of them good. All of them filled with regret and grief. "I found myself dumping everything about my family and growing-up years on Bill. It was a long walk and by the time we came back to HQ in the village where we were staying, he knew the good, bad and ugly sides of me. I'd never dumped any of this on anyone except my counselor. I was shocked and worried afterward that he'd gossip to the other guys. But he never did. He treated me like I was sacred or something." Dev petted Bella and added, "He gave me confidence, Sloan. That nine months in the field with him helped me get so much that was wrong with me right. And he did it with his observations, his own life experience."

"He cared deeply for you," Sloan offered.

"Yes…it was love. I didn't realize it at first, but the last three months we had together, I knew it was love. And I was so afraid to admit it to myself…to him."

"Because of the nature of your deployment? The daily danger?"

"Yes." Dev pushed strands of hair off her brow. "Bill had no trouble admitting it to me, however." She smiled fondly. "He came up to me one day after we'd gotten off a six-hour patrol and had this handful of blue wildflowers. He gave them to me and then crouched down in front of me and asked me to marry him. I was so shocked, but I knew he was serious. I think he saw my surprise and told me he'd fallen in love with me. That he wanted to spend the rest of his life with me. And that he could offer me not only his heart, but his big happy Italian family, too. He swore that his family would love me to pieces, like he did." Tears burned in her eyes and Dev closed them, remembering that day so vividly. Pressing her fingers gently against her eyelids, she willed them away. Later, she opened her eyes and whispered unsteadily, "You have to understand, Sloan, that I didn't think I was lovable. I know it sounds stupid, but at nineteen, I didn't really know who I was. So his wanting to marry me just took me by complete surprise."

"I think he knew what he wanted," Sloan said. "And he loved you. Even if you didn't see yourself, he did."

Anguish thrashed through her and Dev choked out, "Yes… I saw that later…after…after he was killed."

Sloan slowly sat up and put the plastic container away. "Do you want to talk about that?"

With a swift shake of her head, Dev said, "No…not today…"

"Fair enough," Sloan murmured. Looking up, he asked, "Are you about ready to start the ride back?"

Relief jagged through Dev and she rose to her feet. Bella leaped up, staying close to her thigh, as if sensing she needed a little doggy support right now. "Yes, I'm ready." Dev saw the thoughtful expression on Sloan's face. There was such a powerful urge to walk across that red blanket and into his arms as he stood. In that moment, Dev realized just how much Bill Savona and Sloan Rankin were alike. Both men possessed a quiet confidence that radiated around them like warming sunlight. Both men had deep insights into people and animals. Bill had been like the father confessor to all the men in that Marine company. She would bet that a lot of other forest rangers just naturally gravitated toward Sloan in the same way. God knew she had.

Her heart opened as she picked up the blanket, shook it out and then quickly folded it up and handed it to him. When their fingers met, Dev greedily absorbed the contact. Somehow, she knew Sloan would be a tender lover. Her lower body stirred, as if to reaffirm that knowing deep within her. She saw compassion in Sloan's dark blue eyes—compassion for her. And that same wonderful, invisible embrace surrounded her as she got ready to mount Goldy. Now, she recognized it for what it was: Sloan's care for her.

As Dev mounted, she was careful not to try to name *what* she felt coming from Sloan. Settling into the Western saddle, she watched him bonelessly mount lanky Rocky, as if born to the horse. The Stetson darkened his upper face; his profile was strong and rugged. There was nothing to dislike about him. Sloan now knew her fears of commitment, of losing a man she had loved once. He seemed content to be her friend. As she turned Goldy around, with Bella leaping and catching up to them, Dev realized in that moment that Bill had been her friend first, too, before they fell in love with one another.

As they rode slowly across the sunlit meadow, the lake behind them, Dev luxuriated in the sunlit warmth vying against the coolness of the mountains. At this altitude, it never got really hot. She heard birds calling to one another, but no warning calls from blue jays. She was grateful to Sloan as he trotted up to ride at her side. He was teaching her the finer points of being in this park. This one had more dangers to watch out for than her last assignment in the Smokys. Still, as her mind touched upon events in her life, Dev felt far more threatened by a human named Bart Gordon than any grizzly. She'd felt worry around Sloan when she'd told him about Gordon. Sloan was concerned about it, and she sensed his worry even now. Why?

Dev watched Mouse and Bella gallop ahead of them and dive down onto the trail at the edge of the meadow. It was a narrow path, allowing only one horse and rider at a time. Sloan moved ahead of her and took the lead. Dev was content to follow. She was still amazed by the fact that being around Sloan dissolved all the anxiety that normally hung like a choke chain around her throat twenty-four hours a day.

The shadows of the forest quickly swallowed her and Goldy up as they started down the thin, rocky trail that would eventually, in three hours, bring them back to the parking lot where her horse trailer was parked. In some ways, Dev didn't want this day to end. She liked Sloan's company. He was intelligent and he asked good questions and made insightful comments.

What were the chances she'd meet a second man so much like Bill? Dev had thought it was an utter impossibility, and now that she knew it wasn't, it triggered real fear. Fear of losing Sloan like she'd lost Bill. Oh, being a ranger was dangerous sometimes, but nothing like combat in Afghanistan. The fear was eating at her gut, which was a ridiculous overreaction. They were safe in the United States, unlike that war-torn country in the Middle East.

She watched Mouse and Bella trot shoulder to shoulder down the trail, pink tongues hanging out, their eyes bright, ears up and noses in the air, sniffing the abundant scents. They made a good team and Dev smiled. The dogs got along like she and Sloan did. There was a quiet ease between them. Good. Beckoning. Terrifying.

Sloan rode his steel-gray gelding with that look that cowboys usually had. His hips moved in accord with his horse, his upper body straight and his shoulders thrown back with inherent pride. He was a powerfully built man and yet she didn't cringe around him. Bart Gordon was built similarly, though far more muscle-bound because he worked out with heavy weights, and she'd instinctively feared him. Dev turned Sloan's questions over in the back of her mind as she rode. Maybe she should find out if Gordon was still back East. But how? Once he was fired by the Forest Service, most of the rangers had probably lost track of him. And Dev had no idea how to find him otherwise.

As the horses turned down another switchback, Dev frowned. Sloan's questions had upset her whether she wanted to admit it or not. What if Gordon was *still* stalking her? Out of sight, somewhere around here? Compressing her lips, Dev felt a niggle of fear shoot through her. No, he wouldn't do that. Would he? He'd already been in jail for stalking and assaulting her once before. Would he come out here? To Jackson Hole? To find her? And then do what?

Her throat went dry with possible answers. Dev would never forget the insane look burning in Gordon's eyes as he'd pinned her down on the floor of the mow. It was like an unchained monster staring down at her, lusting after her, and it had scared the hell out of her. Even now, her skin crawled, and a chill rippled down her spine.

CHAPTER TEN

BART GORDON SMILED. He had Saturday off and he was well hidden near the first apartment complex of The Pines, casually observing the second one. His eyes narrowed as he spotted Dev McGuire getting out of a truck. It wasn't hers. Bart had purposely worn green clothing to blend in to his surroundings between the wall of the complex and the high shrubbery. Last week, he'd taken a ride around the towers early in the morning, at dawn, and spotted Dev's blue-and-white Ford pickup truck parked at the second complex. He knew she was somewhere in that building. Bart had not been able to get into it as he had the first building. He had called over to the visitor's center at Teton Park and asked for her, but she hadn't been on duty. It was a good time on his days off, to hang around here and wait. And watch.

His lips curved triumphantly as he saw Dev emerge from the truck. His attention was instantly centered on the tall, lean man with her. He wondered who he was. On the side of the truck he saw print indicating he was a farrier. Bart made a mental note to check the phone book and trace him. Sooner or later, he'd find out more about this dude. Was Dev in a relationship with him? He knew Dev had been a loner at the other park, never having relationships with men. Someone had once said in passing that Dev had lost the man she loved in Afghanistan. He surmised that was why she was single and available. His erection thickened.

As the couple walked into the second complex, the door shutting behind them, Bart lifted his cell phone camera and took a picture of the door of the man's pickup.

Feeling like it had been a successful day, Bart slipped out of the greenery and walked around the rear of building one. His silver Dodge truck was parked on the other side among many others. Mentally, he rubbed his hands in glee. Tomorrow, he had to drive to Idaho Falls with a load, but it left the rest of today to search the internet for this bastard who was with her. Jealousy ate at Bart as he stepped up on the sidewalk and casually strolled down to his truck. He was still learning about Jackson Hole, its nooks and crannies. And he still didn't have enough money to make a deposit down on the apartment he wanted. Instead, he'd rented a dingy room on the other side of town.

Right now, he had no firm plan for kidnapping Dev. This time, he had to make sure of every step so law enforcement would not catch up to him. He'd been stupid to attack her in that barn. His footprints had shown he was there. Further, the bailing hook she'd struck him in the shoulder with had had his DNA on it. Another nail in the coffin that had earned him the prison time. And a lost job. Anger seethed through him. There was real pleasure in allowing his next kidnapping of her to unfold slowly. Because he wasn't going to get caught this time.

DEV'S PHONE RANG just as she got herself and Bella into her apartment. Taking off her baseball cap, she dropped it on the top of her couch and picked up the landline phone on the small walnut desk next to it.

"Hello?"

"Dev? This is Gus Hunter. What are you doing tomorrow afternoon for Sunday dinner?"

Smiling, Dev sat on the edge of the overstuffed couch. "Nothing. Why?" She loved Miss Gus. Everyone did. She was a lot like Iris Mason, who was also a greatly loved and respected valley grandmother to everyone.

"Well, Val and Griff would love to invite you and Sloan over to our ranch for dinner. We always have a special midafternoon meal on Sunday and would like you and Sloan to show up. Are you game?"

Dev grinned. "Of course. It sounds like fun."

"You need to see Sloan, though. See if he can make it, too?"

"Sure. What would you like us to bring? A casserole? Dessert?"

"Just yourselves. We eat at 4:00 p.m. Why not come around three and bring your dog? We're gonna have the Holts here, as well, and Talon's bringing Zeke, his dog, along. Plus Daisy, the golden retriever that Sandy owns. I think all three dogs will get along fine, and Talon's wanting to socialize Zeke more."

"Sure, I don't have a problem bringing Bella, and I'll let Sloan know. Okay?"

"Okay, see you then!"

Dev felt warmth invade her chest and she looked over at Bella who was intently staring at her. "Well? You heard we're invited to dinner with Miss Gus and her family?" Dev grinned and leaned over, ruffling Bella's thick yellow fur.

Bella panted and excitedly thumped her tail.

"You've already met Zeke and he likes you. But then, you're a girl and he's a boy. You're a dog with two male admirers, Bella." It was clear Bella liked Mouse, too. She stood up, wanting to get out of her clothes, take a shower and change. But first, she'd walk across the hall and knock on Sloan's door.

Sloan opened the door and Dev gave him the message. He had a towel wrapped around his neck, his upper body naked. A rush of pleasure flowed through her as she tore her gaze from his powerful chest sprinkled with dark hair. She forced herself to look up into his eyes. He had obviously been on his way to take a shower when she'd knocked. Mouse was at his side, watching her with friendly curiosity, wagging his tail.

"Sure, we can make it, but I wouldn't put Mouse and Zeke together when there's two female dogs around," Sloan told her, looking down at his dog. "Probably get into a fight. Combat dogs are highly competitive, a lot of testosterone, so I think we'll leave Mouse here."

"Will Bella be okay with Zeke, you think?" The man's muscles flexed and she felt herself go hot in her lower body. Sloan's shoulders were well defined, his upper arms attesting to his hard work as a farrier, tight and ropy. His hands were on either end of the towel around his neck. It struck Dev that he was utterly comfortable with his maleness, who he was. And it was beckoning to her.

"Sure. Zeke will probably think he died and went to heaven." Sloan chuckled. "You okay with it?"

"Yes. Bella was spayed at a year old."

"What? Wouldn't you want some half Belgian Malinois, half yellow Lab puppies running around?" he teased.

"No. I'm not ready for six to twelve puppies," Dev said with a laugh. "But I don't have to worry about that."

"Zeke will be a happy guy to see Bella." He looked down at Mouse. "And he's gonna be mighty unhappy his girl is with another male dog."

"Bella is the belle of the ball. I'm looking forward to the dinner." And then Dev added wistfully, "It's like the home I always dreamed about, but never had."

Nodding, Sloan gave her a tender look. "I think as people get to know you over time, you'll have more Sunday dinner invites than you can fill," Sloan promised.

"Does Miss Gus invite you out to their ranch all the time?" Dev asked, inhaling the scent of him and the perspiration and dust from their earlier ride. It did funny, delicious things to her as a woman, and that yearning ache began once more. It always did when she was around Sloan.

"I usually eat with Iris and her family two weeks out of the month and the other two, I'm over at the Bar H with Miss Gus and the Holt family."

"That's a lovely way to spend a Sunday," Dev said, her voice soft.

"It's a great Western tradition," Sloan agreed. "Take pity on us poor, lonely single people."

Dev didn't want to leave, but she knew she had to. Sloan agreed to meet her Sunday at 2:00 p.m. and they'd take a leisurely truck ride out to the Bar H. She wanted to stay. Wanted to kiss this man. Dev saw something else in Sloan's eyes, something that told her he wanted to kiss her, too. She wasn't naive. She could interpret when a man wanted her. Her hands fluttered nervously.

"I'll see you tomorrow." Dev quickly turned around and left. Her whole body was quivering internally. How

long had it been since she'd made love? Once in her
apartment, Dev went to the kitchen sink and poured herself a glass of water. Being so sensitive, she could feel
Sloan wanting her as much as she wanted him. After
gulping down the water as if it would put the fire out in
her body, she set the glass down. She gripped the granite counter, hung her head and closed her eyes. Did she
dare get involved with Sloan? Every time she was with
him, she was happy. Her anxiety disappeared. She felt
at peace, and she hadn't felt that way since before Gordon's assault on her.

Opening her eyes, Dev pushed away from the sink
and walked to the bathroom to take a quick shower. As
the water sluiced down across her head, Dev felt so much
regret about Bill and not consummating their relationship
before he died. Just because they were in a combat area
didn't mean Bill didn't know places where they could
go to make love with one another. But Dev had resisted
for a lot of reasons. Now those reasons seemed so lame.
She grieved because they did steal kisses from one another. And his kisses had enflamed her and made her
ache for so much more with him.

Stepping out of the shower, her hair smelling of nutmeg from the shampoo she'd used, Dev toweled off,
caught in the misery and grief of her past. The look in
Sloan's blue eyes had been clear. He wanted her. Now
there was no combat, no other concerns for her to worry
about with him. She patted her face dry and walked to
the steamy mirror, picking up a comb, moving it through
her limp, damp hair.

While she chose a soft pink pair of jersey trousers and
a white tunic with a cowl neck, her heart and her mind
dwelled on Sloan. He'd never made a move to tell her

that he wanted her. But dammit, she *felt* it around him! Being sensitive like this was miserable. Dev knew she would have to make the first move. She would have to let Sloan know that she wanted something more from him…if she was reading him accurately. Dev grimaced as she pulled the blow dryer from the bathroom drawer. She ran her comb through her drying hair, the bluish highlights glinting in the mirror. She knew her ability to read people was far from perfect. She'd not picked up on Gordon's real intentions, had she? At best her "knowing" was spotty and not to be fully trusted.

Was Sloan any easier to read? Or was she fooling herself? Maybe she was reading him all wrong. And how embarrassing that would be! Dev would have to face him nearly every day because he was stationed with her at Teton Park. What a mess. Dev didn't see any way out of it, either. If Sloan wasn't interested, she would be mortified by her assumptions.

It had been Bill who had pursued her, not the other way around. They'd worked together, which gave them a lot of time with one another. Dev clearly remembered seeing that same look in Bill's eyes when he looked at her—that look that had said he wanted her. And remembering back through those years, Dev knew she had felt his love for her, but it had been different than what she felt from Sloan. Bill had been a jokester and a teaser, and Sloan was not. He was a salt-of-the-earth kind of guy, quiet and attentive. She liked Sloan's humor when he shared it with her, though. Since the assault, her sense of humor had fled. Or maybe it was buried? Like so much of the rest of her.

Pulling the brush lightly across her black hair to shape it, she stood there, observing herself in the mirror. The truth was that she was very bad at choosing men. Dev didn't know why she couldn't read them. After all, she was an empath. She picked up on people's emotions and intent. But her gift, or curse, was not reliable. And maybe it was her. She hadn't had a whole lot of relationships through the years. Bill had been her first serious one. She'd fallen in love with him. Making a face, Dev placed the brush on the counter.

Bella was lying sprawled out on her side, nearly blocking the entire hallway. Grinning, Dev stepped quietly over her, knowing her Lab was tuckered out from the six-hour trail ride. But she was a happy dog. Her snores echoed up and down the hall. Dev sometimes wished she was a dog instead of a human. They were much more alert and sensitive to humans and their surroundings. She hadn't even heard Gordon sneaking up on her. *God.*

"Why, don't you look pretty all gussied up, Dev."

"Thanks, Miss Gus. Here, these are for you. From Sloan and me."

Dev smiled shyly as she carried a bouquet of flowers that Sloan had stopped at the grocery store to buy, so she could give them to Miss Gus at the door. She was glad she'd dressed up in a pair of drapey cream-colored Tencel pants, with a soft belt around her waist. It suited the warmth of the season. She loved her short-sleeved sunrise-colored jersey top. The small pearl buttons from the boat neck downward made her feel very feminine.

Gus, dressed in a bright red dress with an embroidered white sash around her waist, nodded and peered intently up at Sloan, who stood in the foyer behind Dev. "Well now—" she cackled "—I don't think they're from this cowboy." Her eyes danced with mirth. "I think it was *your* thoughtfulness, Dev. The only thing Sloan has ever brought to this ranch house is his considerable appetite!" She chortled, giving Sloan a merry look.

Dev laughed and looked over her shoulder at Sloan. He'd put on a clean, pressed white cowboy shirt, wore a pair of jeans and even wiped the dust off his well-worn cowboy boots. The red neckerchief around his strong neck just about matched the ruddiness that flooded his cheeks as Miss Gus teased the daylights out of him. "No, it's from both of us. He helped me pick them out for you. Said you really liked white daisies."

Gus raised her white eyebrows. "Well, that's new. Isn't it, Sloan? You helping Dev out like that? Hmm, sounds like a serious relationship forming here."

Sloan smiled lamely and removed his freshly brushed Stetson. "It was Dev's idea to get the flowers," he admitted. "But when I saw the white daisies, I knew they were a favorite of yours." He gestured out the open screen door where he stood. "In fact," he murmured, "if I don't miss my best guess, there's a ton of Shasta daisies growing right inside the fence line out there."

"Right you are," Gus praised. Eyes twinkling, she pulled Dev to her side. "You have to watch this hombre. He's a mite slow about social graces, but he catches on fast." And then, she gave Sloan a hard look. "So, next time you come? Might be nice to show up with flowers. And I do like chocolates, you know. So does Val. Good chocolate," she noted, giving him a coyote smile.

"I'll remember that," Sloan promised, serious. "Otherwise, next time you invite us, you might not let me get a boot inside your ranch house door?"

Shaking her finger at him, Gus said, "I haven't thrown you out yet, have I?"

Sloan gave her a warm look. "I will never show up here again without flowers or chocolate for you, Miss Gus. That's a promise. I've learned a good lesson today."

"*Good* chocolate, Sloan. You men just think you can grab a box of chocolates outta a grocery store and that'll do."

"It doesn't," Dev agreed, feeling for Sloan's discomfort. It was the first time she'd ever seen him blush. He looked like a little boy who had been caught with his hand in the cookie jar. Gus had a genteel way of chiding a person so they didn't feel completely humiliated, she noticed. Still, Dev felt it was proper to bring something to a dinner she'd been invited to, and couldn't believe Sloan hadn't thought to bring his elder something before this time.

"See? She knows," Gus said, indignant. "Ask this pretty little gal about good chocolate. She might know a whole lot more about it than you Wild West cowpokes who talk to your horses all day do." She turned and laughed. Dev moved next to her. Gus had a slender oak cane that she leaned on. "Can I help you, Miss Gus?"

"Oh, Lordy, no! My hip is fussin' at me today, so leanin' a little on a cane takes the pain away. Val says I need to have a good, hot bath and that's probably so, but I'm hungry! Everyone's in the kitchen. Let's go eat!"

Dev followed the elder as she hobbled down through the foyer. She inhaled the mouthwatering scent of yeast-risen rolls, a baked country ham and, she was pretty sure, sweet potatoes. Glancing over her shoulder, she saw Sloan come in and hook his hat on a peg. He smiled at her. Heat went straight through Dev and she felt that intense yearning once again. Soaking it up, she gave Sloan a soft look and followed Gus into the massive kitchen.

Sloan's hand fit lightly against the small of her back
as he strolled up to her, guiding her into the kitchen.
Her skin tingled in the wake of this unexpected contact.
Even more, Dev felt a sense of being his woman. She
wondered if she was really picking up on his feelings
or, because she wanted a closer relationship with Sloan,
she'd made them up.

Lifting her hand, she saw Val holding her eight-
month-old daughter, Sophia, in her arms. Griff was
nearby, talking with Talon and Sandy Holt-Reynolds.
Her husband, Cass, was standing with them. Cat Holt
was at the kitchen counter doing the food prep.

"I'm going to go help Cat," she told Sloan.

"Want another set of hands?" he asked.

"No. I think two of us can handle it." She drowned in
the liquid look in his blue eyes. Yes, Sloan wanted her.
There was no doubt about it. A soaring feeling of being
desired flowed like warm, sweet honey through Dev.
She felt her breasts tightening and was glad to be wearing a cotton bra beneath the colorful top that lovingly
outlined every curve of her upper body.

In no time after donning bright green aprons, Dev
and Cat had a huge ham that was drizzled with a thick
red cranberry glaze set on the table. Talon went to work
slicing it and Griff McPherson held out a huge platter
to place the slices upon. Dev had been right about the
fancy sweet potatoes. She inhaled the aroma of the huge
casserole as she brought it to the table and placed it on
a bright blue metal trivet. It had been made with orange
juice, and sprinkled with coconut and pecans, which had
browned just right in the oven.

Cat brought over three huge baskets of freshly baked
yeast-risen rolls and placed them at three different points

along the twelve-foot trestle table. Val had put her red-haired daughter into a chair, then brought over two jars of honey for the rolls and sat down next to her child.

Dev found a large bowl of cranberry-grape salad and pulled it out of the fridge. The European greens were mixed with pineapple and crushed walnuts, as well. It was a pretty salad and Dev took it to Miss Gus first, who had sat down at one end of the table. Talon had sat at the other end. Untying her green apron, Dev smiled over at Cat, who looked beautiful in a short-sleeved purple tunic that draped down over her hips and her white linen trousers.

"Let's go sit down before there's nothing left," Cat said with a laugh, slipping her arm around Dev's shoulder for a moment, giving her a big thank-you hug for helping her. Cass seated his wife, Sandy, next to Miss Gus and then took the chair next to her.

Sloan hadn't sat down yet, and seemed to be waiting for her. Dev had never had a man be so gentlemanly toward her. He pulled out her chair, smiled down at her and she sat. Sloan eased his bulk into a chair to her left. Opposite them were Val, Griff and their daughter. On Dev's right, Cat sat down next to her husband, Talon.

"Okay," Gus called, "let's hold hands."

The table immediately quieted and every one created a circle of hands around the table. Gus said a short prayer of thanks and then said, "I don't want to see any leftovers!" She eyed Sandy's six-month-old golden retriever puppy, Daisy. Bella and Zeke sat near the opening to the kitchen, watching them. Daisy romped around them, never still, happy for the company. "Well," Gus amended, "maybe a few leftovers for the doggies?"

Talon groaned. "Gus…"

Cat laughed. "Oh, come on, Talon! Zeke's been doing well with a few scraps of real food every now and again. He started out on marshmallows from my cup of hot chocolate, if you remember?"

Talon rolled his eyes and held up his hands. "Okay, okay. I surrender. But don't feed him too much. He's been on a dry dog food forever."

"Yes," Gus said, stabbing at a thick piece of ham as Sloan held the platter toward her, "but he's a civilian like you are now. And if he survived Cat's marshmallows, I don't think that a teeny, tiny piece of leftover ham is gonna make him go belly-up. Do you?" She waggled her silver eyebrows in Talon's direction.

Everyone laughed as the food was passed around the table.

"Busted," Cat told her husband, grinning.

Talon eyed her. "You're enjoying this way too much."

"Miss Gus is the only one who can get you to loosen up on Zeke and feed him real food," Cass noted with a grin toward Talon.

He gave Cass a grudging look. Cass had at one time been an Army Special Forces operator, but she said nothing. And with Talon having been a SEAL, they got along just fine because they'd both been in black ops.

"Every Sunday when you come over for dinner, he gets good vittles," Gus agreed, pleased. "Why, I think Zeke's even gained a little weight, Talon."

Talon filled his plate with a little of everything. "Yes, about five pounds."

"See?" Gus said, pleased, stabbing her fork in Talon's direction. "It's good to bring Zeke here for Sunday dinners, too."

"Do you think Bella might like a few bites of ham?"

Sloan asked Dev. "Or do you have her on a real strict diet, too?"

Bella lifted her head, eyes bright with expectation, ears up.

Everyone laughed, watching the dog's reaction.

"Bella's a foodie," Dev informed everyone with a chuckle. "She was trained with food because that's the most important thing in her life."

"That's a dog I can like," Gus said. "She's a pretty yellow Lab, Dev. And it looks like Zeke and Daisy are real pleased with her company, too."

Dev nodded. "Bella gets along with everyone. She's easygoing."

Cat pointed her chin toward the two dogs. "Good thing she's spayed. Zeke looks at Bella like he wants to have a batch of puppies with her."

Gus burst out laughing, slapping her knee. "Zeke's an alpha male. He thinks he owns every female who waltzes into this ranch house whether she has two legs or four legs."

Cat slid her husband a wicked look. "Somewhat like his owner, huh?"

More titters riffled up and down the table. Sly looks and grins were exchanged.

"What *is* this?" Talon demanded, laughing. "Pick on Talon time?"

"Ohhhhh," Val crooned, "a SEAL can't take a little ribbing? Give me a break! SEALs invented the most gruesome teasing I've ever seen."

"Well," Talon said, shrugging, "we are a little cruel at times with one another."

Val snorted and fed her daughter some of the yummy sweet potato casserole after blowing on it to make sure it was cool enough for her. Sophia's blue eyes shone with pleasure over the food Val gently spooned into her bow-shaped mouth. "Listen, I worked with SEALs when I was an intelligence officer in the Air Force. You guys were just plain brutal with one another."

Talon had the good grace to remain silent and pay attention to his food. Cat was snickering while she ate. She reached over and patted Talon's broad shoulder through the dark blue cowboy shirt he wore.

"You'll live, darling," she soothed.

Gus chuckled. "Maybe this will make him ease up on poor ole Zeke. The dog's nose is in the air and he can smell everything on this table. You gotta give him a little of everything, Talon. So the dogs can have their Sunday dinner, too."

Talon grimaced.

Cat smiled widely and nodded her head.

Dev got the feeling that Miss Gus was leading the charge to continue to socialize Zeke, to take him out of his world of combat-assault and make him more a house dog. She knew that Zeke, like Mouse, had had two to three years of training starting at birth and both had seen a lot of combat. It was hard to get a dog to leave what he knew behind and embrace something new. And yellow Labs were a lot easier to retrain than the intense, competitive Belgian Malinois breed. She turned to Sloan.

"Did you have a hard time retraining Mouse?" she asked.

"Some," Sloan admitted. "Part of the equation of retraining is the man who partnered with him. We were trained, too."

Gus gave Sloan a narrow-eyed look. "Well, seems to

me you're real retrainable. Dev's already got you pick-ing out special flowers for me."

Dev felt sorry for Sloan as Gus aimed her gun sights at him. Gus enjoyed putting the guys on the spot, she was discovering. Sloan's cheeks went ruddy as he tried to take her teasing with good grace.

"Well," Sloan began awkwardly, "I just suggested the daisies was all, Miss Gus."

"Horse feathers!" She jabbed her index finger into Sloan's upper arm. "I think you're kinda sweet on Dev. Not that I think that's bad. She's a beautiful young woman. Maybe you ought to think about buying *her* some flowers in the future? Hmmmmm?"

The whole table snickered and exchanged knowing glances with one another, all glad that Sloan was the center of Miss Gus's attention and not them.

"Thank God she's picking on you now, Sloan," Talon muttered with mock relief, grinning like a fool.

"Let's talk about something else?" Sloan suggested politely to Miss Gus.

"Phooey, I might be in my mideighties, young man, but I still have a set of eyes in my head that work! You're sweet on Dev. You got moon-dog eyes for her."

"Uh-oh," Val whispered dramatically to everyone, "Sloan's got that awful male disease called moon-dog eyes."

Dev gave the elder a confused look. "I've never heard the term. What does it mean, Miss Gus?"

Gus smiled gently over at Dev. "It's a Western term from my day, when I was as young and pretty as you are. Moon-dog eyes mean a man is yearning and pining away for the woman he loves. He's got that dazed, far-away look of dreaming in his eyes for his lady."

Instantly, Dev felt a flush of heat fly up her throat and into her face.

"I don't know which of you," Griff said, pointing in their direction, "is redder at the moment."

Val raised her brows. "I'd say Dev is."

Cat turned and twisted a playful look at her. "Dev, you really blush well."

CHAPTER ELEVEN

THE WARM SUMMER BREEZE lifted strands of Dev's hair as she walked at Sloan's side. She touched her stomach. "I feel like a stuffed turkey. How about you?"

Sloan cut his gait to remain in step with Dev. The western sun was hanging low over the Tetons and robins were singing their melodic songs around the main ranch area. "About the same," he said, smiling over at her. "Miss Gus doesn't take any prisoners at Sunday dinners, does she? I think she thinks it's open season."

Their hands sometimes brushed against one another as they strolled around the large ranch house. Sloan had suggested a walk down the dirt road that led to Long Lake, about a half a mile north of them. Dev was more than willing to walk off some of the delicious food. She'd eaten far more than usual and maybe that was because of the love that reigned at the table. "Her teasing isn't mean, though. She's sharp and she calls it as she sees it. Val is in the kitchen making each of us a nice to-go box from the leftovers. I'll get at least two meals out of mine."

"I'll get one."

She grinned. The warmth of the breeze felt good and she absorbed Sloan's nearness, cherishing the time she spent with him. "That was such a wonderful dinner. All the dogs got a little ham, too. I think Zeke was smiling from ear to ear. The food was great, but the people, well, that really was dessert for me."

Nodding, Sloan looked along the road, at the evergreens to the right. "The Holt and McPherson family has a good Western tradition."

"Did your family do this, too?" she wondered, looking up into his pensive features.

"They do," he said. "To this day. We have families like that all over Black Mountain. Poppy Thorn usually, about once a month, invites everyone over for Sunday dinner. My ma will invite everyone over the next week. And the other families will do it, too. That way, no one family takes the burden of cooking all the food all the time. It's a great way to catch up with everyone's lives, see if they need help of some kind, share the good and the bad together." He smiled a little. "That way, if bad comes, you have a lot of loving support from the people on the mountain who know you. It helps a lot."

"That sounds so wonderful." Dev sighed. When Sloan's hand brushed hers, this time he wrapped his fingers lightly around hers. And then, he looked down at her, as if making sure it was all right. Her heart took off and she drowned in his darkening blue eyes. Mouth dry, Dev shyly curved her fingers around his. It was such a huge step for her. But nothing had ever felt so right to her, either, despite her past experiences. A molten cobalt look from Sloan and she could feel an incredible sensation of warmth and care wrapping around her. As if he were physically embracing her. But he was not. They continued to walk at a slow pace down the center of the dirt road.

"I think," Sloan said, "that allowing yourself to be drawn into Iris's and Gus's families will do you a lot of good. Maybe make up for all those missing years when you didn't have a loving family around you?"

Dev absorbed their hands fitting together. Hers were a little damp from excitement and giddiness. Dev could feel the thick, rough calluses on Sloan's hand, feel the latent power in his grip, which he did not bring to bear on her. "I sat at the table thinking about how much I missed."

"But you won't miss it from now on. I'm sure Miss Gus will always ask you to come to Sunday dinner with me."

"I'd love to start a new tradition," Dev admitted, her voice suddenly emotional. The evergreens lined a well-used footpath down to one end of the lake. Half of Long Lake was on McPherson property and the other half, she understood, was on US Forest Service land. When they arrived at the edge of the lake, which reminded her of the shape of a long, fat finger, Dev noticed the six cabins that Gus and her family rented out weekly to tourists. There were a number of cars parked next to each log cabin, with families at picnic tables and children playing along the sandy beach. It was an idyllic scene to Dev.

"Come on, we'll go the other way," Sloan urged, tugging a little at her hand. "Talon and Griff built a real nice sturdy swing at the end of the lake." He gestured toward a group of pine trees standing near the bank.

The path was wide enough for two people and Sloan moved to the left of her, so she could walk close to the grassy, wildflower-strewn bank. Dev could see a great blue heron in the shallows near that swing in the distance. There were long, hairlike strands of clouds high above them. The breeze was off and on, and she enjoyed seeing the otherwise smooth lake surface riffle here and there. It reminded her of the sparks of fire traveling up her fingers and into her hand where Sloan held it. The sensation surrounding her at this moment made her want to kiss him. All Dev could think about was kissing Sloan. She'd seen the desire in his eyes earlier. He had wanted to kiss her, too. Her heart took off a little faster as she felt a sweet anticipation rise within her, like tendrils curling around her heart, which had been dormant for too long.

By the time they reached the end of the lake, the great blue heron took off with graceful flaps of his seven-foot wingspan, skimming the surface of the lake. Dev spotted the huge pine rocker suspended on chains built on a solid pine foundation. The six fragrant evergreens made a semicircle around where it sat so people could sit in it and look out across the lake. The polished pine was smooth and when Sloan sat down at one end, he released her hand, allowing Dev to make the decision whether she wanted to sit close or far away from him. Her heart pounded with anticipation and Dev was feeling inwardly rocky. She wanted to sit right next to Sloan, hoping he'd put his arm around her shoulders. Was that too forward? Didn't they need to talk? Dev felt utterly inept at this and she chose to sit about midway between the other end of the rocker and Sloan. He'd leaned back and she could see the enjoyment in his expression as he gently pushed the rocker back and forth a little with his boot.

"Do you come out here often?" Dev wondered aloud, calling herself a coward for keeping her gaze on the lake and not Sloan.

"No. I want to, but usually I've got five or six animals to shoe and by the time that's done, I only have time to get home, get a shower, cook up some grub and then hit the sack." Sloan slanted her an amused glance. "This is the first time I've ever brought someone down here. I've got to say, it's far nicer than sitting alone."

Dev drowned in the warmth of Sloan's blue gaze, feeling her heart tug. How desperately she wanted to kiss this man. He'd held her heart so gently from the beginning, never making a move until right now. "I guess," she began tentatively, giving him a shy glance, "that Miss Gus and everyone else thinks we're a couple?"

Grimacing, Sloan stretched out his long legs and hooked his arm across the back of the rocker. "Miss Gus has the eyes of an eagle. She misses nothing." He gave her a wry look. "You were blushing pretty well."

Laughing unsurely, Dev opened her hands. When she got nervous, they always fluttered. "Is she psychic or something?"

"You'd think." He chuckled, holding her gaze. "Is she right or wrong, Dev? You tell me."

His voice was deep and mellow, nothing divisive or challenging in it. Just like the gentle breeze that came and went around them right now. Her eyes fell to her clasped hands in her lap. "No," she said, her voice barely above a whisper, "I don't think she's wrong." God, Sloan deserved someone who wasn't so cowardly. Taking a deep breath, Dev held his inquiring gaze. "I feel something between us, Sloan. I did from the beginning. And I couldn't identify it. I can feel it, though."

"Did it upset you?"

Shaking her head, Dev took another deep breath and plunged on. "No. In fact, it felt—wonderful." She cut Sloan a quick glance. "I fell in love with Bill Savona over time. We worked together. I was with him every day. We faced death together in different ways, but we had one another and that helped so much. He was a lot like you,

Sloan. He never crowded me, gave me lines or chased me. I guess, well, over time I just fell in love with him."

"And then he was torn from you."

The words hurt to hear and she felt her heart crumple a little. "Yes," she admitted hollowly. "In an instant."

"And it takes years to get over someone who was taken from you, Dev. I saw it in other instances around me."

"No question. I was just coming out of what felt like a long, dark tunnel emotionally when I got assigned to Great Smoky Mountains National Park. I was at the end of my grieving for Bill, I guess. But I'd done so much inner work on myself, the tears, the memories, confronting the reasons he'd died, that I wasn't really paying much attention to things around me." With a weak shrug, Dev added, "And Bart Gordon was there, watching me all the time, but I honestly wasn't aware of it at first. Wanting me for all the wrong reasons."

"So," Sloan said, moving his right hand down his thigh, "you reeled from one tragic trauma to another with Gordon."

"Yes, it was a slowly occurring disaster even though I didn't realize it at the time. I'd never been stalked. Never been around that kind of person. I didn't know what to look for, the signs…"

"Most people wouldn't, gal, so don't go so hard on yourself."

She drowned in his dark blue gaze. It looked like clear, deep ultramarine Pacific water. "Yeah, I get a little hard on myself sometimes."

"And then," Sloan said gently, "you met me."

Gulping, Dev forced herself to hold his gaze. She felt nothing but that incredible blanket of warmth swirling around her. It was the most wonderful sensation she'd ever felt and she hungered daily for it. "I've been living in an unsafe world for so long, Sloan."

"Do I make you feel safe, Dev?"

Her heart rolled in her chest. Her voice became stronger. "Yes. Ever since we met, I've always felt... protected...when I'm around you. You even made my anxiety go away and I still can't figure out how or why it happens." A sweet keening fluttered through her lower body. "Part of me wants to run to you, Sloan. The other part questions my ability to know a good man from a bad one. Not that you're bad, but I'm just scared."

"That's what I thought," Sloan murmured, giving her a sympathetic look. "You just need time to sort everything out, Dev. There's no hurry. Never has been."

She stared at him, the silence growing between them. "Then, how do you feel about me?" Her throat constricted, the last word coming out strained. Dev tried to prepare herself for being wrong. The expression on Sloan's face softened.

"It's mutual, Dev. Miss Gus wasn't wrong, bless her heart."

She didn't know whether to scream and yell with joy or retreat. Dev tried to tell herself Sloan was nothing like Gordon. And he wasn't. It was just the memories, those dark clouds of suffocating terror that popped up, unwelcome and unwanted. "I guess I needed to come clean. I've felt something toward you from the moment you pulled up and helped me out with that flat tire on my horse trailer." She tried not to convey her nervousness, gripping her damp fingers together. "I didn't come here expecting to find a relationship."

Sloan nodded. "Even misfits find one another in this world, gal."

"Am I a misfit, Sloan? Are you?"

"Naw," he teased, "it's just an expression, is all. I think you're still reeling from Gordon's attack. That was recent. It takes a long time to deal with something like that, Dev."

She tilted her head, staring intently at him. "When I'm with you, all that anxiety goes away." Tears suddenly sprang to her eyes. Shocked, Dev wiped her eyes. "I don't know what it is," she blurted. "I get so emotional when I'm around you, Sloan. No one has ever done this to me before..."

The look on his face grew tender. "Come here," he said, his voice low and thick.

As Sloan turned and eased his arm off the back of the rocker and curved it around her shoulders, he didn't try to pull Dev toward him. Instead, he allowed her the decision.

Dev's throat tightened, a lump forming as his long arm slid lightly across her shoulders in invitation. Her heart twisted in her chest, caught between the past and the present. Lifting her lashes, she sank into his stormy-looking eyes, feeling him monitor the weight of his arm against her shoulders. And then something deep within her snapped. Dev wasn't sure what it was, what it was about, but she found herself moving so that her leg was pressed against the length of his hard thigh. Her hand drifted to his starched, pressed white cowboy shirt, her palm resting near his slowly thudding heart beneath it. His eyes changed, narrowed, and Dev knew he was going to kiss her.

And that was exactly what she wanted. It was as if

he'd silently read her and knew what she needed. As
Sloan lifted his other hand, sliding it against her jaw,
Dev closed her eyes, her skin skittering with tiny flames
of pleasure. She felt such tension within Sloan, as if he
were holding himself in tight check. Without thinking,
because her pounding heart had taken over, she flowed
against him, her breasts meeting the wall of his chest as
she lifted her chin, wanting him to kiss her.

Sloan skimmed her lips lightly. Nothing crushing.
Not controlling her. Rather…inviting her to respond.
His mouth was strong, curving lightly across hers, testing her, seeing how much she wanted, seeing how far
she wanted to go. Her nostrils inhaled the clean scent
of soap along with his masculine scent—it flooded her
as she dragged it deep into her lungs. Dev slid her hand
across the cotton of Sloan's shirt, feeling his muscles
tense beneath her exploring fingers. There was such a
sense of power and urgency thrumming around her and
yet Sloan's mouth was tender, searching, silently asking
her what she wanted.

No man had ever kissed her like this, gently intro-
ducing himself, allowing her to respond as little or as
much as she wanted. Sloan's breath was moist against
her cheek, a little ragged, the tension tightening between
them. The ache in her lower body flared to life each time
his mouth took slow, leisurely sips from her lips. A low
moan of pleasure caught in her throat as he cupped her
jaw, angling her so that he could kiss her more surely, if
that was what Dev wanted. Her heart was galloping in
her chest and her fingers slid up his corded neck, feeling his heavy pulse beneath.

Dev parted her lips, opening to him, opening to possibility. She felt Sloan lurch inwardly and place a steel

grip upon himself, his arm sliding a little more strongly
around her shoulders, holding her just so, taking her lips,
savoring the first real taste of her.

Dev felt as if she were a flower slowly unfolding to
his slow exploration of her. He was taking his time, enjoying the physical act of sliding his mouth across her
lips. The sensations radiated outward and downward, engaging her yearning heart and gnawing lower body. This
man knew how to kiss a woman, there was no question.
She brushed against Sloan's recently shaven cheek, feeling the sandpaper quality of it. Every subtle touch sent
waves of heat and hunger surging down through Dev. His
fingers moved slowly through her silky black hair. He
treated her as if she were some beautiful, fragile being
to be worshipped and given back to, not taken from.

Her entire body burst open from the deepest levels
within herself as Sloan positioned her head just a little
more, his mouth able to capture hers more deeply, urging
her to explore him at the leisurely pace that was setting
her on fire. Dev had been so right! She'd known Sloan
would be a man who knew how to kiss a woman. And
now, there was no question that he would be an incredible lover, taking her to places she had never been with
a man before.

Dev's breath was becoming short and ragged. She
slid her fingers around his nape, drawing him closer to
her, her breasts pressed insistently against his chest. She
felt them tightening with need, the nipples puckering,
begging to be touched by Sloan. Lost in the enveloping
fire he was creating with just his mouth and the way he
held her, cherished her, as if she were the most precious
woman on earth, Dev felt herself sinking deeper and
deeper into his mouth, his hands, his body galvanized

with tension. And when she opened her lips more, at the shy brush of her tongue against his flat lower lip, Dev sensed a powerful trembling move through Sloan, as if the pleasure were nearly too much for him to handle.

Sloan took her mouth more surely and she dissolved into the texture, taste and heat of him. All the sounds of nature around her faded away. Only the pounding of her heart and their ragged breaths mingling ruled her sensory universe. There was such yearning between them and Dev felt as if at any second, it would snap and break. Need, lust and arousal surrounded her, tunneled through her needy body, and her mind dissolved into that boiling cauldron.

SLOAN HAD TO ease away from Dev's mouth or he wouldn't be able to control himself much longer. Agony in his lower body commingled with fierce need for her, and he slid his fingers slowly through her hair, gently easing his mouth away from hers. He barely opened his eyes. He was shaking inwardly, his breath uneven, heart stuttering. Never, in all his life, had Sloan fallen so quickly into a woman's heat as with Dev. He allowed his hands to curve around her shoulders, watching her eyes slowly open. Her lips were parted, slightly swollen from the power of their kiss. Dev had surprised him completely. Only when she sank into their fevered state had she allowed him to see how hungry she was for him. And when she had, she'd taken Sloan around a sharp bend filled with raging lust.

Her eyes were drowsy looking, filled with arousal. It was the luminous look in them that made his heart turn over and swell with an unknown emotion that sent him soaring. He didn't want to name the emotion. He didn't

dare. It was far too soon. All they'd shared was a kiss.
A kiss that had rocked and fractured the world he knew.
As he drowned in her forest green eyes that took his
breath away, Sloan felt as if she had made him punch-
drunk. *One kiss*...

He noticed how dazed Dev had become. Their kiss
must have sent her somewhere intensely pleasurable because he saw a faint upward crook at the corners of her
mouth. Allowing his hand to fall away, he smiled a little unsurely at her. "I feel like lightning struck us." His
voice was low and roughened with passion, there was no
denying that. Dev's cheeks had become flushed and she
touched her brow, running her fingers slowly through
her mussed hair. The expression on her face could only
be interpreted as wonder. At least it wasn't shock, Sloan
thought wryly. Their kiss had been something out of this
world. *Extraordinary.* Sloan swore he was floating. Her
lips were ripe, full, and he ached to lean down and capture them once more. The knowledge that he couldn't
bed Dev, that he had to wait, made him slow down. She
wasn't the kind of woman that could be crowded, cor-
ralled or pushed. Dev had come to him. Sloan had felt
her need, her yearning, and that was when he'd risked
everything by catching hold of her hand, holding it in his.

Dev could have jerked her hand out of his, but she
hadn't. And when her slender fingers had shyly curled
around his large scarred ones, he'd known. He'd known
this wasn't one-sided. It wasn't just him wanting her. It
was mutual.

His heart raced with a dizzying joy that made him
feel like he was an untethered balloon joyously surging
skyward in celebration of that knowledge. Hope infused
him as he saw Dev smile wonderingly up at him, amaze-

ment shining in her half-opened eyes, her pupils huge and black. She was so beautiful to him. Every square inch of her Sloan ached to lick, nibble, kiss and nuzzle, letting her know just how exquisite she was to him.

Lifting his hand, he smoothed a few errant strands of hair on the side of her head. The sun was setting behind the majestic Tetons in the distance, sending golden shafts of light shooting boldly across the wide valley. The shadows were growing deeper along the lake. And it was getting cooler.

Sloan wondered what Dev thought of their kiss. He could see her nipples pressing against her orange-and-fuchsia tunic. His hands fairly ached to slide around the curve of those full breasts of hers. He barely brushed her cheek with his thumb.

"Coming back to earth?" he teased in a thickened tone.

Dev made a happy sound in her throat and closed her eyes, her hand pressed against her upper chest.

"We probably need to start walking back, gal. It's getting chilly out here." The last thing Sloan wanted to do was get up and go anywhere. He desperately wanted to sit and listen to Dev, explore where they were with one another. That kiss meant everything to him. And he sensed it did to her, too, but he wanted to hear it come out of Dev's mouth. If anything, Sloan had learned the hard way in his lost marriage that if he didn't communicate often, the end result was assumption by both partners. And that was the first major fault line in a marriage going wrong. A slow-moving disaster toward hell.

Just sitting there watching the play of expressions across Dev's face told him so much.

"Oh," Dev whispered, finally opening her eyes, her

fingers resting against her throat. "I've never been kissed like that."

A faint curve came to Sloan's mouth as he held her spellbinding gaze. "Me neither," he confided, mirth in his voice. "It was nice. Real nice. Was it for you?"

Dev licked her lower lip. "Oh, yes. I'm still floating, Sloan."

"Can you walk?" Sloan asked in jest, standing and offering her his hand. The air was turning chilly now that the sun was behind the Tetons.

Dev slipped her hand into his. "I'll try," she murmured.

"I won't let you fall," Sloan promised as Dev eased to her feet. She wavered a little and he slid his arm around her shoulders, pulling her gently to him. Dev flowed against him. His skin burned everyplace she touched his body with hers. Sloan was sure Dev wasn't fully aware of how much she incited him because she still had that transfixed look in her eyes, was still coming down from the lust and the firestorm of arousal their mutual kiss had created.

Sloan eased his gait for her. Dev slid her arm around his waist, leaning against him. The happiness that threaded through him was profound. It filled him with hope. He'd never thought he'd ever meet a woman like her. Dev trusted him. Sloan knew enough about her past, about her mistrust of men thanks to Gordon. She felt soft and flowing against his angled body. Silent pleasure thrummed through him. Dev nestled her head against his shoulder. It felt like there was some kind of silent infusion going on between them even now. It was all good.

As Sloan led her back to where the path moved up a slope, he removed his arm and grasped her hand, pulling her up onto the dirt road. The sky was turning a deep pink in the clouds high above them. It was a beautiful, chilly evening. Dev seemed content to hold his hand. Judging by the clarity in her gaze, she was starting to come back down to earth. She no longer felt tense. No, Sloan felt a melting kind of bonelessness in Dev and it reflected in the grace of her walk alongside him.

His head spun with shock over how one kiss with her had upended his world. Had it done the same for her? Or would this kiss scare her off at some point? Sloan knew there was a minefield between Dev and himself. Part was due to Gordon, part from her nearly dying in Afghanistan when that IED was set off by her dog King, who had lain down near it. Bomb-sniffing dogs were taught to sit or lie near the ordnance. Only this time, Sloan knew, the dog had lain too close and set it off, killing him and wounding Dev.

No, he had a long, hard road to slog through with Dev, but Sloan didn't see it as insurmountable or impossible. In less than two months, she had come to him on her own terms and of her own accord. Patience was a virtue and he knew that in spades. Now, if he could just get his body to settle down and accept that pace, things would be great.

CHAPTER TWELVE

"YOU LIKE SLOAN, don't you?" Cat Holt asked Dev as they worked in the kitchen two weeks later, for another Sunday dinner at the Bar H.

Dev was making a huge salad for the family, who were chatting and visiting with one another in the living room. Sloan had offered to help, but they'd both shooed him out of the kitchen. Dev wiped her hands on her green apron. "I do."

"But it's complicated?" Cat asked, giving her a wry sideways glance as she stirred a pot on the stove, making the gravy for a huge pot roast that was still baking in the oven.

Dev's mouth quirked. "Is it that obvious?" She moved to the counter and washed the Roma tomatoes off beneath the faucet and then set them beside the wooden cutting board.

Shrugging, Cat continued to stir the gravy, dipping the spoon into it and blowing on it to cool it enough to taste it. She added a bit more salt. "Just a feeling, is all. You kind of remind me of me and Talon. The first time I saw him in that blizzard, I felt like someone had put an electric charge on my heart. I was so drawn to him that it scared the hell out of me."

"Sloan said you had an abusive ex-boyfriend you were

trying to get rid of?" Dev ventured, picking up the knife to begin slicing the first tomato.

"Yes." Cat sighed, shaking her head. "Beau Magee. He stalked me. I hated it." She gave Dev a sympathetic look. "And you've been stalked, too. You know the terror. The uncertainty. I never knew when Beau might silently reappear and scare the hell out of me."

Dev became grim. "Only Bart Gordon isn't here, thank God."

"But you're dealing with the aftermath of his attacks?"

"All the time." Dev lowered her voice, making sure only Cat could hear her. "I'm so drawn to Sloan. It's scary sometimes because I've never felt that way about any man, Cat. Not that I've had tons of men in my life, but the ones I have had relationships with were not like this."

Cat picked up a bottle of dried basil and shook some into the thickening dark brown gravy. "And you're scared?"

"To say the least. I'm on unknown ground with him. There are days when I'm happy to have him around, but there are others when my past, the assault by Gordon, leaves me scared."

"You're questioning your ability to see a person accurately. Right?" Cat pushed some hair away from her brow.

"In a nutshell, yes."

"I've known Sloan for two years, Dev. What you see is what you get with that guy. He's been shoeing Gus's horses for all that time and you know, she's a very good judge of character."

Dev nodded. Gus was in the living room with everyone else and Dev loved the warmth, the laughter drifting into the kitchen, which was always part of the Sunday gathering. Even little Daisy, the puppy, was in there with them, licking every human hand she could find. "Yes, she sure is. I wish I had her clarity, but I don't."

"Two weeks ago," Cat began, a little hesitant, "you and Sloan were holding hands when you came back from your walk to the lake." She studied Dev for a moment. "Was that something new between you?"

"Yes," Dev admitted, blowing out a breath of air. She cut up six tomatoes and then sprinkled them into the salad. "We kissed…" Cat's face lit up, a smile forming across her lips. "Now," Dev said quickly, "it was one kiss."

"But?"

"Nothing," Dev muttered. "I just need time, Cat."

"I think Sloan knows that. Don't you?"

Nodding, she went to the refrigerator and pulled out six carrots. "He's been patient with me, Cat."

"Does he know what happened to you? What Gordon did?"

Dev brought the carrots over to the counter and used a peeler to take the skin off each one. "Yes. I told him. I didn't mean to, but when I'm around Sloan, I just start blurting stuff out."

"He's a good listener," Cat assured her, testing the gravy again. "Like Talon."

"Maybe it's a black-ops thing?" Dev wondered aloud, cutting off the greens from the carrots' tops. "Sloan worked with a combat-assault dog like Talon did. Though I guess he wasn't black ops. He worked with an Army company."

Cat set the gravy aside. Wiping her hands on her red

apron, she went to a cabinet and pulled down a huge porcelain gravy bowl. "I just think Sloan is built that way.
I've watched him around our horses and they all settle
down and relax in his company. He never makes quick
movements around them, like some people do. Sloan is
real quiet and gentle with them."

Laughing a little, Dev said, "He's that way with me."

"But you frighten easily, too. I was the same way
with Talon. I didn't want to tell him about my ex. I was
ashamed of myself. I couldn't control the situation. I felt
helpless. Not to mention embarrassed."

"But Talon is black ops," Dev pointed out, cutting up
the carrots into thin cylindrical slices. "I'll bet he found
out sooner than later."

"He did," Cat agreed wryly.

"And he liked you, Cat. Talon could probably tell you
were worried about something."

"Yes. I was good at hiding it up until the point Beau
attacked me out in a parking lot outside Mo's Ice Cream
Parlor. If it hadn't been for Talon coming out there after
paying our lunch bill, I think Beau would have done a
lot more damage to me than he did."

Shivering, Dev whispered, "I know exactly how you
feel. You're lucky he's still in prison."

Cat frowned. "I worry about when he gets out in two
years."

Dev looked over at Cat as she poured the steaming
dark brown gravy into the bowl. "I don't know where
Gordon is. I'm jumpy. My imagination runs wild. Sometimes I feel like he's here, in Jackson Hole."

"Have you spotted him?"

"No." Dev gave her a frustrated look, dropping the

carrots into the salad. "It's me, Cat. My imagination goes wild."

"Well, mine does, too," Cat said, taking the empty pot to the sink and running cold water into it. "Even now. At least I can talk to Talon about it." Cat motioned to the opening to the kitchen, where Bella and Zeke sat on the same doggy cushion. Daisy came bounding up to them with her puppy energy, jumping all over the two patient dogs. They weren't allowed in the kitchen, but they could sit just outside it and watch them. "Talon is reassuring, but I still, to this day, have horrible nightmares about Beau finding and hurting me. It's stupid, but there it is."

"I don't think anyone who's been assaulted or attacked ever completely gets over it," Dev admitted softly. She brought out the red peppers from the fridge next. "And I get horrible nightmares a couple of times a month, re-playing what Gordon did to me, and how I escaped." Shaking her head, Dev muttered, "I wish… God, I wish they'd stop."

"It's shock," Cat said, patting her shoulder gently. "The good news is I'm having fewer nightmares now. A lot of it is because of Talon, his loving me, making me feel safe. I never felt safe with a man before that. But I do with him."

Dev's heart warmed and she saw the love shining in Cat's green eyes for her husband. "That's funny you should say that. When I'm with Sloan, my anxiety goes away. And I'm no longer jumpy. He makes me feel safe, too. That's amazing."

Cat's eyes sparkled as she took the huge gravy bowl and walked it over to the trestle table, which was already set. "Hmmmm. Well, that sure sounds like you love one another."

FREE Merchandise is 'in the Cards' for you!

Dear Reader,

We're giving away FREE MERCHANDISE!

Seriously, we'd like to reward you for reading this novel by giving you **FREE MERCHANDISE** worth over **$20** retail. And no purchase is necessary!

It's easy! All you have to do is look inside for your Free Merchandise Voucher. Return the Voucher promptly...and we'll send you valuable Free Merchandise!

Thanks again for reading one of our novels—and enjoy your Free Merchandise with our compliments!

Pam Powers

Pam Powers

P.S. Look inside to see what Free Merchandise is **"in the cards"** for you!

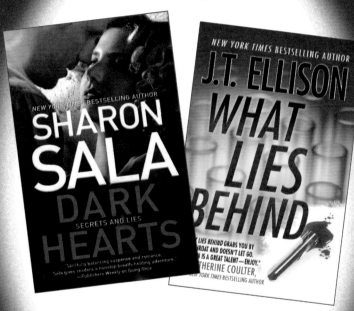

Jolted by her comment, Dev frowned as Cat came back and washed her hands at the sink. "No... I don't think so. I mean—" Dev stumbled over her words. "It's too soon. I've only known him two and a half months, Cat."

Snorting, Cat grinned and lathered up her hands with the herbaria soap she loved so much. "Heck, the first time I saw Talon, I fell in love with him. I just didn't realize it is all. Over time, I did. We both fought the attraction to one another for different reasons." She grabbed the towel on a hook near the sink. "Love has a way of making the impossible possible."

Dev shook her head, dicing up red pepper on the wooden cutting board. "I don't know what to call what's between Sloan and me. It's different than anything I've ever experienced before, Cat."

Cat dried her hands and rested her hips against the counter near where Dev was working, a thoughtful look on her face. "There's different kinds of love, you know? Because of my childhood, I couldn't tell real love from fake love. I had two relationships before meeting Talon and I thought I was in love with each one of those guys. But it wasn't love. I was so ignorant."

Dev glanced over at her. "You're a very intelligent woman, Cat. I came out of an ugly family situation. Sloan has been trying to get me to talk more about it and he's helping me see the patterns in my family and how they affected the way I see things, even now." Dev's lips compressed. "My father is an alcoholic to this day. I've pretty much disconnected from him. My mother still flies. She's a pilot with a regional airline."

"But you're in touch with her?"

"Oh, yes," Dev said. She scooped up the rest of the

diced red pepper and sprinkled it across the salad. "I just don't go home. I don't want to deal with my father."

"That's sad," Cat said, reaching out and patting her shoulder. "I'm sorry, Dev. It sounds like real love, the good kind, didn't exist in your family. It didn't in mine, either. I had this skewed idea of what love was and I was all wrong."

Dev told her about Bill Savona. By the time she was done with the salad and had taken it over to the table, Cat knew her whole story.

"Does Sloan know about Bill?" Cat asked, pulling down the salad bowls and placing them on the table.

"Yes." Dev's gaze moved across the table. It was set with beautiful blue-and-white plates that were, according to Miss Gus, nearly a hundred years old. They had been in the Holt family all that time. Some of them had chips on them here and there, but like Gus said, it was just a sign of age and wear and she wasn't going to throw out a perfectly good plate just because of a few nicks. She made the argument that all humans got nicked up pretty good by the time they hit old age, too. No one argued with her and those plates were used for every Sunday dinner.

Cat smiled a little. "Well, I think Sloan is really sweet on you, but I also think he's a lot like Talon. He's being patient with you, Dev. Speed isn't always the answer. Besides, I think you're a little like me. I can't be crowded or rushed. I have to build trust with a man. And that's how it happened between Talon and me. He had the patience of Job."

Glancing toward the entrance to the kitchen, Dev heard a roar of laughter drift down the hall toward them.

She felt such warmth and love in this household. "Sloan knows I'm unsure."

"He's more sure of you than you are of him," Cat murmured, holding her gaze.

Taking off the apron and folding it up, Dev whispered, "Yes."

"Well, let's get Talon in here to cut up the roast. We're about ready to call everyone in to eat."

Rousing herself from her glum thoughts, Dev nodded. "I'll pull the roast out of the oven. It should be ready."

"YOU'RE THINKING A LOT," Sloan said to Dev as they walked down the road toward Long Lake after Sunday dinner. She'd been in some kind of inner turmoil since they'd kissed two weeks ago on that swing at the lake. He made no attempt to hold her hand, although they ambled along the dirt road close to one another. Dev had been called out the very next day after their kiss, a Monday, to track a lost child near Jenny Lake. Sloan had gone with her and after three hours they'd located the adventurous red-haired boy of five who had taken off to go explore outside the camping area.

Her schedule and his were nearly opposites of one another, thanks to the July shift changes. Sloan hadn't seen much of Dev and had been wanting to sit down and talk with her, to find out what was going on inside her head. And her heart. He knew how he felt. Since that kiss, all he could do was want more of her. The shadows that lurked in the recesses of her green eyes waved him off, a warning. He knew they didn't have as much to do with him as they did her past. And most likely, he guessed, Gordon.

The sun was just above the Tetons in the west and

there were fluffy clouds hanging around most of the peaks, which were still covered with snow. Sloan knew he couldn't press Dev. As much as he'd like to pick up her hand, pull her into his arms, he had to wait. Wait and let her make the first move. It was a different kind of relationship than the others he'd had.

"I think we're going to get a beautiful sunset tonight," Dev told him, gesturing toward the clouds on the peaks. She lifted up her pocket camera. "I've decided I'm going to start a photo book of the sunsets. When they happen around the Tetons, they are spectacular."

Smiling a little, Sloan nodded. "They don't happen every day, but you're right, when the sun sets and every-thing's just right, the colors are mind-blowing." He drank in her profile. Something was bothering Dev. He'd seen it when he'd walked into the kitchen to sit down with the Holt and McPherson families for dinner. For whatever reason, Dev hadn't been as outgoing and connected with everyone as usual. Was it their kiss that was bothering her? His gut clenched because Sloan was afraid that Dev would run. He knew she wasn't that confident in herself when it came to men in general. And he kept question-ing himself. Maybe he'd pushed her too hard, too fast, taking that kiss she'd offered him. Second-guessing was a special hell all its own, he grimly decided.

"Miss Gus outdid herself with that coconut cream cake, didn't she?" Dev asked, touching her stomach.

"That lady is one fine cook," Sloan agreed, grinning over at her. "I see you ate every last crumb off your plate, too."

"Yeah." She laughed. "I didn't take any prisoners, did I?" Dev glanced up into his eyes.

Sloan felt yearning in Dev whenever their gazes connected. He swore he could see that she wanted to kiss him again, but something was holding her back. "Well," he said, amused, "no one left anything on their plate."

"I'm hoping Miss Gus will let us take a slice home for each of us."

"Did you ask her?"

Dev chuckled. "Not yet. I'm working up to it."

Laughing, Sloan said, "Only the brave and foolhardy are willing to go ask, but Miss Gus, I'm sure, will parcel out what's left of that three-tiered cake and split it among all of us. At least, that's what she's done before." They turned and ambled down the sloping dirt path that led to the lake. Sloan halted at the bottom of it. "Where would you like to go?" Because he wasn't assuming anything with Dev. She might not want to go back to the swing, thinking he would automatically want to kiss here there again.

"Just walk this way," Dev said, motioning to the path that led around the end of the lake. "I really need to walk off everything I ate. If I keep this up, I'm going to gain weight."

Sloan nodded and allowed her to take the inside of the path so she could be nearest to the lake. Behind them, he could hear kids shrieking and laughing. The small beach in front of the six rental cabins was a perfect place for children to dip in and out of the cold water. "Well," he said wryly, "I don't always cook great dinners at night in my apartment, so I always look forward to Sunday when I know I'm going to get a good meal."

"I wished I could have gone with you last week."

"You were feeling under the weather," Sloan murmured. He watched Dev's black hair move in the languid breeze off the lake. He remembered the silkiness of it through his fingers, her reaction to his massaging her scalp. Sloan had seen the pleasure in her eyes. Dev liked being touched. And God knew, he wanted to touch her everywhere.

"Pretty embarrassing to get summer flu," Dev muttered. "I was really looking forward to going out and having dinner with you at Iris's ranch."

"Well, she said you always have a return invite."

They rounded the lake and the swing came into view. Dev pointed to it. "Can we sit a moment?"

"Sure," Sloan said. He could almost feel Dev getting up the courage to talk. The more he was around her, the more he was getting to see the subtle signs she gave off, and he was getting better at interpreting them accurately. She hid a lot, but he wondered if it was because of her childhood. Sloan had no way of understanding what it was like to live in an alcoholic family, so he was willing to be taught by Dev so that he could understand her on a deeper, more intimate level. She sat down at one end of the swing so he took the other end, stretching his arm across the back of it. His fingers were about a foot away from where she sat.

Dev tucked one of her legs beneath her and wrapped her arms around her drawn-up knee. She tipped her head against the swing and closed her eyes as Sloan gently rocked it back and forth with the toe of his boot. "I just love this place," she murmured. "I love being around water. Listening to the ducks quack. The birds singing in the trees."

Sloan relaxed, waiting. He knew Dev was building up to saying something important. He just hoped like hell it wasn't to tell him that whatever had been between them was gone. He didn't feel that between them, but he knew

Dev was chewing on something big. "Water always has a calming effect on me, too."

Dev opened her eyes and moved her head to the right, engaging Sloan's gaze. "I was talking to Cat earlier, in the kitchen. She has a past somewhat like mine. We were telling each other about our skewed choices in men along the way. The only man I ever loved was Bill. And I think it was love. When Cat told me about her horrible childhood, being beaten by her father, I felt lucky in comparison."

"But it still changed you," Sloan told her quietly, holding her unsure gaze. He could see the nervousness in Dev, the way she kept opening and closing her fingers around her drawn-up knee. Anytime she started to flutter her hands, he knew that it was about nervousness and perhaps confusion.

"Yes," she whispered, "I'm seeing that now more than ever."

"Cat had a really bad childhood," Sloan agreed. "And she's remarkable. She's come so far despite it."

"Cat has talked to you about it?"

He smiled a little and shrugged. "She'd sometimes come out to the barn when I was shoeing their horses and we'd just start jawing with one another."

"You're easy to talk to," Dev said. "You hold a confidence. You don't gossip about it."

"No, I'd never do that," Sloan agreed. "So what did the conversation with Cat today bring up for you, Dev?" He saw her eyes darken and she looked away, her lips pursing for a moment. A niggle of fear went through him because Sloan didn't want it to be about them. He was afraid Dev would tell him it was over before it had even begun. Sloan knew it was the past driving her. She was the one who had kissed him first. Maybe that's what had scared her, her sudden boldness toward him? He really had no sure answers so he waited while she cobbled her thoughts together.

"Being able to talk to another survivor," Dev said, holding his gaze once more, "is helping me to see things I haven't seen before."

"Like?"

She opened her hand and gestured toward the lake that now had a glass-smooth surface. "Like how much of my past runs me to this day." Her voice dropped into a tone of disgust. "Cat said because her father beat her, she distrusted all men."

"That would be a natural reaction," Sloan said. Pain came into Dev's eyes and then she frowned. "Do you think because of your father, you ended up the same way? Not trusting men?"

"Yes," she forced out. "I do. I was just starting to get my feet under me, Sloan, when I met Bill. He was nothing like my father. He was so different and I was so drawn to him." And then she slanted him a glance. "Like I'm drawn to you."

"Because I'm nothing like your father?" he guessed.

"Exactly." She rubbed her brow. "But dammit, Sloan, how could I not see Gordon coming at me? What kind of huge blind spot do I have that I didn't know? If I'd just seen him. Recognized the stripe of animal he was…" Her voice grew hoarse.

Sloan heard the anguish, the questioning of herself, and it made him flinch inwardly with pain for Dev. She was haunted. "I'm not a therapist, Dev. And I've never been around an alcoholic, so I don't know their behavior. Is it possible your father was like Gordon in some ways?" He opened his hands and added, "Not that your father laid a hand on you like Gordon did. But what's got you tied up in knots is the fact when you met Gordon you didn't recognize how dangerous he was to you. Am I right?" He held her wavering green gaze. Even her lush mouth was tightened into a line, as if to try to protect herself.

"That's it," Dev admitted, releasing a breath of air. "My father wasn't who I thought he was. He had this… this…mask on. The mask is just another word for manipulation of me and everyone else around him. Part of the alcoholic's personality." She ran her fingers distractedly through her hair and shook her head.

"Well," he said gently, leaning forward and resting his elbows near his knees, "as a child, how could you know that? I don't think you could. You just accepted him at face value."

"Yes," she said bitterly, "I did. I was too young…"

"You were innocent, Dev. All children are. They can't be expected to have an adult's mind. They don't have the experiences behind them to see when something like that is wrong. You can't be hard on yourself like this."

"Gordon manipulated others, Sloan. Just like my father did. Only he wasn't an alcoholic, he was a sexual predator in disguise."

"Gordon is a stalker, too. He uses camouflage to hide what he really wants from someone, Dev."

"Why couldn't I see it coming?"

"Why would you?"

"Because I grew up with it," she muttered, disgust in her tone.

"Gordon was different from your father in some respects," Sloan suggested. "He was after you. Your fa-

ther wanted to manipulate everyone in the family so as
to continue his drinking. There's a huge difference there,
Dev. Do you see that?"

Glumly, she released her hands from around her knee
and stretched her legs out in front of herself. "I didn't...
but I do now that you mention it. They both manipulated
for different reasons and outcomes."

"Yes, they did." He saw her chewing on the realiza-
tions, absorbing them, and Sloan felt good that he could
help her parse some of these issues.

Sloan took a huge risk. "Dev? Do you think I'm hiding from you in some way?"

She stared blankly up at him, her lips parting.

He felt her stunned reaction and clearly saw it in her
expression. Maybe it was the wrong thing to ask, but
Sloan had to know where he stood with Dev. Without
knowing that, he had no way of knowing how to work
with her, how to gain her trust. Did she see Gordon or
her father in him in some respect?

CHAPTER THIRTEEN

Dev felt her throat close as Sloan asked the question, but she pushed through the fear. "Cat was saying that with you, what you see is what you get." She shrugged. "I can't fully trust myself to see people very well, Sloan. But I do trust Cat. And I know the Holt family loves you. You're one of them."

"Is that what you believe?" Sloan asked gently.

Her heart thrashed in her chest and Dev desperately wanted to move into Sloan's arms. She knew he'd open them, allow her to crawl into them to hide. To feel safe. "Yes," she whispered, her voice choked sounding, "I do believe that."

"So what's got you so bothered, Dev? I see fear in your eyes sometimes."

She stood up, wrapping her arms around herself, looking out over the Tetons now covered with thickening, fluffy clouds at their peaks. The sun had set behind them. The light was bright here and there in that constantly swirling, changing mass of clouds. Dev turned toward Sloan. "This is going to sound stupid," she warned him. "But for the last three weeks, I feel as if someone has been watching me, Sloan. I don't know if it's my wild imagination or if it's real." She opened her hands, feeling confused. "It feels like Gordon. Honest to God, it does." She watched his tightening features. A flash of concern flared in Sloan's narrowing blue eyes.

Pacing back and forth on the path in front of the swing, Dev said, "Now I'm waking up some nights, having nightmares about the bastard again. Sometimes, I think I hear him at the door, twisting the doorknob, trying to get in. But Bella isn't barking, so I know it's in my head. It's horrible, Sloan." She pressed her hand to her brow and halted in front of him. "I feel some days like I'm going crazy because I feel his eyes, feel his eyes on my back again. Watching me."

"Have you seen him?" Sloan asked, frowning.

Giving a shake of her head, Dev said, "I wish I had! If I'd seen him, then I'd know I wasn't making it up. It would be real. When I leave the apartment to go to work, I'm looking around like a scared animal, Sloan."

"Why didn't you tell me about this before?" he demanded.

"Because I didn't think you'd believe me. I thought—" Dev shrugged "—you'd think that I'd gone off the deep end or something."

Sloan rose slowly. Opening his arms, he said thickly, "Come here, Dev."

A lump formed in her throat. There was nothing she'd rather do than go to Sloan. Without a word, she stepped into his arms, pressing her cheek against his chest, wrapping her arms around his narrow waist. Just the sensation of his hard, muscular arms around her allowed her to release a sigh of relief. Inhaling his scent, part sweat, part clean soap and his maleness, Dev shut her eyes tightly.

"It's going to be all right," Sloan soothed, grazing her hair and sliding his hand lightly up and down her back.

"I feel so ashamed," Dev muttered into his shirt. "Like I'm losing it or something."

"I believe you are picking up on something," Sloan confided to her in a low voice. "There are things we can do to prove it, one way or another, Dev. We can go to Cade Garner, the deputy sheriff, and you can tell him your story. He won't think you're crazy, either. I'm sure Cade can check up on Gordon's whereabouts."

She sagged against Sloan, who felt like a protective oak tree. His arms held her gently, not too tightly, helping her ratchet down her anxiety and worry. Lifting her head away from him, she looked up. "What could Cade do?"

"Find out where Gordon is located. He spent time as a felon. He's out of prison now and probably has a parole officer. And he no doubt has to check in with him weekly."

"Okay, that's a good idea. He was also supposed to wear an ankle device that would show his whereabouts." Dev felt so good in his arms. And then she whispered, "Sloan, thank you…for everything. Right now, the way I feel, you're like a rudder in my life." He smiled faintly, his eyes burning with so much more than he was acting upon. She didn't want to pull out of his arms, but Dev didn't dare stay, either. It wasn't fair to Sloan to tease him. She knew it was a special hell he was caught within, too. As she released her arms from around his waist, he allowed her to step away from him.

"You're an empath, Dev. Let's find out the facts and we can go from there."

DEV'S HANDS WERE damp as she sat nervously in Cade Garner's office a week later. The morning sunlight was strong and from his glass-enclosed office, she could see the rest of the busy sheriff's department gearing up for the day. Sloan was standing nearby since there was only one chair at the front of the deputy's desk. Even after a week, she was still frazzled by that sense that someone was watching her. Earlier, when looking in the mirror, she'd noticed there were shadows beneath her eyes because she wasn't sleeping well at night, either. Her only comfort was Bella, who was a watchdog of the first order. Glancing to her right, she saw Sloan was leaning casually against the doorjamb, watching the comings and goings of civilians and deputies up and down the polished-tile hall.

Dev eyed him worriedly. "What if I'm wrong? What if Gordon isn't anywhere near here?"

"I believe that someone is watching you. Maybe you're still working through some of the shock that's still surfacing from your last attack, Dev."

She immediately settled down beneath his low, soothing tone. Most important, Sloan wasn't questioning her. He had no idea how much that meant to her.

A deputy as tall as Sloan with black hair and gray eyes entered the office. It had to be Cade Garner. He shook hands with Sloan and then halted at her chair.

"I'm Cade Garner, Miss McGuire. I'm sorry we couldn't see you sooner. I was following up on your complaint," he said, holding out his hand to her.

"I—I'm sorry to take up your time on something that is probably my imagination," she rushed on, giving him an apologetic look.

"Not so fast," Cade cautioned her, coming around the desk and sitting down. He nodded toward Sloan, who quietly closed the door, giving the three of them privacy.

Dev felt Sloan's hand come to rest gently on her shoulder. He was standing so close she could feel the heat off his body. Automatically, she inhaled his scent and it steadied her nerves. Cade had a file on his desk and opened it, his expression serious. He held up a color photo.

"Is this Bart Gordon?" he asked her.

Instantly, Dev's stomach clenched. Her mouth went dry. "Yes…it's him. And please call me Dev."

"Okay," Cade said grimly, sliding the photo into the folder. He held her gaze. "Gordon's parole office reported him missing a month ago, Dev."

Gasping, she came out of the chair. "That's when I started feeling him around me!" she cried out, her heart frantically pounding. She jerked a look up at Sloan, terrified. His eyes were dark with concern.

Cade nodded. "I've got an APB out on him in Teton County, Dev. No one has seen him around here. At least, not yet." He opened his hands. "And he may not be here, but maybe he's in the general vicinity. We just don't know, yet."

"His parole officer? The ankle bracelet he had to wear?" Sloan asked, guiding Dev back to the chair. "Has he checked into Gordon's family?"

"He has," Cade said. "He cut off the ankle monitor. It was found in his apartment. His mother had no idea where he is. His brother, Justin, who is a car mechanic in Martinsburg, West Virginia, hasn't a clue, either. And the brother doesn't like Bart too much, from what the parole officer who dropped by his shop and interviewed him said."

"Did Gordon have a car?"

"A silver Dodge Ram truck," Cade said. "We've got the make and the license plate." He gave Dev a gentle look. "Have you spotted him at all since we last talked on the phone a week ago?"

She shook her head. "No. But…I feel him. I know this sounds weird, but I feel his energy around me." She slid her arms around her waist, feeling as if she were slowly suffocating once more. Only Sloan's reassuring hand on her shoulder helped her stop going down that path.

"As law enforcement, many times we're working off our hunches and intuition, too, Dev. I believe you. Okay?"

Relief tunneled through her. Two people believed her. "Thank you. What do I do now? What if Gordon's around here? Watching me? Stalking me again?" Her voice grew hoarse as she asked the last question. Sloan's fingers move lightly across her shoulder, comforting her.

Cade remained resolute. "Just stay alert. Don't go anywhere without someone with you, if you can."

"I think," Sloan said, slanting a glance down at her, "that we need to talk to our supervisor, Charlotte Hastings, about this. She can't be putting you in situations where you're alone until this situation is resolved, Dev."

Licking her lip, she gave a jerky nod. "Yes…okay… that's a good idea. I'll do that Monday."

"I'll go in with you if you want," Sloan offered, holding her distraught gaze.

"I'd like that. Thank you." Because right now, Dev felt like she was splintering apart within herself once again.

"You know that Gordon had sealed juvenile court documents? That we can't touch them? But he did something illegal when he was fifteen," Cade added.

"Did the officer interviewing the brother ask him about it?"

Cade shook his head. "No. And unless we get a con-

firmed sighting of this man, I can't go back and demand
to have those sealed records opened."

"I understand," Dev said. "I—just feel so horrible,
like it's happening all over again. Only this time, I know
he's out there and he's stalking me. The first time, I was
completely blind to it until he sneaked up behind me and
attacked me in the barn, Cade."

"I understand," Cade murmured, sympathetic.

"Listen," Sloan said in a deep voice, holding her moist
gaze, "you have me. I'm not going to let anything happen to you, Dev. This time around, you have Cade and
his department out looking for this guy. They're going to
find him if he's around here. They're good at what they
do." He moved his hand soothingly across her shoulder. "And I have your back, Dev. Take a couple of deep
breaths and we'll work through this situation. You're
going to be fine."

Dev's insides felt like so much jelly. Now the terror
was flowing strongly through her. She had sensed Gordon. It had felt like a thick, oily film surrounding her,
closing in on her, slowly suffocating her. She desperately
needed some fresh air, was unable to sit still much longer. When she got rattled like this, she had to walk. "I
need some fresh air," she told them, her voice unsteady.

Cade rose. "Of course. Can I get you a cup of cold
water?"

Sloan slid his hand around her upper arm, helping
her stand.

"No… I just need air. I need to move around. I guess
I feel like if I sit still too long, I'm a target," she joked
weakly. There was no way she could force this fear down
and make it go away. She was grateful that Sloan placed

his hand in the small of her back. Cade opened the door for her.

"We'll be in touch," he promised her. "The moment we get eyes on this guy, you will be called. I'm going to see what I can do about getting his juvie court records opened."

"Good," Dev whispered, reaching out and squeezing his hand. "Thanks so much, Cade. It feels good to have some protection this time around." Because there had been none before. She felt Sloan's large hand, warm and comforting. Dev didn't mean to, but she leaned into him, the fear so great she couldn't get her feet working right until she really focused on them.

DRIVING ON THE way home, Sloan tried to keep his emotions hidden from Dev. He saw her wrestling with the situation, her fingers in constant motion in her lap. Her lips were set and she was tense.

"Talk to me?" he urged. "What's going on inside your head, Dev?"

"I'm angry. I'm so pissed I can't see straight, Sloan. How *dare* this bastard come after me again!" She threw up her hands. "I realize I don't have proof he's here, but I feel him! That's enough for me."

"And it was enough for Cade Garner," Sloan reasoned with her, glancing over at her. Normally, Dev's cheeks were a pink color, but right now, she was pale. Her green eyes that normally reminded him of a deep emerald were dark and scared looking. "You have people who will protect you this time around, Dev. It isn't a forest supervisor taking Gordon's side of the argument this time around. Cade will do everything within his legal power to find this bastard. So will Charlotte. I'm sure she'll hand out a photo of Gordon throughout the USFS system, both here and in Yellowstone Park."

"Gordon's hiding in plain sight," Dev muttered defiantly. "That's what he did at our park HQ. He waited until we were alone. Or he'd follow me into a room or office when no one else was around, to entrap me."

Sloan scowled. "That supervisor should have been fired."

"Oh, he's still there, believe me. I feel sorry for all the other women rangers who are forced to work under him. He's prejudicial as hell against women in general," Dev said angrily.

"Charlotte will believe you. We should go to see her Monday. I think she'll want to know for a lot of good reasons."

Cutting him a glance, she demanded, "Is Hastings one of those women who is a good ole boy at heart? That will take a man's side over a woman's word? They're out there, you know."

"I know they are. But I've been here for two years and Charlotte has never been like that from what I can see. She's fair and evenhanded and doesn't consider gender in her decisions. People get promoted based upon their abilities, not their sex."

"That's good to hear because frankly—" Dev pressed her hand against her stomach "—I'm terrified of seeing Hastings. I worry she'll be like my other supervisor and blame *me* for Gordon stalking me. Will say that if I wasn't such a pretty young woman, if I didn't have such a great-looking body, that it wouldn't have happened." Her mouth flattened. "I'm so sick of that kind of attitude."

He reached out, gripping her tightly fisted hands in her lap. "There are a lot of good people who respect women as equals. You have me, you have Cade Garner and many more besides us. There will be plenty of others who will support you." He squeezed her clasped hands gently and released them. "I know Charlotte will back you on this. She'll do everything in her power to see to it that you are kept safe and are not anywhere alone while on duty."

"It's a start," Dev whispered. "Maybe if these men could put the face of their wife, their daughter, mother, aunt or grandmother on the woman they're stalking, they'd think twice about doing it."

"That would be helpful," Sloan said. "But those kind of men are sick. They've been taught that it's okay to abuse a woman, take what they want from one, that they won't be held accountable."

"I got some of that when I was in the Marine Corps," Dev said, her voice sounding exhausted. "If it weren't for Bella, who's a great watchdog, there were guys in my company who might have raped me. I saw it in their eyes, the way they treated me, the way they hinted around that, when they found me alone, they were going to force me to have sex with them. One sergeant tried, and Bella attacked and bit him. He drew his knife and was going to slit her throat because she'd defended me. I started screaming and it brought the gunny sergeant running. He saved us."

Dev shivered. "Thank God our gunny intervened. I pressed charges. But it went nowhere. The captain of the company buried it. The Marine got his ass chewed, but that was all. The only thing that stood between me and that group of Marines was the gunny and he had a little "talk" with them one night. From that time on, everyone left me alone, but I could feel their hatred, their anger.

They wanted to get even with me for reporting the Marine who attacked me. As it was, my rate was frozen and I didn't make sergeant like I should have. It was just too much, Sloan. Too much."

"It would be for anyone," Sloan agreed, shaking his head.

"That was why, when my enlistment was up, I got out. I loved doing what I did with my dog, finding IEDs and keeping everyone safe, but I had to deal with daily sexual harassment in the military. And now there's a statistic from 2014 that shows twenty-six thousand military women were raped in the services. One out of every eight women who joins the military can expect to be raped. And those men are usually in the same company as the woman. Hell, I didn't just have to be scared of the enemy hurting me. I had to be afraid of the men in my own company raping me. That's not acceptable. I got out."

"It's completely unacceptable," Sloan growled.

"If I were a mother, I'd never allow my daughter to serve in the military. Not with that kind of good-ole-boy system protecting the rapists and blaming the survivors." Her mouth curved downward.

Sloan heard the steel in her lowered voice. Felt the outrage around her. And he was glad to see the anger rising because so many women had been brainwashed and taught that it wasn't all right to show their anger. Or to act upon it in a healthy way when they did feel it. "Keep your anger out in front of you like a shield, Dev. You've a right to feel it. No man should use his power against you for any reason. You're a human being. You deserve to be respected."

"Can I clone a billion of you?" Dev asked, giving him a grateful look. "Replace other men with your kind?"

Sloan chuckled. "Oh, I have my warts, gal, that's for sure. I'm far from perfect."

"That's okay. I like you just the way you are."

Sloan smiled. "And I like you just the way you are, too." His heart warmed and he ached to draw Dev into his arms, give her the sense of support Sloan knew he could give her. But there were so many fine lines to tread with her. If he acted on his protective instincts too aggressively, Dev might lump him in with men like Gordon, or those who had sexually harassed her in the Marine Corps. The stress and hurt in Dev's face tore at him. What the hell was wrong with men thinking they could do this to any woman? He kept his anger to himself. It would do no good to show it.

"Would Bella protect you if Gordon found you?"

"I'm sure she would. At the time of the attack, she was in my truck, not with me. When I got away from Gordon, she was barking, trying to get out of the truck, sensing something was wrong. Bella bit that Marine sergeant that tried to corner me in a deserted Afghan home. She didn't wait. She lunged and grabbed his lower left arm and left four huge puncture holes in it."

"That's good to hear," Sloan said. "Because she's your first line of defense. Bella may well sense Gordon before you do. Better hearing. Better sense of smell."

"You're right," Dev admitted. "But I can't take her into the grocery store or restaurants or the other places I have to go to do my business in town, Sloan."

"I know." And Sloan didn't like the idea of Dev being without her brave dog who would give her life for her if she needed to. Damn, he'd like some confirmation that someone, somewhere, had seen Gordon. His hands tightened on the wheel as they drove into the southern end of town, heading back to their apartment complex. "Look," he said, catching her gaze for a moment, "I'm right across the hall from you. If you feel scared or you feel Gordon around, you need to come over and tell me. Will you do that for me?"

"What? And wake you up in the middle of the night, Sloan? You need your sleep. I don't get that much sleep since I've felt Gordon around. Why wake you up? There are times I have nightmares and I'm so caught up in them, I don't know what is real and what is a dream."

"Bella will know," Sloan told her patiently, frowning. "If Gordon really is stalking the halls of this place, Bella will take off barking at the door."

"That's true and I know that. When I get jerked out of sleep by one of my nightmares, Bella comes into the bedroom. She licks my hand, whines and tries to comfort me." Her voice softened. "Usually, Bella sleeps right by my bedroom door. And you're right, she'd be the first to hear someone moving in the hall outside my apartment and sound the alarm."

Sloan nodded. "Mouse would hear him, too, believe me. And when he barks, he shakes the rafters. There's nothing meek about my dog's bark. He can sense if someone is out in the hall and up to no good. He's been trained to know an enemy by sensing alone and he's good at it, Dev."

"Well," she said wryly, "between our two dogs, if Gordon thinks he can come up to my apartment and break in, he'll get the surprise of the century."

"Mouse would tear that door of mine apart trying to get out to reach you," Sloan said. "He likes you. And he'd know if someone was coming to harm you."

"Mouse has already made me part of his pack," she agreed.

"He has. But he's a big alpha male and he's the head of the pack." Sloan saw a little bit of hope come to her eyes. The more he could rally the resources they had around her, the easier it would be to keep her safe. And there was nothing like a dog as a first alarm. "And you have me, you know."

"Believe me, I wouldn't be feeling very strong right now if you weren't in the mix, Sloan. And I appreciate you so much. I'm just so torn up by all of this. I thought by moving out here I was leaving it all behind me."

"Until Gordon is caught," Sloan told her, "you need to surround yourself with people who care about you, Dev. You don't have to fight this alone, this time. You have Iris Mason and her family. And you have Miss Gus and the Holt and McPherson families. They all love you like a daughter or a sister." His eyes twinkled as he saw her rally. "And you have me and my big bad guard dog, Mouse." A faint smile pulled tentatively at her lips. As much as Sloan wanted to tell her to come and live with him, he couldn't go there. Dev wouldn't do it because she had battled all her life, alone and without support, starting with the family she grew up in. And it would take Dev time to adjust to the idea that others would not only be there for her, but damn well protect her if that's what it came down to.

"They're all the family I wished I'd grown up with," Dev admitted. "I so look forward to Sundays now, Sloan, with you."

"It's a great time out." He wanted to talk more about precautions but saw Dev was pretty much overwhelmed at this point. As a ranger, she carried a pistol on her at all times. And Sloan was positive it was in her apartment. He wanted to speak to her about getting a concealed weapons permit so that she could keep it in her truck, or on herself, depending upon where she had to go. Sloan was positive that with what had happened to her already, and the possibility Gordon was here stalking her again, that law enforcement would allow her such a permit. She was well trained in the Marine Corps and knew how to handle any number of weapons besides just a pistol.

Those conversations could wait for a bit, but Sloan felt pushed to speak sooner, not later about them. And did he want Dev going into town by herself when she wasn't working? Not really. Not right now. How would she feel about being constantly shadowed by him or other rangers who would have to be with her if she did tracking in the Tetons? Would Gordon go so far as to try to kidnap her out there in the forest? He was, after all, an ex-ranger. And he knew how to hunt and use weapons, as well. Worse, the man was mentally unstable and couldn't be counted on to do the logical thing and stay away from Dev.

Fear ate at his heart. Sloan tried to ignore it, but he couldn't. He pulled into the apartment complex and automatically looked for a silver Dodge Ram truck as he slowly drove through the area. Dev was alert, looking at people going in or coming out of the buildings with far more intensity than before. It was a helluva strain on her to have to live like that. Damn, but he wanted to protect her. He could keep her safer if she'd only think about moving in with him. Right now, Sloan knew the idea wouldn't fly. But he sure as hell wanted it to for a basket of reasons, some unselfish and some completely selfish. Dev was a decent person caught in the snare of a man who not only hated her but wanted to destroy her.

CHAPTER FOURTEEN

WHEN DEV ENTERED her apartment, she instantly had a bad feeling. Bella also came in and walked casually into the living room. Maybe she was just being ridiculous? Perhaps the interview with Deputy Sheriff Garner had shaken her up, made her imagination take off. Turning, Dev made sure the door was shut. The noontime sunlight was indirect because her apartment sat on the west side of the complex. She had a beautiful picture window where she could see the Tetons rising off to her right. The sky was a pale blue and the July temperature was in the mideighties. Placing her purse on the foyer desk, she felt her neck hairs rise. That was her first line of defense when in Afghanistan. If her neck hairs stood up, it meant danger. Immediate danger.

Looking around, she saw Bella lie down on her doggy bed in the corner of the living room. If someone were in here, a stranger, her dog would have heard him and gone after him, barking loudly. Instead, Bella was lying down to go to sleep.

Shaking her head, Dev felt that same oily, sticky energy around the apartment. It happened every time Gordon was nearby. Was she making this up? Dev sighed and wandered into the kitchen, torn.

Something was out of place. She sensed it.

Her throat tightening with fear, Dev looked at the five

cookbooks she had between two polished agate bookends sitting on the granite counter in the corner of the
kitchen. She walked over to them and frowned. She had
always placed them in a certain order.

Now, they were out of order. The dessert cookbook
was first, not last.

Rubbing her brow, Dev hesitated, unsure. Had she
done this herself? She gazed around her small kitchen.
Nothing else was out of place. She walked into her dimly
lit bedroom and turned on the light. Nothing was disturbed in there, either. Going next to the bathroom, she
peered in and flipped on the light.

Nothing was amiss.

It had to be her.

Feeling depressed by all the pressure building within
her, Dev figured she might have misfiled her cookbook
herself and let it go at that. That oily, dreadful sensation
that always enveloped her when Gordon was around was
now just shock over the fact he was missing and no one
knew where he was.

But she knew he was here, in Jackson Hole. Or was
he?

Her imagination was working overtime.

How could she trust herself anymore? She hadn't
picked up on Gordon coming up into the barn and
sneaking up behind her to attack her. Tears burned in
Dev's eyes as she turned off the light. She made a muffled sound and turned, going back to the kitchen. Even
though it was around noon, her stomach was tight and
she had no appetite. But she had to eat.

As she made herself some tuna for sandwiches at the
counter, Dev's heart turned to Sloan. If he wasn't in her
life right now, she didn't know what she'd do. She wanted

so much more from him, but there were so many other obstacles staring her in the face. Gordon was missing. He was somewhere. Was it fair to Sloan that she was leaning so heavily on him right now? He didn't seem to mind, but Dev was afraid to say how much she was attracted to him. She refused to call it love. It was just too soon to know that. And even if it was love, meeting Sloan right now was bad timing, especially now that she was threatened by Gordon. Dev couldn't focus on Sloan or what was building slowly between them. But whatever it was, it was good. Wonderful.

As she added pickle relish to the bowl of tuna, Dev stirred it with a fork. Feeling naked and vulnerable with Gordon on the loose and no one knowing where he was, she focused on making herself a tuna sandwich.

There was a quiet knock at the apartment door.

Bella barked and galloped to the door, hackles up, growling.

Dev's heart jumped in her chest. She jerked in a breath, turning as Bella kept barking. At least she was a very good alarm system.

Peeking out the peephole in the door, she saw it was Sloan.

Confused, she opened the door. Bella leaped out, licked his offered hand and wagged her tail, thumping it against the jamb.

"Sorry to knock," he said, gesturing to his open door. Mouse was sitting in the entrance, alertly watching them. Sloan had told him to sit and stay.

"What's wrong?"

Sloan grimaced. "Well, something happened and you need to know about it. Do you have a moment to come over and I'll show it to you?"

Bewildered, Dev wiped her hands on a small towel. "Sure." Making a gesture to her dog, she said, "Sit, Bella. Stay."

The yellow Lab whined and sat down in the entrance. Mouse thumped his tail as she followed Sloan into his apartment. He gestured for her to walk down the hall. He gave Mouse an order, and the dog followed her.

"Turn around," Sloan told her after shutting the door.

Dev's eyes widened. The inside of his apartment door held deep claw scratches. "Oh, my God. What happened?" she whispered, pointing at it. She saw how grim Sloan had become.

"Mouse was leaping at the door, trying to get through it, is what happened."

Blinking, Dev looked down at Mouse and then over at Sloan. "I don't understand."

Sloan came up to her. "Did you see anything in your apartment that was out of place? Is anything missing?"

Her heart dropped and she gasped, her hand flying to her chest. "Oh, God... Why do you ask?"

"When Mouse feels a threat, he's been trained to go through a window or whatever is in the way in order to reach the enemy. He apparently felt or heard a threat out in the hall sometime while we were gone. Maybe a stranger was in our hall? Maybe he or she turned or twisted the knob on my front door. Mouse wouldn't have attacked the door like that if it was you or me. He knows the sound of our footsteps. He can smell us through a door because no door is fully leakproof."

Dev's mouth went dry. "I—I... Oh, God, Sloan. When I got home, I felt this oily, slimy feeling that I always associate with Gordon, inside my apartment." Immediately, Sloan's eyes narrowed and became intense. "I thought it was me. Bella went to lie down in the living room, like there was nothing wrong. I went into the other rooms looking for anything out of place, and I found nothing." She gulped. "Then in the kitchen I saw my cookbooks were out of order. I always make sure I put them back in a certain order, where they belong. I thought it was me. I thought maybe I'd made a mistake and didn't put them back in the same way after using them." She touched her brow, her heart galloping in her chest. Gordon had been in her apartment. Terror shot through Dev as she looked pleadingly up at Sloan.

"C-could Gordon have been up here on our floor? Could he have by mistake twisted the doorknob on your door instead of mine?"

"I don't know." Sloan moved his hand across her shoulder, giving her a squeeze, hoping to make her feel a little safer than she looked right now. "What I am going to do is put Mouse in harness and I'm going to have him smell the doorknob and then see where he tracks the scent. Do you want to come with me? Put Bella on a leash?"

"Yes…" The fear ate away at her. "What if Gordon was here? What if he was in my apartment while we were gone? How did he get in?" Her voice thinned with terror. Sloan pulled her more tightly against him and she savored his closeness.

"Let's take this a step at a time," Sloan urged her, holding her anxious stare. "Go get Bella? What I want to do is use Mouse to track the scent. Let's see if he tracks it from my door into your apartment or not. I'll meet you out in the hall in a few minutes. I want to get my pistol and holster."

That brought it all home for Dev. She had one, too, but

hadn't even thought of reaching for it. Reminding herself that Sloan had a combat-assault dog, that he was used to being in the fray of combat, unlike her, Dev gave a brief nod and slipped out from beneath his arm.

SLOAN TRIED NOT to relay his worry. He wore his pistol on his right hip and he had Mouse in his working harness. The Belgian Malinois knew what that harness meant and was all business as he walked expectantly out into the hall. Sloan allowed the apartment door to shut and then pointed to the knob.

Instantly, Mouse was sniffing it.

"Seek," he told the dog, giving him plenty of room on the leash to go wherever the scent led him.

Mouse had his long black nose down on the carpet, following it to Dev's closed door. He smelled it, sitting down in front of it.

"That means he's linked the odor on my door to your door," Sloan told Dev, glancing up toward her pale features. Bella sat at her side, alert. Fear leaped to Dev's eyes. Sloan took a handkerchief, not wanting to disturb any prints that might be left on the knob. They were all probably destroyed earlier when Dev opened it with her bare hand. But the scent was still on it. Opening it, Sloan pushed the door open.

Instantly, Mouse was following the scent down the hall. He turned sharply into the bedroom.

Dev followed them.

Turning on the light in the bedroom, Sloan watched his dog work, following the scent around the bed, then to the dresser and then to the other side of the bed. Dev came and stood next to Sloan. Her hand was pressed against her throat, her eyes huge with fear.

"He was in here," Sloan gritted out.

And then Mouse quickly whipped out of the bedroom, moving to the bathroom.

Sloan watched his dog working around the toilet, and then the bathtub. Then Mouse turned, thrusting his snout upward, sniffing strongly up above the lights over the basin counter. Mouse lifted his front legs, paws resting on the counter, whining and looking pointedly up at the light array.

"What is it?" Dev asked hoarsely.

Moving forward, Sloan, who was taller, craned his neck, carefully checking out the light fixtures all bound together. "Something…" He peered intently at it. He told Mouse to sit. Dropping the leash, Sloan eased his bulk up on the granite counter so he could get eyes fully on the fixture. "There appears to be a small camera assembly up here."

"No…" Dev breathed, eyes widening.

"I'm not touching it." Sloan got down. He turned to her, his hand on her shoulder. "I'm calling Cade right now. They need to get a forensics team out here to go through your apartment, looking for fingerprints. Someone has been in here and—" his voice lowered to a growl "—they put that camera in here to see you naked while you took a shower or bath."

Dev made a small, desperate sound, wrapping her hands around herself.

"Look," Sloan told her quietly, guiding her out of the bathroom, "I want you and Bella to stay in my apartment until Cade can get out here with a forensics team. The less you move around in your apartment, the fewer things you touch, the better the chances of finding fingerprints that were left behind. Okay?"

"Y-yes, that sounds good."

"Let me finish up checking the apartment?"

"I want to stay and watch."

Nodding, Sloan picked up the leash. "Mouse. Seek."

The dog instantly stood up and bolted out of the bathroom and down the wooden hall, his nails clacking noisily on the surface. Sloan watched him go into the kitchen. There, Mouse instantly stood up on his hind legs, whining and trying to get to the five cookbooks in the corner. Sloan praised him and told him to get down and continue his investigation. The dog went next to the refrigerator, which he started pawing at.

"Did you open the fridge?" Sloan asked.

"Yes, to get the pickle relish."

"Okay, but the handle might have a print on it."

"I just blew that, didn't I?"

"You didn't know. It's all right."

Mouse bounded out of the kitchen and went into the living room next. He sniffed the couch, around the coffee table and then went to the large flat-screen TV across the room, against the wall. The dog once more got up on his hind legs, whining, trying to get between the TV and the wall. Sloan told him to get down and peered behind the TV.

"Something's back there," he murmured, lifting his head and looking at Dev. "Did you touch this TV? Anywhere around it?"

"No."

"Good." Sloan let Mouse continue his hunt and the dog strained against his leash, heading to the door.

"Now," Sloan said, picking up his cell phone from his pocket, "he's going to follow the scent of the intruder outside your apartment. I'm calling Cade right now. Stick close to me?"

Dev nodded.

Mouse followed the scent down the carpeted hall to the emergency exit stairwell door. Sloan was careful to use the handkerchief to open it. He then pulled his pistol as he and the dog slowly started down the concrete stairs to the narrow exit area. Dev was behind him. Watching his combat dog, Sloan knew if Mouse heard anything, he'd go into full attack mode, and the bristling hairs on his shoulders and all the way down his back to his tail would instantly rise. As he slowly took the stairs, watching and listening, Sloan sensed the intruder was gone.

They reached the door to the entrance leading out into the parking lot. Sloan pushed it open with the handkerchief once again. The sunlight was bright and Sloan blinked, giving his eyes time to adjust from the dim light of the stairwell area to the outdoor light. He made sure that Dev remained close to him. She was almost paralyzed with terror. There was no mistaking the fright in her green eyes. Giving her a gentle look, he said, "Follow me. But don't get in front of or beside us."

"Right."

Mouse went from the cars parked along the sidewalk of the second apartment building and scrambled, wanting to run, hauling Sloan along as he moved across the huge black asphalt parking lot to the corner of the first building of the complex. He went into thick brush and shrubs on the corner, sniffing loudly. Sloan saw footprints around the edge of one bush and called Mouse back. He took out his cell phone and took photos of the prints, sending them to Cade. He ordered Mouse to sit. Sloan thought it was a perfect hiding place for someone who wanted to observe Dev's movements. Was it Gordon? He thought so, but he wasn't going to tell Dev that.

Dev was so frightened right now and Sloan didn't want to add to her stress. The haunted look in her expression ripped at his heart. A fierce sense of protection rose in him and he had to do everything not to grab her, hold her hard and tight against him, to let her know he'd never allow her to be harmed again. But he couldn't. Sloan had to remain focused, find out all he could about her stalker, the man who had broken into her apartment. Worse, he realized the person knew how to jimmy open a door and could do it again. That meant her intruder could enter the apartment when Dev was asleep. While it was true she had Bella as a watchdog, the intruder could very easily kill the dog. And still get to Dev. Dammit!

Carefully searching the area and keeping it free of their own paw and footprints, Sloan had Mouse seek once more. The Belgian Malinois leaped ahead, straining mightily at the leash once more, on a scent. His dog got excited when the scent was powerful, or the enemy was nearby. Sloan kept an alert lookout as the dog lunged repeatedly toward the nearby forest. The area had been clear-cut around the apartments. In a crescent-shaped circle behind the complex, there was a mix of deciduous trees and pine trees. The area was thick with grass and weeds, untrodden by humans—a perfect place to hide. Sloan slowed his dog and Mouse tugged hard, wanting to follow the trail into the darkening woods.

"Is someone in there, you think?" Dev asked in a low, unsteady voice.

"I'm not sure," Sloan said. "But I'm going to wait until Cade arrives with some deputy reinforcements. There's no sense in us going in there alone right now.

No Kevlar vests, no protective vest on Mouse, either. It's not worth the risk if the intruder is still in there." Sloan called Mouse back and the dog reluctantly obeyed the order, twisting his head toward the forest, not wanting to give up the scent.

Sloan positioned himself in front of Dev in case the intruder was still hidden in the forest and watching them. If he took a shot, he wouldn't strike her. Sloan was in combat mode, just like his dog. Glancing up, he could see that the window of Dev's apartment was in complete alignment with the forest behind the building. The intruder could have a Wi-Fi device that was looking through that small camera he'd tried to hide in the bathroom lamps, right now. A huge part of him wanted to send Dev back to his apartment, return to the forest with Mouse and hunt the bastard down. But that wouldn't guarantee he would find the stalker, however. He could have gone back to her apartment and could be hiding in it right now. Waiting for Dev.

Every protective gene in Sloan was screaming for him to shield her. He cared deeply for Dev even though they'd never had a chance to fully explore their feelings with one another. God knew Sloan wanted to, but Dev was in free fall with this stalker situation exploding around her once again. What he could do was give her a sense of safety by being around her, supporting her the best he knew how, right now.

DEV GNAWED ON her lower lip as she watched the sheriff's forensics team come down the hall. Two women in white one-piece suits carried their equipment, their expressions serious. Dev had the door open to her apartment. They said hello to her and went to work on the outside of the door. She remained in Sloan's apartment, sitting on the couch, with Bella at her feet. Cade Garner had come in to take her statement. Then he took Sloan's. Two more deputies showed up later in black Chevy Tahoes. Sloan left with Mouse in harness, returning to the wooded area with the deputies. Dev couldn't even watch the activity from her apartment. Anxious and worried, she paced in Sloan's large living room. Sloan and Cade would not allow her and Bella to go with them. What would the forensics team find in her apartment? A second forensics team focused on the corner of the first complex building, going over it thoroughly for fingerprints and making plaster casts of the boot prints discovered in the mud.

She was more anxious about Sloan, Mouse, Cade and his two deputies going into the woods. That was the great unknown. Some of her worry had been reduced when Cade handed Sloan a Kevlar vest to wear—just in case. Only Mouse had no protection. The sheriff's department didn't have a K-9 unit, so there was no bulletproof vest that Mouse could borrow.

Pushing her fingers through her hair, Dev hated what was happening. Even now, she wore her holster on her hip, and the pistol had a bullet in the chamber with the safety on. Sloan didn't want her helpless or unable to defend herself in case the intruder was still around. She felt it would be stupid for Gordon or whoever it was to try coming back into the apartment complex. There were four Teton Country deputies with SUV cruisers in the parking lot. Still, Dev didn't fight Sloan on his request for her to remain armed until they returned from the forest investigation.

Bella slept for nearly an hour while Dev paced. When Sloan and Cade reentered the apartment, she stood tensely, waiting for one of them to say something. Mouse was panting heavily, his cinnamon eyes glinting with the look of the apex predator and hunter that he was.

"We found more boot prints," Sloan told her, leaning down to remove the work harness from Mouse.

"There was also a couple of cans of soda and food wrappers," Cade added, holding up the paper bag that held the contents. "We'll take these back to our lab and run them for prints and DNA."

"But you saw no one?"

Sloan shook his head, ordering Mouse over to his bed in the corner of the living room after he took a long drink of water. Straightening, he said, "No. But it looks like the guy was either watching you from the corner of apartment one or changed positions and watched you from the woods. Both were well-concealed areas and you probably would not have seen him."

"But he could see you," Cade said.

"What should I do?" Dev asked the deputy.

"If it's not too uncomfortable for you, I'd prefer you stay with Sloan for now."

"I'll sleep out on the couch," Sloan told her. "You get the bedroom."

Cade gestured to the door. "My forensics team has removed the camera put into that lamp fixture in your bathroom. And another unit behind your flat-screen TV was removed, as well. They are both Wi-Fi gadgets with lithium batteries. All the suspect would have to do is have a receiver strong enough to pick up on the signal and he'd see you in the bathroom and living room."

"I wonder how long they've been in there?" Dev asked them, her voice bleak.

"Mouse picked up on everything today," Sloan

soothed her. "He must have gotten into your apartment while we were gone."

"I think the same thing," Cade told her. "We're going to set a trap for this suspect in your apartment. What I'd like you to do now is go get your clothes, any food or anything else you need, and bring it over here to Sloan's apartment."

"I'll help you," Sloan said, setting the harness on a small table near Mouse's round bed.

"Because once we set the trap, Dev, you can't go back in there," Cade warned. "We've got motion-sensor cameras being mounted in there right now. They'll record anyone coming into your apartment. And we have a silent alarm that will trip when someone opens that door to alert us of an intruder. We'll send two cruisers over here immediately as well as alerting the two of you."

"But so far, we don't know if it's Gordon?"

"No," Cade said, "but I'm hoping these items will prove what we all think." He held up the sack. "If I get any kind of confirmation it's Gordon, you'll be called immediately. I can't afford you twenty-four-hour police protection, but Sloan is good backup. You're both rangers and I'm calling your supervisor, Hastings, to let her know what's going on. I'm going to ask her to keep you two paired because you need the protection right now, Dev, until we can capture the suspect."

Dev felt comforted. "I really appreciate all you're doing, Cade." She gave Sloan a warm look. "Are you okay with a roommate for a while?"

Sloan nodded. "I'm okay with it, Dev. Anything that will make you feel safer, until Cade and his deputies can find this guy and put him behind bars, is fine with me."

Never mind the attraction she felt for Sloan. Dev

wasn't sure she could keep herself together under Sloan's roof. He was so masculine, the way he cosseted her, that one, galvanizing kiss that had melted her soul… Taking a ragged breath, Dev nodded and said nothing. Her whole world was crumbling around her once again.

CHAPTER FIFTEEN

"HOW ARE YOU DOING?" Sloan asked Dev later. The deputies were gone and it was nearly 5:00 p.m., dinnertime. They had brought Dev's clothes, food and anything else she needed over to his apartment. Sloan had emptied the top two drawers of his dresser for her. Luckily, he had few hanging clothes and he placed hers on one of the two rungs in the closet, so she had plenty of room. The move had gone well but she had been quiet, which was unlike her.

Dev forced a slight, jagged smile. "Could be better. Just stressed-out," she admitted, closing the upper drawer of the dresser.

"I'm going to fix us something to eat," Sloan said. "You probably aren't hungry, but you need to keep your strength up, Dev." Sometimes, he'd see moisture come to her eyes and assumed she needed to cry. But then Sloan would see her battle them back, force them away and keep on folding or hanging her clothes in the bedroom.

"I can't eat, Sloan." Dev touched her stomach. "I'm tied in knots."

He stepped aside as she move past him into the hall, heading for the living room. "Anyone would be," he agreed, following her. "I'm a pretty good cook for a single guy," he teased, hoping to ease some of her strain. "I was thinking of a chicken and vegetable stir-fry? Does that sound good to you? I put in a little ginger, a few other herbs for taste."

Dev sat down on the couch and Bella came over, the Lab wriggling herself between her open legs. Petting her dog, Dev said, "Okay, I'll give it a try. Do you want any help?"

"If you want, you can cut up the red and green peppers and red cabbage. I'll cut up the chicken breasts and make the orange-hoisin sauce."

Giving Bella a quick kiss on her head, Dev rose. "Thanks. I need something to do, Sloan. I feel like I'm going crazy. Doing normal things helps me settle down and focus."

He smiled faintly, holding her dark green eyes that clearly showed how upset she was. "Good enough. Come on. I'll get you a good cutting knife, give you a bread board and you can go to work."

Sloan watched Dev relax as he put her to work in the roomy kitchen. They worked side by side and he enjoyed her closeness. She was quick with the red and green peppers, putting the slices in a bowl. Sloan gave her the shiitake mushrooms next. He cut up the chicken breasts into thin strips.

"What do you think they'll find?" Dev asked him.

"I'm hoping there will be prints and DNA on those aluminum cans we found."

"What if it's Gordon?"

Sloan heard the closeted terror in her voice. "It probably is, but we can't go there without proof," he cautioned, glancing to his left, holding her large, shadowed gaze. "At least we'd know, one way or another."

"Yes," she whispered hollowly, cutting up the mushrooms.

"You'll stay with me until it's over, Dev. I think that will help you."

"I feel bad you've got to sleep out on the couch."

Sloan smiled a little, pulling the bok choy over to cut it up. "Listen, we're both used to sleeping on the ground or on a piece of cardboard if we could find it over in Afghanistan. You, more than most, know it's great to have a couch to sleep on."

"True," Dev murmured, giving him a concerned look. "But I'm kicking you out of your bedroom."

"It's temporary." Sloan wanted to say, *Sleep with me every night. I'll hold you safe. I'll make all that fear go away because I'll love you.* None of it could be said, as much as he wanted to broach the topic. But the timing couldn't be worse.

Dev dropped the mushrooms into the bowl.

"Why don't you get the rice started?" He pointed to a box on the counter. "The pots and pans are beneath where you're standing." He saw her rally. The act of cooking, doing something familiar, was helping Dev enormously. "And after you get that started, can you bring me that jar of honey on the lazy Susan on the corner of the counter? I use a quarter cup of honey, grate some ginger, mince some scallions and chop up a pair of lemongrass stalks. Does that all sound good to you so far?"

She laughed a little. "You're actually making me hungry, Sloan. It will not only smell wonderful, but it will be yummy to eat."

His heart swelled with a fierce need for Dev. Already, Sloan could see some pinkness creeping back into her wan cheeks. Her green eyes no longer looked as haunted and dark. He smiled over at her. "I like to cook. My ma taught me early and I was always in the kitchen with her if I wasn't helping my pa after school on a chore or some project. She was fantastic with herbs and spices. Now I always feel like a chemist before I cook something, wanting to try new spices or herbs on chicken, which is pretty bland meat without them."

"You're actually a chef in disguise," Dev said, giving him a proud look. "Who knew?"

"What?" Sloan teased, wanting to distract her from the stress. "That a backwoods boy could be a decent cook?" Her eyes shone and an ache built in his lower body. Dev was so easily touched. It didn't take much to make her respond and right now, that was a good thing. Washing his hands, he started on making the orange-hoisin sauce.

After pouring the water into the pan, Dev placed it on his gas stove. "There's just so much more to you than I first realized, Sloan," she said.

He placed chicken broth and orange juice into a small pan. "Don't you think it's that way with everyone? We all have many facets. Sort of like a diamond. Maybe some folks have more facets than others, but we all have them." Sloan added a bit of soy sauce, hoisin sauce and sesame oil to the mixture. Taking a whisk, he stirred it together and then added fresh orange zest and a bit of cornstarch.

After turning the burner on, Dev poured the dry rice into a measuring cup. "You're right. I guess I just don't expect men to cook like this, that's all." Sloan reached around her and turned on the heat to cook the sauce ingredients.

"I saw you brought over a fancy-looking camera case and tripod. Are you a photographer?"

"I try," Dev said, wiping her hands on a small towel on a hook near the sinks.

"What do you like to shoot?"

"Wildlife." She gestured toward the bedroom where there was a king-size bed. "I brought over my photo albums of some of what I think are my best shots."

"Then sometime let's sit down at the dining room table and go through them." Sloan held her surprised gaze. "I want to see how you see the world, Dev. Through your eyes." He didn't mean for his voice to go thick with emotion, but it had. He saw a luminous quality enter Dev's eyes, and realized his comment had made her feel good.

"Okay, but they're not very good... Really, they aren't..."

"Beauty is in the eye of beholder," Sloan assured her, stirring the sauce briskly now. The citrusy scent of the oranges filled the kitchen.

"I've never shown them to anyone," Dev admitted, lifting the lid on the water to see if it was boiling yet.

"No? Why not? Were you too shy, I wonder? Worried that others wouldn't see what you saw?"

"You're pretty astute," Dev grumbled, and then grinned over at him. They stood close, almost close enough to brush one another's elbows. "My mother got me into photography when I was ten. She is an excellent amateur photographer and I was always hanging around her, asking questions. I guess she got tired of it and bought me a small Canon camera, a tripod, and we'd go out into the field together."

"That's nice that you have a connection like that with your mother," Sloan said, taking the pot off the burner and turning it off. He placed the pot on a metal trivet on the counter. Opening a cabinet above his head, he picked out a bright red ceramic bowl and then poured the steaming sauce into it.

"It is," Dev admitted softly, seeing that the water was now boiling. Taking off the lid, she put it aside and poured the measuring cup of rice into the pan. Reaching, she turned off the gas. "She wouldn't be home for three or four days at a time and I'd really miss her. I always looked forward to spending that time with her when we'd go out together and photograph nature."

"Being an airline pilot is like being in the military," Sloan said. "A lot of time away from home because of flight schedules." He took out the wok pot and placed a few dollops of coconut oil in the bottom of it, moving to the gas stove.

Dev stirred the rice, their elbows brushing against each another. "I hated her being gone so often as a kid."

And Sloan knew her alcoholic father had been there all the time. No wonder Dev looked forward to seeing her mother. Wanting to keep the conversation light and positive, he asked, "What sort of wildlife do you like to shoot?" He added all the ingredients to the wok pot, stirring them briskly.

Dev moved away from the stove, resting her hips against the counter, watching Sloan work. Already, the air was filling with marvelous scents of ginger, oranges, lemongrass and soy sauce. "I love the buffalo around here. We didn't have them back East, of course. I haven't been able to photograph them yet, but I really want to, once things settle down around here."

"I know where there's a nearby herd," he told her. "Maybe sometime next week, I'll take you out on Gros Ventre Road, and if we get lucky enough we'll intersect with them. They often cross the highway and you can get out and be within ten or twenty feet of them. Sound like a good offer?"

"Does it ever," Dev said, suddenly excited. "Everyone over at the visitor's center was warning me that the buffalo are extremely dangerous. That I should be really careful around them. Is that true?"

Stirring the veggies and chicken briskly, Sloan nodded. "They're what we refer to as 'twitchy.' That means they're unpredictable. A buffalo might look docile eating grass, but they can suddenly turn on a dime and charge you, out of the blue. It puts a whole new perspective on them. The rangers around here know that. They're constantly warning tourists not to approach them. It's a dangerous game. And you don't want to have a one-ton buffalo charging you. You'll lose that round. Guaranteed."

Dev took the lid off the rice and stirred it. The kernels were white and fluffy and ready to be eaten. "Then you're going to show me how to work with them? Show me the little signs that they're getting twitchy, so I don't get stomped?"

Sloan chuckled. He watched Dev empty the fluffy rice into a dark blue ceramic bowl and place it on the dining room table. Soon, the wok veggies and meat would be done. "Yes, I can share with you what I've observed and learned about them. We'll have to keep the dogs in the truck, though. Buffalo don't like dogs at all and will usually charge them if they feel threatened by them. They see a dog as a wolf. And the Snake River wolf pack can and do go after buffalo."

"Maybe leave them home?" Dev asked, coming back into the kitchen. She pulled out bright yellow ceramic plates from a cabinet and retrieved flatware from the drawer.

"Probably best," Sloan agreed. He smiled a little. "I think Bella and Mouse are going to really like this new arrangement, don't you?"

Smothering a laugh, Dev nodded, eyeing the two dogs sitting side by side on Mouse's large round doggy cushion. "I think it's already a done deal, don't you?"

Sloan nodded. He transferred the contents of the wok to a rectangular Pyrex glass bowl. "I think so, too. Well? Ready to eat? Hungry yet?" He brought the Pyrex out to the dining room table and set it down on a quilted hot pad to protect the maple wood.

"It really does smell wonderful," Dev admitted. She hurried back to the kitchen and located two red linen napkins. When she returned with them, Sloan was standing, her chair pulled out from the table.

"Thank you," Dev said, placing the napkins beside each plate. Sitting down, she watched Sloan retrieve two large ladles and the hoisin sauce from the kitchen.

Bella whined, sitting up on the cushion, ears up, eyes on the prize.

Dev laughed. "Oh, no! You do not get any of this, Bella."

Entering the dining room, Sloan saw the yellow Lab lie back down, her full focus still on the food. He grinned and placed the spoons in the rice and the Pyrex bowl. "Do you give her scraps?" he asked, sitting down. He picked up her plate and placed a heap of rice and then the wok contents over it, then handed it back to her.

"Sometimes," Dev hedged. "She's such a foodie."

"She's not overweight and looks good. I think we'll have some leftovers for her, if you want?"

"And you feed Mouse human tidbits?"

"Now I do. Yes. Not a lot, though," Sloan admitted, piling his plate high. "Go ahead, try the food. Let me know if you like it." He wanted Dev's focus on her own well-being. She was like most people when they got upset: they lost their appetite. He tried to ignore her grace as she picked up the fork. And the way her soft lips opened, but he was already remembering their kiss at Long Lake. Damn, he'd give anything to strengthen their emotional ties to one another. Sloan didn't see a way for that to happen presently. Dev was completely distracted and had a right to be, under the circumstances.

"Mmm," Dev whispered, slowly chewing the food. "This is delicious!"

Sloan ate a bit of it himself, pleased with the outcome of his cooking skills. "I think it's the coconut oil. It gives a very subtle tropical touch to the wok ingredients. What do you think?" Sloan felt his pulse arc upward. There was pure pleasure shining in Dev's eyes.

"I can barely taste the coconut, but for sure, it does give it an exotic flavor. I love it!" And she dug into the food with relish.

Sloan was secretly thrilled to see her eat. Dev was underweight for her height. She was medium boned and yet she was almost skinny. He was sure it was due to the stress in her life since Gordon's attack. "Eat all you want, gal."

Dev raised her brows. "There's a *lot* of food in this wok, Sloan!"

"Don't worry about them," he urged. "Put some meat on your ribs." He shot her a teasing look. Her cheeks reddened. Sloan was discovering when he was intimate with Dev, her enjoyment showed in her expression. And that was a good thing. He could sense she liked him, but there was nothing like a physical reaction to confirm it.

DEV WAS HELPING Sloan clean up after the unexpectedly delicious dinner in the kitchen when the phone rang. Instantly, her hands froze in the suds of the water she was washing the dishes in.

"Could you get that, Sloan?" He was closer to the wall telephone and his hands were dry. Her gut twisted. Was the call from Cade Garner? Her breath hitched as she heard Sloan talk in low tones, his brow wrinkling.

When he hung up, he said, "They positively identified Bart Gordon's fingerprints on one of those soda cans we found in the forest." He walked over to her. "At least we know," Sloan said, placing his hand on her shoulder.

Desperately needing his touch, Dev dried her hands on the towel and turned around. "Did he say anything else?"

"Well, there were no fingerprints in your apartment. Cade thinks Gordon wore latex gloves. He didn't think to wear them in the forest, though. It means he's sloppy, and that will get him caught sooner, not later."

Dev moved toward Sloan, wanting his arms around her. He didn't disappoint her. Closing her eyes, she leaned into his chest, placed her cheek against the roughened weave of his shirt. She inhaled, wanting the scent of him filling her because it automatically chased the fear out of her. "At least we know…" Dev slid her arms around his waist, exhausted by the terror. There was no safe place and Dev knew it. "Now," she whispered unsteadily, "I worry about the person who will be assigned to protect me, Sloan." Dev pulled away, drowning in the dark, stormy blue of his eyes. When he lifted his spare fingers and threaded them through her loose hair, it soothed her rising fear.

"Gal, don't go there. Whoever is with you, knows the score. You aren't going anywhere without an armed escort." He caressed her hair, leaning down, placing a kiss on the top of her head. "It's going to be all right."

"I just want it to go away," Dev whispered, her voice taut with barely concealed emotion. "I don't want anyone else hurt. All I want is to be able to live my life in peace and not keep looking over my shoulder, Sloan. God, I'm so tired of this!" she choked out, burying her head against him.

Sloan's arms tightened around her. She felt his lips trace her hairline, sending tiny flames wherever he barely brushed her skin. He stirred her affection for him. Despite everything, her heart ached to share so much more with him, but she was putting Sloan in danger. She lifted her head, staring up into his narrowed eyes. "I've put you in danger, too, Sloan. We've barely known each other three months." She grimaced. "This probably wasn't what you signed on for with me." Dev saw a lazy smile tug at the corners of his mouth.

Sloan lightly traced the high curve of her cheekbone with his finger. "Gal, don't you go worrying about me. All right?" His voice deepened and he released her, framing her face with his large hands. "I am *exactly* where I want to be with you, Dev. By now, you know without question that I care for you, don't you?"

As his warm, roughened hands cradled her face, they sent streamers of heat down her neck, flooding into her breasts, the flames turning molten in her clenching lower body. "I—wasn't sure. I wanted a serious relationship with you, Sloan. We haven't had much time to talk…to really sit down and hear what's in one another's heart and mind." Dev felt mesmerized by his large black pupils ringed with cobalt blue as she felt the intensity of Sloan's emotions swirling around her. He was so close. All she had to do was lean scant inches upward and.. kiss him. How Dev wanted to kiss him again! She'd never been kissed like that in her life, and she hungered for more, right down to the tips of her toes.

"You're right," Sloan said thickly, staring into her widening green eyes. "But time doesn't always matter. I've been attracted to you since the day I met you, Dev. I've been hoping all along what I was feeling wasn't just me wishing it was so. I needed to hear those words from you, gal." He lifted his chin, staring over her head for a moment, struggling to find the right words. His gaze swept across her sweet face, those deep green eyes luminous with something he was afraid to name. It was love. Sloan was sure of it. He swallowed. "Don't ever question my loyalty to you, Dev. I have your back. I always will. I'm here for you in any way you need me to be. Just say the word…"

Dev couldn't tear her gaze from Sloan's, feeling an incredible, almost euphoric energy suddenly embrace them. Her heart was pounding and she wanted to kiss him but was afraid to. She was more afraid of herself, worried she'd be unable to stop once she invested her heart in Sloan. But she knew she would do just that. His mouth was so strong looking and yet his touch so gentle. Right now, Dev needed that, but she couldn't ask. Instead, she lifted her hand, gently curving it down the expanse of his hard jaw, watching his eyes suddenly constrict upon her. She felt Sloan tense, as if controlling himself for her sake.

"I didn't want you doing this because you thought you had to," Dev admitted unsteadily, searching his face, feeling the heat and masculinity of him surrounding her. Wanting her. Right now, she felt dampness between her thighs, shocked that just being in his arms could cause that kind of powerful sexual reaction. Dev trusted Sloan with her life. Literally. He was sensitive to her and seemed to know what she needed, even if she didn't.

Sloan released her and caught her hand, pressing a kiss to the back of it. "You're hardly a burden, Dev." He released her hand. "Feel like some dessert?" Because if he didn't get on some safe ground with her, he was going to slip his arms beneath Dev and carry her into his bedroom and make love with her until they were exhausted. Her cheeks were flushed and he felt her sudden yearning for him. It was clearly etched in her green eyes. And her lips had parted moments earlier, as if silently asking him to kiss him. Oh, Sloan had seen the signs, but he'd waited. Because in their situation, Dev's stress was coloring their need for one another, and he knew it. Maybe not in a bad way, however. The danger was pushing them together a lot faster than normal. But he needed to be careful. Did Dev see him only as her protector, and not someone who could hold her heart? Sloan didn't know yet.

And above all, he wanted Dev's heart, not just her body, although it was hell on him not having her right now, the painful tightness in his lower body proof of that.

"Dessert?"

Even Dev's voice was wispy sounding, that far-off look in her eyes telling him that her body was just as riled as his from their touching one another. Kissing her lightly along her hairline and her brow had been his private pleasure. Oh, how much more Sloan wanted to kiss her. "I've got some vanilla ice cream in the freezer and some good hot fudge. Kind of a sundae without the nuts and whipped cream?" he coaxed, moving into the kitchen.

Mouse whined.

Dev turned, looking at the dog as he sat up, his big black ears pointed up and his eyes intently watching as Sloan walked into the kitchen. She heard Sloan laugh as he opened the refrigerator and bent down to look into the freezer for the ice cream.

"What are you laughing about?" Dev asked, walking in to join him.

"Mouse. He's a sucker for ice cream. It's his downfall." He pulled out a half gallon of it and handed it to Dev.

She smiled a little, warmed by that information. "And you know this how?"

Straightening, Sloan shut the refrigerator and gave her a merry look. "I spoil him." Going to the cabinet he drew down two bright yellow bowls and set them on the countertop. Dev came up and handed him the ice cream.

"How much do you give him?"

"Oh," Sloan said, digging out a couple of scoops for each bowl, "maybe a tablespoon. No fudge, because as you know chocolate can kill a dog. He only gets some after I finish my bowl."

"Big alpha male here," Dev teased, pulling two spoons from the drawer.

"That's right, in his eyes, I am," Sloan said, raising a brow as he took the ice cream back to the freezer. "If I gave it to Mouse first, he'd think he'd been upgraded to alpha and I'd be instantly demoted to being a beta male."

Smiling, Dev took the jar of fudge and opened it. "Feed yourself first around your dog so that he or she always knows you're the alpha," she said, as if reading from a manual. All handlers were taught that rule. Alphas always ate first in dogdom and in wolf packs. All the beta dogs and wolves were second and waited their turn until after the alpha had eaten and was sated.

Walking over to her, Sloan watched Dev drizzle the thick fudge over her three scoops. Nothing Dev did wasn't beautiful to watch. Her hair shone beneath the lights, blue color dancing here and there among the thick, full strands. She was relaxed now, no longer focused on Gordon. Inwardly, Sloan breathed a small sigh of relief. As he took the jar of fudge from her, their fingers touching, he wanted to do much more for Dev. "Are you an ice-cream gal by any chance?" he asked.

Dev smiled and picked up her bowl and spoon. "Like Mouse, ice cream is my downfall."

"Well," Sloan said with a chuckle, "we'll let you eat when I do. You're the alpha female around here."

CHAPTER SIXTEEN

Dev TRIED TO sleep in Sloan's king-size bed, but her mind was churning and wouldn't shut down. She twisted and turned beneath the cotton sheet, watching the clock on the dresser move from midnight to 1:00 a.m. More than anything, she wanted Sloan here, beside her. She knew he would take her mind off the haunting terror eating at the fringes of her terrier-like brain. And she wanted to love him fully and completely because there was something beautiful that hung silent but unfulfilled between them. She wanted to tear at that unspoken yearning they both had for one another and expose it. He meant more to her at this stage than Bill had to her. What was love? She'd thought she'd known with Bill.

Dev didn't try to hide from the word any longer. What she felt for Sloan was real. It wasn't a figment of her imagination. The look in his eyes tonight had told her that. The ache between her legs intensified. It stunned her that in the midst of all this mounting danger, she was thinking of sex with Sloan. Wanting him. All of him. She sensed he'd be a tender lover and that was exactly what she needed. Even now, the yearning for him was always palpable, always there. No matter what. That was love, and Dev knew it.

How had she fallen so hard? So quickly? It took her breath away. She'd never loved anyone except Bill, and it had taken her nearly two years to realize it. It had been two months with Sloan. Dev trusted herself at this age far more than she had when she'd met Bill, years earlier. There was such a powerful attraction between her and Sloan. She couldn't give it words, but she could feel it as if it were hot sunlight shining down upon her, embracing her, flooding her with the need to have him in every possible way. How badly she wanted Sloan with her, right now. And she was such a coward for not telling him what she wanted.

Pressing her face into the down pillow, the sheet and blanket twisted around her legs, Dev wondered if how she felt was fair to Sloan. Did danger make a person want sex? She'd been in plenty of danger in Afghanistan and had never felt one inkling of sexual hunger in the midst of it. Not one iota. It had to be Sloan. Her attraction to him. Or was it because she felt vulnerable to the threat of Gordon being around again?

Making a sound of frustration, she turned onto her side, jamming the pillow beneath her head, staring off into the darkness. Finally, Dev came to the conclusion that her attraction to Sloan had started on the day she'd met him. It didn't happen instantly when Gordon appeared on the scene. She was falling in love with this easygoing cowboy who always seemed to be there to catch her when she stumbled or fell.

There was more to it than just the physical, and Dev knew it. Her heart widened with a wild array of feelings toward Sloan. He invited her trust. He was painfully honest about himself to a fault. And his sensitivity toward her amazed Dev. She'd never met a man like him. Bill had been sensitive, too, but not to the degree Sloan was. Closing her eyes, Dev wondered why her world was falling apart around her again. Hadn't she paid enough of a price with Gordon's first attack? She'd gathered the courage and testified in court against him and he'd been put away. The sentence was too short in her opinion, but the good-ole-boys network had stuck together, protecting their Gordon, not her, the victim. Dev had seen the amusement in the eyes of the judge who'd presided over the case. She'd known then Gordon would get a slap on the hand. And now he was out and hunting her down once again. The male judge had *not* done his job.

Somewhere between all those thoughts, Dev finally fell into an exhausted sleep, her mind finally shutting down.

THE INSTANT SLOAN heard Dev's scream through the closed bedroom door, he bolted off the couch, the covers flying. Disoriented for a moment, sleep tearing from him, he vaguely heard Mouse growl and leap to his feet, hackles rising.

"Stay," he ordered his dog thickly.

Sloan twisted the knob, throwing the door open. In the bare light from a small bulb in a wall socket near the dresser, he saw Dev sitting up in bed, pushed up against the massive wooden headboard, terror in her eyes. Her breathing was explosive and ragged. Sloan saw she wasn't here but caught in the vise of the nightmare. He was familiar with flashbacks in military vets and Dev had the same look etched in her frozen features as they'd had.

"Dev?" he called gently, sitting down on her side of the bed. Sloan knew better than to touch or try to hold her. Flashbacks meant she could still be caught up in a horrific event, and if he reached out for her, Dev might think he was the person in her nightmare instead. It would cause her more stress and fear. In a low voice, Sloan called her name, reassuring her that she was all right and that she was in a safe place.

Slowly, her chest stopped heaving. Sloan saw her eyes change and he purposely kept his voice low, talking her down. Talking Dev back to the here and now, helping her loosen herself from the crushing event that she was trapped within. Tears streamed unchecked down her taut, pale cheeks. He felt helpless in so many ways, wishing to hell he could slip his arms around Dev and haul her into the safety of his arms. But he couldn't do it. Not yet. She pressed her hands to her face, a sob escaping her contorted lips.

"I—I'm sorry I woke you," Dev choked out brokenly, dropping her hands from her face, giving him a look of abject apology.

"Don't be, sugar. It's all right. You're back now and you're safe." Sloan saw pain come into her glistening eyes, the way her mouth twisted. Dev needed to cry. Sloan opened his arms a bit as a silent invitation to her. He didn't know what Dev wanted or needed right now, and wasn't about to assume anything.

She lifted her head and her eyes met his. There was such regret in them.

"Come here." Sloan offered his outstretched hand to her.

Dev hesitated and then slowly loosened from her frozen position against the headboard. Tears continued to leak out of her eyes. She reached out and gripped his proffered hand. His warm, rough fingers wrapped around her damp ones, drawing her forward to her knees.

"I—I had a nightmare," Dev whispered unsteadily,

needing Sloan's offered embrace. Dev saw the sympathy burning in his shadowed eyes.

"I know. It's okay, Dev. Come on. Let me hold you
for a bit. It'll make you feel better."

Never had an invitation sounded so necessary in her
life. Heart still pounding because the adrenaline was
keeping her tense, she gave a jerky nod. In moments,
Sloan had settled her across his lap and brought her up
against his naked upper body. She sighed brokenly and
rested her head wearily against his broad, strong shoulder. His flesh was warm and taut beneath her cheek,
his scent masculine and steadying as she breathed it in
deeply. Sloan wore nothing but a pair of light blue pajama
bottoms. As she slowly wound her arm around his waist,
wanting to be as close as she could get, she felt his hand
settle against her hip, drawing her fully against him.

All the terror bled out of Dev then. Sloan's large hand
moved slowly up and down her thigh to her hip, soothing her, making her feel shielded and grounded. It wasn't
sexual at all. It was one human comforting another. Closing her eyes tightly, fresh, hot tears spilled, wetting his
flesh. Dev couldn't help herself and one sob after another started to pull out of her, jerking her body. And
every time, she would feel Sloan's arm tighten a little
bit in reaction, as if to silently absorb that hurt and con-
sole her. His lips pressed against her hair. Dev sobbed
a little more, unable to control the shaking of her body.
She had never cried in a man's arms before. Right now,
she had never felt more loved. She'd been so caught up
in her terror, the years of pain and fear locked inside her,
and now the tears poured freely out of her for the first
time in her life.

Dev had no idea how long she cried, only that after-

ward, she sank limply against him as her sobs ebbed.
Sloan lightly skimmed the strands of her hair, his hand
curving slowly up and down her back as she lay in his
arms. Her body began to hum with each stroke from her
head to her hip. It comforted her. But her breasts against
his darkly haired chest began to tighten, as well. For long
moments Dev lay with her eyes shut, absorbing Sloan's
warm, taut flesh beneath her cheek, now gleaming wet
with her endless tears, and a new urgency awakened
somewhere deep inside her.

Her breasts ached for Sloan's touch each time his long
fingers moved slowly through the strands of her black
hair, lingering to gently massage the sensitive nape of
her neck, then following the line of her spine downward.
Everywhere Sloan's fingers skimmed, her skin grew taut,
and flames fired through her, spreading ever outward
with the pleasure he was giving her.

Time lulled and Dev became lost in his languid
strokes across her body. With each graze, her tension
dissolved a little more. Sloan's scent mingled with the
sage soap he'd used earlier. His moist breath cascaded
softly across her damp cheek. Her brow was pressed
against his jaw, his beard chafing her skin, making it
come alive with awareness. Dev whispered Sloan's name,
sliding her arm across his shoulder and fully pressing
herself against him. She felt so empty inwardly but getting as close as she could to him eased that sense of being
suspended in nothingness. With Sloan, she came alive
in every possible way.

As Dev twisted her hips against him, silently letting
him know she wanted him as more than a comforter, she
tried to prepare herself for his rejection. Sloan had come
in to give her solace, not to love her. But love was what

Dev wanted from this quiet country man who saw life simply through his intelligent blue eyes. She thought he saw her the same way. It was a sense, that was all. But it was strong within her and she shifted her head to his shoulder, opening her eyes, meeting his concerned gaze.

"Dev," he rasped thickly, "is this what you really want?"

She drowned in his gleaming, shadowed, cobalt gaze. Saw him conflicted between giving her comfort and giving in to the longing he held for her. His hand came to rest on her hip as he continued to hold her close. "It's exactly what I need, Sloan." Dev lifted her hand, wiping the last of the tears from her lashes. "I've wanted you for so long…" She saw his expression shift to one of surprise. And then, it was quickly replaced with a new tenderness she'd not seen before. It gave her the courage to go on. "I was afraid to discuss it with you, Sloan. I thought it might only be me feeling this way…" Her voice trailed off into silence.

"You weren't the only one thinking along that line, gal. So was I." Sloan frowned, his tone becoming more serious, searching her eyes. "Dev? This has to be about more than just you wanting safety and comfort after that nightmare. I feel it's more than that, but I need to hear that from you."

Dev dragged in a deep, steadying breath. "Tonight just triggered all of it, Sloan. I've been wanting you for as long as I've known you. I was just too chicken to tell you." Dev wiped her cheek dry. She was surrounded and absorbed by Sloan's powerful male body. She could feel the leashed power around him, that intense yearning in his eyes and flowing through his tensed body.

Sloan lifted his hand from her hip, cupping her jaw,

looking deep into her eyes. His voice was low. "You're one of the bravest people I've even known, Dev." His thumb caressed her cheek as he leaned down, his mouth a breath from her lips. "I want to love you, too…"

Closing her eyes, she lifted her chin that scant inch to meet his descending mouth. The warmth of his breath flowed across her nose and cheek as she opened to his nudging lips, desperately wanting another kiss just like the last one.

Dev wasn't disappointed. Her heart started pounding unevenly as heat thrilled and streamed throughout her body, flooding hotly into her channel, making her thighs clench with need. Sloan's kiss was grazing, absorbing her lips, her taste, and Dev felt cherished. No man had ever made her feel as priceless and beautiful as he did. Her fingers slid up his jaw, threading into the dark, clean strands of his hair above her ear. Sloan stiffened and though he was clearly trying to maintain rigid control over himself she felt him react powerfully to her tentative, searching touch.

As he moved his tongue across her lower lip, testing her, Dev moaned and felt her breasts grow taut with need, and she pressed her nipples wantonly against his broad chest. She became lost in the fire between them, the hunger of his exploring mouth taking her slowly, as if he were sipping a fine wine, allowing the taste of her to fully flow through every cell in his body. Sloan was not in a hurry like so many other men always were. He wanted to get to know every square inch of her as he cupped her jaw, angled her such that his tongue moved sinuously against her own.

Instinctively, Dev arched into Sloan as he drew her solidly against himself. She could clearly feel the hardness of his erection straining tautly against his pajamas. There was no mistaking Sloan's need for her. Moisture collected swiftly between her thighs. As his tongue rocked gently against hers, waiting for her to respond, she breathed in his ragged breath, his long fingers anchoring her, holding her captive against him. She felt as if he were going to eat her like a delicious, sinful dessert. The seduction of his mouth sliding against hers allowed Dev to sink fully into her exploding senses.

She moaned as he eased from her wet lips, barely opening her eyes, lost in the lightning heat bolting through her. Sloan had only kissed her and she knew without a doubt her panties were soaked. That was the intense yearning they synergized between one another. Dazed and breathless, she stared into Sloan's intense-looking eyes, and Dev became lost in the turbulent blue and gold within them.

"Are you protected?" he asked, his voice low, urgent in tone.

It took long seconds for Dev to come back to Earth. "I'm on the pill. I'm clean, Sloan, no diseases." She saw one corner of his mouth hook upward.

"Same here. Do you want me to wear a condom?"

With a shake of her head, she said, "No."

He nodded and released her, allowing her to sit fully on his lap, his one arm around her waist, holding her so she wouldn't fall.

Dev slowly eased off his thighs. Her legs were unsteady because she wanted him so badly. Gripping his shoulder, she pushed off her socks. "I haven't had many partners," she admitted, standing and tugging at her pajama bottoms.

"That's okay. No sin in being picky."

She grinned down at him, her whole body consumed by the sensual fire racing through her. He eased her trembling fingers away from her drawstring waistband.

"Let me untie that for you?"

"Your hands are more steady than mine are. That's a compliment to you…your kiss…"

Sloan's mouth curved faintly as he loosened the string and let the pants fall. "Not for long. You make me burn, sugar."

His words drenched her like liquid flames. Sloan stood and he began to undress, as well. If Dev had thought she'd feel embarrassed about getting naked with Sloan, she wasn't. Instead, as the clothes piled up around their feet, she admired him fully naked, feeling nothing but raw desire. The play of muscles throughout his shoulders and chest was hypnotic to Dev. There was something so mesmerizing about Sloan, though she couldn't define it because her mind was useless at this point. She felt like a primal female in heat, wanting her mate.

The look in Sloan's eyes, that gleam of appreciation for her as he stood naked, made Dev tingle all over with a keening ache. Her nipples puckered beneath his intense look as his gaze swept her from head to toes. If Dev had had any worries about being ugly, or not perfect enough, or her breasts being too small for him, they all dissolved beneath that one sweeping, blistering look he gave her.

Sloan walked toward her, sliding his fingers through her clean black hair. "Sugar, you are beautiful to me in every way," he murmured, pressing light kisses across her hair, massaging her scalp, allowing his fingers to caress her sensitive nape. "You were beautiful in my dreams, but in real life?" Sloan leaned down, licking that exquisitely sensitive spot behind her ear, and drew an immediate gasp from Dev. "You are ten times prettier..."

Dev moved forward, gliding her breasts against his chest sprinkled with dark hair. When her rounded belly met the hard, warm length of his erection, her knees suddenly went weak. Sloan must have sensed her reaction because in one smooth, unbroken motion, he lifted her into his arms. He turned and settled Dev into the center of his bed. Sloan's face was deeply shadowed, with only a night-light on, and she thrilled at his primal expression. He wanted her. It was such a delicious discovery. And never had Dev wanted anyone more than this man.

SLOAN INWARDLY TENSED, ruthlessly controlling himself for Dev's sake. He kept telling himself to go slow, to take his time with her. If she hadn't had many partners, it became a question of just how experienced she was. He didn't mind himself one way or the other, but Sloan did care for Dev's possible innocence. She might not be used to certain positions or the many ways a man could love his woman. And he wanted this first time to be special for both of them.

As he came and lay at her right side, skimming his hand from her shoulder then capturing her hand, he watched for her reaction. He opened her palm and licked the center of it, and her pupils grew large and black. Her eyes fluttered half-closed for a moment, as if she were enjoying the sensations he was creating in her opened palm. So much of what he knew about loving a woman involved foreplay, getting her so hot and ready that she wanted to scream. A woman was slower than a man to come online sexually, but when she did, she could have as many orgasms as she wanted compared to his one. Slow start, but a damn strong finish.

"Is there anything that you especially like?" he asked, raising his eyes from her palm, holding her languid gaze.

Confusion came to Dev's eyes and he got it: she was truly a neophyte. A woman with more experience would have no trouble telling him what she desired. He smiled and leaned down, caressing her lips. "It's okay," he whispered against her mouth, "you just tell me what pleases you as we go along. Or, if I make you uncomfortable, tell me right away, Dev." Sloan gave her a light kiss and drew back enough to engage her gaze, which burned with need for him.

"Yes, I can do that. But I want to please you, too. This isn't a one-way street, Sloan."

He nodded, mouth hooking upward. "Fair enough, sugar, but this first time? Let's just get to know one another. You okay with me taking the lead this one time?"

"Fine," Dev answered, "this one time."

He liked her spirit. Dev might be less experienced in some ways, but she was able to share and his heart swelled. There was no question in Sloan's mind about her natural unselfishness and generosity. "Sounds like a plan," he murmured, moving his mouth across her parted lips. She was so sleek, soft and responsive as he pressed her to open her mouth so he could taste her fully. Instantly, her body slid urgently against his. He caressed the curve of her breast. She purred deep in her throat. The sound hardened him and Sloan left her lush mouth and settled his lips upon the taut nipple just begging for his attention. The moment he suckled her, Dev about came undone in his arms, her hips clashing urgently against his, sending a hot blaze up through him.

If Sloan had thought that neophyte meant shy, he'd been delightfully mistaken. Dev moved sinuously against his hips and erection like a cat rubbing against him. Her fingers slipped though his hair, sliding downward, gripping his thick shoulder muscles as he continued to tease her nipple. Her moan shuddered through him, sending a spike of heat throughout his rigid body. Lifting his lips, he paid an equal amount of time and attention to her other nipple. Dev twisted and writhed beneath him, her small cries sending a flurry of pounding heat through him. She had turned wild and wanton, completely immersed in the intense pleasure rippling through her. It made Sloan feel good and strong as a man that he could please her like this. Nothing meant more to him.

Taking her mouth, Sloan crushed her lips against his, her breasts raking across his chest, fire searing through him. He moved his hand downward, eased her thighs open. His fingers met her dampness. She was more than ready. Sloan wanted to do so much more with Dev, but he cautioned himself to keep it simple. Basic. To let her guide him to what she desired from him. The moment he caressed her wet entrance, a strangled cry erupted from her. She arched upward, pressing against his fingers with her woman's strength. Sloan was surprised at her power. Her sleek, firm thighs, curved with muscles honed from riding a horse, made him salivate. Heat surged through him, making him groan as she thrust her hips toward his wet fingers. He began to tease her.

Nearly losing his concentration, Sloan kissed the length of her neck, nipping the flesh, soothing it with his tongue, feeling Dev move boldly against his fingers, asking for more. He heard her moan in frustration, wanting him to explore her further, to feel him inside her.

Sloan took one of her nipples at the same moment he gently slid his finger into her.

A cry tore from Dev and she clutched frantically at his shoulders, hips moving powerfully against him, wanting more, much more of him. A powerful drumlike rhythm sheared through Sloan as he felt how small and tight she was. His own body was on the edge of exploding. Withdrawing his finger, he lifted his body across her damp one. He saw the desperation in Dev's half-open eyes, saw the lust shining in them. Taking her hands, he held them gently above her head, opening her thighs with his knee, gauging her reaction. The moment he pressed his erection against that hot, welcoming gate of hers, she shut her eyes, arching hungrily, silently inviting him into her.

Sloan froze, feeling the tight grip of her around him, knowing it had to stress her. But one look at Dev's flushed features, the ecstasy across them, and he pulled back and then eased forward once again. He wanted to introduce himself slowly to her body. He wanted to avoid causing her discomfort, or worse, pain. With each slow, pumping movement, her cries turned to whimpers of pleasure, her hands opening and closing as he held her wrists captive. Increasing the rhythm, he felt her lower body beginning to contract, a sign she was close to orgasm. Beads of sweat trickled down his temples and his teeth clenched as he held himself in check for Dev's sake.

Sloan pushed deep into her, feeling her body accommodate him, hearing Dev's sobbing and panting. Her hips were restless and urgent beneath his. And as she slid her long, slender legs around his waist, Sloan knew he could take her now. He thrust deeply into her. His entire body shook and broke out in a sweat as he felt her hurtling toward that orgasm, groaning as he fought to withhold his own reactive release.

Dev gave a long, keening cry, her entire body flexing upward, paralyzed as Sloan felt her body blossoming from within, that thick, hot fluid drowning him in the most pleasurable of ways. He kept up the rhythm, holding her hands in place, watching a flush sweep across her chest, across her exposed neck and into her taut face that mirrored ecstasy. And it was then, as she rocked into him, that Sloan released her wrists, and her hands settled around his narrow hips. He kept thrusting, understanding Dev would automatically come again, very quickly. And just as he released himself into her, she cried out, fingers digging into his flesh as a second, even more powerful orgasm flooded her. Eyes tightly closed, his teeth clenched, Sloan gripped the bedsheets on either side of her head, surging deep within her, feeling fire rip down his spine, erupt within his lower body, making him growl like the animal he'd become in these scalding moments. His mind turned to jelly and he strained, every muscle screaming as the red-hot intensity jetted through him, taking her, loving her, never wanting to let Dev go.

CHAPTER SEVENTEEN

SLOAN WATCHED DEV SLEEP. She lay on her right side, black hair a frame against the white cotton pillow beneath her head, emphasizing her sensitive features. Her lashes shadowed cheeks that had remained flushed. His heart overflowed with a fierce joy, something he'd never before felt after making love to a woman. *Not like this.* Sloan's hand lay across her hip. The bunched sheet had gathered around her waist. Her left arm rested across his rib cage, her other arm between her breasts, fingers slightly curved toward her palm in sleep. It was her profile that held his heart. Head slightly bent forward, brow resting against his torso, the clean line of Dev's nose, her slightly parted lips, tugged powerfully at Sloan.

Even though he wanted to slide his fingers through her ebony hair, he didn't want to wake her. Dev had been on an emotional roller coaster the past few days. But as his gaze swept over her sleeping features, what amazed Sloan was that the stress lines around her eyes had disappeared. The tension she'd carried around her mouth was gone. Right now, Dev looked like an angel who was visiting her earthbound lover, like she could magically disappear from his embrace in a heartbeat. There was nothing not to love about this woman and his fingers itched to glide down the smooth flesh of her upper arm.

He glanced at the clock on the dresser. It was 3:00 a.m.

Sloan was wide-awake, his body radiating pleasure in small concentric ripples that were somehow continuing well after they'd made love. He lightly smoothed the sheet across her hip. Dev was exhausted, sleeping so deeply that even as he caressed her, she didn't move. Her breathing, the slow, easy rise and fall of her partially exposed breast, told Sloan she was deep in the arms of her dreamworld. And he sincerely hoped they were good dreams, not nightmares.

The shadows were deep in the corners of the inky room, but the bare night-light showed the clean curve of Dev's high cheekbones. Where strands of her hair had slid back, pooled on the pillow like ebony water, he appreciated her small, delicate ear. There was nothing overtly powerful about Dev. Sloan remembered his first impression of her at the horse trailer, that she possessed willowlike suppleness and fragility. After getting to know her, Sloan knew differently. She possessed inborn strength. There was so much hidden about her. Sloan wanted to discover all of Dev's delicious nuances. Wanted her to trust him enough to open herself up fully to him on every possible level. She was worth getting to know. Getting to savor.

What had happened to his wariness about falling in love again? He'd married Cary Davis at twenty-two, right after he'd become a forest ranger. For so long after the acerbic divorce at twenty-seven, Sloan had been sour on women. He'd shrugged off Cary's behavior as part of her natural personality. The fact she'd hidden it from him still left him bitter. He came from a family where honesty and integrity were foremost in a person's life. Lies were not tolerated or accepted.

Sloan quietly lay down, his arm curved around Dev's

shoulders. Her presence was incredibly comforting to him. She trusted him. And Cary had never trusted him. Ever. That pain still gigged him every once in a while, even three years after his divorce from her. He was upset with himself for not having seen her drug problem. Was it ignorance on his part? He'd never been involved with drugs or people who took them. So how could he have spotted such a pattern of abuse?

Closing his eyes, Sloan dragged his arm across them, trying to sort it all out as he had attempted to do thousands of times before. His mind moved toward Dev. Was he seeing her accurately?

A faint flow of desperation moved through Sloan. He was lonely. Humans weren't meant to live alone or apart from one another. They were social animals who thrived in relationships. And he'd been alone for the past three years, focused on his ranger work. The only reprieve from that loneliness had been being part of Iris Mason's and Gus Hunter's two ranch families. Their kindness and inclusiveness had eased some of his biting loneliness. Sloan was more than grateful for them taking him, a stray, into their familial embrace.

Dev, he realized, didn't have much of a home life, either, thanks to her alcoholic father. In many ways, she'd been cut off from her family, through no fault of her own. He wondered why her mother refused to jettison her husband. Lily had made a choice to keep her sick, addicted husband despite her innocent and unprotected daughter. Sloan knew that cut deep into Dev's heart. It had to. He couldn't imagine being estranged from his own family like that. There was a deep love and care between all of them.

And somehow, romantic love had seeped back and taken deep root in his heart when he'd met Dev. Sloan had despaired of ever finding his mate. He'd always wanted marriage, children, but after making such a fatal emotional mistake in choosing Cary, he'd given up on finding the right woman. He smiled a little, remembering his ma shaking her finger in his face shortly after that painful divorce from Cary. She'd told him that time would heal his heart and that eventually the right woman would finally step into his life. Sometimes, she'd counseled, the second marriage was the good one. That people made mistakes and the first marriage was sometimes more like a training-wheels session, prepping you for a much better partner the second time around.

Sloan remembered nodding his head at his impassioned mother, whose eyes had blazed with a fierce love for him. She knew he was hurting badly, blaming himself for the failure of the marriage instead of sharing the responsibility with his ex-wife. He'd taken it all on himself, and the past three years had been a private hell for Sloan. But he always tried to be responsible. He knew that others had trust in him and he wasn't about to let them down.

His parents had been married at age eighteen. And to this day, they loved one another, so many years later. Sloan had grown up wanting the same thing. Only it hadn't happened. Cary had been an extrovert, outgoing, a wild child of sorts and beautiful. She had been like brilliant sunlight to Sloan after his long, dangerous deployments over in Afghanistan. He'd pined for some calm in his life, some normalcy, after he'd left the military. And Cary had been there, blazingly beautiful, stealing his heart. He'd been blinded in an emotional sense to her for so many reasons. He wanted a respite from war and killing. He wanted peace and happiness within a marriage, just like his parents had.

Dev called to him on all those levels. Only this time, Sloan wasn't an emotionally wounded returning military veteran. He was solidly locked in to his job as a ranger and he loved what he was doing. Meeting Dev in a time and place where he was stable, where life was good, although lonely, was markedly different from when he met his first wife. And as much love as he had for Cary, that kind of love wasn't what he felt now for Dev. She was a quiet, peaceful harbor in his life. Maybe her being an introvert like himself was the reason why Sloan felt relaxed. A sense of peace always surrounded him whenever he was with Dev.

Right now, she was here, beside him. Like it should be. Sloan had envisioned Dev with him like this from the moment he'd met her. It had been a crazy dream, but he couldn't fight the powerful connection that throbbed with life, with such fierce promise between them. Her soft, moist breath flowed against his chest and Sloan drowned in all the sensations she created lying beside him. He knew his heart oriented only toward Dev. And after that last thought, Sloan drifted off into a healing slumber.

DEV BLINKED GROGGILY. Sunlight was bright around the edges of the blinds on the window of Sloan's bedroom. Rubbing her eyes, she felt almost drugged, her sleep had been so profound. Glancing up at the clock on the dresser, she started. It was 9:00 a.m.! She never slept that long! And she was late for work!

With a gasp, she flew into a sitting position, the sheet falling around her hips. Sliding her fingers through her mussed hair, Dev tried to think clearly. She pushed off the covers, and her feet hit the cool wooden floor. Memories of last night, of loving Sloan, gripped her and she felt her heart instantly swell with rich emotions. She was supposed to be at work at nine. Hurrying toward the bathroom, she saw her civilian clothes were neatly folded on the counter. Why hadn't Sloan awakened her earlier?

She heard the door to the bedroom open. Sloan entered.

"Hey, relax," he called softly to her, standing in the doorway. "You're getting the day off. Take your time."

Gasping, hand pressed to her throat and realizing she was naked, Dev said, "I thought I was late. Thanks." Sloan's eyes burned with a look that told her he wanted her all over again, and her body reacted swiftly to that look. Dev felt no embarrassment this morning being naked in his presence. It made her feel cherished and desired. "Then I have time for a shower?"

He smiled a little. "For sure. I was just making breakfast." He moved his chin toward the kitchen. "Are you up for some tasty French toast? I coat it in a light crust of peanut butter and then make a syrup for it with Kahlua."

"Sounds great," Dev said, some of the strain leaving her voice. "I can be there in about twenty minutes?"

"That'll do," he said. "See you then." He closed the door.

Her heart was tripping double time and Dev sighed, leaning against the doorjamb to the bathroom, relief flooding her. She closed her eyes for a moment, sleep still fogging her brain. Never had she slept so hard or so deep. She remembered nothing after Sloan had tucked her up alongside himself. Dev blinked and made a turn into the large master bathroom. Sloan's thoughtfulness made her relax. Had he called Charlotte Hastings, her supervisor? He'd thoughtfully brought in a set of clean clothes for her to wear: jeans and a bright pink tee. There were socks as well as her tennis shoes on the floor.

It took a hot shower and washing her hair, for her to finally feel fully awake. As Dev combed and dried her hair, she opened the bathroom door to let the last of the steam escape. The luxurious smell of coffee scented the air and she was dying for a cup or two just to feel more alert. After she dried her hair, she grabbed her tennis shoes and tugged them on. Dev quickly headed for the kitchen, following the fragrant scent of the coffee.

Sloan was just placing four wedges of French toast on her plate when she arrived. There was a full mug of steaming coffee waiting for her, too. As she gave him a grateful look of thanks, he pulled the chair out for her and she sat down.

"I overslept."

"No, you didn't. The last couple of days have been really rough on you, Dev." He walked to the head of the table and sat down at her elbow, his plate piled with a heap of French toast. "You still look sleepy," Sloan teased, a grin lurking at one corner of his mouth.

Picking up the mug of coffee, Dev sipped it and said, "I feel almost drugged."

"Drinking the coffee and putting food in your stomach will help," Sloan coaxed, digging into his plate of food.

"What time did you get up?" Dev asked, eagerly slicing into the fragrant French toast that smelled like peanut butter, along with the chocolate-vanilla taste of the Kahlua syrup. It was mouth-meltingly delicious. Sloan was far more than the average guy in the kitchen opening a can of soup for dinner.

"About 6:00 a.m. You were sleeping so deeply I didn't have the heart to wake you up. I called Charlotte at 8:00 a.m. and I explained the situation to her, and how exhausted you were. She said for you to take the day off and just rest. It will be marked down as a vacation day and she's fine with it."

"Thank you," Dev said.

Sloan had shaven and her gaze automatically went to his mouth. Her body radiated with the scalding memory of his mouth upon her and she felt her body clench. The look in his clear blue eyes was warm and Dev swore she could feel that wonderful, invisible embrace surrounding her once more. Sloan was his usual calm self. As if nothing had happened last night. But it had, and she wanted to wake up enough to discuss it with him later. He wore his jeans and a light blue cowboy shirt, the sleeves rolled up to his elbows. Sloan's masculinity was blatant and she absorbed it, still shimmering from the pleasure he'd given her last night. Dev didn't want to forget or push away those beautiful sensations and feelings. Sloan had been a wonderful lover.

"Is there any more news from Cade?" She was discovering just how hungry she'd really been, eating the second piece of French toast with relish.

"I called him earlier," Sloan said. "They're still running the DNA. It takes forty-eight hours. He's got an APB out in the counties surrounding ours, which is a good move. We don't know where Gordon is, or where he's going."

Some of her hunger dissolved. "I feel like he's around here, Sloan. Close, not far away."

"Wouldn't be surprised." Sloan reached out, stroking

her cheek and giving Dev a concerned look. "We're taking this one day at a time, sugar. You and me. You won't be left alone. You'll always be with someone. Charlotte and I discussed the situation this morning, and she's in agreement that you need a full-time guard. Until Gordon is apprehended, you will always be with another ranger."

Grimacing, Dev muttered, "Sometimes, Sloan, I think it would be better if I just disappeared. Went someplace he couldn't find me. Right now, I'm putting *another* person at risk, and that's you. I'm not comfortable with it."

"Charlotte thinks it would be better if you were focused and busy, that it would probably help you in the long run. There's no sense in holing up. You'd go stir-crazy."

"She's right about that," Dev muttered grudgingly, her plate clean. Pushing it aside, she slid her hands around the warm mug of coffee. "I thought that by leaving my other ranger station out East, I'd get the break I needed."

"But he's followed you. So there's really no safe place to hide from him, Dev. It's better that you're here with me. And the other rangers who will be with you while you're on duty? They will know the lay of the land. I don't think Gordon is going to attack you while someone else is with you. He's got a bully mentality. His kind likes to pick on vulnerable or unarmed women who are alone with no way to call for backup or help."

"I was that way once," Dev said, frowning. "He caught me completely off guard in that barn. And I wasn't defenseless. I got away. I'm *not* going to let that happen again, Sloan."

"No, you won't." He slid his hand down her forearm. "Let's talk about something good, sugar. Let's talk about us. About what happened last night."

Dev turned her hand over, lacing her fingers between his. Euphoria stole through her heart as she drowned in Sloan's stormy blue eyes. "I loved it." *I love you.* The words hung sweetly in front of Dev. How badly she wanted to say them to Sloan, but she didn't dare. Everything was so new, so different between them. Her maturity told her it would be wiser to wait.

Sloan cupped her hand between his, moving a finger slowly around her open palm. "Last night was special for me, too, Dev."

She felt the roughness of his fingers, sending the fire skittering from her palm into her lower arm. "I'm still high from it," she admitted shyly. "I've never been loved so well, Sloan." His eyes glittered with male pride and it made Dev feel good to give him a compliment he deserved. "I know I'm rough around the edges. I'm not exactly superskilled like you are."

"When you love someone, Dev, that shouldn't matter one whit," he said thickly. "It should be about one heart meeting the other. When that happens, things will just magically work out between us as we go along. They sure did last night."

"You make me feel so good, Sloan…thank you. When I was younger, I lived in fear of not meeting anyone's expectations of me." She gave a painful shrug. "And I never did…"

Lifting his hand, Sloan caressed her hair. "You are perfect for me just the way you are. You need to know that."

Sloan's quietly spoken honesty, the sincerity in his eyes and voice, washed across Dev. He released her hand and she already missed his amazing touch that had sent her into another world of nothing but burning arousal and pleasure.

"Thanks," she whispered, giving him a look of relief.

"I don't take what happened as an invite to be with you nightly, Dev. To be honest, I never expected what happened last night." One corner of his mouth tipped upward. "Well…that's not exactly true. I've been dreaming of loving you from the moment I met you. I just never thought it could come true…"

Her heart stuttered as she held his frank gaze. The men she'd known before didn't have Sloan's maturity. Dev understood he was giving her control of the situation. "I couldn't keep my eyes off you out there at the horse trailer," she admitted, giving him a wry glance.

"You too, huh?" He grinned a little, leaning back in the chair, warmly studying her.

"I've always been drawn to you, Sloan."

"Same here."

"So? What does that make us?" Dev felt her throat tighten with fear of rejection.

"A work in progress?"

She smiled a little. "That's about right."

"I know things have been a little compressed because of the situation," Sloan said. "You have to stay with me until we can find Gordon. It's not safe for you to live by yourself right now. He got into your apartment too easily."

Dev didn't disagree. "Can we take this a day at a time, Sloan? I'm torn up enough about everything. And it's not fair to you or me under the circumstances. I can't put my whole heart and focus into us right now even though that's where I want to be." She held his understanding gaze. There was no recrimination in Sloan's face, but she felt his reaction. Sadness, yearning, though he was man enough, mature enough, to give her space and allow her to set the pace.

"It's a crappy situation," he agreed. And then, he smiled a little. "So, I'll stay on the couch until or if you want some company. Fair enough, gal?"

Reaching out, Dev slid her fingers across his arm, feeling the muscles tense beneath his flesh. Already, her body was aching to love Sloan once more. "Yes… I'm sorry, Sloan…"

"Hey, there's nothing for you to apologize for." He gave her fingers a slight squeeze. "We're in a dangerous situation. We need our focus. There will be other times when you're finally out from under this threat. No hard feelings from my end. Okay?"

Her throat tightened. Of all the people in her life, Sloan had been the most loyal. He deserved better. Dev wanted to extend her relationship with him. Anger chilled her as she thought about Gordon, and how he was once more staining her life. "Okay," she whispered, giving him a look of longing. "But I worry Gordon might attack us here in this apartment once he finds out I'm not over at mine."

"The dogs will give us early warning of his presence," Sloan soothed. "Especially Mouse."

"But if it was that easy to break into my apartment, Gordon could get in here just as easily." A shadow came to Sloan's eyes as he absorbed her worry.

"He could. But there are ways to know if someone has entered this place. And if we're home, the dogs will be our alarm."

Sipping her coffee, Dev muttered, "I still wish there was a place I could go and hide."

"If we find Gordon has broken into this apartment, then we need to consider that option."

"Where could I go?"

Sloan moved uncomfortably. "I had a discussion with Cade Garner about that earlier, Dev. He thinks that you could go hide out at the Bar H. He's already talked to Miss Gus about the situation and how it's escalating. And Griff and Val McPherson want to keep you out there at their ranch. They are all for it. But it would mean you would have to stay on the ranch, not go into town where you might be spotted by Gordon for any reason."

Frowning, Dev said, "But that puts them in Gordon's sights, too. I can't do that, Sloan. I won't place them in jeopardy."

"If you left here under cover of night, we could pull it off. And they know the score. Val was once an Air Force intelligence officer. She knows how to handle a gun. Griff was on the Olympic pistol team at one time, and he's an excellent shot, even though he never went into the military." Sloan tried to lighten her anxiety. "And who in their right mind wants to go up against Gus Hunter? She's mean with that twelve-gauge shotgun of hers."

Trying to smile, but failing, Dev said wearily, "I love all those people so much, but it still surprises me they'd open themselves up to Gordon possibly finding me out there and putting all of them in danger."

"Cade feels you'd be very safe out there."

Searching Sloan's grim face, she asked, "How do you feel about it?"

With a hitch of his shoulder, Sloan murmured, "Well, my answer is purely selfish, gal. I'd much rather have you here, with me. I like your company. I know I can defend you. But if I find that Gordon has broken into this place, you will have to go to the Bar H."

Shaking her head, Dev felt miserable. She didn't want to put anyone else in danger. "Gordon would kill them, Sloan. Think of Sophia, their little girl. My God…"

"Look, at the ranch next to them, the Triple II, there's a number of black ops men there who fought in Afghanistan. Talon Holt is a former Navy SEAL. Cass is a former Special Forces soldier. And he has a foreman there who was Delta Force at one time. All Gus has to do is call them, and they'll be over there in minutes. There's more protection for you there than you realize, Dev."

Glumly, she shook her head. "All of you are putting yourself at risk for me."

Sloan gave her a gentle look. "Back East, no one had your back, sugar. This is the West. We protect our own. It was smart of you to move out here."

"Then I need to talk to my supervisor about all of this."

"Already done," Sloan said. "Cade called her and told her the lay of the land."

"Is Charlotte in agreement with me taking a sabbatical if I must?"

"She's in agreement. She understands this is an extraordinary event in your life, Dev. She knows you are the victim here, and she wants to protect you as much as the rest of us do."

Sloan was right: things were different this time around. A tiny thread of relief wound through Dev. "Well…okay…"

"Charlotte said you can come back to work tomorrow, if you feel up to it. If this threat escalates, then she'll suspend you with pay until we nab Gordon."

Rubbing her face, Dev muttered, "God, I hope it doesn't take long, Sloan. I hate living in a limbo like this. Hate that other good people are in the cross fire, as well."

He smiled faintly and captured her hand in his. "You're such a worrywart, Miss McGuire."

Rallying beneath the dark warmth of his voice, Dev said, "I can't help it, Sloan."

"Don't change a hair on your head, gal. We'll muddle through this together with you. You have a lot of people who love you and think the world of you. They're more than ready to stand with you in this showdown with Gordon. Okay?"

CHAPTER EIGHTEEN

"HEY, JOHN," Dev called as she hesitated at the door to the main office at ranger HQ, "I need to go to the bathroom. I'll be back in a minute."

John Welborn, working nearby at his desk, grinned. "Yeah, I don't think I need to follow you into the bathroom, do I, Dev?"

She laughed. "No way! I'll be right back." Dev turned and hurried down the white tiled hall to the first floor of the long rectangular two-story building. It was 10:00 a.m., and it felt good to be back at work. Yesterday she'd spent the day with Sloan, which hadn't been bad at all. They'd made love yesterday afternoon and even now her body glowed from his skilled hands and mouth. The man knew how to tune her body like a finely honed instrument of utter pleasure, no question. And she'd slept with Sloan last night because it felt so right. They belonged together. He'd left it up to her to decide, and she appreciated that Sloan wasn't pressuring her.

As she walked down the hall, she passed several people from the same office, coffee cups in hand. It felt good to be wearing her dark green gabardine trousers, her long-sleeved tan shirt and black leather boots. She'd been wearing a uniform one way or another since she was eighteen. Dev aimed herself toward the last door located near the outside entrance to the rear of the building.

She kept a watchful eye, however. Sloan had warned her that Bart Gordon could still get inside the park. He had been a ranger at one time himself, and he knew how to sneak past the gate entrances.

John, who was in his forties, a father of two girls and happily married for thirteen years to his wife, Susan, had been a great watchdog for Dev. He had been a Marine at one time before joining the Forest Service. And he knew how to use the pistol he carried on his hip. Best of all, John was easygoing, much like Sloan was, and it had served to allow Dev to relax, despite the circumstances. As she pushed the light green door to the women's rest-room open, her boots sounded hollowly against the tiled floor. She leaned down, looking to see if anyone else was present. There were ten stalls, but they were all unoccupied. She was the only one in the facility.

Her heart lingered on Sloan. Today, he was out at the corral of Grand Teton Park, shoeing six mules. She was glad that he was nearby. Dev was going to go to lunch with him at a nearby restaurant within the park. Her heart sang with happiness. She washed her hands in the sink afterward. She stared at herself in the mirror. Her green eyes were clear and she saw gold flecks of happiness deep within them, put there by Sloan loving her. She'd never made love in the afternoon before, and it had been a delicious experience. Never had Dev laughed so hard as when they lay in one another's arms afterward. Sloan had a wonderful sense of humor. He got to talking about his growing-up years as a boy in the woods of the Allegheny Mountains, sharing some of his silly adventures.

I love him.

There, she admitted it as she dried her hands on the

paper towels. Her black hair was pulled back into a ponytail, so it was out of the way. Wishing she didn't have
to wear a pistol, but knowing she always had to, Dev
wished the threat of Gordon's would just go away. How
badly she hoped Cade and the Teton Sheriff's Department would spot and capture him. Throwing the paper
towels into the receptacle, she turned to go to the door.

A scream lodged in her throat.

Bart Gordon stood five feet away from her, his face
dark and intense. He held a Glock 19 pistol directly at
her.

"Well, good morning to you, too, Dev," he snarled.
"Don't make a sound. If you do, I'll kill you right where
you stand."

Dev felt her heartbeat roaring in her ears. Felt the
shattering effect of adrenaline crashing through her
bloodstream. *Oh, God!* Her mind whirled with a hundred questions. How had Gordon gotten in here? Why
hadn't she heard him enter the restroom? Her eyes were
wide with fear, her mouth going dry. She saw satisfaction burning in his dark brown eyes. He was dressed like
a civilian. Instantly she noticed he'd dyed his red hair
and beard a brown color. The beard, now scraggly, made
him look even more dangerous. On his back was a big
black knapsack bulging with unknown gear. He had a
long knife on one hip, a holster on the other. Everything
he wore was camo colored. The boonie hat on his head
fit the camouflage of the rest of his attire.

"Don't do this," she whispered unsteadily, tense,
wanting to run. But there was no place to run. A gleam
of triumph came to his slitted eyes.

"Why not? You put me in jail, doll face. You have no
idea how long I've been waiting to extract my special re-

venge on you. Walk toward me. And if you try anything, I'll kill you. This pistol has a silencer on it. They'll just find you dead in here in the restroom at some point."

Dev believed him, and her knees suddenly started to go shaky. Try to escape? Or go with Gordon and be raped and then be killed? The hatred in his eyes guaranteed that was a possibility. Her cell phone was in her back pocket. She had a Buck knife on her belt. But it was a small knife in comparison to the one he carried. Forcing her feet forward, Dev walked toward him.

"Stop. Turn around."

Her heart was pounding so loud Dev could barely hear his low order. She halted, slowly turning her back to him. Gordon yanked the safety off her pistol and removed it from her holster. He unsnapped the case that carried her Buck knife, removing it, as well. Dropping both of them in a washbasin, he returned, raking her from head to toe with his gaze.

"Any other weapons on you?"

"N-no…" Dev felt his hatred wash over her as he loomed over her. Gordon was six feet tall and heavily muscled. She remembered the last time he'd attacked her from the rear, his brute strength and power. And he'd shoot to kill. The drive to stay alive filled her terrorized mind. Somewhere in her tumbling thoughts, Dev knew if she stayed alive, she might be able to escape. Maybe…

The instant his hands roughly began groping at the top of her shirt, moving across her breasts and back, searching her, Dev jerked away in reaction.

"Damn you," he hissed, grabbing her by her ponytail. "Stand still!"

Muffling a cry, Dev was yanked against Gordon as he continued his frisking of her, even the insides of her trouser legs. Humiliation and embarrassment shot through her. Stiffening, Dev tried to evade his hand between her thighs and heard him growl a warning.

"Bitch."

Her scalp burned with pain as he held her head against him with her ponytail. After he leaned down, thoroughly checking her back pockets and finally around her ankles, he released her.

"Now," he said, glaring at her, "you're going to turn right and go out the rear door. I'll be right behind you. If you so much as make a sound, it'll be the last one you make. Got it?"

Giving a jerky nod, Dev started for the door on wobbling legs. She had to think! She had to get a grip on her escaping emotions! Tears burned in her eyes. *Oh, God, Sloan!* She loved him! She hadn't told him! Her hands flattened on the door, pushing it open. Gordon was so close it nauseated her as she walked into the hall. Glancing swiftly down it toward the office where John was, she saw him with his head bent over his paperwork. There was no one else in the hall. Without hesitating, Dev made a right turn and pushed open the glass door.

The moment they were outside, she swiftly glanced around, looking for help. The rear exit was backed up to a long black asphalt parking lot. There were thirty or so cars and pickups parked in it. But no one was out there. It was deserted. Gulping, her throat tight with terror, she felt the grip of Gordon's hand wrapping tightly around her upper right arm.

"This way," he hissed, shoving her ahead of him, aiming for the nearby line of trees.

Dev moved quickly. Gordon's breath was rancid, making her nauseous. His fingers dug hard into her arm and she whimpered in pain. He practically shoved her into the dark, thick woods. She stumbled, and he caught her and jerked her back onto her feet. Pain arced up Dev's arm, her shoulder burning from the wrenching power of his strength.

"Straight ahead," he ordered.

The forest closed in around them, hiding them. Dev knew she was lost now. No one would see her. No one.

"Where?" she demanded breathlessly, Gordon forcing her into a trot.

"The river."

The Snake River. It was only about a hundred yards from the building. Her mind twisted. Why there? Did he have a raft? That was all that was allowed in this area of the river. And then, it hit Dev. Gordon would never be able to drive in or out of the park because he knew they were looking for him. He'd somehow found a raft and would float out beyond the boundaries of the park, home free. And her with him.

Dev searched the woods and saw an opening ahead. The Snake River was about a hundred feet wide, deep and swift moving even though the surface didn't look that disturbed. But rafters were well acquainted with the deep currents that flowed through it, unseen. How could anyone find her once Gordon had taken off in his raft with her? It felt as if a knife were being twisted in her gut and she felt tears burning in her eyes. She was going to die soon. Gordon would have his way with her and then kill her.

"Halt." Gordon pulled her against him, his hand like a claw on her shoulder. Quickly, he scanned the parking lot where the rafts would land from upriver. A number of rafting companies used this docking area as their final place to come ashore with their group of rafters. Dev saw nothing. The parking lot was half-full, but no people were nearby. "Okay, we're going to trot toward the bank." He pointed straight ahead.

Dev was pushed forward. Her knees felt like so much jelly as she trotted quickly across the parking lot, weaving in and around cars. As they got closer to the bank, she looked upstream, hoping to see rafters coming in to dock. She could yell for help, but there was no one in sight. Gordon guided her to the ramp and she spotted a river raft tied nearby. It was a big one, about twenty feet long. A rafter would stand in the middle of it with two long oars. He would then guide the raft in and around islands and logs that had fallen from the banks into the Snake.

"Get in!"

Dev clambered into the soft, squishy bottom of the raft.

"In the front of it! Just ahead of the center of it. Hurry!"

She felt and heard Gordon's panic. He was looking around. His gun was holstered. She knew the Snake River was comprised of glacier water and would be deadly cold. Anyone staying in that deep, swift-moving water for longer than ten minutes would go into hypothermia and drown. Scrambling over the wooden seat and missing the oar handles, Dev went and knelt down in front of the spar, facing the bow. She felt Gordon's weight move into the raft. He pushed by her and released the rope from the branch it had been tied to onshore. Throwing it in front of her, he quickly shoved it away from the loading dock.

The sun was warm and the sky cloudless. It was a beautiful day, but Dev didn't see any of it. Within a minute, Gordon had taken his position in the center of the raft, grabbed the long oars and guided the raft to the very center of the river. The bridge across the Snake was just ahead of them. There was tourist traffic on it, but no one would hear her if she yelled for help. Oh, God, if only Sloan knew!

They drifted silently beneath the busy bridge. There was a lot of foot traffic on it. As they floated beneath it, Dev saw a young boy of ten lift his hand and wave at them. She didn't dare respond. Others were watching them, as well, some clicking photos with cameras or cell phones. Dev knew many tourists had never seen a river raft before. If only one of them could get those photos to a ranger, someone would know she'd been kidnapped.

The swift current carried them far away from the bridge. Dev heard Gordon chuckle as he expertly guided the raft, keeping it in the center of the Snake.

"Well, we're outta the park boundary. No one is gonna know where you've gone." He laughed heartily, enjoying the triumph of his plan. "They'll never find us."

SLOAN WIPED THE SWEAT off his brow with the back of his sleeve, straightened up and patted the last mule that had to be shoed. The morning sunlight lanced brightly into the huge barn, where the doors were open at both ends to allow air to circulate throughout the facility.

He placed his tools in a wooden box, pulled off his thick leather gloves. He took a well-earned swig of water from a bottle nearby. Just as he finished drinking nearly all of it, his cell phone vibrated in his rear pocket. He pulled off his leather apron, dropped it on his toolbox and answered the call.

"Sloan here."

"Sloan, this is John Welborn. Dev is missing."

Instantly, Sloan's heart dropped. "What happened?" he demanded, swiftly leaning over, picking up his tools and placing them in the tack room. Moving to the mule in the ties, he unsnapped the animal and led him by his halter out to the corral where the other mules were standing.

"Dev didn't come back from the bathroom," John said, his voice taut. "I went in there to find her just now. We found her pistol and Buck knife in a sink. No signs of a struggle."

"Damn," Sloan growled. "Have you called Cade? Alerted the rangers at the entrance and exit gates?"

"Already done. I need you down here. Can you make it?"

"I'll be there in five minutes," he rasped, settling a black baseball cap on his head. Sloan clicked off his phone, running down the long, wide concrete breezeway. In thirty seconds, he was at his truck, climbing in. *Dev!* Gordon had somehow gotten into the park and found her. His heart wrenched in his chest as he hauled the truck out of the parking lot, tires smoking and screaming.

By the time Sloan pulled into headquarters, there were two black sheriff's department Tahoes there along with four green forest ranger pickups. He parked and got out, trotting over to the group of men and women. He spotted Shelby Carson, a well-known tracker and deputy sheriff. Her blond ponytail stood out from the men huddled together.

Cade Garner looked up as Sloan squeezed into the group. "We're assuming Gordon kidnapped Dev."

"Yeah," Sloan growled, hands on his hips. "What's being done to find them?"

Shelby said, "Sloan, we've got two deputies canvassing the bridge to the gate. It goes across the Snake River."

She gestured toward the visitor's center across the street from them. "Two more rangers are canvassing people there to see if they saw Dev and Gordon."

"Have you got photos?" Sloan demanded, finding it hard to stand still.

"Yes," Cade said. "We're asking everyone for their camera cards if they photographed the river area. The rangers are taking the cards over to the visitor's center to dump them and see if there are any photos of Dev on them with Gordon."

Sloan looked to John. "There were no signs of a struggle in the restroom?"

"None," John said, his voice defeated. He gave Sloan an apologetic look. "I'm sorry. I thought she'd be safe enough going to the bathroom by herself. It's only a hundred feet down the hall from our office."

Giving a curt nod, Sloan said, "It's all right, John." Most men wouldn't have gone into the women's bathroom. The man looked contrite enough about it, heavy guilt in his expression.

"So, Dev is unarmed. Defenseless against Gordon," Sloan said to them. "Is there anyone around HQ that might have seen them leave? A strange truck that wasn't usually in the parking lot?"

"We're on that," John promised quickly. "We're canvassing right now."

And every second, Dev was in greater and greater danger. Frustration tightened his throat. "I'm taking Mouse to see if we can't track her scent." Sloan had left Mouse with one of the rangers at the front desk of HQ. His dog would lie on his bed behind the counter and bother no one.

Shelby said, "Great idea! I'll go with you." She looked over at Cade who gave her the nod of approval.

Sloan trotted quickly down to the main entrance of the HQ, Shelby on his heels. He lifted his hand to Ann, the ranger behind the desk. She was stressed, having heard what happened to Dev.

"You're coming for Mouse?" she asked, hope in her voice.

"Yes," Sloan said. He moved around the counter. Ann handed him the leash and he bent down, snapping it onto Mouse's leather collar. Shelby waited nearby.

"I think we should start at her office desk, Sloan. Let Mouse pick up her scent. Then follow it wherever it goes."

"Right," Sloan said, guiding Mouse from behind the counter. The dog knew he was now in combat mode— ears up, eyes glinting, panting with excitement. He followed closely at Sloan's side as they walked down the hall and into the office where Dev was working. The rest of the employees all looked up. Sloan could see the worry in their faces.

"Mouse," he ordered, pointing to Dev's chair at her desk.

Instantly the Belgian Malinois sniffed it and whined, wagging his tail briskly.

Good, he had her scent. "Seek," he ordered Mouse, releasing the tension on the leash.

Nose to the floor, Mouse leaped and strained against it, practically dragging Sloan down the highly waxed hallway. People saw the dog coming and stopped, hugging the wall, giving him the room he needed. Sloan nodded to the rangers, silently thanking them for getting out of the way. Every second was of importance.

Shelby followed swiftly as Mouse leaped up on the bathroom door, whining.

Sloan allowed the dog in and he moved to one stall, then out to a sink, and then he wanted out of the door again. Sloan propped it open with his foot and Mouse was sniffing once more. He made a sharp right, leaping at the glass entrance door.

Shelby unholstered her pistol and took the safety off, wary as she looked outside. "This leads into the woods."

Grimly, Sloan said, "Yes." He threw open the door. Mouse leaped outside. Within a minute they were deep in the woods, following Dev's scent. Shelby was jogging to keep up, always alert, looking around. Sloan didn't want to take out a pistol yet. Shelby was a fine deputy and he felt she had this situation under control.

They broke out of the woods, Mouse whining and lunging against the leash as they ran across the asphalt parking lot toward the river. Sloan's mind tumbled over why Gordon had led her here, to the river. No one could swim across it since the current was too strong. The river was well known for swimmers who'd thought they could cross it drowning.

Mouse lunged down the concrete boating ramp. He turned right and then twenty feet down along the thin edge of the gravel and sand bank, he sat down, looking downstream toward the bridge less than a quarter of a mile away.

Sloan jerked to a stop, his heart hammering in his chest. Shelby skidded to a halt, holstering her pistol. *What the hell!* Terror flooded Sloan as he craned his neck, looking as far down the winding river as he could. He saw no raft on it. Looking upstream, he noticed two tourist rafts coming into the landing ramp, their float trip at an end.

"Oh, no," Shelby breathed, giving him a horrified look, "he had a raft!"

"Yes," Sloan rasped, his hand clenching the leash until his joints ached. "He had this all planned. He had a raft, went in that rear exit door and waited for her. He could have easily seen me drop her off at HQ this morning." Anguish soared through him. Sloan couldn't let his emotions dictate his behavior. *Not now.* Dev's life was on the line. Turning to Shelby, he said, "You have a helicopter. Right?"

"Already ahead of you," Shelby assured him, pressing on her radio attached to the shoulder of her shirt. "I'm calling Cade now. We need to get it up in the air and follow the Snake River downstream. They're on it somewhere."

Sloan looked at his watch. "Fifteen minutes have gone by," he muttered. "The Snake is a fast river. They could be a mile or more down it."

Nodding, Shelby made the call to her boss. Her voice was husky with urgency.

Sloan listened, giving Mouse a healthy pat and praise for his good work. The dog looked up, eyes shining with happiness, pink tongue lolling out the side of his mouth. Sloan listened intently to the radio conversation. Cade was going to get the helicopter up and it would land here, near HQ, where there was a helipad. Hope rose sharply in Sloan. The faster they could find Dev, the more chance they had of finding her alive.

How could this be happening? He rubbed his chest, the pain in his heart so real he thought he might be experiencing cardiac arrest. He'd just found the woman he wanted to spend the rest of his life with. Why hadn't he told Dev that? Why had he hesitated? Life was so precious and no one knew better than Sloan that it could be snuffed out in a millisecond. Why the hell had he hedged his bets and not shared how he really felt toward her? He'd thought it would be too soon. That Dev would see it as just another pressure she had to deal with presently. Dammit!

His reasoning had been good and solid. More than anything Sloan hadn't wanted to distract Dev with personal things. But now, it was too late…

"Okay," Shelby said, pleased as she looked over at him, "it will be at least twenty minutes before the Black Hawk will arrive. They've got the helo crew on call and they'll get there as soon as possible."

Nothing would be soon enough as far as Sloan was concerned, but he harnessed his violent anxiety. "That sounds good, Shelby. Thank you." He reached out, touching her arm. The woman smiled sadly at him.

"I can't know what you're going through, Sloan, but I can see it in your face. Dev means a lot more to you than you've let on."

Turning, he asked Mouse to stand and come to his side. "I love her, Shelby, pure and simple." He followed the deputy across the thin strip of the bank and then they climbed the boat ramp, heading quickly toward the HQ once more.

Shelby gave him a compassionate look. "Listen, love has its way with us. I never expected to fall in love with Dakota. It sneaked up on me."

"Same thing happened between Dev and me," Sloan admitted, unable to keep the strain out of his tone. "It happened so fast."

Shelby smiled a little. "It did with us, too. Out of the blue. It took a few months and me being in jeopardy for both of us to get it."

"I feel a little better, then," Sloan told her wryly as they moved down toward the other end of the building. Beyond it was a huge cleared area that had an asphalt landing pad for helicopters. There was a white circle painted in the center of it, a guide for the helo to safely land. "That's the way it happened to us."

Shelby placed her hand on his shoulder as they came upon Cade, who was waiting nearby. "Does Dev know you love her?"

"No." Sloan wiped his mouth, sadness serrating him. "I didn't want to tell her just yet, Shelby. I thought it was too soon." He gave her a pained look. "I didn't want to distract her from what was going on with Gordon being in the area."

"And that was the right choice to make," Shelby said firmly, giving him a sympathetic look. "Don't feel guilty about it."

Sloan drew to a halt near Cade. How could he *not* feel guilty about it? Saying nothing, he turned to Cade. "I want to go along with my dog."

"Already a done deal," Cade promised. "The chopper can handle the three of us, plus Mouse. They've got M-16 rifles on board, ammo, and we're set." He glanced at his wristwatch. "Another fifteen minutes."

Fifteen minutes. Sloan stood there, feeling like they had to hurry, but everyone was doing the best they could right now. Out of the corner of his eye, he saw a ranger coming toward them with a set of parents and a ten-year-old boy.

Sloan remained near Cade as the ranger showed Cade

a digital photo that the parents had taken earlier on the
bridge. Eyes narrowing as he looked across Cade's
shoulder, Sloan saw a river raft. His heart plummeted
with fear. There was Dev sitting in the front of it with a
stricken look on her face. Gordon was at the helm with
the oars in his hands behind her, a look of triumph on
his face. Rage flowed through Sloan. He looked closer,
and to his relief, he didn't see any injuries on Dev's face.

Cade praised the family and thanked them for their
information. He had the ranger take their camera card so
they could make copies of it and then email it out to all
of law enforcement, not only in Teton County, but anywhere the Snake River flowed further south of the park.

Sloan heard the approaching Black Hawk helicopter
that had Teton Sheriff painted in bright yellow on the
shining black surface of the fuselage. Luckily, Mouse
had been on many helo trips and would remain calm.
Right now, Sloan wished he had the working harness on
his combat-assault dog, but the leash would have to do.
Urgency thrummed through Sloan.

*Hold on, Dev. Just hold on. Don't make Gordon
angry. Just be quiet and try to hang on...*

CHAPTER NINETEEN

JUST THE LAP, lap, lap of water against the inflatable raft would lull anyone into a tranquil state as they floated down the Snake River. Anyone except for her. Dev felt the radiating rage and hatred of Gordon against her back, that oily, suffocating sensation that made her swallow hard and nearly choke on it. Sitting tensely in front of him in the bow, she willed her hands out of being clenched fists, her mind running wild with ways to escape.

"Where are we going?" she demanded, twisting a look up toward him.

"I've got my car parked about six miles from here. That's where we're headed."

She bit down on her lip, trying to discreetly look at the river they were on. The water was a dark, opaque green because of the glacial water that ran between its banks. If they got to his car, Dev knew she would be lost. She had to escape before that. But where? How? It wasn't lost on her Gordon had a pistol on his hip and he'd use that Glock on her if she tried to escape.

She had to try. Dev couldn't stand the other choice. She'd already felt his strength, his roughness and his hands hurting her. And he'd hurt her ten times more this time. And then, he'd kill her. Not the way she wanted to die. Dev stared in the face of her lousy choices. If she tried to escape, Gordon would shoot to kill. An image flashed across her mind, of her lying on the bank, bleeding out, sending chills down her back. And yet she'd faced death every day in Afghanistan. So what was the difference?

Dev understood this was a life-and-death war, and that she was in combat once more. She had to raise herself mentally to that level in order to make a daring attempt to escape. Looking at the long, straight stretch of water, she noticed forest on either side of the Snake. The banks were about ten feet high, made of gravel and sand. It would be hard to climb swiftly because of all the loose rock. Dev needed an island to appear. They were dotting the river off and on. More important, she needed to distract Gordon. Or push him out of the raft and into the freezing water as she leaped out the other side of it to escape.

Dev couldn't do it without a nearby island, because if they were both in the water, Gordon would try to come after her and drown her. No, she had to have an island because the water would be shallow on her side of the raft and deep on the other side. Mind racing, Dev tried to concoct a plan that would get her to shore. Once there, she could run for the other side of the island, swim or run through the shallow water between it and the bank. And then scurry up and over it and disappear into the woods. From there, she thought she would go north, run within the forest paralleling the Snake River and head back toward the Grand Teton Park entrance and that bridge across it. She estimated they were a good one and a half miles away from the bridge at this point.

God, it was such a risk! Her heart ached as she thought of Sloan. How much she loved him! Desperation clawed through her because more than anything, Dev wanted a life with this man. She knew by now Sloan had probably realized she'd been kidnapped. And she knew he'd move heaven and hell to find her. Everyone would. That gave her some solace, but not much. Time was of the essence. Once Gordon got to his car, abandoning the raft, no one would ever find her. She wanted to cry. Her eyes were burning with tears, but Dev forced them back. She had to focus. Had to wait for an island to appear.

As the Snake River made a lazy curve to the right, Dev spotted a small island filled with ten-foot-high willows growing across it. On the other side of the oval-shaped island, she saw about five feet of water between it and the bank. The bank was high and gravelly. That would slow her ascent. Her mouth went dry.

This was her chance.

Even more hopeful? The thick stand of willows. Glancing out of the corner of her eye, not wanting to tip off Gordon, Dev saw that on the right side of the raft the water was deep. She strained to see how shallow it was on the left side. If the water was too deep, she could be swept out to the center of the river, carried downstream, unable to reach the island in time.

Her heart rate arced upward. She heard the drumming beat of it in her ears. Adrenaline began to shoot into her bloodstream, making her feel tense and rigid.

Oh, God, let this work. Please…

The moment the raft's nose came parallel with the gravel island, Dev turned suddenly, leaping to her feet and violently shoving her hands at Gordon's chest.

He yelped in surprise, dropping both oars. He teetered for a moment.

Dev watched him fall backward into the raft instead

of into the water. It was impossible to get to the pistol he carried. She groaned.

She had to make a break for it now!

Leaping out of the raft, she splashed into knee-deep water. Flailing, sobbing for breath, Dev scrambled up onto the island, lunging for the safety of the willows.

Gordon screamed, "*Stop!* You bitch! I'm going to kill you!" He rolled over on his hands and knees as the raft started to turn around in the swift current. Reaching for his Glock, he yanked it out of the holster.

Dev dove into the thick willows. The thin, flexible branches smacked against her body, stinging her face, whipping against her arms and neck. She dug the toes of her boots into the soggy soil, unable to stand. Scrambling on her hands and knees, she heard Gordon's curses behind her.

Just as she reached the other side of the willows, she heard the *pop*, *pop*, *pop* of his Glock going off. No! Had he gotten out of the raft? He could have and Dev knew it. And if Gordon did, he'd easily catch her. And then he'd kill her. With a small cry, she shoved to her feet, her knees shaking so badly she was afraid she couldn't run at all. The five feet between the island and the bank was shallow! Leaping into it, Dev surged forward in the ankle-deep water.

Lunging for the bank, she heard the gun go off again. Just as she clambered unsteadily onto a rocky and sandy slice of cliff and bank, her left arm went numb. Dev paid no attention to it, her focus on climbing the six-foot bank looming in front of her. She grabbed at a small bush sticking out of it, hauling herself upward. Her breath exploded from her. Slipping, falling, hauling herself up that slope, she wriggled on her belly to slither over it.

Pop, pop, pop!

Bits of dirt shot up in geysers all around her.

With a cry, Dev jerked a look across her shoulder. Gordon was on the raft, firing at her. He was past the island, the raft pulled by the current into the center of the swift-moving river. Relief plunged through her. She could do this! She could make it to the forest line in time!

Grunting, she scrambled, thrusting one toe of her boot into the soft grass, heaving herself forward. She sprinted, crouched, wove and raced into the dark forest. And she didn't stop there.

Pop, pop, pop!

Bark exploded right in front of her. Slivers of bark struck her face and neck.

Screaming, Dev stumbled and fell over a fallen limb, her hands automatically coming up to protect her face.

As she slammed into the pine needles on the ground, the breath was knocked out of her.

Dazed, Dev rolled over on her back, gasping for air, floundering weakly, trying to get her breath back. Looking up, she saw Douglas firs surrounding her, their narrowed tops like spears pointing up at patches of blue sky above her.

Get up! Get up! Run!

Dev groaned, forcing herself onto her hands and knees, reeling. She knew Gordon would try to get the raft to this side of the shore and then come after her with a vengeance. She had to put as much distance between them as she could. Her knees were wobbly. Her left arm ached. Ignoring her body's protests, Dev felt a surge of adrenaline shoot through her and she got to her feet. Mouth tight with determination, she dug in, hurling herself north, running hard.

Dev didn't know how long she ran, only that she wanted to put as much distance between herself and Gordon as possible. There was no more firing from the Glock. It would be impossible to hit her from this range with thousands of trees so closely packed together. Focusing, she kept her gaze down, intent on not being tripped up by another fallen limb on the floor of the forest. Even more, she had to be quiet. But that was impossible, and ragged, noisy gasps tore out of her open mouth as she ran.

For a moment, Dev was disoriented. Where was the Snake River? She was deep in the belly of the forest and it had closed in on her. So many people got directionally confused in a situation like this, and she was no stranger to it. Slowing for a moment, she rested her hands on her knees, bent over, trying to catch her breath. It was so hard to hear anything! Her heart beat was pounding furiously in her ears.

Her gaze caught the sight of blood on her upper left arm. Frowning, Dev straightened. *What?* Shock bolted through her. She'd been hit by a bullet! Blood was staining the upper sleeve of her shirt, dribbling down her forearm.

Dammit!

Dev tried to assess her wound. It had bled a lot. Had the bullet hit an artery in her upper arm? Sudden terror deluged her. Jerking her glance around, she knew she had to do something fast or she might bleed to death. Gasping for air, she peered into the forest, trying to find a place to hide in case Gordon was tracking her. Dev wasn't sure he could track, but most rangers had that skill in place, more or less.

Spotting a bunch of bushes at the edge of a tiny opening in the forest, she realized it was willows growing at the edge of a swamp. If she could hide behind the screen of those willows, she'd be undetectable unless she made too much noise. She trotted toward it, worried about the numbness of her arm. It wasn't broken, but the bullet had done damage to her. *Oh, God...*

The closer Dev got to the willow stand, the spongier the ground became beneath her boots. As she pressed her hand over the bullet wound, she felt the pain now beginning to appear because her adrenaline was fading from her bloodstream. She rounded the end of the stand. In front of her was a small pond. Moving parallel to the center of the twenty-foot-long stand, Dev found a rock sticking out of it, and it was flat enough for her to sit down upon.

Her knees felt like jelly and she knew she was exhausted from her efforts. Having no idea how long she'd run, she began to try to unbutton her shirt. Her fingers were trembling so badly she had a lot of trouble. Worse, her fingers on her left hand felt wooden and nearly unresponsive, making it harder to slide a button through a hole. It felt like it took forever. Dev worked the shirt off her shoulders and pulled it off, laying it across her lap. She got a good look at the bullet wound. Thank God she'd been in the military or she'd probably be freaking out completely by now.

It was a through-and-through, meaning the bullet had passed through the meat of her arm without striking the bone and breaking it. All that was good news, but she continued to critically examine the area. Blood was oozing out quickly and that told Dev the bullet had probably nicked a major artery. And blood loss over time could kill her. She leaned down, washing her hands in the puddle of water around her boots, wiping them off on her gabardine trousers.

Lifting her head, she listened, her hearing becoming better as she rested and her heart rate subsided. There was a blue jay in the distance, shrieking a warning. Was it Gordon coming after her? Terror shot through Dev. She forced herself to examine both ends of the bullet wound. On the inside of her arm, it was barely bleeding. Most of the loss was on the other side. Dev knew what she had to do. She'd made friends with an 18 Delta combat medic in Afghanistan. He'd shown her how to stuff a wound with cloth to help halt the bleeding. She also remembered that if an artery was sliced in two by shrapnel or a bullet, the ends of it would close within a few minutes—usually. The only way it wouldn't close within minutes of being torn was when the artery was sliced cleanly through and not torn open at an angle. Then it wouldn't automatically close down and halt the bleeding. Was this what happened to her? Or was it a just a nick? Dev didn't know.

She grabbed the end of her shirt and jerked hard at it, trying to tear it. Without her Buck knife, which was an essential tool to have in situations like this, she had nothing to rip the material. Frustrated, she saw a small branch from a fir tree nearby. It had a jagged end. Picking it up, she jammed it repeatedly into the material until the fabric began to fray. Finally, there was a hole in it and she took her fingers, jerking it again and again until it opened up and tore. In minutes, she had a strip of material. Taking a deep breath, knowing it was going to hurt like hell, Dev gritted her teeth and jammed the piece of fabric into the wound.

Fire and agony tore through her arm. Gasping, closing her eyes, she continued to jam it into the hole to stop the bleeding. Nausea stalked her. Dev knew pain could make a person vomit, as well as faint. She couldn't stop! She had to arrest the bleeding or she'd die from it sooner or later. Grunting with pain, Dev leaned her head downward, feeling dizzy as she punched the material as deep as she could into the hole.

Feeling faint, Dev groaned and sank her head against her knees, feeling dark spots dancing and edging her tightly shut eyes. She shoved the material into the other side of the wound. For the next five minutes, she did nothing but try to handle the grating pain, the throbbing in her upper arm, to breathe through it and fight off the faintness. Damn, it hurt! But Dev needed this rest. Needed to ramp down and think. No longer did she feel a trickle of warm blood down her arm or dripping off her fingers as she allowed that arm to hang loose and free at her side.

Slowly lifting her head and opening her eyes, Dev critically studied her wound. The blood had halted, thanks to the material inside the bullet holes. She took a shaky breath, leaned over and sluiced water over her arm, which washed away the blood. Knowing she had to drink as much water as she could, she decided she would walk around the small pool later and drink her fill. The water would have bacteria and parasites in it, most likely. She wrinkled her nose. Dev didn't exactly want them inside her, but on a survival scale, she knew it would take two to three days for any of what she drank to give her symptoms. And if luck held for her, she'd find that bridge within an hour or so. Then she could take medicine to kill the bugs inside her.

Pulling on her shirt, Dev slowly rebuttoned it with

badly trembling fingers, her hearing aimed at the sounds around her. Everything was so quiet in the forest right now. Dev heard the soft whisper of wind through the tops of the firs above her. It was always a soothing sound to her. She no longer heard the blue jay. They were her best early-warning system if someone was nearby. But jays weren't always present. Allowing the shirttails to hang, Dev pushed to her feet. Standing still, she listened intently. Her knees felt stronger, not so wobbly any longer. Pain was a constant throb in her upper arm. Nothing she couldn't work with.

She moved slowly, not wanting to make any sloshing sounds. Dev knew she would need to expose herself at the end of the willow stand in order to get to the other side of the pond. Hesitating, she crouched down, hidden, gazing around.

Where was Gordon?

He wouldn't give up on her. He'd beach that raft on this side of the river sooner or later. He hated her. And she'd seen the murder in his eyes for her. Shivering, she slowly rose to her full height, making no quick movements. She could be spotted if she moved too quickly. Worrying about how close Gordon was, if he was ahead of her somewhere, Dev made it to the other side of the pool. She knelt down and cupped water into her hands, drinking silently. Always, after every drink, she'd halt, look around, and when satisfied no one was nearby she'd drink another handful of water.

Her senses were wide-open and ultrasensitive. Dev could feel that oily, heavy feeling around her, knew it was Gordon.

Where is he?

BART HALTED, BREATHING HEAVILY. He'd holstered his Glock and maneuvered the raft from the center of the Snake River to the left bank half a mile down from where Dev had made her escape. Rage boiled through him. He was pissed off at himself that he'd underestimated her courage, her will to survive. Hauling the raft up on a sandbar so it wouldn't be taken out again, he quickly cut swaths of willow and covered it, trying to hide it. It was easy for the long blade of his Bowie hunting knife to slice through the thin willows. In no time, he had the bulk of the raft covered. Law-enforcement officers would have realized Dev had been kidnapped by now. Bart understood the game. They would be trying to find them, no question. Tugging at the raft, he moved it close to the willow stand, trying to make it look like a part of it. The raft was a dark green, so camouflage-wise, it blended in well. They'd use a helicopter if they somehow found out they'd escaped via the Snake River by raft.

Looking at his handiwork, he felt the urgency to locate Dev. She was a helluva lot smarter than he'd given her credit for. The first time he'd jumped her in the barn, she'd surprised him there, too. Anger fueled him as he hoisted the heavy backpack onto his shoulders and strapped it around his waist. Grimly, he looked north, figuring she would try to head back to the bridge to get help. She was smart enough to know to do that. His tracking skills weren't good and that worked against him. He figured she'd parallel the river. But people got lost in the forest, too.

Pulling out his compass, he made a check and then pocketed it. He had plenty of food, water and ammunition for five days. Dev had nothing. No water. No food.

And he hoped like hell he'd winged her when he'd shot at her with his Glock. But he didn't know for sure. Moving along the bank, Bart didn't dare remain in sight and angled toward the edge of the forest about twenty feet away. He'd stay within the tree line and trot northward. Sooner or later, he had to run into her.

Keeping his hearing locked on to the natural sounds around him as he trotted into the tree line, Bart knew if he heard the sudden cry of a blue jay somewhere ahead of him, it would lead him to where Dev was located. As he loped along, feeling strong and vital, Bart smiled a little. He'd find her, no question. It was just a matter of when. If she made the mistake of coming out of the forest, driven by thirst from her run, he'd easily see her heading for the river. His gaze swung from the bank of the river and into the gloomy forest. Where was the bitch?

He had all kinds of fantasies about what he'd do after he found her. Rape her first. Beat the hell out of her afterward. And then put a bullet into her head. Yes, that satisfied him. That would fulfill the revenge that had eaten at him since she'd put him in prison by testifying in court against him.

DEV KEPT UP a slow, steady trot. She had no food to power her and if she tried to run fast, she'd deplete her strength very quickly. As much as she wanted to run as fast as she could, she didn't dare. There was very little to eat in a forest and she knew it. Her only chance was to get to the Snake River and look for freshwater mussels. She'd never be able to catch a fish with her hands, that was for sure. Her left arm was screaming like a banshee now, and every time she pumped it forward and back as she trotted, the pain jagged up into her shoulder. If only she had some aspirin to dull the pain a little.

Keeping her mouth open as she jogged, Dev tried to remain a quiet shadow within the embrace of the forest surrounding her. Right now, she was angling, she hoped, toward the west, trying to find the Snake River once again. Light played funny tricks on someone in a forest and one was never sure what direction they were really moving in. Wishing for a compass, Dev swore if she ever got out of this, she would always carry a small one on her person at all times in the future.

Her mind moved to Sloan. What was he doing? Did he know she'd been kidnapped by Gordon yet? Was Cade Garner involved? She recalled that little boy on the bridge waving at her, his parents photographing her in the raft. Was it at all possible that the rangers or the deputies had been shown that picture?

Her heart swelled with a fierce love for Sloan. Would she ever see him again? Would they find her someday in these woods, dead? Grief and loss sheared through Dev. All she wanted was to get home to Sloan's arms, to be with him in his bed, to be loved by him and to love him fervently in return. Was it too much to want? Was it that she didn't deserve love for some unknown reason? Dev had always tried to do right by others. She never lied, cheated or stole from people. Well, maybe she did tell white lies so as not to hurt other people, but that was the extent of it.

Mind swinging back to her family, she wondered if someone had contacted her mother, Lily. She'd be devastated by the news. Dev didn't care one whit what her alcoholic father thought one way or another. But she did care for and love her mother. What must she be going through knowing she was kidnapped? Tears burned in her eyes again. The horrifying reality that she might not ever see Sloan or her mother again tore through Dev. The anguish was real, like a knife slowly twisting savagely in her quickly beating heart.

But as she trotted over the slippery pine needles, taking her time, keeping focused and keeping her pace steady, Dev felt indomitable will rising within her. She deserved to live! She deserved to have a chance with Sloan! Knowing he loved her just as much as she loved him, Dev wanted a second chance with him. To tell him in person that she loved him. Just let her survive this. Let her get back to Sloan, talk to her mother on the phone, reassure her that Dev was okay.

Wiping her sweaty upper lip with her fingers, Dev felt a trickle of perspiration down her temples, as well. She kept a lookout for more water. She didn't dare show herself between the tree line and the river. The likelihood was slim she'd find another pond. While ponds did exist in this forest, they were few and far between insofar as she knew. But Dev was new to the Tetons and didn't know the region intimately. If only there was another water source within an hour of her, it would help. But like with everything else, Dev knew there were no guarantees. *None.*

Swinging her gaze from side to side, Dev wondered where Gordon was. Could he have gotten ahead of her? A cold terror jagged through her and Dev felt hunted. She could feel him near. How near? If only she knew! She was constantly looking for a place to hide in case he suddenly showed up. What would she do? Try for the river? Run and leap into it?

Her clothes and boots would drag her down. Her left

arm was only partially usable and the Snake had a strong current. Dev knew she would tire quickly, swiftly get hypothermia, and she could drown before ever reaching the other bank. Plus, Gordon had a pistol. He could stand on the bank and fire at her. And rangers knew how to shoot accurately because they trained with pistols all the time.

Disheartened by her options, Dev buckled down and kept her pace no matter how weak her legs were beginning to feel. Now she didn't have adrenaline to support and fuel her. She would crash soon. And when she did, she'd have to rest for at least half an hour…maybe more, before she had the returning strength to push on. Plus, she had no food. But she'd eaten a heavy breakfast that Sloan had made for her that morning, and she was grateful he'd cajoled her into eating more than usual.

Let me live. Please…let me live. I love Sloan. I want to go back to him so badly… Let me live…

CHAPTER TWENTY

SLOAN HELD ON to his deteriorating patience as he stood with Cade Garner at the flight circle where the sheriff's helicopter was landing. It had taken nearly forty-five minutes before the Black Hawk had arrived. Mouse was used to the slapping gusts of wind against him as Sloan hurried forward. The crew chief slid open the rear door of the Black Hawk and Mouse eagerly leaped in like the combat veteran that he was. Sloan followed.

There were two jump seats in the rear of the cabin and he settled into one, guiding Mouse to sit between his opened legs. Cade sat in the other one. He was grateful that the sheriff's deputy had had a spare protective Kevlar vest in his cruiser. Sloan was glad to be wearing it. Prior to boarding, he'd put a bullet in his .45 pistol and then snapped the safety on it. They were handed helmets to pull on and had plugged their cords into the ICS, intercabin system, so the four of them could talk to one another over the noise of the vibrating bird. Sloan placed protective cotton in Mouse's ears for the flight. The sound in the cabin could create deafness in both humans and animals. The crew chief slid the door shut, locked it and gave the pilots permission to take off. In moments, they were lifting off, the gravity pushing them downward in their seats. Mouse sat obediently next to Sloan's leg, panting and alert. He knew what was up. His combat-assault dog thought this was just another mission. It was. To save Dev.

Sloan wrestled with his emotions as the Black Hawk quickly flew to an altitude of one thousand feet, but a little relief slid through him. They were up and now they could begin looking for Dev and Gordon. The pilot swung the bird over the water, and they began to follow the Snake River below them. Cade stood up, walked forward and leaned between the two front seats, speaking to the pilots and gesturing down toward the river.

Sloan moved to the window on his left, craning his neck, gazing down below. From the air, the Snake looked like a lazy, quiet dark green ribbon of a river. But that was nothing close to the truth. The Snake was deep, the currents wicked and powerful. It was a river of consequence, and more than a few people had been fooled, had either nearly drowned or fully given their lives for failing to respect this mighty river. He saw the forest tree line about a hundred feet from the shore. In some places, huge meadows pushed it back a quarter of a mile.

Where was Dev? How was she? Sloan rubbed his chest, his heart aching because he swore he could feel her terror. What would Gordon do to her? He didn't want to go there, the answer too gruesome for Sloan to contemplate. His fingers tightened on the leash as he struggled not to allow his feelings to overwhelm him. If not for his years in the military, Sloan couldn't have been doing what he was doing right now: focusing on the hunt for Gordon. And it was only because of his background that Cade had asked him to come along with his dog. His heart was nearly beating in time with the blades above them.

They had gone a mile and not seen any rafts on the

river. The raft trips began within the Grand Teton Park and ended at the main entrance gate to the park. But no raft tour companies were allowed on this part of the river, so if they spotted someone, it would be Dev and Gordon. Straining his eyes, the sunlight bright and blinding, Sloan tried to peer ahead of the shaking, vibrating helicopter. He saw nothing. Not yet. He wasn't sure what Cade would do if they spotted them. The Black Hawk was a law-enforcement helo and carried weapons on it. He saw the M-16 rifle above the sliding door. And the two pilots and air crew chief were armed, as well.

The other worry Slade had was if Gordon had a rifle. At a thousand feet, the Black Hawk *was* a target. Yet they had to fly low enough, slow enough, to try to find the couple. Gordon was an expert marksman, had been in the Army for four years and had seen a lot of combat action in Iraq. Sloan knew not to underestimate the man in any way. His heart swung to Dev. She was a survivor. She was a military vet and had seen combat many times over in Afghanistan. She would take advantage of any situation to try to escape if she could. She would not go down without a fight. But he felt his heart ripping wide-open with fear for her plight. Gordon was sick and twisted. Sloan was sure he was blaming her for his time in prison, which was what Cade had surmised earlier. And he didn't doubt he had come back to kidnap—and punish—Dev for putting him there.

"There," Cade said, his voice rising with excitement. "Do you see that? It looks like a partially hidden raft on that island!"

Instantly, the pilot swung wide so that Sloan could also see a sliver of a gravel-and-sand island thick with willows across it. Frowning, he saw the nose of a dark green raft partially covered with cut willows. His heart rate amped up. Searching the area, Sloan saw no one around. And he had been watching the tree line all the way down the river in hopes of spotting Dev if she'd escaped Gordon.

"Go ahead and land on that sandbar," Cade ordered the pilots. He twisted a look toward Sloan. "We're going to exit. The helo will take off and they'll search further downstream, but I think Gordon deliberately hid the raft here for a reason." Cade pointed toward the tree line. "Dev might have escaped from him, forcing Gordon to beach the raft and go after her."

Sloan nodded. "Unless this was his destination." He hated saying it, knowing what that meant. If Gordon had some kind of hideaway in these woods, he would be taking Dev to it. His mind didn't want to go there. It just didn't. Giving Cade a grim look, he saw the deputy nod, his mouth tightening. Sloan knew he was thinking the same thing: that Gordon had a hideout somewhere in the forest and he would take Dev to it, rape her and then kill her. His stomach knotted. Nausea rose in his throat and he swallowed several times.

"When we land," Cade told him, "let's see what Mouse picks up. We'll draw weapons as soon as we disembark."

"Got it," Sloan said. He lowered back into the seat and Cade sat down, as well. They would unsafety their weapons outside the bird. The helo took the other end of the sliver of a sand spit and quickly landed. Sloan kept his gaze on the tree line because Gordon could be just inside it with a rifle. He could shoot at the helo or at them once they egressed. He lifted the baseball cap he wore, wiped the sweat collecting on his brow and then settled it back on his head, the bill shading his narrowed eyes.

He felt as if he were back in Afghanistan. Often, Sloan would ride in a Black Hawk, being ferried to an area where black ops was operating. Sometimes, it was with CAG, the Delta Force operators, or the SEALs or Army Rangers. Everyone needed a dog like Mouse when they were hunting down the fleeing enemy. Now, he wished he had his 9 mm Beretta on him, but the .45 pistol was as good, if not better. Just heavier and more unwieldy to use.

"Can we take that M-16 with us?" Sloan asked Cade. He wanted a good military rifle in this mix, not just pistols.

"Yeah," Cade said, "good idea. I'll grab it as we dismount."

Sloan felt a little better. "Gordon was in the Army. He's a good marksman. I don't think he would kidnap Dev without carrying some kind of small arsenal on him."

"I was thinking the same thing," Cade muttered, shaking his head. "He'll have a pistol and a rifle on him, for sure."

Sloan watched the ground come up in a hurry. The pilots weren't interested in staying on the ground long because they, too, were targets. As soon as the tricycle landing gear touched down on the sandbar, Sloan took off his helmet. Cade opened the door, got rid of his helmet, removed the M-16 from above him and hopped out. Sloan got up and Mouse instantly leaped to his feet. In seconds, they were on the sand-and-gravel surface.

Crouching, Sloan followed Cade, who was already putting a bullet in the chamber of the M-16. He was leaving the safety off and in an unknown situation like this, that was smart in Sloan's book. Mouse trotted alongside of him. They entered the thick stand of willows covering the bar. Crouching down on one knee, Sloan heard the whistling engines of the Black Hawk start to shriek as it quickly lifted off, heading across the river, gaining altitude.

The willows slapped Sloan smartly in the face and flailed like stinging whips across his back as he brought Mouse closer to protect him from the swinging branches. The blades were turning at over a hundred miles an hour and giving off bruising gusts, nearly knocking Sloan off his one knee planted into the ground. In less than a minute, the whipping winds and the roar of the helo's two engines eased. Sloan looked to his right where Cade was couched. The deputy had a radio on his shoulder and was checking in with the department, giving them their GPS position. Once done, Cade gave him a thumbs-up and slowly stood. The willow stand was eight to ten feet high.

Sloan got Mouse pointed to the closest area they could get out of the willows and yet remain hidden from the tree line opposite the island. His hearing was keyed and he heard birds singing here and there. That meant nothing was amiss. Only when it became silent around him would Sloan know there was a threatening influence to the birds, who would suddenly stop chirping or singing.

Standing outside the willows, Cade approached him, pointing to his right where the partially hidden raft was sitting. The M-16 was strapped to his back and he held his pistol in his right hand, safety off. Sloan wasn't going to draw his weapon unless it was necessary. Mouse, when on the hunt, became excited and could pull hard on the leash. The dog weighed seventy-five pounds and could jerk and lunge powerfully, almost knocking Sloan off his feet on some occasions.

"Let's check out the raft," Cade said in a low voice. "Let Mouse get a sniff of it."

Mouse leaped forward, hauling hard on Sloan. He kept the dog steady, not allowing him his head. The raft was empty but Sloan allowed Mouse to sniff excitedly around the outside of it. Cade moved forward, pulling the willows away from it so the dog could sniff everywhere.

Mouse whined and sat down, looking up at Sloan with his bright brown eyes.

"He's got her scent," Sloan told Cade, his voice thick with sudden emotion.

"Good," the deputy said, relief in his low tone. He pointed to a bunch of tracks farther down from the raft. "Two sets of prints. Let me get cell phone photos and send them back to base."

Sloan saw the tracks. Forest rangers wore a certain type of boot and it had a certain tread pattern on the bottom of it. Once Cade was done and had stepped back, gesturing him toward them, Sloan released Mouse to follow Dev's scent. He went straight to the mix of tracks. The sand was heavily disturbed and Sloan easily identified Dev's boot. "This is Dev's boot tread," he said, motioning toward it. The other boot had to be Gordon's because it was not the Forest Service tread design and had a much larger print than hers.

"Okay," Cade said quietly, searching the tree line, "take the lead, but let's be alert."

No worries there, Sloan thought as he gave Mouse a hand signal. The dog lunged hard against the short leash. Normally, with a working harness and leash, Sloan would have the dog on a sixteen-foot retractable lead.

But not today. All he had was a six-foot nylon leash. He could feel Mouse's frustration as he tugged and jumped, wanting to rush ahead and follow Dev's scent to find her. He didn't dare let Mouse go because the dog could run much faster than they could and would quickly disappear into the thick forest. Sloan would have no idea where Mouse might have gone. Plus, Sloan knew Gordon was also tracking Dev because he could see imprints in the grass.

"Dev escaped," he told Cade, glancing over at the deputy. "Her tracks are here. Gordon's are paralleling hers. He's following her."

"That's what I thought," Cade muttered, frowning, his gaze searching the gloomy forest just ahead of them.

Sloan didn't want to say the obvious. Had Gordon found Dev? Had he recaptured her? Or was she still running? They entered the pine forest and were quickly closed up within it. Slowing, he could no longer see clear tracks, only impressions left in the soft pine-needle-covered forest floor here and there. Sloan could tell by the way Dev was digging in with the toes of her boots, the length of her stride, that she was running hard. Running to get away from Gordon. Who was now following her.

"Is Gordon a good tracker?" Cade wondered in a quiet tone, his head swiveling, looking for trouble.

"From what Dev told me earlier, he isn't."

"That could work in her favor."

Mouth tightening, Sloan nodded.

God, let it be so.

DEV HEARD WHAT she thought was a Black Hawk helicopter's blades thunking in the distance. Her heart leaped as she heard it coming down the length of the Snake River to her left. She was easily a mile inside the forest and was far from the river. She'd never be able to sprint fast enough to break out into the open, waving her arms, hoping to be seen. The other challenge was Gordon might be close enough to see her bolt from the forest, trying to wave the helo down. He could shoot and kill her.

The risk wasn't worth the reward to Dev. So long as she could keep this pace, avoid being seen—she hoped that Gordon was still a poor tracker—she was going to try to make it to the Teton Park entrance gate and the bridge that led to it. Breath ragged, her calves cramping from the hard trot, she halted near a huge Douglas fir. The girth of the trunk more than hid her. She sat down, resting her back against it, wiping her sweaty face, wincing as she lifted her wounded left arm. Blood was still trickling out of the stuffed wound, but it had nearly slowed to a stop. She narrowed her eyes, but with the treetops so close together, she couldn't even see the helicopter. Praying it was coming from the Grand Teton Park HQ, she heard it fly south.

Was Sloan on board? Frustration made her grimace because she couldn't even see the helo to know if it was the sheriff's department bird or not. Estimating she'd traveled a long way, her heart pounding in her chest, Dev tried to control her terror. She knew without a doubt that Gordon was somewhere behind her. She could feel him, that oily sensation enveloping her head to toe. Shivering, she wanted so badly to step to the banks of the Snake and drink. Her mouth was dry and she was craving water.

Dev couldn't do it. Gordon would probably be close to the tree line, trying to follow her. She waited, listening to the helicopter. The sound became farther and farther away, and her heart dropped. They had to be looking for her! Or was it a civilian helicopter with paying tourists on board giving them a scenic tour of the area? Groaning, wishing she knew, Dev desperately prayed it was the Teton sheriff's helicopter. Sweat trickled into her eyes, burning them. With a muffled groan, she wiped her dirty fingers on the side of her trousers and then cleared her eyes. Blinking rapidly, Dev looked around. Everything was silent. That was a bad sign.

Shoving to her feet, Dev turned and glanced behind her. Her heart was pumping with fear. She didn't want to see Gordon's dark form anywhere near her. Nothing moved. There was no sign of him. Relief sizzled through her. Dev was a target. She knew if Gordon caught sight of her, he'd fire his weapon at her. The only thing in her favor was that the trees were growing close together, making it tough for anyone to sight and shoot. As she pushed herself off from the tree, she felt fully exposed and wished mightily that she had a protective Kevlar vest to keep her back from being an easy target.

The land started becoming bumps of hills here and there. Dev trotted in what she hoped was a zigzag pattern so that her prints would be harder to follow. She made a point of going around the small hills topped with trees. Some of the hills had holes in them, some small, some large, telling her animals of some variety were making their homes in them. It could be foxes, wolverines, badgers or bobcats. Or something much larger: a bear. And if she came upon a grizzly and startled it, the territorial animal could charge her.

Nothing was safe right now and Dev felt excruciatingly vulnerable. There was no defense against the terror she was feeling. She was a hunted animal. Rounding a hill, she saw a much larger one ahead. There was a huge hole in it that had been dug out some time ago. Rocks and dirt were all around it and she recognized it as a bear den. That put her on warning. Every bear had a hibernation spot. Grizzlies normally headed up the rugged Tetons, finding rocky holes, digging deep, to hibernate on the upper slopes. If it was a sow, she would birth her cubs in it. As Dev jogged toward the hill, she wondered if maybe it was a black bear's den, because they intermingled with the grizzlies in this region.

Her arm was aching constantly now, and Dev would check it every now and then for blood leakage. Her fingers on her left hand were stiff and it was hard to flex them. She was sure the muscles that had been destroyed by the bullet were the reason. At least she could feel her fingers, telling her that the nerve had not been destroyed. For that, Dev was grateful.

A sound caught her attention. Instantly, she stopped and hid behind the nearest tree.

What did she hear?

Her heart rate ramped up. Her fingers digging into the rough bark of the tree, she looked around. The sound had been different. Like someone stepping on a limb on the floor of the forest and cracking it. *God, don't let it be Gordon!* Almost paralyzed with fear, Dev remained where she was, her gaze trying to find any movement. And then, her breath choked in her throat as she caught activity to her right.

A huge grizzly bear! With two cubs in tow. And she was less than two hundred feet from where she stood hiding behind the tree.

Oh, God...

Her mind blanked out for a split second. Dev's fingers dug into the bark as she watched the seven-hundred-pound sow moving slowly away from her, heading south. Her two one-year-old cubs, both cinnamon colored, romped and played around their mother. Had the bear picked up her scent? Adrenaline surged through Dev. The bear's most powerful implement was its nose. They had very poor eyesight, but their noses more than made up for that weakness. Which way was the wind blowing? Was she upwind or downwind from the bear?

BART CURSED SOFTLY as he tried to follow the shallow soil depressions on the forest floor. He hated tracking, but that was exactly what he had to do in order to find Dev. It was costing him a huge amount of time. She was somewhere ahead of him. He'd heard the helicopter off in the distance but couldn't see it due to the thick wall of forest. It sounded like a Black Hawk, but he couldn't be sure. Then it flew past him, and the noise disappeared as it went a lot farther south from his position. Probably just a tourist copter on a visual tour of the Tetons, he thought.

As he slowly moved his gaze outward, looking for slight, almost invisible depressions into the pine floor, Bart knew he had to find Dev. He'd been damned surprised at her balls when she nearly pushed him overboard. She was a helluva lot stronger than he'd ever given her credit for. But the look in her eyes had been sheer terror, so he knew her desperation. Because he'd been floundering around in the suddenly tipping raft, he hadn't gotten to his pistol fast enough. Although he'd eventually fired repeatedly at Dev, he wasn't sure he'd hit her. And he probably hadn't, judging from the speed of her escape. Dammit!

The sun was slanting past noon. There was no question she was heading back toward the Teton Park main entrance gate. Gordon estimated it was roughly three miles ahead. But how far ahead of him was Dev? It irritated the hell out of him that she was moving this fast. Women were weaker than men. She shouldn't have gotten so far, so fast. The bitch!

Suddenly, there was movement ahead and to his left. Bart quickly dropped to one knee, pistol ready. What was it? He could just barely see a shadow moving slowly between trees. His eyes widened in shock. A damn bear! And two cubs. Shit! His lips drew away from his teeth as he watched the dark brown sow ambling, nose to the ground, looking for food beneath the surface. Her two cubs were spunky, running playfully around the sow, oblivious to her search for food.

The grizzly was coming straight at him. Son of a bitch! What to do? They were nothing to mess with, that much he knew. And although he carried a .30-06 rifle in a sheath on the back of his rucksack, Bart didn't want to fire at the animal. If he just wounded the grizzly, she'd tear him apart. Raw fear trickled through him.

Cursing softly, Bart lifted his pistol. He fired it about five feet in front of the sow.

The grizzly grunted, jerking sideways at the popping sound. She woofed, stood up to eight feet tall on her hind legs, front paws hanging in front of her with five-inch claws revealed. Testing the air with her sensitive nose, she whuffed. Her cubs scuttled up two different trees, with an instinct to get off the surface of the land where they could get killed.

Bart watched them. The sow had a huge nylon tracking collar around her thickly furred neck. It meant the rangers could track her. And he'd just fired his pistol. But what the hell kind of choice did he have? She was only two hundred feet away from him and Bart knew the bear could suddenly sprint at twenty-five miles an hour, easily overtaking his effort to run away from her. He'd had to fire the pistol! Angry about it, knowing that now Dev would be onto him tracking her, Bart clenched his teeth and watched the bear. She finally got down on all fours, turned and looked at her two treed cubs, and called them down with several grunts.

The babies half slid and half fell down the pine trunks. When they hit the bottom, they rolled, scrambled to their feet and quickly scampered to the bulky safety of their mother. The sow looked around warily, testing the air one more time.

Bart wanted to will the sow either east or west of him. He didn't care which way she went, only that she didn't come *his* way. His breath jammed in his throat, his mind whirling with options. Would he have enough time to grab his .30-06 from his ruck? No. Two hundred feet was a couple blinks of a person's eyelashes. Not near enough time. His hand became sweaty around the pistol. He had five bullets left. The .45 pistol was a good one, but not against a bruin of this size and weight. It wouldn't kill the sow, only enrage her if he emptied the bullets into her.

The sow looked his way, her small eyes studying him intently. Bart wasn't sure she could see anything, as their eyesight was poor at best. She lifted her nose, sniffed once, twice, and then turned toward the river, her cubs scrambling to keep up with her quick, trundling escape.

Wiping his brow, Bart suddenly felt shaky. The hunter had been hunted. And now, Dev knew he was near. But how near was she to him?

CHAPTER TWENTY-ONE

SLOAN JERKED TO a halt, crouching, weapon drawn as he heard the crack of a gunshot at least a mile ahead of them.

Cade hissed a curse, also crouched, intent.

A cold feeling snaked through Sloan. Adrenaline started leaking through his bloodstream. He twisted a look to his side where Cade remained. "Gordon?" Mouse whined, shivering with excitement, sitting but tense, ears pointed toward the gunshot.

"I don't know," he rasped. "There's no hunting right now. Out of season. But that doesn't stop some illegal hunters from doing it, either."

"That wasn't a rifle," Sloan said grimly. "It was a pistol." More than likely, Gordon's. Dev didn't have any weapons on her.

"Yeah, I know."

His gut was screaming at him to get up and start running toward the sound. "I think it's Gordon. He might have found Dev." His voice dropped and he said hoarsely, "She could be in deep trouble. I want to go ahead. Now."

Cade slowly stood up. "Let me call this in. Then we'll take off."

Sloan didn't want to wait but knew he had to. Mouse was whining, jerking and jumping against the leash. Even his dog knew it had to do with Dev. God, had she just been wounded or killed by Gordon? Had the bastard found her? The sound was in alignment with her tracks, that much Sloan knew. And Gordon's tracks were following hers. This was a no-brainer for him, and he chafed as Cade finished his call. The deputy's eyes were narrowed, his face set.

"All right, let's hoof it," Cade grunted, gripping his pistol.

"Let me lead," Sloan rasped.

"I'll be right behind you, watching our back."

Nodding, Sloan unsafetied his pistol. He gave Mouse the signal. The Belgian Malinois leaped mightily against the leash.

DEV JERKED AND nearly screamed when the pistol was fired nearby. It was no more than two or three hundred feet behind her. Instantly, she began to sweat, her heart rate soaring. Sitting paralyzed and crouched up against the wide trunk, she knew it had to be Gordon. The bears had headed south, away from her. Logic told her Gordon would be coming from that direction. And he'd be following her tracks. Her throat ached with tension, terror racing through her.

What should she do? Dev's mind swung to options. None of them were good. If she tried to run now, he might see her. All her years of being in the military, being in danger's path over in Afghanistan for so long, came to the forefront. This was a matter of simple tactics and strategy. She had an enemy nearby. Swinging her gaze around, Dev realized she was completely hidden by the massive trunk. No one could know she was behind it. Her elbows and shoulders did not stick out on either side of it. That was lucky. She had the advantage of surprise.

Shakily wiping her mouth, she heard the grunt and whuff of the grizzly bears, the sound of them running away from her. Had Gordon seen them? Fired his pistol to scare them off? Because a pistol would never bring down a grizzly. And right now, she heard the bears hightailing it in the direction of the Snake River.

Gordon was somewhere right behind her. She moved her head slowly to the right and then to the left, twisting her body slightly, using the trunk to continue to hide her while she carefully surveyed the area. Dev wanted to make sure he wasn't coming at her from an angle because then she'd be a target for sure. If he were following her tracks, then he would be directly behind her. Heart pounding in her ears, it was hard for Dev to hear. If only she could be cool, calm and collected. That wasn't going to happen.

Reaching out in front of her, Dev quietly picked up a four-foot-long, slightly curved branch that had fallen off the tree. It had enough heft and weight to it that Dev knew if she swung it at an unsuspecting Gordon as he passed by her, she could at least knock him out. *Hopefully.* She grimaced as she wrapped her left hand around the limb below her right one, pain arcing up her arm from the slowly bleeding bullet wound. The terror over her strategy made her mouth go dry. She had no one to rely on but herself. There was no help coming that she was aware of.

If she didn't get that pistol away from Gordon, she was dead.

Closing her eyes tightly, Dev willed herself to settle down. Her hearing improved. Would she hear Gordon coming? Was this all her imagination? That oily slime covered her. Dev didn't know, and she held the thick limb in her hands, resting it against the trunk, near her head.

A branch snapped nearby.

Her breath jammed in her throat, eyes widening.

It *was* Gordon!

She strained to hear, not daring to move.

Another, smaller branch broke, slightly to the right and behind of her.

Yes, Gordon was following her tracks, no question. She had gone to the right of the tree.

Slowly easing her head toward the right, trying to catch sight of him before he saw her, Dev choked on her breath. Adrenaline poured through her. Her fingers gripped the limb hard, knuckles whitening. If she couldn't swing it hard enough, Gordon would be conscious and he'd turn and fire, instantly killing her.

BREATH TORE OUT of Sloan's mouth as Mouse tugged mightily, straining to race even faster. The dog was digging up pine needles and soft, damp black earth with his hind legs, trying to move faster than a human could run. Sloan didn't dare allow his dog to run free because Mouse had no Kevlar vest to protect most of his body. He was not going to sacrifice Mouse like that. Instead, he ran hard, stretching his long legs, willing himself forward at top speed. He could hear the heavy footfalls of Cade Garner right behind him. The man was in top shape, like himself.

Sloan swung his gaze right to left, looking for a shape or movement. But Mouse seemed intent on lunging straight ahead. They were no longer visually following the tracks. Instead, his dog was in complete combat mode, his nose close to the ground as he ran on Dev's scent. Sloan's heart hammered in his chest. What if they were too late? What if that one bullet had killed Dev? Anguish ripped through him and he faltered, nearly stumbling. Catching himself, Sloan hurtled forward, pushing himself beyond his physical limit. Tears burned in his eyes and he rapidly blinked them away.

Dev could be lying on the ground, bleeding out. All the horrors he'd seen in his military days in Afghanistan were haunting him right now. Grief and anguish entwined in his heart. He loved Dev. She couldn't be ripped out of his life this soon.

BART CURSED TO himself as he stepped on a second small twig on the forest floor. He knew better. He was distracted by that grizzly bear. He was breathing harder than normal, his adrenaline screaming through him from the close brush with the bear and her cubs moments earlier. He heard a noise to his left as he approached a massive pine tree, its girth huge. Looking anxiously toward the river, he didn't see the sow and her cubs. Relief trickled through him. The grizzly could circle back and attack him from the rear. Sows were known to protect their cubs at all costs, being ten times more aggressive than any male grizzly. Eyes down, Bart caught impressions of Dev's boots as they swung wide of the tree in front of him, so he changed course, turning to follow them. He held the pistol in his right hand, close to his body. The forest was silent. But then, he'd just fired his gun.

Where the hell was Dev? Had she heard the pistol report and taken off ahead of him? Gordon's attention was on the curve of her tracks, looking downward, continuing to follow them.

He heard another sound. A slight one, to his left. Unable to identify it, he turned. Gordon's eyes widened enormously.

Dev swung the club in her hand as hard as she could, bringing all her body weight into it. She'd made a sound by slowly standing up, her shirt catching on a piece of bark at her back. Gordon was angling away from the tree, no more than three feet from her when she'd lifted the limb in preparation. He'd halted and turned toward her.
Too late!
The club smashed into the side of his neck and jaw. There was a sharp cracking sound.

A powerful vibration shot up both Dev's arms as she connected solidly with Gordon. Dev let out a gasp, seeing the murder and hatred in his eyes as he realized it was her. But it was too late for him. The limb was solid and didn't snap as she brought it down with all her might. He uttered a cry, jerking, his knees suddenly collapsing from beneath him.

Dev leaped back, breathing erratically, holding the limb in her white-knuckled hands. She watched Gordon drop into an unconscious heap, the pistol falling out of his nerveless fingers. Leaping forward, Dev kept the limb in her throbbing left hand and kicked the gun away from Gordon with her boot. He didn't move. She saw blood and scrapes along his jaw. The cracking sound was probably the breaking of it or his nose. Or both.

Dev didn't care. Relief splintered through her as she rushed far around Gordon and grabbed the pistol out of the pine needles. After dropping the limb, she made sure there was a bullet in the chamber.

Dev scowled, hearing panting. Lifting her head from

where she stood ten feet from where Gordon lay unconscious, she saw dark shapes running toward her. Blinking, she realized it was Sloan and Cade! And Mouse!
The dog was jerking and leaping wildly in his leash,
desperately wanting to reach her.

Suddenly, her legs felt like mush. Dev collapsed to
her knees, not wanting to faint. But black dots were suddenly dancing in front of her vision. She saw relief etched
deeply on Sloan's face as he raced up to her. Mouse
reached her first, whining and licking her face and hand.
Cade wasn't far behind.

Kneeling down, Sloan gripped her shoulders. "Dev?
Are you okay?"

It was the last thing Dev remembered. The moment
Sloan held her, blackness overwhelmed her.

SLOAN REMAINED AT Dev's side as Cade handcuffed the
still-unconscious Gordon. He'd placed a jacket beneath
her neck to keep her breathing passage open after gently
guiding her limp form to the ground. Sloan had a first-
aid kit on him and used the blanket within his ruck to
cover her and keep her warm since she was clearly in
shock. Because he'd been a combat-assault K-9 soldier,
Sloan had EMT training. He'd taken her blood pressure, which was below normal. Her pulse was slow, too.
Everything indicated she'd fainted. Either from lack of
water or food, or both. All he could do was monitor her
and keep a close watch on her. Dev was so damned pale.
He'd quickly examined her from head to toe, front and
back for wounds. Sloan's heart ripped open when he discovered her bloodied left upper arm. He saw Dev had
tried to stop the bleeding by stuffing the holes with fabric. Mouse lay next to her, opposite him, panting heavily,

his eyes never leaving Gordon. Cade had already called the Black Hawk. It would be twenty minutes before it could land near the GPS coordinates he'd given the pilot, well outside the tree line.

Keeping his hand on her right shoulder, Sloan leaned down, pressing a kiss to her dirty, sweaty cheek. "Dev? Come back to me, sugar. Come on, you're safe now…" He moved his fingers through her stiff, dirty hair. He picked several brown pine needles out of her black, dust-coated locks, tossing them aside. The lips he'd kissed and worshipped were parted and slack. The black lashes fanning out across her wan cheeks made her look like a pale porcelain doll, so fragile. He ached to take her into his arms, but keeping her still was the safest thing for her right now.

Cade came over, leaning down, hands on his knees. "Did she faint?"

"Yeah, I think dehydration played a bigger part than the wound, most likely." He gestured to her left arm. "She's lost blood, but I don't think that much. I already examined her head to toe and there's nothing broken and no more wounds, thank God."

Cade straightened up, his gaze never leaving Gordon. With his hands cuffed behind him, he was going nowhere when he awoke. "I need to find out how far we are from the tree line. Can you keep an eye on both of them?"

"Yes, go ahead," Sloan said.

Cade turned and trotted west, toward the unseen Snake River.

Allowing a gutted sigh to slip from his lips, Sloan moved his fingers in a grazing motion across Dev's cheek. He willed her to return to him, willed her to con-sciousness.

Her lashes fluttered in response to his touch.

Instantly, Sloan's fingers froze. Dev's eyes slowly opened, their green depths cloudy and pupils large and black.

"Dev?" he called, cupping her cheek. "It's Sloan. You're okay. Can you look at me?" And he watched her gaze slowly move toward him. His heart leaped with hope. She slowly licked her lips and a small frown began to form and spread to between her eyebrows. Sloan waited, allowing her time to return, to become fully conscious. He grazed his hand across her hair, caressing her.

"We've got Gordon. You're safe," he rasped. Her eyes began to focus, as if someone were coming home. To him. Sloan managed a shaky smile as her gaze clung to his. "Welcome home, sugar." He leaned over, lightly caressing her lips, needing desperately to feel her warmth and softness. He loved Dev so damned much his chest ached. Sloan had almost lost her. Easing away, he touched her cheek, watching it begin to flood with pinkness. His hopes rose even more. "Do you want to sit up or stay lying down?"

Dev closed her eyes, lifting her right hand, touching her brow. "Gordon?" she rasped.

"Handcuffed." Sloan raised his head, seeing the man had started to regain consciousness. He shifted his attention to Dev, who was dazed. "You didn't kill him. But he's not going to hurt you ever again, sugar." He couldn't stop touching her, knowing it was stabilizing to another human being. Pressing several strands of hair away from her cheek, he watched her eyes wander back to his gaze. Her pupils were still much larger than normal, a thin crescent of green around them, making her eyes appear even larger.

"I—I hit him," Dev whispered.

"You sure did," Sloan praised. "From the looks of the left side of his face, I'd say you've busted up his jaw, but good. It's pretty swollen." He watched Gordon's eyes snap open. He might have been coldcocked by that limb Dev had hit him with, but his eyes were hard. Bart continued to glare at Sloan, jerking and trying to get his hands free. That wouldn't happen.

Pressing his hand down on Dev's shoulder, Sloan murmured, "Cade has a helo coming in to pick us up. Matter of fact, I hear it coming right now. I'm going to tend to Gordon. Stay where you are, Dev."

Dev didn't want to move at all. Her legs felt like sawdust. Her mouth was cracked and dry. She heard Gordon's snarling voice nearby and more movement. Her heart started to pound with terror. Lifting her head, she saw Sloan pull him to his feet by the shoulder of his shirt, his hands cuffed behind him. Sloan took Gordon to the huge pine tree where she had originally hidden. Closing her eyes, Dev felt like the weight of the world had just been taken off her shoulders. Sloan was here. He had come to rescue her. Him and Mouse. And although he hadn't saved her directly, Dev had never been so glad to see him as when she woke up. Her heart swelled fiercely with love for him.

Dev heard something near her head. Turning slowly toward the sound, she met Mouse's cinnamon-colored eyes. He was panting heavily, his flanks heaving in and out. She weakly placed her hand on his brindled side, petting him. Mouse leaned over and eagerly slurped her fingers several times, whining. Dev could feel the dog's worry for her, she was that sensitive. Her brain was coming back online. She remembered now how she had hid and plotted to strike Gordon as he'd passed near the tree where she'd crouched. And she had. Pain was throbbing in her left arm near where Mouse lay, inches between them. Guarding her. Sloan and his dog loved her, and it had never been more evident than right now. She gave Mouse a soft, trembling smile because she felt like the dog wanted to crawl up into her arms and lie on her to protect her. Sloan had placed his body physically between her and Gordon, who was sitting down at the trunk of the pine tree.

A helicopter approaching the area snagged her wandering attention. Sloan rose after making Gordon remain sitting against the tree. Sloan's face was hard and unreadable. Now, she was getting the taste of the warrior deep inside him. Like his dog, who could be so warm and loving, Sloan had a deadly side to him, as well. She managed a wan smile as Sloan crouched down near her head, always keeping watch on Gordon.

"How are you doing?"

"Better… My brain's starting to work again. Do you have any water?"

He touched her hair. "Yeah, hold on…" He moved to his pack beyond where Mouse now lay. Dev automatically tried to get up, pushing weakly and finally rising to her elbows. She was so damned exhausted it was pitiful. Why?

Sloan motioned for Mouse to move. He didn't want his dog's back to Gordon at any time. Instead, Mouse would keep an eye on their prisoner at all times because Sloan sent him over to sit three feet away from Gordon and stare at him, growling. Leaning down, Sloan slid his arms around her shoulders, easing Dev up into a sitting position. She grimaced in pain because he'd brushed that wounded arm of hers.

"Okay?" he asked, supporting her for a moment.

Leaning forward and pulling up her knees, she nodded. When Sloan handed her that bottle of water, Dev thirstily gulped it down, water sliding out of the corners of her mouth, wetting her shirt, but she didn't care. Dev felt Sloan rise. When he returned, she was finished with that bottle and he'd handed her another open one. Gratefully, she took it, drinking nearly all of it, too.

"Thank you," she said hoarsely.

"You were dehydrated," he murmured, picking up both bottles. "That's probably what made you faint."

"Yes," she said, wiping her mouth with her dirty hand. Dev could hear the unseen helicopter landing, the reverberations rippling through the area.

"How close are we to the river?"

Sloan stood and tucked the bottles in his ruck and closed it. "About a tenth of a mile." He glanced up. "Here comes Cade and another deputy." He smiled a little at her. "Ready for a ride?"

Was she ever. And yet, as Dev looked wearily over at Gordon, who sat with hatred in his eyes for her, she shivered inwardly. "Yes, I am," she said, her voice a little stronger. Drinking the water was doing wonders for her. Her heart expanded as Sloan gave her a tender smile meant only for her. He hefted the ruck over his shoulders, strapping it on.

Cade walked up.

"How are you doing, Dev?"

"Better now," she said, her voice still raspy.

Cade told the deputy to go get Gordon to his feet. He turned to Sloan. "Can you take care of Dev? Get her to the Black Hawk? They're going to take her straight to the hospital. I want you with her."

Sloan nodded. "What about you two?"

"Got another helo coming in to take us directly into Jackson Hole," Cade said. He nodded toward Dev. "She's our priority."

Dev felt relief that she didn't have to ride in the Black Hawk with Gordon near her. She didn't trust him. He was angry and snarling at the deputy who had his arm. Mouse stood, growling menacingly at Gordon, his hackles up from his neck all along his back to his tail, which was up and straight out in warning to the man. If Gordon tried to escape the deputy, Mouse would attack and bring him down.

Before she knew what was happening, Sloan leaned down, slipped his arms beneath her legs and back, lifting her easily into his arms. She gasped, her left arm against his chest, pressing against the wound.

"Sorry, sugar," he said roughly, holding her lightly, "we'll be there in just a few minutes." Sloan called Mouse to his side. The dog hesitated, as if wanting to take a chunk or two out of Gordon. Then he turned, obeying his owner.

"I can walk, Sloan," Dev protested.

A faint smile hovered at the corner of his mouth. "I'm sure you can, sugar. But not right now. You're pretty weak from the looks of everything. We need to get you on an IV of fluids."

Just being in his strong, caring arms made Dev relax. The wounded arm continued to throb, but the love in his eyes made her feel so much better. "My legs are wonky," she admitted as he began taking long, lanky strides. Mouse followed obediently at his side, sometimes looking up toward her to ensure she was all right. Wearily, Dev laid her head on Sloan's shoulder, inhaling the sweat and male scent of him. It intoxicated her in the best of ways and she placed her right hand against his chest.

"That's better," Sloan murmured, pressing a kiss to her hair. "All I want you to do is just rest, Dev. You've been through hell."

Closing her eyes, Dev barely nodded. "I was so scared, Sloan. God… He jumped me in the bathroom at headquarters. I never expected him to come after me in there…"

"He's insane," Sloan muttered. He cleared the tree line, where the Black Hawk was idling, the blades slowly turning. Gusts of wind pummeled him and he leaned into them, head down, protecting Dev against him. To his relief, the ER doctor, Jordana McPherson, was just inside the cabin, waiting for them. She was in a dark green one-piece flight suit. He'd recognize that woman anywhere. The fact that she was head of ER at the hospital in town made him feel even better for Dev's sake. Jordana was the best when it came to any type of emergency medicine. A litter had been attached to the inside of the cabin fuselage wall and was waiting for Dev. He looked down and saw Dev was asleep. Completely out. His heart ached with love for her.

At the door of the Black Hawk, Sloan crouched and stepped inside with help from the crew chief. Mouse knew what to do, leaping in beside him, taking a spot between two empty jump seats at the rear of the bird. Jordana smiled a hello at Sloan. She moved aside as he laid Dev on the awaiting stretcher.

Dev woke up from the movement, drowsy and slightly disoriented as Sloan deposited her on the litter. He helped her get the helmet on her head to protect her hearing and then stepped aside so the doctor could examine her. The crew chief slid the door shut and locked it. He gave Sloan a helmet and he plugged it into the ICS unit overhead so he could hear all the conversations going on within the cockpit and rear cabin.

Sitting in one of the two jump seats in the rear, Sloan heard and felt the shuddering of the helicopter surround him as it got ready for takeoff. Mouse sidled in between his legs and he placed his hands on the shoulders of his brave dog. The vibration pulsed through the bird, which relaxed Sloan. He was glad Jordana McPherson was here. Sometimes she volunteered for life flights. The physician took Dev's blood pressure, talking to her, smiling and putting her at ease. He sat there, the afternoon sunlight streaking through the cabin for just a moment as the helo lifted skyward a thousand feet above the forest floor and then banked. The Black Hawk headed across the dark green Snake River and aimed directly at Jackson Hole, to the hospital on the outskirts of it. Sloan began to feel exhaustion stealing upon him, combined with sheer relief. They'd found Dev, but not before she had had to defend herself. He wished he could have been there to do it, but she had an inner strength and toughness honed by her military days. And it had served her well today. He was so damned proud of her.

Mouse lay on the deck, panting and keenly keeping watch over Dev. Laying his hand on his dog's head, Sloan turned and smiled down at the Belgian Malinois. Today, Mouse was all combat-assault dog. Even now, his hand and elbow ached from the dog pulling and lunging constantly, wanting off the leash, wanting to race to Dev's side to defend her. As much as Sloan wished he could have released his dog to run ahead, he knew Gordon would not have hesitated in killing him. And what would that have achieved? Nothing except to alert the bastard that he and Cade were closely trailing him. Mouse would be dead, and Dev would still be in danger. Yet he knew his combat dog could fearlessly take down an enemy. Without a protective Kevlar vest however, Mouse might have died, and nothing would have changed the stakes for Dev's life as a result.

Rubbing his face, Sloan saw Dev close her eyes as Jordana quickly inserted an IV into her good arm to give her fluids she was badly missing. All he wanted to do was take her home, stand with her in a shower, wash her hair, wash her and give her a sense of safety. He was glad he and Cade had believed Dev about her stalker. Gordon had been a potential murderer on the loose. And if Dev hadn't done what she did, she wouldn't be here with him right now.

His gut twisted with angst because Sloan had put off telling her so much more about how he felt toward her. Now, he wondered if, after Dev came out of the shock and trauma of this event, she would still want a relationship with him. Sloan wanted it more than ever. Dev was priceless. She was going to be a permanent part of his life, if that was what she wanted. She owned his heart, whether she knew it or not. The green countryside swiftly skimmed below them, and the four-story redbrick hospital would be coming up soon. Sloan slumped wearily against the seat, allowing his own shock to begin to dissolve.

He saw Jordana lightly move her hand across Dev's mussed hair as she slept. Placing a second blanket across her, Jordana turned and gave Sloan a nod.

"We'll take a look at her bullet wound in a bit," she promised him, standing near Dev's litter. "I don't think she'll need to stay in the hospital for observation."

"That's good to hear," Sloan said. "Dev needs to be home. With me."

CHAPTER TWENTY-TWO

"I DIDN'T THINK I was going to live," Dev quietly told Sloan as she sat with him on the couch in his apartment. He'd made her a cup of coffee after they'd driven home from the hospital. Her left arm had a nice, clean bandage on it, the pain much less because of the medication Dr. Jordana McPherson had ordered for her. Touching her hair, still damp from the shower they'd taken together, Dev wanted nothing more than to be in Sloan's arms. He sat in the corner of the couch, his arm around her shoulders while she tucked her legs beneath her, thick, warm socks on her feet. Mouse and Bella lay nearby on their doggy cushion, their combined gazes trained upon her.

Bella had been beside herself once Dev had come home. Another ranger, John Welborn, had thoughtfully driven her Lab home and brought her to Sloan's apartment. John knew where the extra key was kept at the manager's office and was able to bring Bella into the apartment to wait for their arrival. It was a wonderful welcome home for Dev to have her beloved Lab greet her at the door.

"We didn't even know where you were at first," Sloan confided. He inhaled the fragrant scent of nutmeg in her softly shining hair. It was nearly 5:00 p.m., and he was glad to finally get Dev home where she could begin the decompression from the life-and-death trauma.

"I can't even imagine what you went through, Sloan," Dev whispered, lifting her chin, meeting his dark, worried eyes. He had showered with her, lovingly cleaned her dirty hair, gently washed her from head to toe, because she had problems lifting her wounded left arm above her breast. It was exactly what Dev needed: tenderness. And Sloan didn't disappoint her. His touch has been caring, not sexual, as if he were giving her his energy, his love, with every stroking touch of his fingers upon her stiff, badly bruised body. Being able to climb into a pair of old gray sweatpants and a loose-fitting yellow T-shirt, no bra or panties, was exactly what Dev needed. Sloan had thoughtfully placed heavy warm socks on her cold feet. He'd warmed each of them up first, placing each of her sore, bruised feet between his long, large hands. Her heart spilled open with so much love for this man.

"It took a lot of swift work by a lot of good people," Sloan said, skimming his hand lightly down her right arm. Dev was pensive, still in shock. But her cheeks had color in them now, and there was life returning to her once-cloudy eyes. "I brought Mouse in to trail your scent at the headquarters. He's the one that led us out to the boat ramp area."

Dev smiled down at Mouse. "He helped save me, too."

"Everyone wanted to save you," Sloan said thickly, pressing a kiss to her damp but drying hair.

She sipped the hot coffee, relishing it. Dev knew she could be dead right now, not enjoying the quietness of Sloan's apartment with him, his love for her as he held her on the couch. Dev no longer tried to avoid the fact she had fallen hopelessly in love with this man. "I knew you would," she whispered, leaning her head against his shoulder. "I felt it. I knew I just needed to survive long enough for you to locate me."

"You were within a mile of the bridge, did you know that?"

Shaking her head, Dev said, "No. I must have run a lot of miles, then. I knew the only way to get help was to go back to the bridge and get to the main entrance of the park. And I knew Gordon would know that, too." She dragged in a ragged sigh. "God, Sloan, I was so afraid…"

"I know you were. We all were, too. If we hadn't had that family on the bridge who snapped that digital photo of you and Gordon in the raft, we wouldn't have gotten on this as fast as we did. They were a huge help."

She finished the coffee and eased out from beneath his arm, setting the cup on the coffee table parallel to the couch. Slowly turning around, Dev crossed her legs and reached for his left hand. "I need to fess up," Dev offered, giving him an earnest look. "All the while I was with Gordon, my only thought was escape and getting back to you." Dev squeezed his roughened fingers. "I was so scared I'd die, Sloan. I kept crying off and on as I ran, because I'd never told you that I loved you." Searching his narrowing blue eyes, feeling a shift of energy around him, she gave him a trembling smile. "I knew from the day we met that we were meant for one another. I fought it for a lot of reasons. Mostly because it was too soon for a relationship. But I'm hoping you feel the same. Because life's too short. That was proven to me for a second time in less than a year."

Frowning, Dev looked away for a moment and then met his burning gaze. "Sloan, do you love me?" She was so scared to ask and yet Dev knew this was exactly what needed to be discussed with him. His eyes widened a little, but she saw tenderness come to them. Sloan lifted his hands, framing her face and leaning down, capturing her lips.

Closing her eyes, Dev melted into his strong mouth that slowly, deeply cherished hers. His breath was moist, warm and comforting across her cheek and jaw. Tiny prickles of delight skittered across her flesh where his roughened hands cupped her face. His mouth curved gently across hers, giving to her, letting her know of his love even though he'd not spoken the words yet.

Sloan eased away, drowning in her luminous green eyes, seeing so much love reflected in them for himself. He felt like shouting out his joy. Instead, he gave her a wry look and said huskily, "Dev, you have more courage than I do. I love you. I was going to wait until another time to tell you, maybe later after you got some sleep under your belt."

"I'm always impatient," Dev managed brokenly, tears jamming into her eyes. Sloan caressed her cheek and released her, capturing her two hands in his, holding them warmly within his grasp. "I wanted so desperately to live, Sloan. I swore if I got out of that, it would be one of the first things I'd tell you…"

"It's mutual, sugar. I figured out that the day I met you out there on the highway that I'd started falling for you." He tucked errant strands of her black hair behind her ear. "Then, I got tangled up in my own past, my failed marriage, and I didn't want to rush anything with you. I knew you were still traumatized by Gordon jumping you in that barn, and that you were skittish around men in general. I thought I'd wait it out. I never questioned that I was falling in love with you, Dev. I was."

He shrugged. "It was me. My past, and my coming to grips with it and getting real about it once and for all."

"I kinda figured that," Dev admitted, feeling his love like warm sunshine embracing her. "We both thought we had all the time in the world to let our relationship open up and bloom naturally, but that didn't happen."

Sloan dragged in a deep breath, squeezing her hands gently. "No, Gordon took care of that. We should both thank him for that one thing. For me, it pushed me beyond my past, those experiences that were holding me back. I got very clear about you and me. What I wanted to share with you, Dev." Sloan looked around the quiet apartment and then gazed at her. "I don't want you to be anywhere but living here with me. Are you all right with that?"

Nodding, Dev said, "I'd love to stay with you and Mouse." She gestured to the dogs. "I think from the moment Bella and Mouse met, they liked one another. Maybe," she said, giving Sloan a soft look, "a sign of things to come later between us?"

"Dogs are a lot more up front about it than we were, that's for sure," Sloan agreed, a smile edging his mouth. "I love you, Dev. Never, ever doubt that." He leaned forward, giving her a tender kiss meant to heal her. He tasted her salty tears and withdrew from her lush lips. "Come here," he told her gruffly, turning her around so that she could fit beside him once more. Sloan understood Dev needed to cry and that was a good thing, not a bad thing. He enclosed her in his arms. "Go ahead," he rasped against her hair, "just let it go, sugar. I'm here. I'll hold you through it…"

Sloan's heart winced with each of her sobs. Dev pressed her face against his chest, her arm going around his waist, clinging to him, as if afraid she would be torn away from him again.

Whispering soft words near her ear, he continued to gently wipe the trailing tears away from her cheek, loving her so damn much. As the initial shock began to dissolve, Sloan knew her raw emotions would start coming back online. He had anticipated her weeping. He saw both dogs rise and come over, standing as close as they could get to Dev on the couch. Bella leaned forward, her cold nose against Dev's pant leg, as if to give her doggy support, wanting her to feel better. Mouse sat down, whined a little, worry in his intelligent eyes as he thumped his long, thick tail.

Closing his eyes, feeling her shake, Sloan absorbed her sobs. He was so grateful to be here for her this time. It still bothered him he hadn't been able to protect Dev before, but at least now he could be here to help her through this part of her long healing process. It would take Dev time to work through the combined traumas. She'd come out West to escape Gordon. And he'd followed her. Grimly, Sloan held the woman he loved more than life gently in his embrace. In the coming months, Dev would be fragile, would need his quiet support, his love to shore her up in order to get through all the legal hurdles that would now begin with Gordon's capture. In time, she would have to face him once again, in another trial, and put him away, he hoped, for the rest of his life this time. For whatever sick reasons, Gordon had fixated upon Dev.

Sloan had already made a phone call earlier from the ER at the hospital to Dev's mother, Lily, explaining everything. In another week, Lily would be flying out here to stay and visit with Dev. That was a good thing, Sloan felt. Right now, Dev needed her family. Even though her father was missing in action, her mother had immediately stepped up to the plate and been compassionate toward her daughter. Dev needed the wagons circled around her right now, and Sloan was going to make sure that she would feel not only safe, but cosseted by those who truly loved her. That was when true healing took place.

DEV AWOKE SLOWLY the next morning to sunlight peeking around the drawn drapes of Sloan's bedroom. She missed his presence. She smelled food being cooked outside the partially open door. Her tummy grumbled. Yesterday she hadn't been hungry at all. Sloan had coaxed her to eat a tiny bit of last night's light dinner he'd prepared for them. Shock made a person lose their appetite. Sliding her palm across the cool sheet where Sloan had lain beside her last night, she smiled softly into her pillow, closing her eyes, caught in the love thrumming through her heart for him. She heard movement on her side of the bed and heard Mouse's long, low whine.

Rubbing her eyes, Dev slowly sat up. Her left arm was achy but more serviceable this morning. She saw Bella with her head resting on the edge of the mattress, watching her. Mouse sat next to her, happily thumping his tail, his eyes bright and shining with what she interpreted as happiness. "Well," she laughed huskily, reaching out and petting each of their heads, "I can see how this is going to go."

"Good morning."

Sloan leaned casually against the doorjamb, smiling over at her, his arms across his powerful chest. Instantly, her body warmed to that sensual male smile of his. He wore a pair of clean jeans, a dark green cowboy shirt with pearl buttons, and looked so damned good to her. "It is," she murmured, slowly pulling the covers aside. She was naked and didn't mind his admiring look. It felt good to be seen as beautiful.

Sloan shoved off the jamb and walked to the end of the bed, handing her his dark blue robe, helping her on with it. "Sleep well?" he asked.

Pushing some hair off her face, Dev stood and tied the sash around her waist. "I died." And then her mouth quirked. "Let's not use that analogy," she muttered, giving him a longing look. Sloan read her accurately, taking her gently into his arms so she could curve her arms around his waist and rest against his tall, strong body. "I slept really well," Dev admitted. "Thanks to you. I always sleep better when you're with me, Sloan."

He kissed her cheek after moving some of her ebony strands aside, easing them across her shoulder. "Love always makes a person sleep better. Did the dogs wake you up?"

She laughed a little. "No, not really. They both must have been in here earlier?"

"Yes, they were at the door this morning when I got up. Mouse was whining and I was afraid it would wake you up, so I let both of them in. I made them lie on the rug. I didn't want them jumping up on the bed and waking you up."

Dev eased away just enough to reach up and kiss his mouth. Luxuriating in the strength and emotions behind Sloan's returning kiss, Dev drowned within his arms. Breathless after the kiss, she glanced down at the two adoring dogs who stood expectantly nearby. Both tails wagged in anticipation. "I woke up on my own," she told him, reaching out, patting both of them. "And I think they felt me wake up and then came over to my side of the bed to give me a doggy good morning."

"They love you, too, sugar. Are you hungry? I'm fixing ham, scrambled eggs and toast. Sound good?"

This morning, it did. "It does…" Dev slid her feet into his too-large soft leather slippers, warming them.

"Got coffee for you, too," he teased, leading her out of the bedroom.

"You really know what will get my attention," she said, grinning. Walking out into the airy, sunlit kitchen, Dev felt some of the heaviness dissolve from around her shoulders.

"How's the arm doing this morning?" Sloan asked, pulling out a chair at the table for her to sit down upon.

"No so cranky. I can even lift it higher. Look."

Sloan gave an approving nod. "Good. You sit here and I'll get you some coffee."

Dev looked out the huge picture window. The sky was a powder blue, the sunlight strong, no clouds in the sky. She would never tire of looking at the nearby forest or the wide Wyoming sky above them. Bella came and sat on one side of her chair, Mouse on the other. "What are you," she teased them, "guard-dog bookends?"

"They know you need a little more TLC than usual," Sloan offered, placing the large red mug with coffee in it before her.

Making a muffled sound, Dev caught his serious gaze. "I do. I feel like an egg without a shell right now."

"In time, that will pass," Sloan reassured her. "And while you're in that mode, you need to do things that make you feel safe and happy."

"Then," Dev murmured, reaching out and catching

Sloan's work-worn hand, "I'm in the best possible place for that to happen."

"Speaking of nice places to be," he said, going back to the kitchen, "Miss Gus called an hour ago. She wanted an update on you. I told her you were doing well considering everything." Sloan fixed up two plates with the breakfast food. He brought them over to the table and then sat down at Dev's right elbow. "She's invited us over for dinner tonight if you feel up to it. Do you?"

Tucking the green linen napkin across her lap, Dev said, "Of course. They're people I will always want in my life. I feel very safe and well loved by all of them." The salty ham smelled heavenly to her and she picked up her fork and knife to cut into it.

"She'll be happy to hear that. I'll call her as soon as we're done with breakfast. I think everyone from the Triple H and Bar H are going to come to see you, make sure you're doing all right. You okay with that crowd?" He searched her eyes.

"They're like family to me, Sloan. I'm going to love seeing each and every one of them. Yesterday, I didn't think I'd see anyone again."

"Good, because you need to put yourself with people who care about you, Dev."

She frowned. "I need to call Charlotte and find out when she expects me back on the job."

"I called her this morning. Jordana wants six weeks off for you and Charlotte's granting her that medical request. It will give your arm time to really heal up properly, get you physical therapy, plus give you some emotional space to recollect yourself, sugar."

Relief tunneled through Dev. "That's great." Her eyes sparkled as she met Sloan's concerned gaze. "But what am I going to do with six weeks without something to do?"

"Oh," he said mysteriously, digging into his pile of fluffy scrambled eggs, "I think you might find out more about that tonight when we go over to see Miss Gus."

Tilting her head, she gave Sloan a confused look. "What do you mean?"

"Well," he drawled, "you know Miss Gus. Her and Iris Mason are a lot alike. They're the fairy godmothers of this valley, always doing good turns for good people who need a little helping hand every now and then." He smiled a little. "But it's a surprise, Dev, and I don't want to spoil it. I'll let Miss Gus tell you. Okay?"

"Okay," she said, hungry and appreciating the eggs. "Well, if it's a surprise from Miss Gus, then she'd kill you if you let it slip out."

Chuckling, Sloan nodded. "Oh, yeah. I'll do what Miss Gus asks of me."

Suddenly, Dev felt so much of the heavy weight lift from her shoulders. She was sitting and having breakfast with the man she loved. The dogs were nearby, loving her too. "I'm really surrounded with love, Sloan." Her voice trembled a little. "It feels really nice…" Dev reached out, briefly touching his hand, holding his tender blue gaze.

"It's long past time, sugar. It was good you transferred out here. I think Wyoming is the place where you'll not only find love but people who want you in their lives from near and far. You'll bloom here." Because Sloan knew the wounds left by her father were still alive and well within Dev. He understood when a parent jettisoned his own child, the child carried a lifelong heart wound. And even though Sloan knew he couldn't heal that wound in her, he could love Dev, and over time she would make peace with her past and release it.

DEV WAS SHOWERED with love and affection as everyone encircled her after Sloan drove her to the Bar H. Miss Gus wrapped her thin, strong arms around her and gave her a very powerful hug. Next came Valerie McPherson and her baby, Sophia, and then Griff, her husband. It felt so good to be embraced, hugged and have her cheek kissed. Talon, Cat, Cass and then Sandy were next. They guided her to the huge living room where everyone sat down. She was glad to have Sloan's hand in hers. They sat at one end of the massive U-shaped leather sectional.

They brought Bella along because they knew Zeke would be present. Sloan left Mouse at home because the two males would not get along under the circumstances. Bella was wagging her thick yellow tail, thumping it on everyone's legs as she eagerly licked their proffered hands hello and readily accepted all pets available while she remained at Dev's side. Zeke was a happy dog.

The smells emanating from the huge warm kitchen made Dev's mouth water. Miss Gus had told her it was a celebration-of-life meal for one and all. Just being with all these people who cared for her drove tears into Dev's eyes. She tried to circumspectly wipe them away with trembling fingers. Sloan offered her his white linen handkerchief, which she took with a grateful look. He then rested his arm around her, keeping her close, understanding she was emotionally vulnerable as never before.

Miss Gus took the rocking chair which faced the U-shaped sectional. She was wearing a bright purple apron, her silver hair glinting beneath the hurricane lamp chandelier hanging above the area. The rest of the family crowded around Sloan and Dev. Val had brought a file to her and Gus thanked her. She placed her parchment-like hands over the file resting in her lap.

"Well, you're looking a bit peaked, Dev, but under the circumstances, that's to be expected," she told her gently.

Dev smiled a little, giving Gus an apologetic look. "It's been a little rough of late," she agreed.

"That's gonna end," Gus said firmly. "And this is a happy dinner, planned especially for you. I found out from Sloan this morning that your favorite meal is tuna and noodle casserole." She slanted a lively glance toward her rapt audience. "Cass helped me a lot since that's not something I know how to cook very well. We also have corn relish, and I'm sure you can smell the homemade yeast rolls he's made, just starting to bake in the oven." Her hands fluttering, she added with a wide smile, "And yes, your favorite dessert, German chocolate cake. We have Cat to thank for that. Thank you, Cat."

Cat grinned over at Dev. "In truth, Talon helped me out. He's a better cook than I am." She gave her husband a warm look of thanks. Talon returned her loving look.

"It's a family affair," Gus told them sternly, waving her finger at all of them. "And that's what families are for. We help one another out when things get tough on one of us."

"Gosh, Miss Gus," Dev said, "this is even better than Christmas! Thank you, everyone." She glanced around and made eye contact with each of them, smiling.

Everyone smiled and nodded.

"It is Christmas in summertime," Gus agreed sagely, giving Dev a serious look now. "We all know your story, Dev. And you've been hounded almost to death by Gordon. That no-good is gonna get slammed away for a long,

long time. Wyoming judges don't put up with our women being stalked out here. I know the judge who's taking this case, and he'll hit him with the maximum sentence."

"Couldn't happen to a better person," Dev whispered. She felt Sloan's arm squeeze her gently. Everyone nodded in grim agreement.

"On to happy things, now." Gus cackled, smoothing her hands over the file. "I've been working with Sloan on the sly for a bit. You didn't know anything about it, and he wanted to keep it a secret from you for a bit."

Confused, Dev twisted a look up at Sloan. His eyes gleamed with amusement and he gave her a kiss on the brow. "What did you do?" she demanded.

Sloan had the good grace to blush, his cheeks growing ruddy. "Well, actually, it's Miss Gus who can tell the whole story, sugar. Go ahead, Miss Gus. We're all dog ears." He gave Bella and Zeke a fond look.

Chuckles flowed around the room.

Dev frowned. She looked at all her friends and they were smiling, eagerness in their expressions. *What* was going on? Cat could hardly sit still, wriggling around, happiness in her expression. Dev felt the love and care radiating from Sloan, who had an enigmatic look on his face. The man knew how to keep a secret.

"Okay," she said. "Are you playing Mrs. Santa Claus today?"

Gus give her the biggest smile, her eyes dancing with merriment. "Indeed I am." Gus slowly got out of her rocker and walked over to Dev, handing her the file. Turning, she walked back and sat down. "Go ahead, Dev, open it up. See what's inside there for you."

Brows moving down, Dev unfolded the file in her lap. There was a color photo of some land. It was flat and covered with lush green grass. In the background was a stand of tall, elegant Douglas firs. Confused, she looked at Gus. "What is this, Miss Gus?"

"Do you like what you see, Dev?"

"Well…er…yes, it's beautiful. But what is it? I don't understand."

"If you like it well enough, then Sloan is going to build a house on it for you and him. Plus, of course, your two dogs." She grinned a little. "That is, once he asks you to marry him."

The room grew very quiet with anticipation.

Dev gasped, jerking a look over at Sloan.

"I think it's time I gave you a set of rings, Dev," Sloan said, handing her a small dark blue velvet case, placing it in her hand. "I have to make this official. Will you marry me? Be my best friend? My lover? My wife? Forever?"

Her heart melted over his huskily spoken words filled with so much barely held emotion. She swallowed, gripping the ring box between her hands. "You know I will, Sloan!" Dev lifted her wounded arm just enough to embrace him and accept his chaste kiss. Tears jammed in her eyes as the room exploded with cheering, hoots, hollers and clapping. Sloan's mouth slid gently across hers and she felt incredible love contained within it. As he eased away, he rasped, "Take a look at the rings, sugar. See if you approve of them."

Gus cackled and slapped her knee. "Hurry up! I've been dyin' to see 'em myself, Dev."

A grin crossed Dev's lips and she opened the box. The engagement ring was studded with small dark green stones that sparkled in the overhead light. Next to it was a thicker gold ring that had leaves embossed around it.

"Oh," she whispered, touching them delicately, "these are beautiful, Sloan."

"Good," he said, relieved. He picked the engagement ring from the box. "These are small faceted emeralds for you, Dev." He met and held her moist eyes as he slipped it on her ring finger. "Thanks to Talon, who went with me to the jewelry store in town—he's got a lot of knowledge about gemstones. I didn't know what to look for, but he did." Giving her a loose smile filled with love, he added thickly, "When Talon asked the jeweler to show us his emeralds, I knew right then and there they exactly matched the color of your eyes." His fingers tightened around her hand. "I'm glad you like them."

Dev sniffed, holding up her hand, showing everyone the engagement ring. "Thank you, everyone..." She got up and walked over to Talon, leaned down and chastely kissed his cheek. "Especially you...thank you," she choked out.

Talon patted her shoulder. "It was a labor of love, Dev. I enjoyed helping Sloan pick the stones out for you. He's great at horseshoeing but awful when it comes to gemstones."

Everyone laughed.

She gave the cowboy a warm look, then took Cat's hand and squeezed it. "You two are something else. I don't know what I did to have you come into my life, but I'm so grateful you're both here for Sloan and I. Thank you..."

"You're a part of our family," Cat said, tears in her eyes. "The Holts, McPhersons and Hunters just attract strays like us, absorb and love us. Welcome to our family."

Dev hugged Cat fiercely and wiped her eyes.

Sloan handed Dev the file when she sat down next to him.

"Good, we got the serious stuff outta the way!" Gus crowed, jabbing her finger at the file. "Now, Dev, take a look at that piece of land in that photo. Sloan came to me a month ago, wanting to buy a five-acre parcel off us here at the Bar H. Since we've just bought the Circle R, a ten-thousand-acre ranch east of us, I was fine in selling him this parcel." She pointed toward the west. "After dinner? I think we should all take a couple of trucks, drive down to that piece of land and let you walk it? I think seeing it in person is better than any photo, don't you think?"

Dev could barely hold on to her emotions. "O-of course, Miss Gus." Tears ran freely down her face. "I'm sorry," she whispered brokenly, dabbing her eyes. "Just so much has happened."

Everyone gave her sympathetic looks of understanding.

Miss Gus nodded and said gently, "Well, from now on, Dev, only *good* things are gonna happen to you. Mark my words!"

CHAPTER TWENTY-THREE

"IT'S SO PEACEFUL and beautiful out here," Dev whispered, tightening her arm around Sloan's waist. It was almost sunset and everyone had trooped out to the newly bought parcel after dinner. After walking the land, Miss Gus and her family, plus Sandy Holt-Reynolds's family, had left them alone to appreciate the land. Bella sat near Dev's leg.

Sloan leaned over, pressing a kiss to her hair. "It is. How are you holding up?" He searched her face as she gazed up at him. He was concerned because so much had been piled on Dev at one time. Miss Gus was gung ho to show Dev the land he'd just bought for them. Sloan had wanted to wait. Anyone who had been shot had a lot to work through, and he knew Dev hadn't even started that life-churning process.

"Exhausted, if you want the truth," she admitted wearily. "But happy." Dev gestured to the five acres of green grass where their house would eventually be built. "It just seems like a dream, all of it." Holding up her hands, she eyed him tenderly. "Except for this, the ring and you."

Understanding, Sloan turned and brought her against him, taking Dev's offered mouth, caressing her with all the love he held for her in that kiss. Her lips were opening to him, lush with promise, and he felt her move sensuously against his hips. His woman was a total turn-on.

All Dev had to do was look at him with that pixie-like smile, the deviltry shining in her green eyes, and he was lost. Hopelessly, but happily lost. As he left her wet lips, he stared deeply into her large, exhausted-looking eyes. "Come on, let's get you home. You've had one heck of a day, sugar."

Nodding, she allowed Sloan to tuck her beneath his right arm and guide her back to the truck. Bella led the way, her big yellow tail waving from side to side like a proud flag.

"How's your arm doing? Is the pain coming back yet?" Sloan asked, opening the door for her.

"It's cranky," Dev admitted, climbing in. She gestured and Bella leaped in, making herself comfortable on the floor between her legs. "I need to take my pain pill."

Sloan shut the door and climbed in the driver's side. Her purse was between them and he dug into it, finding the bottle. Opening it, he handed her a tablet and then leaned over, retrieving a bottle of water from the door. "Take it now."

Dev gave him a look of thanks, making quick work of it. "You're a big mother hen, Rankin."

He drove the truck down the wide dirt road and slipped her hand into his on the seat. "But you love me, anyway?" He slanted her a teasing glance, his mouth pulling into a grin.

Rallying, Dev whispered, "Oh, very much…"

"Do you like the plot of land I've bought for us, Dev?"

"Yes." She shook her head and gave him a wry look as they slowly drove by the main Bar H ranch house. Everyone was inside for the evening. "You knew."

"Knew what?" He released her hand and pulled up

at the stop sign. Turning right, he drove them toward Jackson Hole.

"That I loved you. You had to. Why else would you have bought that land, Sloan?"

"I was hedging my bets, sugar. I wasn't positive you loved me like I loved you, but everything was there in plain sight. I was just hoping I was reading it right."

As Dev tipped her head back on the seat, Bella laid her head across her thigh. She rested her hand on her dog's warm fur. "I knew, too, but I was afraid to admit it, Sloan." She rolled her head to the left, catching his momentary glance. "I thought it was too soon." Sighing, she stared up at the ceiling. "But after getting kidnapped by Gordon, I was wishing with my life that I'd let you know before it happened." She reached out slowly with her left hand, resting it on his hard jean-clad thigh. "It was my biggest regret of all, Sloan. I thought Gordon was going to kill me and I'd die without you knowing that I love you." She swallowed hard. "I had so many regrets."

"Well, sugar, it didn't happen." Sloan patted her hand. "Why don't you close your eyes? See if you can catch a quick nap before we get home?"

Home. That word sounded so good to Dev. It was easy to allow her lashes to fall shut. She felt as if she were on a whirling carousel and there was no way to get off or stop it. Just the roughened warmth of Sloan's hand over hers comforted her and allowed her to fall into a quick slumber.

DEV WAS TOUCHED beyond words when Sloan led her back into his apartment. Mouse was delirious with joy at seeing them. Sloan let him out of his crate and he went over and licked Bella hello, wagging his tail. Making sure he had a bath started for Dev, Sloan then took Mouse outside to do his business. Bella remained behind with Dev, lying just outside the bathroom door.

Just sinking into the very warm water made Dev groan with utter pleasure. Every bone in her body hurt. She had so many purple and blue bruises. After arriving by helicopter at the hospital, Jordana had taken care of her in ER. She'd cleaned out the bullet wound and put a nice new waterproof dressing around it. Giving her a shot of antibiotics and pills to take for the next seven days, she had teased Dev about her many colorful bruises. Jordana could make an iceberg smile, Dev decided, grateful for her warmth and maternal care. It was exactly what she'd needed at the time.

Dev washed herself with fragrant lilac soap, filling the bathroom with a scented, steamy haze. Later, Dev stepped out and toweled off. Sloan's dark blue terrycloth robe hung on her, and it felt wonderful because she could smell his scent lingering in the fabric. Slipping on clean socks and shoes, she pulled out a dark red tee and a clean set of cream-colored slacks.

Sloan came back with Mouse while she was washing her hair, albeit awkwardly, at the kitchen sink. He walked over, running his hand down her curved back.

"Let me help you." He guided her hands to the sink and finished shampooing her hair.

Dev absorbed his body next to hers, leaning against Sloan as his fingers wreaked magic across her sensitive scalp, sending sweet shafts of pleasure tingling down her head, past her neck and flooding the rest of her body. Sloan carefully rinsed her thick black hair beneath the warm water of the faucet and she closed her eyes, hungrily absorbing his touch. How badly she needed this. Needed him.

"There," Sloan murmured, pleased, placing a towel around her hair as she straightened up. "You're clean from head to toe, sugar." He took the towel from her hands, gently beginning the process of drying her hair.

"My arm isn't up for being above my head yet." She sighed, giving him a loving look. His face was rugged and weathered. Yet Dev knew she would never tire of the dancing glint in Sloan's amused blue eyes. His chiseled mouth was crooked.

"Don't push the river, Dev. You need to rest."

"I know," she uttered, wrapping her hands over his hips while he continued to dry her damp strands. "I feel like I could collapse into a heap. That dinner with Miss Gus and everyone was huge, and it tasted so good."

"Come on over to the couch. I'll get the comb and brush from your vanity and I'll work these snarls out and tame them."

Dev sat down on the couch. She watched Sloan walk with his casual, easygoing gait, knowing there was a warrior hidden beneath that facade. He'd come for her yesterday, and he'd helped to rescue her. Her heart thudding with a fierce love for him, Dev settled against Sloan, her back to him as he began to gently unknot her damp hair with the comb.

"When I first saw your hair," he rasped after he finished, moving locks across her shoulders as he pulled Dev into his arms, "I thought you might be part raven. I saw blue highlights dancing across the waves of it."

Dev snuggled into his arms, brow against his jaw, surrendering completely to him. "I love ravens," she murmured, closing her eyes, never more safe than right now.

Caressing her smooth, silky hair across her shoulders, Sloan leaned back into the corner. "You're slurring your words, sugar. Do you want me to carry you into the bedroom? Tuck you in?" He smiled as his mouth moved in small kisses across her pale cheek.

"Mmm, no…" Dev protested, resting her palm against his chest. "I just want to be quiet. Not move… Just be with you, Sloan…"

"You got it," he promised her thickly, sliding his hand across her hip and down her leg. "Go to sleep. I'll hold you safe…"

Dev woke up sometime during the night from a bad dream. She found herself naked in bed with Sloan, the covers across her shoulders, lying as close as she could get to him. Rubbing her eyes, she felt Sloan awaken. It wasn't a jerking motion, but she felt him instantly go on guard and become alert.

"Sorry," she mumbled against his chest. "I was having a bad dream."

Sloan curved his arm around her, drawing her fully against him. Sliding her leg over his, she made a happy sound in her throat, the terror in the dream fading away.

"I want to be here whenever you have bad dreams, Dev," he said, feathering light kisses from her cheek down her slender neck to her shoulder. "And in time, they'll fade. You'll have another, happier focus, sugar."

Nodding, she moaned as he nipped her shoulder with his teeth. Tiny, rasping shivers scattered like dappled sunlight throughout her. She felt her breasts tightening, his chest hair tangled and teasing her hardening nipples. Sloan eased away just enough to allow him to continue to lick and then press kisses along her sensitive collarbone. This was what she needed: Sloan. Loving him.

Drowning herself in him, having him within her, heart to heart. She moaned and lay on her back, his arm supporting her so that he could continue to lavish her with his mouth and tongue.

Heat began to simmer and then turn boiling in her lower body as he leaned over, cupping her breast. His hand was calloused and streaks of pleasure radiated outward, making her tense and want more from Sloan. It hurt to raise her arm very much, but Dev slid her hand across his nape, drawing his mouth down upon her begging nipple. Her breath caught. How badly she wanted Sloan. He did not disappoint—his lips tugged upon the nipple, making her arch wantonly against him. Just the warm steel of his erection pressing into her belly made her moan with anticipation. Wild spasms of fire rippled throughout her and Dev leaned into him, begging silently for him to continue to ravish her. Slipping her fingers into his short, dark hair, she smiled and tipped her head, soft sounds caught in her exposed throat.

Her world grew hotter as he languidly glided his fingers down her tense, curved thigh, opening her for sensual exploration. Breathing going ragged, Dev arched into his hand as he trailed his fingers down through her wet folds. His mouth captured the other nipple and she writhed in his arms, the scalding heat of his mouth and fingers teasing her entrance, making her cry out. It was a cry pleading for more. Much more.

As HE LIFTED his head, Sloan's eyes squinted through the darkness while he studied her. Dev was turning into his wild woman whom he loved so much. She was artless, her body humming with the pleasure he was giving her. She was the center of his heart's universe. Pleasing her, feeling her tremble, demand, pant and cry out his name, her short nails digging spasmodically into his chest, was all he desired. Easing his finger into her, capturing that sweet spot within her, he heard her gasp, suddenly pushing hungrily against his hand, wanting.

"You're so wet," he growled, feeling her begin to pant, feeling her walls begin to contract. Dev was responsive, so easy to please, and Sloan drove her toward that proverbial cliff that she was swiftly approaching. She had gone through so much in such a short period of time that all he wanted to do was make her forget about all of it. He wanted Dev to enter a realm of roiling, red-hot pleasure instead. Sloan tugged at her nipple, suckling her strongly. Instantly, she keened, hips jerking upward, desperate for more of what he was lavishing her with. In seconds, she orgasmed, her walls contracting powerfully around his finger, her cry of sheer satisfaction reverberating through both of them.

Sloan milked her, pushed her right over the edge of that cliff of ecstasy, her cries turning into wispy mews of utter pleasure. Easing out of her, he lay down, pulling her on top of him. Her eyes were drowsy, her lips parted. She was breathing raggedly, consumed by ecstasy. Gripping her hips, he urged her legs across him, guiding her wet, hot core down upon his thick, awaiting erection. Sucking in a sharp breath, Sloan clenched his teeth as he glided her across him, her honeyed fluids inciting him, her woman's heat driving him crazy with need of her. He wanted to be in her and he watched her eyes barely open and focus on him.

"Ride me," he rasped harshly. "All the way, sugar..." Her lips moved into a faint smile, the satiation gleaming in her eyes as she pressed her hips down upon him.

Every stroke of her body, that fluid silkiness sliding tantalizingly against his erection, making him groan and arch against her, ate rapidly away at Sloan's mind. Dev's long, curved thighs sweetly held him right where she wanted him and he luxuriated in her gliding fluidly back and forth on him, teasing him until he couldn't take it anymore. And just as he gripped her hips to arch into her, she beat him to it. In moments, her woman's scalding heat surrounded him, and she took him deep, without mercy, moving swiftly back and forth, making him growl with gratification.

Dev leaned forward, dragging her nipples teasingly across his powerful chest, nipping his jaw, placing hungry kisses across his mouth. She drew him all the way into her. He groaned, his fingers digging into her hips as she rode him hard and with the focus of a hunter. She wanted him to come and could feel how rigid and swollen within her he had become. As she established that swift, deep rhythm, Dev felt herself starting to fly apart in the process once again. Her fingers dug into Sloan's chest as suddenly her body contracted violently. She cried out, frozen in place with intense pleasure radiating outward throughout her lower body as the orgasm rapidly swept through her.

Sloan guided her hips, urging her to move, eliciting even more friction against that sweet spot deep within her. Dev cried out his name, sobbing and paralyzed with pleasure between his guiding hands. And just as she began to come down off that high place the orgasm had taken her, Sloan released within her, feeling the molten heat slam down his spine and spilling into her. Now, he couldn't move, couldn't breathe, could just…feel the raging, tunneling fire jetting through him, draining him until he felt like little more than sawdust afterward.

Dev lay weakly against Sloan's damp form, gasping, clinging to him, her brow against his, their chaotic breaths commingling with one another. Her entire body quivered as the ripple effect of her orgasm continued minutes afterward. It felt so wonderful to share so much with him. Sloan felt incredible inside and she wanted to remain fused with him forever in this molten moment.

"I love you, Sloan… I love you so much…" Dev weakly framed his face with her hands, placing her mouth upon his, kissing him deeply, her tongue ravishing his. Sloan's hands cupped her face, kissing her hungrily, letting her know just how much she enflamed him. Smiling inwardly, Dev lifted her lips from his, drowning in his hungry, narrowed eyes.

"You're mine," he growled thickly, running his hands across her mussed hair, taming it across her damp shoulders. "You always will be. We were made for one another." He arched into her, reminding her in the sweetest of ways.

Dev moaned, her breasts so close to his mouth. She wasn't disappointed as his lips captured one of her nipples, suckling her, slamming her back into that volcanic heat that still boiled deep within her. She could feel him begin to harden within her once more, stretching her, the sensations escalating, making her sigh and surrender to him in every way, all over again.

WHEN DEV AWOKE, she felt warm and pampered within Sloan's embrace and against his body. Slowly opening her eyes, she stared drowsily up into his. Sloan's face was serene, his blue eyes thoughtful looking, holding her gaze. This morning his face was darkened with stubble, making him look deliciously sexy to her. She reached up with a soft smile, trailing her fingers across the hard line of his jaw. "I love waking up with you like this," she uttered, her voice husky with sleep.

The color of his eyes deepened, a tenderness burning in them for her alone. Dev's lashes dropped closed as he leaned down, worshipping her lips, his breath moist against her cheek.

She now knew as never before what it was like to be truly loved by a man. Sloan had slipped inside her wounded heart and her terror over Gordon stalking her, and his quiet, steady love had silently taken root. As she opened her mouth eagerly to him, sliding her arm around his shoulders, drawing him against her, a sound caught in her throat. A sound of pure joy, a celebration of finding him. Sloan was a warrior, there was no question. Yet, he didn't allow it to overshadow who he was when he was not in a dangerous or threatening situation. That was something Dev loved more about him than anything. He had the ability to remain his essential self, the man she mindlessly loved, who filled her heart to overflowing with joy she'd never known until him.

"Mmm," she murmured, easing from his mouth, her lips tingling, tasting him upon them. Opening her eyes, Dev absorbed the arousal in Sloan's eyes, feeling his erection pressing against her. "I like this. I love you…" Her voice turned tremulous as he threaded his fingers through her hair, cupping the back of her head, drawing her lips to his smiling mouth.

Golden moments spun with the arcing heat coming to a fiery ache within her lower body as Sloan worshipped her mouth. His fingers moved to her sensitive nape and he lifted his mouth from hers.

"In time," he told her thickly, holding her half-closed gaze, seeing the arousal clearly in it, "we'll pick up the pieces of our life together, Dev. It's you and me." And then he gave her a lopsided grin, smoothing hair away from her temple. "Well, let me amend that a little. You, me, Mouse and Bella."

Laughing softly, she caressed his sandpapery cheek. "We're on a journey of discovery, Sloan. And I don't want it any other way." Sobering a bit, she whispered, "I really didn't know love could be this good. This beautiful. You're beautiful, Sloan…"

Dev watched his cheeks turn ruddy as she caressed his jaw. "What? You don't like being called beautiful?" Her mouth curved. He wasn't happy about her calling his hands beautiful, either, but in her eyes and heart, he was exactly that to her. She watched Sloan frown and then shrug his shoulders.

"Well," he mumbled teasingly, "maybe handsome? Beautiful is a term used to describe a woman like yourself, sugar." He kissed the tip of her nose.

"Men can be beautiful, too," Dev insisted, languishing in the heat of his body, within his strong, caring arms. "And in my eyes, cowboy, you have an outrageously beautiful body, beautiful hands, mind and heart. Okay?"

He gave her a lazy grin. "Okay, from you, I'll live with it."

Dev laughed and hugged him hard, her breasts pressed against the span of his chest. Kissing his cheek, his mouth, Dev leaned back. "There's only one man like you in the world, Sloan Rankin, and you're mine. All mine…"

As he swept her hard against him, burying his face in her hair, Dev relaxed fully, knowing Sloan would always love her, give her joy and, finally, a place to feel safe. Inhaling his scent deeply into her lungs, a smile crossed her mouth as she held him with equal fierceness as the morning light silently flooded their bedroom. Hope filled her heart, along with love for Sloan. They had time now, to live together, to get to know one another in so many large and small ways, and to plan for a bright future together. Already, Dev had ideas for that house he wanted to build for her on that parcel of land near the Bar H. Family meant everything to her, and coming from a broken one, just having Miss Gus, Val and Griff McPherson there, along with the Holt family, meant she had a cosmic family of sorts to replace what had been lost so long ago. Now, it was all being returned to her in the most wonderful of ways.

Sloan eased Dev down upon the mattress and he studied her in the silence. "There's one thing I want to do while you're on medical leave. I'd like to take you home to meet my parents and all the good people of Black Mountain. What do you think, Dev? Are you up for that?"

She nodded. "I'd love to meet your family, Sloan. And all those other families, too."

"They'll love you, sugar. My mother will dote on you, believe me." He slid his fingers across her cheek. "We could take a week? I could show you around Black Mountain. Where I grew up. Ply you with wild stories about my childhood?"

She grinned, catching his fingers, pressing a kiss to them. "It sounds like a dream come true. I want to know everything about you, Sloan. That's a good start."

He gave her a warm smile. "Later today, we'll call my parents and see if they're okay with us suddenly dropping in for a visit. I don't think they'll mind at all."

"It has been crazy, hasn't it? I'm so glad it's over, Sloan."

"Well," he cautioned, "there's legal hoops we have to partake in, but this time, I'll be there at your side. We'll jump through 'em together."

Nuzzling his jaw, Dev pressed light kisses against it. "That sounds so good…"

Sloan nodded and slid his hand beneath her nape, positioning her so he could hold her aroused gaze. "From now on," he promised her in a low voice, "you don't have to fight through life alone, Dev. Not ever again. I'll be there every step of the way. Beside you…forever…"

* * * * *

**Tough, rugged and oh-so-sexy...
There's just something about those Western men!**

From Wyoming to Oregon, Texas to Montana, let today's
top-selling masters of Western romance sweep you away with
this sneak peek at ten brand-new novels.

FEATURING EXTENDED
EXCERPTS FROM

Once a Rancher
by Linda Lael Miller

Untamed
by Diana Palmer

One Night Charmer
by Maisey Yates

Rustler's Moon
by Jodi Thomas

Home on the Ranch
by Trish Milburn

Hard Rain
by B.J. Daniels

Texas on My Mind
by Delores Fossen

Texas Rebels: Jude
by Linda Warren

Out Rider
by Lindsay McKenna

Hard Silence
by Mia Kay

The West has never been wilder!

Download your free copy today!

Available wherever ebooks are sold.

Be sure to connect with us at:
Harlequin.com/Newsletters
Facebook.com/HarlequinBooks
Twitter.com/HQNBooks

HQN™

www.HQNBooks.com

PHLLM579

Wrangle Your Friends for the Ultimate Ranch Girls' Getaway

Win an all-expenses-paid 3-night luxurious stay for you and your 3 guests at The Resort at Paws Up in Greenough, Montana.

Retail Value $10,000

A TOAST TO FRIENDSHIP, AN ADVENTURE OF A LIFETIME!

Learn more at
www.Harlequinranchgetaway.com

Sweepstakes ends August 31, 2016

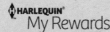 

WCHMR

Same great stories, new name!

In July 2016,
the HARLEQUIN®
AMERICAN ROMANCE® series
will become
the HARLEQUIN®
WESTERN ROMANCE series.

Connect with us to find your next great read,
special offers and more.

f /HarlequinBooks

🐦 @HarlequinBooks

www.HarlequinBlog.com

www.Harlequin.com/Newsletters

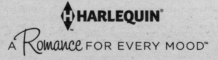

HARLEQUIN®

A *Romance* FOR EVERY MOOD™

www.Harlequin.com

REQUEST YOUR FREE BOOKS!

2 FREE NOVELS
FROM THE SUSPENSE COLLECTION
PLUS 2 FREE GIFTS!

YES! Please send me 2 FREE novels from the Suspense Collection and my 2 FREE gifts (gifts are worth about $10). After receiving them, if I don't wish to receive any more books, I can return the shipping statement marked "cancel." If I don't cancel, I will receive 4 brand-new novels every month and be billed just $6.49 per book in the U.S. or $6.99 per book in Canada. That's a savings of at least 19% off the cover price. It's quite a bargain! Shipping and handling is just 50¢ per book in the U.S. and 75¢ per book in Canada.* I understand that accepting the 2 free books and gifts places me under no obligation to buy anything. I can always return a shipment and cancel at any time. Even if I never buy another book, the two free books and gifts are mine to keep forever.

191/391 MDN GH4Z

Name	(PLEASE PRINT)
Address	Apt. #
City	State/Prov. Zip/Postal Code

Signature (if under 18, a parent or guardian must sign)

Mail to the **Reader Service**:
IN U.S.A.: P.O. Box 1867, Buffalo, NY 14240-1867
IN CANADA: P.O. Box 609, Fort Erie, Ontario L2A 5X3

Want to try two free books from another line?
Call 1-800-873-8635 or visit www.ReaderService.com.

* Terms and prices subject to change without notice. Prices do not include applicable taxes. Sales tax applicable in N.Y. Canadian residents will be charged applicable taxes. Offer not valid in Quebec. This offer is limited to one order per household. Not valid for current subscribers to the Suspense Collection or the Romance/Suspense Collection. All orders subject to credit approval. Credit or debit balances in a customer's account(s) may be offset by any other outstanding balance owed by or to the customer. Please allow 4 to 6 weeks for delivery. Offer available while quantities last.

Your Privacy—The Reader Service is committed to protecting your privacy. Our Privacy Policy is available online at www.ReaderService.com or upon request from the Reader Service.

We make a portion of our mailing list available to reputable third parties that offer products we believe may interest you. If you prefer that we not exchange your name with third parties, or if you wish to clarify or modify your communication preferences, please visit us at www.ReaderService.com/consumerchoice or write to us at Reader Service Preference Service, P.O. Box 9062, Buffalo, NY 14240-9062. Include your complete name and address.